MUSIC
CITY
MADNESS

Jason Melby

Book design by eBook Prep
www.ebookprep.com
Editor: Dave Field
Cover design by The Killion Group Inc.
www.thekilliongroupinc.com

All song lyrics by Jason E. Melby. © Copyright (2016). International Copyright Secured. All rights reserved

June, 2017
ISBN: 978-1-61417-967-2

ePublishing Works!
www.epublishingworks.com

DEDICATION

To my sons,
Follow the music in your own hearts.
You never know where it might take you.

"Melody and rhythm have a vibration that goes beyond 'healing' all the way to super-empowering, it really connects you to the central, limitless core force in the universe. Anyone can tap into this…it's free, and all of human kind has used this power since the dawn of time."

—Rory Block

PART I

A Better Teacher

————— ◆ —————

April 26-30, 2010

CHAPTER 1

Thirteen-year-old Abigail Presley tapped her lilac, high top sneakers on the wet pavement outside an East Nashville rambler with a U-Haul trailer in the driveway. Her left arm hung awkwardly at her side in a long-sleeve top while she held an open golf umbrella in her right hand with her backpack slung over her right shoulder. She wore her strawberry hair in a ponytail with low-cut jeans that barely hugged her lanky hips. Mascara with black eye liner and a dark plum lipstick brought a measure of sophistication to her youthful appearance.

She collapsed the umbrella in light drizzle and stepped toward the brown two-door Stanza rolling up to the driveway. She shifted her backpack off her shoulder and opened the passenger door to hear the thumping bass from an Eminem track. "What took you so long?" she asked the driver, a petite platinum blonde in a white McDonald's uniform with *Nicole* imprinted on a bronze name tag.

"I had to open this morning. Then I had to take an unscheduled break to come get you."

Abby pulled the door shut with her floral print backpack on her lap and the wet umbrella wedged beside her seat. "I think the fast food gods will survive without you."

Nicole adjusted the radio volume and drove away. "I can't always leave work to come get you."

"I can't walk to school from here."

"You could have taken the bus."

Abby unzipped a side compartment on her backpack. "Not on my first day. My dad should have taken me."

"He has an audition this morning."

Abby gazed through her window with tranquil blue eyes the color of a Colorado sky. "I know," she said assertively. She rubbed her hand on her damp pant leg.

Nicole shifted the Stanza into fourth with a noticeable *clunk*. "Are those my jeans?"

"Mine were dirty."

"Where did you get the makeup?"

Abby twirled the end of her ponytail between her fingers. "I'm going to be late for school."

"I don't mind if you borrow my stuff, but your dad doesn't want you to wear it."

"My dad doesn't get to choose my clothes anymore."

Nicole checked her mirrors and changed lanes. In some ways, she saw her former self in Abby's skin—young, naïve, and always mad about something. Cute boys were the center of her universe, and no one understood her problems. "I wasn't talking about the clothes."

"The makeup makes me look older."

Nicole spied Abby reaching for a pack of cigarettes crammed inside a zippered compartment. "Don't let your dad find those."

"Find what?"

Nicole pointed to the red Marlboros.

"They aren't mine."

"You're just holding them for a friend?"

"I'm thirteen. I'm not a kid anymore."

"How's your arm?"

Abby adjusted her position. "It's fine."

"I remember thirteen," Nicole empathized. "Don't be so quick to grow up."

"You sound like my dad."

"Your dad's a great guy."

"When he's around."

"He works hard for you."

"He works hard for his music."

"He loves you more."

Abby curled her hand around the pack of cigarettes and stuffed them in her jeans. "Drop me off before we get there."

"It's raining."

"I can hold the umbrella."

Nicole slowed near the school zone. "Are you sure?"

Abby waited for the car to stop and got out. "I'm good," she said, leaning left to shift the backpack on her right shoulder before she deployed her umbrella with the same arm.

"Your dad will pick you up," Nicole offered as Abby kicked the door shut.

Abby plodded toward the school's main entrance and shook her collapsed umbrella above a non-slip mat inside. She wiped the rain off her face with her forearm and observed the thinning herd of students scrambling to beat the final bell. A moment later, a towering, full-figured woman with a cinnamon complexion, braided hair, and a look to suggest she knew bullshit when she heard it, rolled up like a tank on enemy patrol.

"You must be Miss Presley," the woman greeted Abby. "I'm Principal Hendrix. Glad you could make it this morning."

"My ride was late."

Principal Hendrix extended her left hand, which Abby grabbed awkwardly with her right as the final bell rang out.

"I'm new," Abby stated flatly.

"Indeed."

"My dad's going to pick me up this afternoon."

Principal Hendrix pointed to the clock on the wall. "Let's get through this morning, first."

"I don't know where to go."

"Follow me…"

Abby feigned a polite smile. She hated the *new kid in school* label—one she'd worn more times than she deserved. She trailed her new principal through a labyrinth of hallways with dented lockers and cinder-block walls painted dark brown to hide graffiti. A resource officer roamed outside the empty cafeteria decked with spirit banners. The school looked old. It smelled old, too, like the basement in the house she used to live in.

"You've been assigned to Mrs. Dotti's homeroom," Principal Hendrix instructed Abby outside a class full of seventh grade students. "She'll have a copy of your schedule. She can show you to your locker and answer any questions you have. Your lunch rotation starts at 12:15. Good luck today. I suspect we'll see more of each other soon."

Abby took a hesitant step toward the hangman's gallows, where rows of curious students stared in her direction. She kept a laser focus on the teacher at the front of the room with an open textbook in her hand. *"Welcome,"* she heard Mrs. Dotti greet her, followed by, *"Take any open seat you like."*

Abby loped along the perimeter toward a spot near the back of the class, her adrenaline pumping as she avoided eye contact with everyone in the room. She hated Nicole for making her late. She hated her dad for making her move again. She missed her school in Tulsa, and most of all, she missed her friends in her old neighborhood.

She set her backpack on the floor and leaned her dripping umbrella against the back wall. She shuffled between two desks, her sense of anonymity returning when the class faced forward again. But as she maneuvered to take her seat, she slipped on a patch of wet tile and fell sideways toward a student who pushed off to help break her fall, inadvertently dislodging Abby's prosthetic forearm from the socket in her sleeve.

CHAPTER 2

Leland Presley weaved through morning traffic on Hillsboro Pike with his steel-toed boot gunning the accelerator in his '85 RAM pickup before the light at Old Hickory Boulevard turned red. Worn windshield wipers stuttered back and forth as steady rain swept over the Nashville metropolitan area and continued toward the bluegrass pastures and wooded hills in Middle Tennessee.

He jabbed the buttons on the truck's AM/FM cassette to catch the latest traffic update. Short on time and long on miles to a new club in East Nashville, he raced through yellow lights outside strip malls and modest residential properties built away from the sprawling horse ranches and long stretches of triple-rail fence that framed the picturesque landscape outside the city.

He veered sharply from the slower-moving lane near the I-440 overpass. His construction hat tumbled off the hard shell guitar case buckled against the seat beside him and rolled onto the passenger floorboard. He tapped one hand on the wheel and ran the other through his thick, brown hair with his long sideburns. Razor stubble paved his tan complexion, accentuating his emerald green eyes, vibrant and stirring like the Caspian Sea. A gold cross necklace rested against his well-defined chest.

He brushed his hand on his work jeans and unzipped the orange safety vest he wore over his red flannel button-down. Morning news reported another accident west of his location at Parthenon and Oman, where a two-car collision had brought morning commuters to a halt.

Stuck in the center lane between a packed school bus and a dump truck hauling fill dirt, he checked his blind spot and inched his front bumper behind a black Mercedes S500 coupe with tinted windows and a blinking left turn signal. The vanity license plate spelled *CASHVIL*.

He cut the wheel to go around the Mercedes driver yacking on her cell phone and leaned forward to gauge the distance between his truck and the S500's bumper with the left turn signal still flashing. Too tight to make the turn, he cranked his window down and waved at the driver blocking his path. He bumped his horn to force the issue as precious minutes ticked away on the open audition he'd left his job site to attend.

He pressed the brake with his left foot and pushed his right on the gas, revving the engine to spin the rear wheels in place. When the distracted Mercedes driver finally inched toward the left lane, he lurched in front of her and caught a stiff middle finger in his rear view mirror.

He drove as fast as traffic allowed beyond The District and its ensemble of refurbished restaurants, galleries, and familiar honky-tonks along Broadway. He hung a left onto 2nd Avenue and drove toward the Woodland Street bridge. He snagged the first parking space he could find outside the new venue in the Five Points neighborhood. Then he unbuckled his jet black guitar case and grabbed his silver-sand Stetson from the makeshift hat rack mounted behind the truck's bench seat.

He beat a path to the entrance and dipped his six-foot frame inside the refurbished honky-tonk to claim his spot in the cattle call line. He set his guitar case down and flicked the rain off his hat. He sized up the competition in front of him, aligned single file along a wall with autographed photos of Merle Haggard, Willie Nelson, Dwight Yoakam,

Patsy Cline, and other superstars who'd played in relative obscurity before their careers went supernova.

He shuffled forward in line and spied the usual urban cowboys in button-down shirts and wing-tip Laredo's with boot-cut jeans and tassel ties. He heard guitars out of tune and singers who couldn't find the right notes if someone stapled them to their forehead. He heard the same tired lyrics to the same cover songs delivered without passion or connection to any person, real or imagined, in the live audience.

He watched the group of wannabe artists proceed one-by-one, lock-step toward the stage. And one-by-one, he saw defeated souls slouch away tuck-tailed and tarnished from the lukewarm response to their audition.

Undeterred, he rehearsed a new song in his head, where a few simple chords produced a melody to complement the lyrics he'd composed on a date with his daughter at a Taylor Swift concert.

When he landed his turn in the spotlight, he carried his guitar case on stage and acknowledged the impassive club owner who cracked peanut shells at the bar.

"Name?" the owner asked while he chewed.

Leland tipped his Stetson. "Leland Presley."

"Nestley?"

"*Pres-ley,*" Leland articulated slowly. He opened the guitar case with his sleeves rolled up, exposing a treble clef tattoo on his left inside forearm and a rustic wooden cross on his right.

"What are you singing?"

Leland removed his acoustic Gibson from the blue velvet lining. The scent of pattern-grade mahogany and Adirondack spruce brought the hand-made instrument to life. "I'm going to try something different this time."

"How different?"

"A song I wrote for someone very special to me."

"I'm touched, Mr. Presley. The stage is yours."

Leland lifted the guitar strap over his head and caressed the vintage instrument against his body. He tweaked the steel E string with the nickel white tuner and strummed his pick above the single-ring rosette to produce a warm, balanced tone. Then he drew a steady breath and leaned toward the microphone to sing.

I can feel the music move you
On the country-western floor
A small town girl with big time dreams
Ain't gonna settle anymore

But when you find your heart
All alone at night
Let me take your hand, and ask,
May I have this dance?

May I have this dance?

'Cause you're the one that I've been waitin' for...
And I don't think, I can hold out anymore

A daddy's girl with angel eyes
And a smile to open doors
You want a man who wants to love you
For richer or for poorer...

But when you find your heart
All alone at night
Let me take your hand, and ask,
May I have this dance?

May I have this dance?

I can see the sunshine in your smile
When it comes to life and love I don't keep score
And tonight I want you with me on the floor...

May I have this dance?

You're the only one I'm waitin' for
And I don't think, I can wait here anymore…

May I have this dance?

Leland stepped away from the microphone. "It's not my only song."

"It is for now," the owner replied.

"Are we good?"

"We'll be in touch."

Leland gently placed his guitar in the case and latched the lid. He stepped down from the stage and approached the club owner at the bar. "I hear that a lot. Tell me what you really think."

The owner cracked another peanut shell and chewed. "This ain't America's Got Talent. I have a business to run."

"And you're not the Grand Ole Opry. I've heard one train wreck after another in here. I can out-sing any audition you've entertained today."

"We'll be in touch."

"I really need this gig," Leland persisted.

"So does everyone who comes through these doors," the owner retorted. He wiped a pile of peanut shells onto the floor. "It takes a hell of a lot more than a pretty face to draw new business."

Leland gripped his guitar case handle and adjusted his hat. "Yes Sir. But I bailed from my day job and drove thirty miles to get here. A job I might not have when I get back."

"You from Nashville?"

"The buckle of the bible belt."

The owner sipped his drink and chewed the ice. "You ever take voice lessons?"

"I'm self-taught."

The owner gave Leland a business card with a handwritten phone number on the back. "If you want my advice, get yourself a better teacher."

CHAPTER 3

Melissa Hamilton left her keys inside her Mercedes coupe and tipped the country club valet with a folded five dollar bill from her Dolce & Gabbana clutch. Her mirrored glasses reflected the car's glossy finish and the CASHVIL vanity plate. Dressed more for a red carpet stroll than a meeting with her talent agent, she wore her favorite pumps with her Donna Karan pants and sleeveless top to elevate her slender frame and her brown, shoulder-length hair with red highlights. Part Cherokee and part Irish, her facial symmetry and high cheek bones enhanced her almond-shaped eyes the color of burled walnut.

A morning workout with her personal trainer had segued to breakfast with friends, followed by shopping at Nordstrom's for shoes and a quick mani-pedi before heading to the private country club. Confronted with a choice between a dental appointment or a meeting with her haughty agent—slash personal friend and business manager—she'd reluctantly chosen the latter and postponed the dentist to accommodate her busy social schedule.

Inside the club's posh surroundings, she climbed the staircase to the casual dining area overlooking the clay tennis courts and scouted a familiar figure waving her toward a table for two. "Been here long?" she asked her agent.

Sidney Irving, Esquire wiped his mouth with a linen napkin and stood up from his chair to hug Melissa. He wore his thick silver hair combed back with a neatly trimmed goatee to match. "Since yesterday."

"Shut up…"

Sid moved a chair for Melissa. A big orange "T" advertised his Tennessee Volunteers belt buckle at the front of his pleated wool slacks. "You want a drink?"

"It's ten o'clock in the morning."

Sid scooted Melissa's chair forward, his pinstripe Polo neatly tucked inside his substantial girth. "You look chic."

"I got my hair highlighted."

"I thought you were traveling?" Sid asked.

Melissa unfolded a cloth napkin. "Change of plans." She recognized a movie producer and the young tart captivated by his attention. "You look very, debonair."

Sid patted his stomach. A gold Oyster Rolex rattled on his wrist inside his sleeve pinned with silver cufflinks. "I can't complain."

"I saw your name in the paper the other day."

Sid lifted his drink. "Innocent until proven guilty."

"We're all guilty of something." Melissa scanned the menu in front of her. "I had a late breakfast."

"The eggs Benedict are divine."

"I'm not hungry."

Sid moved his hands when he talked. "You look like you're starving. Every time I see you, you've lost another five pounds."

"Hardly."

"And you don't have five pounds to spare."

Melissa flagged a waitress and ordered a wet scotch and soda, neat. "You're very sweet, but I didn't drive all the way out here to flirt."

Sid pushed his plate away with broken potato chips and a half eaten dill pickle on board. "Who's flirting? I've been busier than a one-legged man in an ass-kickin' contest. Ten percent's getting hard to earn."

"Spare me The Prince and the Pauper routine. If you don't sign me to a new record label, I won't have ten percent to give anymore."

Sid nibbled on potato chip crumbs. "Swapping labels doesn't happen overnight. You can't change horses in mid race and expect to win the heat. It takes time to manage, promote, and network. It's a relationship game. We have to build a broader fan base. Make new connections with the right people."

"My fans are my business. Connections are yours. Speaking of which, did you reach out to everyone for Wednesday's event?"

"I did, but honestly, I'm not sure I like the idea."

Melissa accepted her drink from the waiter. "I haven't played a concert in seven years. I want my career back. Not next week. Not tomorrow. I want it now. I've worked too hard and sacrificed too much to sit around and wait for the perfect opportunity to float along. You're my business manager. Get out there and manage."

Sid leaned back in his chair. "I'll take another bourbon," he said, raising his empty glass to the waiter. "And make it a double this time." He stroked his goatee as if deep in thought. Melissa Hamilton always reminded him of his older sister: obstinate, impulsive, and not afraid to speak her mind.

Melissa sipped her scotch. "What is it you're not telling me?"

"I'm not withholding anything you don't already know."

"I've been off the pills for months."

"I wasn't going there…"

Melissa clasped her hands together. "I heard you signed a new starlet."

Sid relaxed his shoulders to soften his posture. "I can't talk about other clients."

"I'm not asking for her blood-type. I'm trying to weigh the competition."

"Ariea signed her to a one-year deal."

"Who's writing for her?"

"She writes her own material."

"Of course she does."

Sid tapped his finger on his empty glass. "Forget about her. Let's talk about you."

"As long as the next words out of your mouth involve a new record deal."

Sid cleared his throat and prepared for battle. "Do you trust me?"

"I wouldn't be here if I didn't."

"Then I'll be straight with you, Melissa. Hip-hop music has become the David to our Goliath. Gangsta Rap, Dirty South, Old School, West Coast, Latin Rap, Underground, Hard Core…You name it. They're stealing our market share."

"Don't compare me to 50 Cent."

"You're missing the point. The music business is about *business*. Like it or not, it adapts to meet the strongest demand. The baby boomers are out. Generation X has moved in. Half the country music singles we cut never make it to the airwaves. The ones that do, all sound the same."

Melissa turned around to catch a tennis match on the courts below. She could see the iceberg looming, but she couldn't steer out of its path. "You're trying to tell me country music is dead?"

"I'm saying things change. The younger singers are more in touch with the new demographic. Labels are circling the wagons around the most successful artists—the ones with the biggest audience."

"And you think I've lost my audience?"

"Sometimes we're victims of our own success. Your audience has matured. People change. Their tastes evolve. You've been off the grid for seven years. You haven't cut a new album since the accident."

"Now you're blaming me," Melissa's voice escalated. "I thought it was the hip hop moguls. Or my geriatric fans."

"I'm your business manager. I see the facts for what they are. I don't allow my emotions to obscure the truth. And the truth is, your music isn't selling the way it used to. Your royalties are way down, and your merchandise sales flatlined years ago."

"Don't talk to me like an accountant, Sid."

Sid claimed his refill from the waiter. "That's part of what you pay me for."

"What I pay you for is helping me negotiate a new contract. My last album went platinum. I was nominated for female artist of the year. I've played across the fifty states. I've toured Europe four times."

"And you had a great run. I'm not discounting your previous success, but Nashville is all about sales volume. Stockholders control the labels. Labels want big money. They won't record what they can't sell."

"Should I be worried?"

"You need to cut expenses. With a cleaver. Your mortgage is a drain, and after taxes, maintenance, staff salaries, horses, private school tuition, and—clothes—you're spending more than your waning investments can earn."

"I have plenty of money."

"You won't for long."

Melissa rubbed her hands together. Goose bumps covered her arms. "This place is always freezing."

"You need to think about your future. And your boys…"

"I am. They start public school tomorrow."

"The school year's almost over."

"I'm trying, Sid. This isn't easy for any of us."

"You need to cut back more."

"I have."

Sid finished his double bourbon. "A *lot* more."

"How much more?"

"Until it hurts."

"I'm not selling the horses."

"You can't ride them anymore."

"The boys can. And my back feels stronger every day."

"Melissa…"

"Forget it, Sid. End of story."

"Lose the Benz and the Bentley."

"I look nice in those cars."

"Then you'll look nice on your way to the poor house."

Melissa fidgeted with the silverware settings. "I'll think about it."

"Have you spoken to Tomás?"

"He's nonnegotiable."

"He can collect social security. Your boys will be old enough to drive themselves in a few years. Chauffer expenses are the last thing you need right now. Between the outrageous salary and benefits you extend him—"

"Tomás is family. He's been a godsend to my boys. The only father figure they've had since their dad bailed on them."

"You're letting emotions cloud your judgment. As your agent and your business manager—as your friend—you need to make some hard course corrections. Soon."

"Jesus, Sid. You sound like a bad country song. This is my life we're talking about. And my sons'. I've worked too hard for too many years to get to where I am."

Sid gave an empathetic nod. "And where you are is dragging you down a path you can no longer afford to go. Trust me."

"I'm not throwing Tomás under the bus."

"I'm not suggesting you desert him. I'm saying, get him off the payroll. He can remain in your life. Just not as an employee."

"How would the boys get to school?"

"On a bus like everyone else."

Melissa pushed her chair back. "We're not like everyone else. My boys deserve better. I'm a country music superstar!"

Sid rocked his empty glass back and forth on the table. "Not anymore."

CHAPTER 4

Leland stood outside Abby's room and knocked gently on her door. "Dinner's getting cold." He scratched the stubble on his chin. "Abigail…"

He knocked again, more firmly this time. "I'm not mad at you."

"*Go away!*" came the terse reply from Abby's room.

"Nicole brought food home."

"*Good for her.*"

Leland touched the gold cross necklace resting on his black T-shirt and heard movement from within his daughter's room. "I'm sorry I couldn't take you to school this morning." He stepped backward, barefoot in his faded jeans, as the door slowly opened wide enough to let Abby's tiger-striped tabby dart through. "You can't stay in here forever," he said before Abby could don her headphones and tune out the world completely. He walked a tightrope between the need to advance and the urge to retreat. "Can I come in?" He poked his head inside to see his daughter telegraph a nearly imperceptible nod.

"I'm tired of eating dinner from a paper bag," Abby started.

"I'll cook tomorrow night."

"That's what you said last night and the night before that."

"I had a gig."

Abby leaned against the bedpost and brought her knees to her chest with her right arm around her legs. An open bottle of orange toenail polish sat on the nightstand beside her. Stacks of moving boxes labeled *books and things* filled the room. "How did your audition go?"

Leland adjusted the window blinds to block the streetlight at the edge of the driveway. "Win some. Lose some."

"Where was it?"

"Downtown."

"You let me come to your auditions before."

"Not on school days." Leland poked through several boxes before he found the one he wanted and retrieved a pineapple ukulele wrapped in newspaper. "This thing was bigger than you when I bought it." He unwrapped the instrument and plucked the nylon strings to play a Rodgers and Hammerstein favorite from *The Sound of Music*. "Edelweiss...Edelweiss..."

"I hate that song."

"You loved it when you were little."

"I'm not little anymore."

"We should rent the movie again."

Abby rolled her eyes. "The movie's older than you are."

Leland smiled. He could feel his daughter's trepidation melt away, despite her overt objection to his singing. "How 'bout this one?" He cleared his throat and channeled his inner Elvis to play Fred Wise and Ben Weisman's "Pocketful of Rainbows."

"I...don't worry...."

"You're doing it again, Dad."

"What?"

"Trying to sing your way out of the dog house."

Leland rested the ukulele on the dresser. "Old habits."

Abby reached for the orange toenail polish and secured the lid. She jiggled the tiny bottle and reopened it, careful to wipe the applicator brush on the bottle opening to remove the excess. "Tell me about the audition."

Leland dipped his head. "Nothing to tell."

"Did you get the gig or not?"

"Not this time."

"I'm sorry."

"I'll get the next one."

"What song did you sing?"

"'This Dance'."

"You should have sung George Strait."

"I don't like cover songs. And those are very big shoes to fill." Leland pointed to Abby's left shoulder, where her amputated arm formed a stump an inch below her elbow joint. "What happened at school?"

"Nothing…"

"I heard you had an eventful day."

Abby applied the polish to her right pinky toe. "What else did Nicole tell you?"

"She said you were upset."

"Tell her she should mind her own business."

"Your principal left a message on my phone, but I never got a chance to talk with her."

"I'm not going back to school."

Leland let Abby vent. She reminded him of her mother at times. The same stubborn determination to want everything her way or no way at all. "Tomorrow will be better."

"No it won't."

"Abigail—"

"You're not the one who has to deal with all the crap I get in school."

"What happened?"

Abby threw her hand up in frustration. "I got detention."

"For losing your prosthesis?" Leland asked incredulously.

Abby set aside the nail polish and looked away from her dad. "I slipped and fell. Some girl knocked my arm off by accident."

"And the school gave *you* detention?"

"It was humiliating. The whole class started laughing at me like I was some kind of freak."

Leland kissed her forehead. "I'm sorry."

"The girl kept gawking at me, so I took the arm and wacked her with it."

Leland stifled the urge to laugh at the image Abby's story conveyed.

"It's not funny!" Abby ranted.

"I'm not laughing."

"You're about to. I can tell."

"What did your teacher do?"

"She sent me to the principal's office."

"What about the other girl?"

"I barely hit her."

Leland scratched his razor stubble. "You could have hurt her."

"You weren't there. You don't know how embarrassing it was."

"Where's the arm now?"

"The principal took it." Abby rested her head on her knees. "You said this arm would be better. No one would know it was fake. I would look normal again."

"Sweetheart, you are normal. You're as normal as normal gets. You're smart and beautiful and funny."

"I don't want it back. Tell the principal she can have it for all I care."

"You don't mean that."

"I wish mom was alive."

Leland ignored the comment. "You should eat something."

"I liked your old girlfriend better. She seemed more sophisticated."

"She tried to steal my truck."

Abby smirked. "She was doing you a favor."

Leland followed Nicole from the living room to the cluttered bedroom piled with unopened boxes, Marshall amplifiers, electric guitars, and enough speaker cable to lasso Tennessee. Pages of hand-written sheet music covered the top of a knotted pine armoire. Guitar stands faced the corner with the vertical blinds closed to shield the room from the neighbor's view. A floor lamp with a tilted shade cast a glow on the upright mattress and box springs leaning against the wall.

Leland slipped his hand in his pocket to retrieve the business card from his audition. "I'm beat," he told Nicole who stood at the bathroom sink, rubbing a wet washcloth on her face.

"Did you call her yet?"

"I need voice lessons like the Pope needs bible study."

"It couldn't hurt."

"You don't think I can sing?"

"No one's perfect." Nicole rinsed the washcloth. "Don't say it."

"I didn't—"

"But you thought about it."

"She's my baby."

"Abby's a young woman. The sooner you accept it, the better."

Leland stuffed the card in his pocket. "I don't like change."

"Really? How many times have you moved in the last five years?"

"That's different."

"Change is change. You either accept it or not."

"I just want Abby to be happy."

"Did you talk to her?"

"She told me what happened with her arm."

"She'll bounce back."

"She told me she doesn't want to go to school anymore."

"No girl her age wants to be in school, Leland."

Leland took his shirt off and kissed Nicole's shoulder. "You smell nice."

"You need a shower."

"I should have joined yours."

Nicole squeezed a dollop of Crest on her toothbrush and backed away from the sink when Leland retreated to the bedroom. "Did you put the mattress frame together?"

"I'll do it tomorrow."

Nicole put the toothbrush in her mouth and scrubbed vigorously.

Leland lifted his guitar from the hard shell case beside the mattress and slipped his arm through the shoulder strap. He played a new chord sequence, rehearsing the lyrics to a song he'd been practicing for days.

Nicole rinsed her teeth and wiped her face on a towel. "Sounds nice."

"It has potential."

"When are you going to teach me to play guitar?"

Leland gave a devilish grin. "You can't afford me."

Nicole threw her towel at Leland's face. "You're cheap."

Leland waited for her to unpack a box of lingerie. "It goes something like this," he said, softly strumming the guitar. "I'm too tired to make my bed. It's been a long, hard, day. So come have sex, with me, instead. And we'll find our way…"

"Not funny."

"A little bit?"

"No! I have to open tomorrow morning." Nicole dug through a moving box for a clean set of sheets. "Why don't you take a cold shower?"

Leland rested the guitar in its stand and approached Nicole. He touched her face with both hands and kissed her lips. "Why don't you take a hot one with me instead?" He slid his hands to her hips and brought her toward him. He kissed her gingerly on the neck. "I'll go slow."

"What about Abby?"

"She's out cold."

"What if she hears us?"

"It wouldn't be the first time."

"I'm serious."

"So am I. We could go in my truck."

"Gross."

"You liked it before."

"I was drunk. I'm not having sex in your truck again."

Leland walked away. "Are we okay?"

"I'm fine."

"You don't seem like yourself lately."

Nicole pushed him away with her tone. "I'm sick of working fast food. This house is a mess. The litter box stinks. My check engine light is on again. And your daughter hates me."

"Abby hates everyone."

Nicole threw the sheets on the mattress. "I'm serious, Leland. I want more than this. I want a house with a toilet that doesn't run and a roof that doesn't leak. I want a car with gears that don't grind. I'm tired of chasing dreams that don't come true."

"Tell me how you really feel."

"What are we doing here?"

"This house?"

"This house. This city. This life. You keep chasing the same dream while I keep serving burgers and fries."

"Then quit. Do something different."

"Someone has to pay the rent."

"I pay my share."

"Since when? You spend more time and money chasing gigs…"

"Music is my life, Nicole. This move. This city. It's part of God's plan. I want the same things you do. I work when I can, but I need to be close to the action."

"So did Icarus," Nicole snapped. "Look how that turned out for him."

CHAPTER 5

Twelve-year-old Jonathan Hamilton stared through limo-black tint at the cadre of curious middle school students enamored with the über-expensive ride. "I don't like it," he told his eleven-year-old brother, Adam, from the sumptuous back seat of a chauffeured Bentley Mulsanne. Cradled in the opulent cabin of saffron leather and polished wood veneers, he liberated an open liter of sparkling water canted in the champagne cooler between the seats. He unscrewed the cap and drank from the bottle while he surveyed his public school peers dressed in cheap attire. He passed the water to his brother and leaned forward toward their driver, Tomás. "What do you think?"

Tomás touched a sterling silver replica of the Virgin Mary suspended from the rear view mirror. "I think you better go," the sixty-eight-year-old mestizo chauffeur said in his native Honduran accent.

"Why do we have to change schools?" asked Adam, shielded from the outside world. He wore his straight brown hair parted down the middle with an Otis Ledge shirt and Abercrombie chinos.

Tomás repositioned himself to face the boys. "I'm sure your mother has good reason."

"This school looks like a juvenile detention center," Jonathan told the former refugee who'd been involved in his life for as long as he could remember.

"Worse," said Adam, who spotted a group of students pointing in the Bentley's direction. "We don't belong here."

"Perhaps these kids think the same about you?" Tomás proposed.

"Public schools are for poor people," Adam replied. "No offense."

"I grew up in Honduras with pequeño dinero, but I was never poor. School was a privilege. One I never took lightly. Neither should you."

Adam processed what he heard. He loved Tomás, but he lived in Belle Meade, not South America. Things were different for him and Jonathan. "Who brings lunch?"

"The cafeteria."

"What kind of food do they have?"

"The kind you can eat."

"What time are you picking us up?"

"When school is over."

Adam finished the sparkling water. His mouth hurt from his orthodontic adjustment. A torture he endured without sympathy on account of his older brother's perfect teeth.

Jonathan leaned back in his seat. He didn't buy what Tomás was selling Adam. "I'm not attending public school next year. I don't care what Mom says. I'll run away if I have to."

"And go where?" asked Tomás.

"Anywhere but this dump."

"This *dump* is your home for the next seven hours. Make the best of it. Now adiós. Both of you. Before you're late."

Jonathan got out first and waited at the sidewalk while Adam hugged Tomás goodbye.

The boys walked through the school's main entrance together, soliciting unwanted attention and a crack about a *Hardy Boys* reunion.

Adam stayed close to his slightly taller brother, born ten months earlier with the same hair and dark brown eyes inherited from their mother. "Just ignore them. You can't fix stupid."

"This whole situation is stupid," Jonathan lamented amidst the frenzy of students sorting personal effects in their lockers before the final bell rang. "We shouldn't even be here."

Adam checked his phone to read a text from his mom, wishing him good luck at the new school. He tapped his brother's arm when he noticed a large, dark-skin woman with braided hair lumbering toward them.

"We're lost," Jonathan announced in frustration.

"You must be the Hamilton boys," Principal Hendrix replied.

Jonathan raised a hand. "I'm the oldest."

"I'm Principal Hendrix. I believe you're both assigned to Mrs. Dotti's homeroom."

"When do we get our lockers?" asked Adam.

"Mrs. Dotti will work with you."

Jonathan pointed to the cafeteria entrance. "What time is lunch?"

"Mrs. Dotti will have your schedule."

"What do you do?" Adam asked candidly. He could tell by the Principal's stony expression he'd opened a lid better left unscrewed.

Principal Hendrix moved with the urgency of a charging bull, parting the sea of loitering middle school students in her path. "I enforce the rules," she replied without looking back at the boys who marched double-time to keep up.

Jonathan stared at his brother. He wanted his old school back. His old friends. His old teachers. His old locker. Regardless of what Tomás had told him, he hated everything about the new school, including his new principal.

He followed Adam into Mrs. Dotti's room and waited uncomfortably at the front of the class while Principal

Hendrix exchanged words with their new homeroom teacher.

He played it cool, pretending he knew the lowdown on his new surroundings without letting his apprehension consume him. When the principal disappeared, he endured the public humiliation from Mrs. Dotti's lame attempt to introduce him to the class. Then he claimed a seat near the back with his brother. No one spoke. Not even the cute redhead with a missing arm who seemed less thrilled about being there than he did.

CHAPTER 6

Leland parked his truck at arm's length from the access control system outside the gated condominium near Vanderbilt University. He cranked his window down and squinted at the light reflecting off the aluminum key pad as the morning sun crested over the West Nashville horizon. Eager to arouse his long-time friend and agent, he jabbed the call button twice. He waited with the motor running, his hand tapping the guitar case on the seat beside him until he heard a muffled reply through the speaker grill.

"Who is it?"

"You told me to get here early," Leland answered.

"Leland?"

"The one and only."

"If I told you to play in traffic, would you do it?"

"You missed a beautiful sunrise."

"I'll catch it on Netflix. Come back in a couple hours."

"I have a new song."

"It better be good."

Leland nudged his Stetson and dropped his tinted sunglasses on the dash. He wore his work jeans and a flannel shirt with the sleeves rolled up. "Take your hand off your junk and buzz me in. You're making me late for work."

A buzzer sounded, and the steel gate opened in front of Leland's truck, granting access to the upscale property.

Leland cranked his window up and drove to the first open spot he could find. He climbed out with his guitar case, the dented driver's door moaning in protest when he shoved it closed.

He rode the elevator to the penthouse suite inside the luxury condominium tower and found Sid in a silk bathrobe and slippers in the hallway outside his unit. "You look like an extra from *The Walking Dead*."

Sid scratched his ruffled hair. "You're going to *join* the walking dead if you show up this early again." He brought Leland inside the three-bedroom condo with a panoramic view of the city. Platinum albums decorated the walls interlaced with more autographed head shots than the Hard Rock Café. Italian lacquer filled the living space. Granite counters and maple cabinetry complemented the gourmet kitchen. A Steinway, black as the ace of spades, occupied the formal dining room with a Yin Yang canvas print on the wall behind it. "Next time, schedule an appointment with my assistant."

"You don't have an assistant."

Sid poured himself a glass of pulp-free orange juice. "I'm working on it."

Leland propped his guitar case on the leather sofa and unlatched the lid. He lifted the guitar by the neck and slid the strap over his shoulder. He played a pentatonic scale to warm up. "I wanted you to hear this first. Some of the notes are rough, but the song has potential."

Sid drank his OJ. "It better have more than potential."

"I'm tired of playing piss-in-a-bottle honky-tonks."

"Why didn't you say something sooner?" Sid replied sarcastically. "I would have booked you on tour with Kenny Chesney."

"I've paid my dues."

"To whom?"

"Everyone."

"Struggle builds character."

Leland picked at the guitar strings. "How?"

"Thomas Monson. Good timber does not grow with ease. The stronger the wind, the stronger the trees."

Leland arched his head back and strummed his guitar vigorously in protest. "I'm tired of swinging a hammer for a living. I want to write music. I want to perform on a big stage." He stopped abruptly and cupped his hand over the sound hole. "I want to touch people in a way no one has before."

"Sounds illegal."

"I'm serious."

Sid finished his OJ and poured another. "Tim McGraw needs a studio musician on his new album. I floated your name to his agent."

"I'll pass."

"This is a solid opportunity."

"I don't do session work anymore."

"Since when?"

"Since I decided to focus on my music career."

"Session work is bread and butter for your career. Few musicians ever meet a star like Tim McGraw, let alone spend time inside his recording studio."

"I want more."

Sid opened the French doors to the balcony overlooking the city landscape. "You'll have your shot when you've earned it."

"Music isn't something bestowed upon the worthy. Music is something you feel." Leland cleared his throat. "Listen to this…"

I'm here today and gone tomorrow…
More than friendship on my mind
Let me show you what I miss, with a slow and tender kiss
Comin' from inside

I'll kick my boots off for a while
Touch your face and see you smile
To enjoy what I've been given

Been away from home too long
Different verse but same old song
This time, I'm gonna listen

I'm here today and gone tomorrow…
Tuck the kids in bed tonight
Sip wine by candle light
And let me show you what you're missin'

I'm here today and gone tomorrow…
I'll turn the bed and pour your bath
Tell you jokes and make you laugh
While I melt away your sorrow

If I could only find a way
To live forever in a day
I would beg, steal, or borrow
To stay with you and not be gone, tomorrow…

Leland waited for Sid's reaction. "What do you think?"

Sid rubbed his goatee while a dog barked in the adjacent residence. "I think you woke the neighbors."

"I've got another one—"

"Hold your horses, Rhinestone Cowboy."

"I could play it in a different key. Maybe slow the tempo. Add a chorus line."

"It's not a hit."

"But it has potential. If you heard it in the studio with a slide guitar and some background vocals…"

"You can dip it in platinum for all I care. The song doesn't work. Period. Maybe a B-side track at best."

"In your opinion."

"I earn a living with my opinion. Play the cover songs like everyone else. You have to write from what you know before you can write beyond what you know."

"I'm not like everyone else."

"Do you even know any songs from the Country Top 40?"

Leland ran his hand through his hair. "I've paid my dues."

"Son, you haven't begun to pay your dues. You might think you own this town, but this town doesn't know you. Nashville doesn't give a shit about you or your music. This is a business. Music doesn't run on hope. It runs on cash. Plain and simple. Labels want small investments and big returns. No one cares if you've played for thirty days or thirty years. You're just another voice in a crowd of thousands."

"Then tell me what I need to do."

"Keep playing. Keep singing. The more exposure you get, the better."

"I'm tired of playing the honky-tonk circuit."

Sid looked at Leland and spoke with his hands in the air as if holding an invisible ball. "It's not always about what you sing, it's *how* you sing it. How you connect with your audience on a purely emotional level. Artists spend their whole lives chasing dreams they never catch. Talent and desire aren't enough. You have to know your audience."

Leland packed his guitar. "I gotta go."

"I'll set up a meeting with Tim's agent."

"I'm more than a studio musician."

"Don't underestimate this opportunity, Leland. You never know what's on the other side of the door unless you knock."

CHAPTER 7

Nicole sat alone in the quiet confines of her doctor's office, afraid to stay and afraid to leave. She'd received the dreaded phone call weeks ago, when a nurse masked the bad news behind a pleasant, yet insistent, appeal to discuss the mammogram results in person. Nicole wanted answers on the phone and disputed a follow-up appointment, citing bad timing, bad weather, car problems, a crazy work schedule, and anything else she could think of to prompt an immediate dialogue and avoid another sleepless night pondering endless *what ifs*? But for every imploration she threw over the fence, the nurse persisted with steadfast commitment to have the doctor discuss the lab results in person.

She wanted to call her mom again, but she dreaded the condescending lecture from a high school dropout who could barely string coherent sentences, let alone offer meaningful advice about cancer. And with Leland focused on his own ambitions, she had no one to confide in except her stepbrother in Reno with his five kids and an ex-wife with a gambling addiction. Or her married friends embroiled in their own problems—or by teenage coworkers she could barely trust to cook an egg let alone discuss her personal life. That left the studio musician who dropped by at lunch every other day for the same combo meal, with apple slices instead of fries, and some serious flirting on the side. After several attempts, the bad boy drummer had coaxed her cell phone number and continued his pursuit with spoony text messages. She'd obliged with daring snapshots of her cleavage, appeasing any semblance of immorality by engaging in nothing more than a virtual relationship with another man. A relationship she quickly carried beyond the illusory realm to a series of brief, but intimate, encounters. At times, she hated herself for cheating on Leland, but she needed the release.

She tightened her posture in the plastic chair, facing a gun-metal desk with a twenty-seven inch iMac and a goose-neck lamp bent downward. She checked the caduceus wall clock for the tenth time in five minutes. Her gut instinct told her the painful bean-size lump was bad news. Now her heart pounded in her chest with the tempo of a vigorous run. She'd survived the first mammogram. Then the follow-up imaging and ultrasound, which led to a simple biopsy procedure, as the doctor described it.

She sat upright when the man of the hour arrived in green scrubs and a pair of orthopedic clogs. "I really need to get back to work," Nicole blurted, half way out of her chair before the young physician could close the door for privacy.

"Sorry to keep you waiting," the doctor offered in a mildly apologetic tone.

"How bad is it?"

The doctor uploaded the pathology results on his computer. "Let me pull up your records."

"I have no family history of breast cancer. I don't smoke. I exercise three times a week."

The doctor tapped the mouse to open a second window. "Your biopsy results show atypical ductal hyperplasia."

The color slowly faded from Nicole's face. "How bad?" She imagined a horrific mastectomy followed by rounds of chemotherapy. Hair loss. Nausea with persistent vomiting followed by months of emotional pain and suffering.

The doctor retrieved an anatomical mockup of a woman's breast from the cabinet behind his desk. He pointed to the plastic milk duct modeled beneath the transparent nipple. "Alveoli cells within this region feed the milk ducts in the breast. In your case, we found irregular cells lining the milk duct region of your left breast. Pathology determined these particular cells are not cancerous."

Nicole let out a deep breath. "So this is good news?"

"With atypical ductal hyperplasia," the doctor continued, "malignant lesions can exist elsewhere in the breast and are often invisible from the screening mammogram. Your diagnostic mammogram showed micro calcifications, which can represent calcium deposits in malignant tumors."

"What are you saying?"

"The data is inconclusive. I'd liked to schedule you for a second biopsy, but from a different region of the breast this time."

"Do I have cancer or not?"

"I'm not saying you do. I can't say for certain you don't. I won't have a conclusive diagnosis until we run some more tests. You could have benign abnormalities or infiltrating ductal carcinoma."

"Meaning what?"

"I'll know more from the second biopsy." The doctor rolled his chair back. "My staff can set up the appointment for you on your way out."

"I'm not sure if I can get more time off from work."

"I strongly suggest you do." The doctor checked his pager. "If you'll excuse me…"

Nicole remained in the office, mentally processing the news as neither good or bad but somewhere in between. She wanted to run away from her life as she knew it, but running never fixed her problems—a lesson she'd learned more times than she cared to remember. Nothing made sense anymore. Not the doctor's inconsistent analysis or her taste in men. And especially not her move to Nashville with a boyfriend who spent more time playing guitar than he did with her. She needed an exit strategy. A fresh start away from everything and everyone. She wanted more than a new beginning. She wanted a brand new life.

CHAPTER 8

Melissa climbed the staircase in her Belle Meade estate and hollered, "You're going to be late!"

She entered Jonathan's room first, aghast at the sight of dirty laundry strewn about an entire floor space larger than her first apartment. Exotic car posters covered one wall. A Miami Heat poster decorated a closet door. "I want your room cleaned up when you get home today. Put your dirties in the basket and bring them to the laundry room for me."

Jonathan pulled a shirt over his head. "What about Adam's room?"

"Same goes for him."

"Yolanda always does our laundry."

"Not anymore." Melissa advanced through the bathroom to Adam's adjoining cave. "Let's go!"

Adam took his iPhone from the dresser. A Fender guitar stood upright in its stand beside a Marshall amplifier. Criss Angel posters covered the walls. "Where's Tomás?"

"He's bringing the car around."

Adam shoved his dirty laundry in a pile. "I haven't eaten yet."

"You should have thought about that twenty minutes ago." Melissa picked up a shredded air soft target printed with a zombie holding a flask of green toxic goo. "You need to work on your room too. With both hands. And a shovel."

"Today?"

"Yes. And make sure you brush your teeth."

Adam opened his sock drawer with his back to his mom and said, "I know…"

"All of them."

Jonathan raced his brother down the stairs, bumping and shoving his younger sibling along the winding banister.

"It's not a race!" Adam shouted.

"Loser—"

"Boys! Knock it off!" Melissa yelled from the spacious eat-in kitchen downstairs. She wore her hair up with her skinny jeans and a silk top she'd purchased from a favorite boutique. She had a party to plan and a million things to do without having to referee her sons.

"Where's breakfast?" asked Jonathan.

"The big closet with the food," said Melissa.

"Where's Yolanda?" asked Adam. He tucked in his shirt and cinched his belt another notch.

"Yolanda quit," Melissa stated matter-of-factly. "She doesn't work for us anymore."

"Since when?" the boys asked in unison.

"Yesterday."

"Who's going to cook for us?" asked Adam.

Melissa emptied the dishwasher and stacked clean plates in the cabinet above the stove. "You two are able-bodied. It's time you learned to do more on your own."

Jonathan entered the butler pantry to search the well-stocked shelves for a box of Pop-Tarts or a chocolate chip granola bar.

"This sucks," said Adam. "Why did Yolanda quit?"

"Because she caught you jacking off again," Jonathan taunted his brother.

"Shut up—"

"You shut up."

"Boys! Get your stuff together. Tomás is waiting in the car."

Adam peeled the drapes back to inspect the circular driveway for the Bentley. "Which one?"

"Did you finish your homework?" Melissa prodded.

"We didn't have any," Jonathan replied when he emerged from the pantry. He tore open a granola bar and chewed hungrily.

"Did you bring your dirty laundry downstairs?"

"We will," Jonathan mumbled between bites as he chewed.

"Did you feed the horses?"

Jonathan looked at his brother, who mirrored the same perplexed expression. "Tomás always does that."

"Not anymore. You boys will need to start cleaning the stalls too."

"We don't know how," said Adam, pouring himself a glass of milk from the side-by-side Sub-Zero refrigerator.

"Then you'll learn."

"No fair," said Jonathan. He threw his granola wrapper on the counter and took a swig from the milk jug when his mom wasn't looking.

"Don't drink out of the jug," Melissa implored.

Jonathan sheepishly wiped his mouth with the back of his hand. "I wasn't."

"I also want the pool cleaned when you boys get home from school."

"That's not our job either," Jonathan complained.

Melissa ventured toward her music studio. "It is now."

Tomás drove a Lincoln Town Car around the driveway and waited. He snatched a folded copy of *The Tennessean* from the seat beside him and checked the sports section for the basketball scores.

Outside the car, thick clouds lingered with the threat of stormy weather. Then as if on cue, drops hit the windshield in a random stutter start before evolving to a steady rain. The sound reminded him of his parents and his childhood years growing up in Honduras before the El Salvadoran violence began. Now he enjoyed a good life in Belle Meade with the Hamilton family. A better life than he could have ever hoped for, though not without great sadness in recent times as he'd outlived his parents and buried his wife of forty years.

He trimmed the edge of his fingernail with a small pocket knife. When Jonathan and Adam climbed in back, he folded the blade and set the paper down to stretch his arm across the passenger seat. "Buenos días. Cómo estás?"

"Bien," Jonathan replied.

"You bring your umbrellas?"

"Sí," said Jonathan, sliding across the seat to make room for his brother, Adam, who quickly settled in beside him. He shoved his backpack on the floorboard in front of him. "Where's the Bentley?"

Tomás waited for the boys to buckle their seatbelts. "It transformed."

Jonathan looked at his brother and shrugged his shoulders.

"We have a new ride now."

"But I liked the Bentley more," said Adam.

Tomás followed the driveway to the end and waited for the iron gate to open. He looked at Adam in the rear view mirror and winked. "Me too."

"Yolanda quit," said Jonathan. "I had to serve myself."

Tomás arched his eyebrows. "The injustice…"

"I'm serious. Mom said we have to clean the pool, too."

"And feed the horses," said Adam.

"Sometimes we learn the value of hard work by working hard."

"And sometimes life just sucks," Jonathan replied.

Tomás drove through the open gate. "Your life is what you make of it." He merged with traffic and gunned the engine to pass a school bus before it slowed to deploy the mechanical stop sign.

Jonathan watched his home fade from view. "Are you leaving us too?"

"No Sir. I'm here for as long as your mother needs my help."

"Can you cook?"

"Can LeBron James dunk a basketball?"

"Can we skip school today?"

"You trying to get me fired?"

"Never," said Adam before his brother could reply. He leaned forward in his seat. "You're the best thing that's ever happened to our family."

"Very kind of you young man, but you're still going to school today."

CHAPTER 9

Melissa stood beneath the crystal chandelier suspended from her foyer's vaulted ceiling and waved goodbye to a bevy of freeloading guests. She twisted her hand back and forth with her arm raised in a Princess Diana pose, convinced that half of her invite list would never step foot in her home again. She blamed the dreary weather for the low turnout, but she also blamed herself for the poorly executed brunch thrown together in haste without the proper decorum required to adequately disguise her promotional opportunity as a charity event. Despite the advance invitations, the elaborate catering, and Sid's efforts to entice Nashville's music elite to attend, she'd missed the mark. By a football field.

She waited for the trailing limousine to disappear down the sloping driveway. Then she retreated inside to find Sid rooting through leftover hors d'oeuvre on the white lace buffet table. "I thought you hated sushi."

Sid tasted the smoked salmon on potato gaufrette with dilled sour cream. In his other hand, he balanced a plate of deviled egg, maple glazed ham, and carved turkey breast above a tray of champagne flutes. "Where I come from, we call it bait."

Melissa grabbed an open bottle of Crystal from a bevy of ice and sipped the cold champagne. "Did anyone even notice my background music? I spent six weeks arranging that piece." She drank some more. "Too subliminal?"

"Too transparent," Sid maintained with his fork descending toward a tray of seared lobster on lemon thyme risotto cake. "Pretending to solicit money for inner city kids while you socialize your big comeback among our Nashville patricians looked better on paper than in practice."

"I thought you invited fifty people?"

"I *reached out* to fifty people, most of whom declined. Label executives can be an ignorant lot at times, but they're not dumb."

"I should have listened to you."

Sid passed on the crackers and caviar dip. He set his plate down and wiped his silver goatee with a napkin. "These people aren't your friends. Not in the truest meaning. Half your guests would poke their own eyes out if it would push them ahead of their competition. You deserve better."

"No argument there."

Sid noted Melissa's tipsy body language. "How much have you had to drink?"

"Not enough." Melissa downed another swig of champagne. She could almost feel the room begin to move beneath her four-inch heels. "At least my heart's in the right place."

"No. It's not. And your head isn't either."

"Then what do you expect me to do? I'm not feeling the love from my current record label."

Sid grabbed the champagne bottle from Melissa's tenuous grasp. "Wharton Brothers is not the problem."

Melissa made a token effort to retrieve the bottle. "I get it." She looked away. "I've got five grand worth of leftover food and drink in this house and no one but you to eat it."

"Never stopped me before."

Melissa slipped her heels off. "I'm going upstairs. Do me a favor and kill the music."

* * *

Sid finished his plate and cleared a space to park his dish on the buffet table. Melissa deserved better, but her ill-conceived publicity stunt ended as he'd predicted, with an empty house and a shattered diva overcome by pride and a stubborn propensity to ignore reality and persist in a state of disillusionment. He'd seen the results with other clients. Some older. Some younger. All talented but edging past their prime. The music business was a monster lurking in the Garden of Eden, waiting for the inevitable rise and fall of superstardom. A lucky few knew when to get out while the rest languished in denial, possessed by their twisted desire to conquer Nashville without realizing Nashville had already conquered them.

He could have pressured more people to attend, but turning the screws on old acquaintances for another goodwill gesture never faired well. He'd built his career on his reputation, pounding the pavement one block at a time for thirty years to outmaneuver, outsmart, or outlive the competition. He had Melissa's interests at heart, but he had his own status to protect. Nudging a few music executives now and then to draw attention to a demo session was one thing, but trying to push cold product on people who weren't interested came across as disingenuous at best.

He advanced toward the glass-enclosed studio, where a grand piano sat opposite Melissa's Grammy prominently displayed in a glare-free case. He entered the private sanctuary and powered down the stereo broadcasting a new album track to the wireless speakers in the house.

Melissa propped herself with her head above the open toilet bowl. Glass fragments from a broken bottle bedazzled the Spanish tile. Another voluntary purge of her stomach contents ended with a violent gagging motion and a few drops of residual vomit.

She wiped her mouth with the back of her hand and faced the bathroom mirror. She balanced herself with one hand on the bathtub as she stood up to tip-toe barefoot through the mine-field of broken glass.

"*Melissa?*" she heard Sid's voice from the upstairs hall.

"I'm fine," she answered sternly.

"*What's going on?*"

"Nothing."

"*It didn't sound like nothing.*"

"I broke a bottle."

"*Are you all right?*"

Melissa wiped her face with a towel and gargled with Listerine. "I went overboard on the Sushi."

"*That's not what I meant.*"

Melissa opened her prescription and swallowed a blue OxyContin tablet. "I'm good…" She fixed her hair in the mirror and left the bathroom to find Sid in her path. "I don't need a babysitter."

Sid noticed the catastrophe on the bathroom floor. "There's broken glass everywhere."

Melissa stepped around him to approach the banister at the top of the stairs. "I'll get it later. You should get going. Tomás is coming home with the boys."

"Tomás?"

"Don't start."

"I didn't say anything."

"You don't have to. I can read your mind."

Sid started down the stairs with Melissa. "I'll send someone over to clean up the catering."

Melissa escorted Sid to the front door and saw him out. After he drove away, she ventured back into the house, alone in the quiet confines of her private residence, her pride dissolved like the ice in the cold serving trays.

She checked the bay window when she heard a vehicle arrive outside, expecting to see Tomás in the new Town Car. Instead, she saw a younger man pull up in an old pickup truck and get out to approach the house in jeans, dirty boots, and a work shirt with the sleeves rolled up. He looked ruggedly handsome in a Steve McQueen sort of way but with longer hair and tattooed forearms.

Curious, and also mildly concerned, she put her clogs back on and ventured outside to confront her uninvited guest. "Who are you, and how did you get up here?"

"The gate was open," Leland replied.

"This is private property."

Leland took off his Stetson and touched it to his chest. "My name's Leland Presley."

"I already canceled my pool service."

"Pardon?"

"You *are* here to clean the pool?"

Leland fidgeted with his hat in hand. "No ma'am. I tried to call, but the phone kept going to voice mail. I apologize for arriving unannounced."

Melissa kept one hand on her hip. She felt a migraine coming on. "Whatever you're selling Mr. Presley, I'm not interested."

Leland retrieved Melissa's business card from his front pocket. "The owner at the Crazy Horse Saloon gave me this."

"Are you a singer?"

"I play guitar as well."

"Do you play for a living?"

"Not yet, but I intend too."

Melissa relaxed her stance and read her name on the crinkled business card. "I don't do voice lessons anymore."

"Are you sure? I drove an hour to get here."

"I'm quite certain, Mr. Presley. And I only work with agent referrals."

"I have an agent."

"Who?"

"Sidney Irving."

"*Sid* Irving?"

"Yes ma'am."

"Is this a joke? Did Sid put you up to this?"

"No ma'am, but I did cross paths with him as he was leaving. You know him?"

"You could say that. Did he give you my address?"

"I found it on the Internet."

Melissa noticed the wooden cross tattoo on Leland's right forearm and the treble clef on his left. "Now you're starting to creep me out. My chauffer will be back any minute."

"Is this a bad time?"

Melissa folded her arms at her chest. Mr. Presley seemed harmless enough. Too handsome to be threatening but not in a Ted Bundy sort of way. "Can you sing, Mr. Presley?"

"I've been singing since I could walk."

"Then let's hear it."

"Now?"

"That's why you're here, isn't it?"

"I didn't think—"

"Don't think, Mr. Presley. Sing. I don't have a lot of time."

Leland switched his hat to his other hand. Unprepared for the impromptu audition, he debated his options and chose a song he knew by heart. A tune he could belt out unaccompanied and unrehearsed. "Do you know 'Unchained Melody'?"

"Does Duncan know donuts?"

Leland cleared his throat and sang the first bar.

Melissa stood quietly, almost mesmerized by the richness of Mr. Presley's baritone voice. Her face was flush when he finished the song—a sensation she attributed to her alcohol consumption as much as Mr. Presley's soothing vocals. "What do you do for a living?"

Leland smiled. "I do construction. Mostly carpentry."

"Do you like construction?"

"It pays the bills."

"Half this town can sing well enough to play in most honky-tonks. You have to be great to stand out, and even then, you'll be hard-pressed to earn a living at it."

"It's not about the money."

Melissa laughed before a muffled burp escaped through her hand on her mouth. Dismissing the awkward faux pas, she asserted, "It's always about the money, Mr. Presley.

And I don't run a charity. I charge four hundred dollars an hour."

Leland lowered his chin. He crunched the gravel under his boot and put his hat back on. "I'm afraid I can't meet those terms."

"Then why are you here?"

Leland tipped his hat at Melissa and walked back toward his truck. "Sorry to bother you."

Melissa gawked at Leland's truck. "It was you, wasn't it? The one who cut me off in traffic the other day. You kept honking for me to move over."

Leland glanced at the black Mercedes in the driveway and read the CASHVIL license plate. "I was late for the Crazy Horse audition."

"I remember your truck."

"I remember the finger."

"Sorry. I suppose it wasn't very lady-like of me, but you did drive a burr in my saddle." Melissa saw the Town Car approach from the rise in the driveway. "You said you do construction. Can you fix things?"

"Depends on what needs fixing."

"Everything. This house is falling apart inside. Maybe we can help each other?"

CHAPTER 10

Jonathan leaned his chair back until his head touched the wall behind him in the principal's office. So far, nothing about public school excited him. He hated the kids. He hated the teachers. And he hated the food. Most of all, he hated being away from his friends at the Belle Meade private school he'd attended since first grade. "Is she out there?" he asked his brother.

Adam peeked through the blinds at the open office area. "Not yet." He plopped himself in the chair beside Jonathan and picked at his braces. "I miss our old school."

"Me too."

"Why can't we go back?"

"Mom's broke."

"How do you know?"

"Why do you think she fired Yolanda and the pool guy? Why do you think she sold the Bentley? The next thing you know *she'll* be driving us to school in a station wagon and Tomás will be bagging our groceries."

Adam choked on his own words. "She can't fire Tomás."

"She fired Yolanda."

"Yolanda quit."

"That's what Mom wants us to think," said Jonathan. He leaned his chair back. "Mom's been home a lot lately. She hasn't been on tour in years."

"So? She has lots of money."

"Not enough to keep Yolanda or the Bentley."

"Do you think we'll have to move?"

"Maybe."

Adam poked his tongue against his braces, where the wire protruded from the band around his back molar and irritated the fleshy part inside his mouth. He wanted a snack and a sparkling water. More than anything, he wanted to clamp down on a fat wad of grape-flavored gum, the thought of which made him salivate. "How much longer do we have to wait here?"

Jonathan shrugged. "Maybe the principal forgot about us."

"She doesn't seem like she forgets about anything."

"No one saw us."

"Then why are we here?" Adam pondered.

Jonathan rocked his chair back and forth in place. "Check this out."

"You're going to break it."

"You mean like this?" Jonathan lifted his butt off the chair to rip a loud fart at his brother.

Adam grabbed an empty folder from the principal's desk and fanned the air. "Don't crack a rat in here!"

"The lunch food makes me fart."

Adam pinched his nose. "Did you even wipe this morning?"

"Shut up," Jonathan retorted, jabbing his brother in the shoulder. He got up to inspect the prosthetic forearm on the cabinet beside the principal's desk.

"Don't touch it," Adam warned.

"I'm not going to break it," said Jonathan. He picked up the arm, surprised by the hefty weight.

"What are you doing?"

"I'm just checking it out. I've never seen one before."

"Put it back before she gets here."

Jonathan tapped the desk with the prosthesis. "Check this out…" He waved the arm side to side. "I know an eighth grader in our old school who saw a movie where an arm like this came to life."

"Put it away!"

Jonathan bent the fingers back toward the palm, leaving the middle finger protruding in an upright position.

"You're going to break it!"

Jonathan put the arm back and plopped himself next to his brother. "Do you think she knows?"

Adam leaned over to raise his butt off the chair. "I know this much," he said, launching his own fart in retaliation.

Principal Hendrix dropped a crumpled brown lunch bag on her desk and opened a cabinet drawer for an aerosol bottle of Febreeze. "Gentlemen," she started as she sprayed the air inside the closed office space, "you've had quite a day." She checked her office phone for messages. "Is there anything you'd like to share with me?"

"We didn't do it," said Jonathan.

Principal Hendrix moved away from the window and reached inside the brown bag to pull out a large jockstrap. She held it up with two fingers and laid it on her desk. "This was found at the top of our flag pole this morning. Any idea how it got there?"

The brothers looked at each other and moved their heads side to side in unison.

"You sure?" She confronted her accused, unflinching and unwavering in her commitment to prod a full confession. "A student saw one of you climb the pole."

"Wasn't us."

Principal Hendrix took a smart phone from her pocket and played a video for the boys. "You tell me."

Adam leaned in closer to see the image of himself laughing at his brother who shimmied up the pole with the jockstrap hanging out of his back pocket. "We were just having fun."

"You call defacing school property, *having fun?*"

The boys sank back in their chairs.

"We thought it would be funny," Adam confessed.

"I don't find this amusing at all. I find it disturbing how two intelligent young men could exhibit this behavior in light of their previous academic achievements." She squinted at Adam. "You tested out of sixth grade and jumped right into seventh. Somehow your intellect advanced, but your integrity got left behind." She stepped toward Jonathan. "And you, Mr. Hamilton, should learn to lead by example. You are the older brother in this equation, are you not?"

"Barely," said Adam.

Jonathan nudged his brother in protest for the snide remark.

Principal Hendrix leaned against her desk. She eyed the prosthesis above her cabinet and scowled at the boys. "I called your mother and explained the situation. She wasn't happy."

"Are we done?" asked Jonathan.

Principal Hendrix stuffed the jockstrap back in the bag. "This sort of thing might have been sanctioned at your previous school, but I assure you, it will not be tolerated here. Since this is your first offense, I'll let you both off with twenty hours of detention, the first two hours of which you will serve today in the cafeteria after school."

"That's not fair!" exclaimed Adam.

"Fair is me not asking where you procured this article of clothing. Fair is not having you expelled in the last month of school. Fair is not calling the police to have you charged with vandalism."

"Our driver will be here after school," said Jonathan. "What are we supposed to tell him when we're two hours late?"

"Tell him to adjust his schedule. Because you two are going to be running late for the next few weeks."

CHAPTER 11

◆

"This isn't fair," Jonathan complained to his brother while he scrubbed a dirty hood vent filter in the cafeteria's stainless steel sink. He dunked the plastic scrub brush in the soapy water the color of camo green and held the filter upside down to attack the other end. From his vantage point in the open kitchen space, he saw the one-arm girl push a dust mop across the floor.

"We should get paid for this," Adam commiserated. He dried a large cookie sheet and replaced it with the others above the industrial size oven now cool to the touch. Jonathan rinsed the last vent filter with the rubber spray nozzle and washed the soapy residue off his hands. He released the trigger to stop the water and pointed the nozzle at his brother. "See if I can hit you from here."

"Don't!"

Jonathan shot a quick burst at Adam who used a cookie sheet to block the stream. "Wuss."

"You're going to get us in trouble!"

Jonathan wiped his hands on a dish towel. "That horse already left the barn." He unzipped his backpack and retrieved a handful of plastic cockroaches.

Adam looked at his brother. "Put 'em back."

"These are the small ones."

"So what?"

Jonathan crouched under the serving counter to place the first bug where someone would find it. "Get over here."

"You heard what the principal said."

"She's just trying to scare us."

"Well it worked. I don't want to spend the summer in detention."

"She can't do that."

"How do you know?"

Jonathan balanced a rubber roach on the freezer handle and propped another one upside down on the serving counter, its prickly rubber legs pointing skyward. "You worry too much."

Adam scanned the cafeteria for teachers, or God forbid, the principal herself. "You think too little."

Abby glanced up from the floor, pretending not to notice the boys approaching her direction. She recognized both, had no desire to talk with either, and counted the seconds until her dad came to pick her up.

She pushed the dust mop to the far wall and steered one hundred and eighty degrees to make a second pass between rows of cafeteria tables. She kept her head down as the boys drew closer, bulldozing the three foot rectangular mop over crumbs and a tacky patch of flattened bubble gum.

"Need help?" asked Jonathan when he came within earshot.

Abby ignored the offer.

"I saw you in homeroom," Jonathan persisted. "We have the same teacher."

Abby charged toward the opposite wall and thought, *maybe he'll get bored and leave?*

"How many days did you get?" Jonathan prodded with his brother next to him.

Abby drove the mop straight at both boys and shook the dust out at their feet. "The principal said no talking."

"She's not here," said Jonathan.

Abby steered the dust mop around the boys.

"What happened to your arm?"

"What happened to your face?" Abby replied, walking away from the boys.

"You missed a spot."

Abby made a second pass to find what looked like a puddle of vomit on the floor. She moved closer and nudged the rubber appliqué with the mop head. She cracked a faint smile, mostly disgusted but also slightly amused by the phony puke.

The boys started laughing.

"What are you guys, like eight years old?"

"We're brothers."

"I got that."

"I'm the oldest," said Jonathan.

"And I'm the smartest," Adam countered.

"How'd you get detention?" Abby asked.

"We hung a jock strap on the flag pole," said Jonathan. "What about you?"

"I hit a girl with my fake arm." Abby made a fist. "This one's real."

"What happened to your arm?"

"A raccoon chewed it off."

The boys stared at Abby's truncated limb.

Abby kept a straight face. "I'm kidding. I lost my arm in an accident when I was little."

"Did it hurt?" Adam asked.

"If it did, I don't remember."

CHAPTER 12

Leland drove across the middle school parking lot to the vacant bus lane out front, where Abby sat on the curb with her backpack between her legs and her phone in her hand. "I got here as fast as I could," he announced with his window down.

Abby slipped her phone in her pocket and stood up. "I've been waiting forever. I almost hitched a ride home with the janitor." She charged around the front of the truck and climbed inside. "What took you so long?"

"Traffic was a bear."

"It was raining when they kicked me out."

"I'm sorry."

"My umbrella's busted."

"I'll get you a new one."

"I'd rather you get here on time."

Leland pulled away from the curb. "You smell like smoke."

Abby propped her bag on the floorboard. "I have not."

"Abby—"

"A teacher was smoking outside while I was waiting for you."

"In the rain?"

"It stopped before you got here."

Leland drove through the empty parking lot and merged with traffic toward home. "Try again, Dragon Lady. I can smell it on your breath."

"I was bored."

Leland held his hand out. "Give 'em up."

Abby dug through her backpack to find the crumpled pack of cigarettes.

"All of them," Leland demanded.

"Why? You used to smoke when you were my age."

Leland shoved the cigarettes in an empty McDonald's bag. "I used to do a lot of things at your age. Didn't make them right."

"I just want to be like everyone else."

"You are like everyone else."

"Now you make me sound boring."

"Not what I meant."

"So you're saying I'm abnormal?"

"I'm saying you're perfect."

"Then it's okay if I smoke?"

"No it's not. And where did you get this pack?"

"I don't do drugs."

"You didn't answer my question."

"A kid at school."

Leland raised his chin and sighed. "You have to make better choices."

Abby twirled her hair with her fingers. "What are we having for dinner?"

"Food."

Abby rolled her eyes.

"Nicole gets off at eight. You're on your own until she comes home."

"Where are you going?"

"I have a gig tonight."

"I thought you said you bombed the audition."

"This is a different place."

"Where?"

"Downtown."

"Can I come with you?"

"Are you twenty-one?"

"Dad…"

Leland drove through the next intersection and hung a right turn. With more than two hundred thousand miles on the odometer, the '85 Ram left a trail of blue smoke in its wake. "Keep your cell phone on. Nicole's coming home as soon as her shift is over."

"I'll try to contain my excitement."

"Cut her some slack."

"She flips burgers for a living."

"She works hard."

"So you'd be happy if I served fries every night?"

"I didn't say that." Leland nudged the truck's accelerator when the road opened up. The drivetrain shimmied and groaned. "No one's perfect."

"Except me."

Leland ignored the smartass comment.

"Are you still mad at me about detention?"

"I'm not thrilled about it."

"Good. Because the principal gave me another week."

"Jesus Christ Abby! For what?"

"For talking in detention."

"Who were you talking to?"

"It wasn't my fault. These boys wouldn't leave me alone."

"What boys?"

Abby shrugged her shoulders. "They're new. Like me."

"I'll talk to your principal."

"Maybe you can serenade her."

Leland squeezed the steering wheel hard enough to pop his knuckles. "Better choices, Abby."

"Says the dad who just drove past our street."

Leland checked his side mirror and executed a tight U-turn at the next intersection. The truck's power steering pump squealed in protest. "This conversation isn't over."

"When are you coming home tonight?"

"Late."

"Can I stay up?"

"No. But I want you to call me when Nicole gets home. And make sure you lock the door this time."

"I know, Dad. I'm not five years old anymore."

Leland paced inside the visitor's room of a psychiatric hospital a hundred miles outside of Nashville. He'd lied to Abby about the gig as a practical matter, or so he'd convinced himself on the long ride out of town. The less she knew about her mother, the better. Same for Nicole, whom he'd tried to broach the subject with but couldn't bring himself to unravel the whole truth about his past. At least not until their relationship took up permanent roots.

A buzzer sounded when the orderly arrived with Paula Presley dressed in white pajama pants and slippers. "Ten minutes," the orderly announced, leaving Paula alone in the company of her husband.

Leland barely recognized his wife with her locks of brown hair reduced to bare scalp. "What are you doing here?"

Paula faced a bank of surveillance cameras and rubbed her finger against her nose. "The Hilton was booked."

"I meant in Tennessee," Leland clarified his statement.

"I needed a change of scenery."

"How did you get my address?"

Paula pointed to the folded paper in Leland's hand. "You got my letter."

"You shouldn't have sent it."

"You don't take my calls."

"We have nothing to talk about."

"And yet here you are."

Leland opened the hand-written note and dangled it in front of her. "This is bullshit."

"Abby's my daughter too. She has a right to know I exist."

"Not anymore."

"It was an accident."

"You drove our daughter into a lake."

"I was sick." Paula rubbed her hands together. "I'm sorry for what happened. I can't change what I did."

"You belong in a hospital. Away from me. Away from Abby."

"I'm not the same person I was before."

"There's no cure for what you have."

"My new doctor says I'm on the path to recovery. I can manage with the right medication. You can't keep Abby away from me forever."

Leland put his arm out when Paula stepped closer. "The court's decision. Not mine."

"Abby is a product of both of us. You have no right to deny my request."

Leland crumpled the letter and tossed it on the ground. "I have every right! You were never fit to be a mother. Not then. Not now. Not ever. No more letters. No more calls. As far as Abby's concerned, you no longer exist."

"Then why did you come here? You could have written back. You could have called the hospital."

Leland pondered the question. "I guess I needed to be reminded."

"About what?"

"About how much your daughter would hate you if she knew the truth about what happened."

"She's old enough to know the truth."

Leland moved closer to Paula under full view of the hospital's closed circuit surveillance. His eyes tightened. His face reddened with his blood pressure rising. "You know the worst part? Abby doesn't need a mirror to be reminded every second of every day how she's different from every other girl she sees. How people never look at her the same way they look at other kids. This wasn't an accident or a fluke of nature. This was deliberate. You tried to end her life. You can't be cured from that. And you sure as hell can't be forgiven."

"I'm not asking for forgiveness, Leland. Not from you. And don't think for a minute I wouldn't trade places with Abby. I can't change what happened. I can only learn to accept what I did and try to move on with my life."

CHAPTER 13

Tomás hauled bales of alfalfa hay behind a Polaris utility vehicle outside the barn on Melissa Hamilton's estate. When he reached the horse stables, he shut the motor off and stepped down to retrieve the pair of four-tine pitchforks from the trailer. Dark clouds threatened rain. "You ever use one of these?" he asked Jonathan and Adam who gathered beside him outside the weather-beaten structure, where rusty nails protruded through exposed wood planks.

"What is it?" asked Jonathan.

"It's called a pitchfork, Dummy," said Adam.

Jonathan nudged his brother's arm. "I know that. What do you do with it?"

"Shovel snow."

Tomás stepped between the boys. "Grab the wheelbarrow."

Jonathan looked at the wagon, then back at Tomás.

"The box with the big wheel in the middle," said Tomás.

"I know," said Jonathan.

Tomás gave each boy leather work gloves. "Put these on." He handed them their own pitchforks. "Be careful with these."

"How long is this going to take?" asked Adam.

"As long as it takes," Tomás replied. "Start moving the hay from the trailer to the wheelbarrow. And make it grande por favor. We need lots."

"Why do we have to do this?" asked Jonathan.

"Horses can't take care of themselves."

Adam stabbed the pitchfork at the fresh hay pile and made a clumsy effort to transfer what he could to the wheelbarrow, dropping more on the ground than he did on target. The more he worked the pitchfork, the more he resented the manual labor. "I'd rather be in detention."

Tomás helped him reposition his grip on the wooden handle. "Like this. Bend your knees more."

"Do you know if Mom talked to our principal?" Jonathan asked Tomás.

Tomás opened the stable entrance to greet Sabrina, an eight-year-old Black Tennessee Walking Horse with a stocky build, a long, thick tail, and a full mane. He touched the horse with tender hands and exuded a sense of calm. "Bring the hay in here. Be careful where you step."

Jonathan entered the stall ahead of his brother to pet the trail horse their mom bought them for Christmas the year before.

Tomás grabbed a pitchfork and started scooping manure piles to one corner. "Like this…" He moved in a circle around the horse, using the metal tines to separate the soiled bedding from the clean hay. "Start at the door and work around. Separate the good straw from the bad. Don't forget to remove the manure." He looked at Adam. "You try."

Adam lifted his Vans to find fresh manure on the bottom. He dragged his shoe on the floor while Jonathan worked the other side. "How often do we have to do this?"

"Every day," said Tomás.

"*Every day?*" Jonathan pondered out loud, jabbing the pitchfork at the floor, nearly spearing the front of his Nike cross trainer.

"Sí."

"This isn't fair," said Adam. "We'll never have time to ride her."

"Fair is a warm bed and food in your stomach every night."

"When are we supposed to do this?" asked Jonathan.

"After school."

"We have detention after school."

Tomás lowered his head. "Entendido."

"This sucks," said Adam.

Tomás smiled to expose a gold molar on his upper jaw. "Sí. Welcome to the real world. We've been expecting you."

Melissa supervised a boiling pot of angel hair pasta behind her kitchen window overlooking the backyard pasture and a pool nearly filled above the skimmer from recent rain. She poured herself a glass of water from the tap and discretely swallowed another OxyContin tablet while Sid occupied the dining room table covered with accordion files and stacks of financial records sorted by month and year. "Do you think I'm attractive?"

Sid looked up from the printed bank statements. "When's the last time you balanced your checkbook?"

"I know I'm not twenty-five anymore, but do I still turn heads?"

"I think you should put the house on the market."

Melissa dipped her fingers in her glass and flicked water at Sid. "Are you listening to me?"

Sid removed his reading glasses and wiped a drop from his face. "You look like a movie star with the voice of an angel, but you need to monitor your investments more closely."

Melissa touched her ass. "It's not my voice I'm concerned about." She stirred the noodles in the boiling water.

Sid scrutinized the financial statements. "Your records are a mess. The numbers don't add up."

"That's why I have an accountant."

"Apparently not a very good one. Back taxes are eating you alive. And you still owe the studio."

"Bullshit."

"Your last album didn't meet expectations."

"Yours or mine?"

"Your record label's. They're entitled to a refund on your advance."

"That's my money!"

"Technically, it's their money."

"Then renegotiate."

"There's only so much I can do. You know how this works."

"I've never had to forfeit a dime."

"And you've never had an album tank before. Twenty years ago you could sell a hundred thousand records and strike gold. Now it takes three times that many just to break even."

Melissa dumped her water in the sink. The hood fan hummed above the gas range, where steam rose up from the boiling water in the eight-quart pot. "Then negotiate a new contract with another studio. When they hear my new material, they'll forget about the last album."

"Not that easy."

"That's what I pay you for."

"You need to sell this estate. Downsize into something with a lot less maintenance. All things considered, you could do well in a smaller place."

"Says the man who owns a villa in Venice."

"Melissa…"

"I'm not selling the house."

"You could take on a roommate to share the mortgage."

"I'm not sharing my home with a stranger. Especially with my boys living here."

"I'm not talking about a hitchhiker or some cretin off of Craig's List. There are reputable services who provide screened applicants."

"Not in my lifetime, Sid. And if you bring it up again, you're fired. How's that for cutting expenses?"

"I'm just saying…Even if you can't get full market value, you'd make enough to get the IRS off your back."

"Jesus Sid. I fired most of my staff. I sold the Bentley. I have two buyers interested in our horses. Tomás is at the barn teaching the boys how to shovel shit as we speak. If you hurry, you can catch the previews."

"Manual labor builds character."

"Did you read that in a fortune cookie?"

Sid pushed a folder aside and packed his printing calculator. "Do your boys know about the horses yet?"

"Not yet."

"You should tell them."

"They're still mad about changing schools. Their principal's on the war path about a jockstrap on the flagpole." She frowned at Sid's reaction. "Don't ask. I have enough damage to control. Selling our horses will only make things worse."

"Not financially," Sid countered. "You need to take a closer look at your spending profile. When the money going out exceeds the money coming in—"

"I have an idea for a duet," Melissa proposed. "And I want you to pitch it."

"To whom? Your own label's threatening to sue you."

"Then bring it to a different studio."

Sid got up and walked about the kitchen in silence while he pondered Melissa's proposition. "If your last name was McEntire or McBride or Underwood, we might have a shot, but given your sales slump, no one's going to promote a new single."

"You're always so pessimistic."

"I'm pragmatic. There's a difference."

Melissa stirred the pasta with plastic tongs and saw the noodles disintegrate in the boiling water. "How do you know when these are done?"

"When did you put them in?"

"A half hour ago. Too long?"

"Only if you prefer to drink your spaghetti."

Melissa shut the burner off. "This is exactly why I need Yolanda back."

"I'll order take-out."

Melissa jabbed the pasta tongs at Sid. "I'm serious about this duet."

"I'll think about it."

"You'll do more than that."

"Are you threatening to fire me again?"

"Worse. I'm threatening to cook you dinner."

CHAPTER 14

Confined to her doctor's waiting room, Nicole passed the time reading gossip about the Hollywood elite in a recent issue of *Us Weekly*. She focused on celebrity photos revealing everything from wardrobe malfunctions in Milan to nanny issues in Malibu. She had no sympathy for the lifestyles of the rich and famous, whose personal problems seemed like a dream come true among the masses. Between the clothes worth more than she earned in a year and the custom handbags worth more than her car, she could only imagine what life was like on the other side of her eight-dollar-an-hour job.

Dressed in her work uniform, she watched a forty-something woman in mom jeans and sandals leave the water cooler with her cone-shaped cup to inspect the waiting area for a seat. Pretending to be mired in a full page article, she avoided eye contact and discretely placed a magazine on the empty chair beside her. She kept the patient in her peripheral vision—right up to the point where the woman snagged the magazine off the chair and claimed the spot for herself.

Nicole wanted to move without overtly rejecting the stranger encroaching on her personal space in a pink sweatshirt two sizes too big. Instead, she kept to herself and reached for another magazine from the coffee table. This time she opened an issue of *National Geographic*. Before she could skim the first sentence, the woman perked up and said, "My husband worked for *National Geographic*. He does photography. Mostly black and white, but he also shoots color. I always wanted to learn photography. I mean, I know how to use a camera. I just don't know how to take pictures the way my husband does. How hard could it be, right? You don't even use real film anymore. Point, shoot, and done."

"Nice," Nicole replied curtly.

"Are you here for Doctor Sanders or Doctor Hemsky?"

"Sanders."

"Me too. He's the best. If he hadn't caught my tumor, I'd be rotting in a coffin by now. Makes you look at life differently, you know? Like maybe we shouldn't take so much for granted. Doctor Sanders told me his wife had breast cancer at one time. Talk about a lucky woman. I mean, not that she was lucky to have cancer, but that her husband is a doctor."

Nicole kept her face pointed squarely at her magazine, hoping Chatty Patty would take the hint.

"I'm Beth, by the way."

"Nicole…"

"How long have you been with Doctor Sanders?"

Nicole flipped the page. "Not long."

"Are you from Nashville?" Beth prodded.

"Just moved here."

"Are you married?"

"No."

"Any family here?"

"No."

"I have an older brother and a younger sister. Got an uncle down in Baton Rouge. My folks retired in Pennsylvania. My husband's family all lives in East Nashville. Born and raised. What kind of work do you do?"

"Food management."

Beth pointed to the uniform. "Gotcha. The chemotherapy must be stunting my brain. I'm usually not this dense. I had a mastectomy last month." She paused to sip her water. "You're not much of a talker are you? I used to be that way. Before my diagnoses. I lost my stamina for exercise, but I find the energy to run my mouth. Cancer's been in my family for generations. I knew my time would come. My husband has been supportive. He pretends it doesn't bother him, but he doesn't look at me the same. I found a good plastic surgeon. I can give you his name if you want. If you give me your phone number, I'll text his information to you."

Nicole closed the magazine in her lap, her nerves chaffed from the ninety-minute wait for a ten minute follow-up consultation. "No thanks."

"If you change your mind, you'll know where to find me. First I have to finish with the radiotherapy. If the cancer doesn't kill me, my armpits might. Can't wear deodorant because it interferes with the treatment. As if getting flambéed with radiation after having my breasts surgically removed wasn't bad enough, Doctor Sanders makes me stink like a homeless person when I'm here. I guess it's better than the alternative. My mother died from breast cancer. Her mother died from it too."

Nicole crossed her legs and imagined she was sitting on the moon instead of waiting for an appointment that could change her life forever. As much as she tried to ignore her new dance partner, the woman got her point across. Breast cancer wasn't the end of the world, but it was close. And not knowing her fate for certain, one way or the other, made it worse. She'd endured another gauntlet of tests, subjecting herself to more discomfort and doubt than any woman deserved. Now she needed to hear the final verdict. Good or bad, she would accept the outcome.

"If your mother had breast cancer, your chances of getting it increase significantly," Beth continued unabated.

"My mother's fine."

"What about your grandmother?"

"She died years ago."

"From cancer?"

Nicole bounced her leg on her knee and maintained a pinched expression. She dropped her magazine on the table the second she heard her name called out and hobbled on a numb leg toward the nurse who'd summoned her. Her butt tingled from sitting too long.

She found the doctor's office as cold and inhospitable as she remembered it, with the familiar gun-metal desk and the big iMac with the white goose neck lamp beside it. When the nurse left, she took her phone out and started texting the one person she needed most.

"Hands are shaking," she typed. She waited several agonizing seconds for a reply.

"It will be ok."

"What if it's bad news?"

"Don't go there yet."

"I think I'm going to throw up."

"Stay calm."

"Wish U were here."

"Me 2. TTYS."

Nicole slipped her phone in her pocket when Doctor Sanders arrived unannounced and logged into his computer. "Your final lab results are here. Let me just pull them up and take a look." He concentrated on the screen. "Your initial diagnostics showed micro calcifications. I see we did a second biopsy from the lower region in your left breast to look for infiltrating ductal carcinoma."

"No more tests," said Nicole. "I can't stomach anymore of this. I don't eat. I don't sleep. All I think about are lab results. I'm so sick and tired of being squeezed and poked like some kind of lab rat. Whatever the verdict, just tell me and get it over with. I can't take this anymore."

Doctor Sanders moved the mouse to scroll the screen and review the patient profile. He maintained the same stony expression he had when he entered the room, unflinching and void of any concern or emotional response.

"How bad is it?"

Doctor Sanders typed a note. "How are you feeling?"

"Like I'm going to throw up."

"Well don't. Everything looks good."

"What does that mean? No cancer?"

"No cancer. Go home. Have a glass of wine. My receptionist can schedule your next annual screening."

Nicole started crying. "Seriously?" She wanted to hug her doctor. Instead, she went out and sent another text message to her man in all caps. "I feel like I won the lottery!"

CHAPTER 15

L eland lifted a hammer from his leather tool belt and drove a sixteen penny nail through a two-by-four he'd cut to fit a window frame. He wore a hard hat and jeans with a long-sleeve shirt and steel-toe boots. Rubber ear buds muted the loud whirring sound from a circular saw ripping through a sheet of plywood while a backup beeper signaled a bulldozer traversing a muddy patch of rain-soaked gravel in reverse.

He retrieved another nail from his tool pouch and drove it home with the claw hammer. He holstered his hammer when the foreman approached him with an envelope in hand.

"This is yours," the foreman shouted above the construction noise.

Leland removed his ear protection and opened the envelop to find his paycheck inside. "This is light."

"A week's pay for a week's work. You've been punching out early."

"I had some personal stuff to take care of."

"You got someplace else you need to be with that guitar of yours, you do it on your own time. We're already two weeks behind schedule."

"I get it."

"I want the framing done by Monday."

"All of it?"

The foreman spit a glob of brown saliva from the wad of smokeless tobacco marinating between his check and gums. "You got a problem with that?"

"I'll get it done."

"I hate to lose you."

"You won't."

"I had big dreams too, Presley. Wanted to be a major league catcher."

"What happened?"

"I found a real job."

Leland wiped his brow with the back of his hand. "Music is my life."

The foreman sucked on the shredded dip in his mouth. "A man's got to earn a living, Presley. Put bread on the table. This job is who you are. Don't pretend to be something else."

Leland tossed his work belt in the back of his truck and drove off. Grungy from an eight-hour shift on a gritty construction site, he drove the long way to avoid the congestion downtown. He sang the lyrics to a new song he wrote, slapping his hand on the truck's steering wheel to keep time.

He checked his phone for a voice mail or text. No news, good news, he presumed and continued to Mrs. Hamilton's address for his first voice lesson.

This time he found the gate closed when he approached the sprawling Belle Meade estate. He cranked his window down and pressed the intercom to announce his arrival. He heard a garbled reply from a bad Darth Vader impersonation, followed by muffled laughter.

The gate opened slowly. Raindrops pinged his windshield in a slow staccato rhythm.

He followed the driveway along the manicured grounds and parked near the familiar black Mercedes. He carried his guitar case to the door and tipped his Stetson at the surveillance camera mounted above. Still dressed in his work garb, he took his hat off when Tomás greeted him at the door. "I have an appointment with Mrs. Hamilton."

Tomás stepped aside and motioned for Leland to enter. "I'll let her know you're here."

Leland set his guitar case on the floor. He sniffed the air and winced, hoping the cologne he applied would keep him in his host's good graces long enough to finish his lesson. He glanced at the walls with autographed photos of Garth Brooks, Hank Williams, Jr., Johnny Cash, Dolly Parton, and Tammy Wynette. A glass-enclosed case displayed two CMA award plaques: one for Female Vocalist of the Year and one for Album of the Year.

"A gift from Quincy Jones," Melissa called out from the stairs with an empty laundry basket. She pointed toward the Fazioli Pianoforti grand piano in the music studio across the room. "The piano," she said to Leland. "You were staring at it like a kid in a carnival." She descended the staircase and thanked Tomás for waiting.

"Tools of the trade."

"You could say that." Melissa carried the empty basket to the laundry room and dropped it on top of the dryer while Tomás retreated to the kitchen. She wore her hair down with a light concealer and coral lipstick to illuminate her face. "I recorded my first top ten single on that piano."

"I hope I'm not intruding," Leland said as he untied his work boots to place them on a shoe shelf behind an oriental rug. Outside the windows, light rain escalated to a steady downpour.

"I wasn't sure you would show."

"I wasn't sure the gate would open."

"My boys like to fool with the speaker." Melissa pointed to a family portrait on the wall. "You met Tomás. These are my boys."

"They share your smile."

"The one on the left is Adam. His older brother, Jonathan, is on the right."

"Do they get along?"

Melissa rolled her eyes. "Like Cane and Abel. They're supposed to be doing homework upstairs." She pointed to the ceiling as the sound of an electric guitar carried through the house. "You can hear how well that's going."

"Which one plays guitar?"

"They both pretend to. Adam likes it more, but he won't sit through the lessons. Wants to learn by himself."

"I can relate."

Melissa checked the clothes in the dryer and gave the timer another twenty minutes. "Do you have children?"

"A daughter. Abigail. I call her Abby."

"How old?"

"Thirteen going on thirty."

"I can imagine. No girls in this house but me."

Leland reached for his guitar case. "I brought my guitar."

"Did you bring your tools?"

"Pardon?"

"My toilet keeps running. The one in the powder room downstairs. I tried to jiggle the chain on the rubber flapper thingy, but it didn't fix it."

Leland followed her to the open bathroom. "Did you turn the supply valve off?"

"The what?"

Leland took the lid off the tank and inspected the components. He could hear water leaking into the bowl. "You have a bad fill valve."

"Can you fix it?"

"If I had the part." He caught her bewildered expression. "I'm a carpenter, not a plumber. I don't keep parts like this on my truck." He twisted the supply valve clockwise. "I shut the water off to keep it from running."

"But it's still broken?"

"Technically, yes. Until I can get the replacement part. Any hardware store will have it." Leland washed his hands in the pedestal sink and dried them on the neatly folded hand towel.

Melissa stepped away. "Boys!" she shouted toward the top of the stairs. "Turn it down!"

"*We did...*" came a muted reply.

"Then turn it down some more! The neighbors in Memphis can hear you."

The volume subsided.

"Sorry," Melissa whispered. "I feel like a prisoner in my own house sometimes." She brought Leland to her music studio and dimmed the lights before she nestled herself behind the piano. "How did you get into music?"

"My mother used to sing to me when I was little. I guess it took. How long have you been singing?"

"Since before you were born."

"I'm not that old."

"Good answer, Mr. Presley."

"Does your husband sing as well?"

"Ex-husband. And only in the shower. He lives in California with his paralegal."

Leland scratched his razor stubble. "What inspired you to sing?"

Melissa glanced up at the ceiling, then back at Leland. "Singing is all I ever wanted to do. I used to run around the house with a toy microphone and sing to my parents."

"Do they perform?"

"My mom died when I was young. My dad passed away three years ago."

"I'm sorry."

"At least he got to see me on stage. He was in the audience when I won my first CMA award."

Leland touched a metronome on a shelf beside the piano. "Excuse me," he said when his cell phone rang. He read Abby's name on the display and opened the flip phone to endure her teenage wrath. "I'm on my way."

"Everything all right?"

Leland closed the phone. "My girlfriend forgot to pick up my daughter from school. Now somehow I'm the one at fault."

CHAPTER 16

Leland drove across the middle school parking lot to
find Abby hunched beneath a narrow awning with her
backpack and umbrella. He parked a few feet away and got
out to open her door in steady rain. "Your chariot
awaits…"

"This is getting old."

"I got here as soon as I could." Leland motioned toward
the truck bombarded by heavy droplets. "If you don't mind,
I'm getting soaked."

Abby lobbed her backpack on the floorboard and
collapsed her umbrella. She climbed inside the antique
pickup and nudged the sagging headliner to stuff it back in
place. "This ride is embarrassing."

"There's no one here but us."

"Exactly. Detention ended an hour ago. I could have
walked home by now."

"Nicole was supposed to get you."

"Well she failed, epically."

"She had an appointment this afternoon."

"Newsflash, Dad. This isn't the first time she's blown me
off."

"I'll talk to her."

"Like that will do any good."

Leland put his arm around her shoulder and said, "I'm sorry you had to wait. We're all doing the best we can with the time we have."

Abby kept her backpack between her feet and monitored the passing traffic. *At least tomorrow's Saturday*, she consoled herself. She counted the minutes until she could bury herself in her room with the door closed and sneak a cigarette by the window. As if school wasn't bad enough, she feared the summer boredom, parading around town in Dad's rolling death trap—or worse—being stuck in the house with Nicole all night, waiting for Dad's gig to end.

She tugged on her seatbelt strap to tighten the slack around her waist. "Do you play tonight?"

"I'm all yours tonight."

"You forgot your guitar the other day."

Leland drove with one hand on the wheel. "I didn't need it."

"Since when?"

"Sometimes I sing without it."

"Try again, Dad. I'm your daughter not your fool. You were chasing a piece of strange, weren't you."

Leland took his eyes off the road and looked at Abby. "We're not having this conversation."

"So it's true?"

"I didn't say that."

Abby tilted her chin up. "I know about sex."

"Abby…"

"You said I could talk to you about anything."

Leland focused on the road. "There's a time and place for this conversation, and right now ain't either."

"You do know I got my period three months ago?"

"Shit…Why didn't you tell me?"

"You were too busy with your music."

"We'll get through it."

"I'm not dying, Dad. I started my menstrual cycle."

"Is there anything you need me to do?"

"I'm good. I found some tampons in Nicole's purse."

"What were you doing in her purse?"

"Looking for something to plug the dam. You need me to draw you a picture?"

Leland hummed a random tune. "How did school go today?"

"Sooner or later you have to face it. I'm a woman. And handicapped or not, I want to have sex one day."

Leland slapped the steering wheel. "Jesus, Abby. You're not having sex."

"Is that a question or a statement?"

"More like an order. You're thirteen. Sex is the last thing you should be thinking about at your age."

"Sex is the *only* thing boys think about at my age."

"Is your homework done?"

"At some point we should talk about birth control."

"No, we shouldn't."

"Would you rather I get pregnant?"

"I'd rather you not have sex."

"You and Nicole have sex."

"We're adults. What we do behind closed doors is our business."

"If Mom were alive, she'd understand."

"*I* understand, Abby."

"I know you feel uncomfortable, but I don't like talking about this with Nicole."

"Why not?"

"She's not my mom."

"She's a woman. She's more equipped to talk about these things."

"You do know my period happens every month?"

"Yes, I know. Nicole can handle what you need in that department."

"She said I had to buy my own tampons."

Leland shifted uncomfortably in the driver's seat. "Can we talk about this later?"

"Can I have money to buy tampons?"

"Yes, of course. Whatever you need."

"Nicole said you should take care of everything since you're my dad."

"I get it. I, we, you…just have to tell me what you need and where to find it."

Abby twirled her hair. "Do you love me?"

"Of course."

"More than you love Nicole?"

"That's a different kind of love."

"No, it's not. Love is love. You either love someone more than someone else or you love them less."

"I don't love you any less because I love Nicole."

"Does that mean you love me more than her?"

"It means I love you as your father. I love her as my girlfriend. There's a big difference."

"She left me stranded after school."

Leland slowed at the next traffic light. "I'm sure she had good reason. You weren't exactly marooned at sea. I came and got you when you called."

"What if you hadn't?"

"There is no *what if*."

"But what if you got in an accident? Who would pick me up?"

"Nicole. Eventually."

"I don't trust her."

"She likes you."

"She tolerates me."

Leland nudged the gas pedal when the light turned green. "You're not giving her a chance. It's a two-way street."

"Wow…that's deep, Dad. Does this mean I get to come home drunk and stumble through the house when you're not home?"

"What are you talking about?"

"The other night. When you left me home alone to make a booty call."

"There was no booty call!"

Abby rolled her eyes. "Nicole came back super late and started tripping over boxes. I woke up and thought it was you."

"She was probably tired from her shift. Sometimes they keep her longer."

"I know the difference between tired and shit-faced."

"Abigail—"

"I'm just saying."

"I want your room unpacked when we get home."

"Can we go fishing tomorrow?"

Leland grimaced like he swallowed a brick. He remembered the brief discussion he had with Abby several nights ago. A comment he'd made in passing about *maybe* going fishing on Saturday had been permanently recorded in his daughter's memory, remixed to alter the original version, and replayed at the most inconvenient time. "I have to work this weekend."

"You promised!"

"I said maybe."

"You said things would be different when we moved to Nashville. You said things would get better."

"They will."

"How?"

"I'm working on it."

Abby remained reticent. "You should pay more attention to what's important in your life. I'm not going to live with you forever."

"But you'll always be my daughter."

"And you'll always be my dad. I just hope you know what you're doing."

Leland put his arm around her and gave a gentle hug. Then he kissed her forehead and said, "Me too."

CHAPTER 17

Leland propped his guitar in its stand for a five minute break from the stage at a milepost honky-tonk way off the tourist map. The smoky place smelled of beer and vomit with broken peanut shells scattered about the scuffed, hardwood floor. He'd played in worse bars but never imagined he'd find himself unsigned after fifteen years of chasing gigs for gas money and food.

He left the stage and caught up with Sid at the bar. "Are you lost?"

Sid raised his drink. "I've heard you play at better venues."

Leland signaled the female bar tender and ordered a beer on tap. "I've made less money at better dives."

"It's not the Bluebird Café."

Leland accepted the mug of Coors Light. "No doubt." He clinked his glass with Sid's bourbon. "To better gigs and bigger dreams."

"Amen," Sid replied above the drunken banter from the sparse crowd of revelers in bootcut jeans and dirty shitkickers.

Leland drank to quench his thirst and looked around for Nicole. "I've been thinking about the session gig you mentioned."

"Tim went with someone else."

"When?"

"A couple days ago."

"You just told me about it a couple days ago."

"The wheels turn fast in Music City. His people brought on someone else."

"You could have told me."

"I just did. You've been in this game long enough to know gigs like that come and go in a hurry."

"And I'm still playing in dumps like this."

"It's called paying your dues."

Leland took another swig from his beer. "I've been paying long enough. Karma owes me. I can barely make rent anymore."

"That's what your day job's for. You've got skills. And you've got heart. You also have a kid who adores you and an agent brave enough to stick with you."

"Then stick around awhile longer. You might hear something you like." Leland looked out at the ramshackle audience in the blue-collar outpost one bribe shy of a failed inspection from the county health department. "One door closes. Another swings open to smack you in the face."

"Speaking of which," Sid continued, "I had lunch with Brad Siegel from Capital Country Records."

"Never heard of him."

"He's heard of you. I floated him one of your demo tracks. He wants to hear you play in person."

"Don't mess with me."

"This is legit. Capital Country is a small studio, but they have big backers, and they generate a lot of attention."

"When?"

"As soon as he gets back in town."

"Seriously?"

Sid's expression went from jovial to austere. "Do I look like I'm kidding?"

Leland shook Sid's hand enthusiastically. "Thank you. Thank you very much."

Sid held the handshake for several seconds, pulling Leland toward him without letting go. "I had to call in a lot of favors to make this happen. My reputation stands to suffer a lot more than yours if this doesn't go well."

"I won't disappoint," Leland vowed, still caught in his agent's iron grip. "Are you going to let go, or are you coming on stage with me?"

Sid let go. "This opportunity with Brad Siegel is like a duel with black powder pistols. You only get one shot. Make it count."

"I will. You have my word." Leland finished his beer and let the news sink in for a moment. Then he took the stage again and slung his arm through the strap on his favorite guitar. He squinted from the overhead lights. He played the D string and adjusted the nickel white tuner to flatten the note. "Here's a little ditty I wrote about life on the road," he shouted out to the Pabst Blue Ribbon crowd in three-legged chairs on an out-of-true floor. "I hope you like it."

He chuckled to himself, his spirits lifted as he tapped his foot in time with the upbeat tempo and finger-picked the strings on his guitar. "I call this one, my favorite honky-tonk."

Four-wheel trucks and slide guitars
Jim Bean bourbon and cheap cigars
Long-sleeve shirts and boot cut pants
Big belt buckles and wide brim hats

In a place that no one knows
But everybody goes
Where a man can walk the walk...

My favorite honky-tonk

High speed fiddles and two-step clogs
Cold beer bottles and red hot sauce
Chiseled jaw lines and cowboy themes
Rodeo clowns and football teams

In a place we like to go
And everybody knows, by name
Where a man can walk the walk...

My favorite honky-tonk

Snakeskin boots and tight blue jeans
Red Bull cans and prom night queens
Hardwood floors and heel-toe moves
Big-time players and small-time fools

Where a man can walk the walk
In my favorite honky-tonk
That's right...
My favorite honky-tonk

My favorite honky-tonk!

He heard the obligatory clap from the owner and a local fan who whistled through a toothless grin. "Thank you," he spoke into the microphone. He waved to Nicole at the bar and cleared his throat. He moved the microphone stand a little closer and smiled broadly. "Let's go with something a little different this time. A little less country and little more, love..."

He ducked from an empty PBR beer can thrown his way and ignored the drunken hecklers. "I wrote this song for someone very special. Never played it live before, until now." He slowed the tempo with the next chord sequence and locked his eyes on one person in the room.

We met on the fairground
You felt like a long lost friend, of mine
We shared all our problems
You showed me the light at the end of it all

I need you tonight

I need you to hear
A secret I share from my lips to God's ear
With all that we've learned
And all we've been through
At the end of the day, you'll see...
I'm all in love, with you
Hmmm hmmm...with you...

You tingle my sens-es
When I feel the heat from the fire in your eyes
I reach out to hold you
Now I can al-most read your mind

The weight of your smile
The touch of your lips
The way that I feel under your fingertips
I need you tonight
I need you right now
You open the door to my heart somehow

With all that we've learned
And all we've been through
At the end of the day, you'll see...
I'm all in love, with you...
Hmmm hmmm...with you...
Hmmm hmmm...with you...

I've fallen in love with you...
Hmmm hmmm, oh yeahhh...
I'm all in love with you...
I'm all, in love...with you...

Leland rested his guitar on a stand. "I'll be right back," he spoke into the microphone before he followed Nicole from the bar to a side exit that opened to the parking lot. "Hold up. Where are you going?"

Nicole pushed her way outside. "I can't stay."

Leland followed her to her car. "Then why did you come here tonight?"

"I need to tell you something."

Leland hugged her. "I tried to call you but your phone kept going to voice mail."

"I had to work a double shift."

"Abby was pissed when you didn't pick her up from school."

"I'm not her chauffer," Nicole snapped, her demeanor cold and indifferent. She unlocked her car. "I think we should see other people."

"What are you talking about?"

"I want to see other people."

"Where is this coming from?"

"I don't want to talk about it."

"Then why are you here?"

Nicole opened her door. "This doesn't work for me anymore."

Leland ran his hand through his hair. He spoke through clenched teeth. "What doesn't work for you?"

"This relationship. Us. Your daughter. Our living arrangement. Everything."

"What's going on?"

"I don't love you anymore, Leland. I'm sorry."

The words hit Leland like a kick to the face. "Just like that?"

"I said I'm sorry."

"You gotta give me something more than *sorry*. You don't just wake up one day and decide to end a relationship like this without a reasonable explanation. It doesn't jibe."

"I can't explain it."

"Will you be home when I get back?"

"I have other plans."

Leland curled his lips in disgust. "Does your plan have a name?"

"Does it matter?"

"How long have you been—"

"He's going on tour with Carrie Underwood. He's a drummer. He wants me to come with him."

Leland winced, his face taut with anger. "Good for him."

"Good for us. I'm not slinging burgers for the rest of my life. I want something more than hearing about your next audition for another gig. Or your next great song. I'm tired of waiting. You've taken this dream as far as you can, Leland. Some things aren't meant to be. You're a great musician. You'll always have that."

"I'd rather have you."

"You're obsessed with your music. You never stop to think about the people around you."

"Who's going to cover your share of the rent?"

"Our relationship is broken, and all you care about is money?"

Leland threw his hands up. "I care about not getting evicted."

"You'll figure something out."

"Would you stay if I quit music?"

"I don't want you to quit, Leland. I want you to do what you do. Just not with me in your life anymore."

CHAPTER 18

M elissa arrived from church with her boys and brought them to the house before she drove around back toward the barn to meet Tomás. She got out with her open umbrella and stood in her Sunday dress as Tomás closed the back of the equestrian trailer with Savannah, her beloved trail horse, inside. "You sure she's okay in there?"

"Sí. She has fresh hay and a clean feed bucket."

"The boys don't know about this yet. I'd like to wait another day before I tell them."

"No problem."

"I hope she'll be okay."

"The Paisley's are good people. She will be happy with them."

"Thank you for arranging everything and for towing the trailer yourself."

"Lo siento."

Melissa rubbed her eye. "Don't be sorry, Tomás. She's a horse, not my first born child."

"You can ride with me if you want."

"I promised the boys we would do something fun after church. And this isn't fun."

Tomás removed his leather ropers and walked around the trailer to inspect the tires. "What about Sabrina?"

"I have a local buyer who's interested."

Tomás carried his work gloves toward the front of the truck, undaunted by the steady rain. "They're strong boys. They'll understand." He opened the driver's side and climbed in with the window down.

"Wait," Melissa told him. She stepped over a puddle in her three-inch heels and raised her umbrella to clear the truck roof. "Drive carefully." She reached inside the cab and squeezed his hand. "You better go before I change my mind." She stepped back and waited for Tomás to pull away. Then she drove her Mercedes to the house to find Sid by his Escalade in the driveway. "Not a good time," she said, hustling toward the door with her umbrella.

Sid followed her and rubbed his shoes on the doormat with the Hamilton name enclosed by a scrolls coir boarder. "I've been trying to reach you."

"I've been busy."

Sid took off his wet Sperry's in the foyer and wiped his face with his hand. "I'm sorry about the horses, but it's the right thing to do."

Melissa mumbled obscenities under her breath and tossed her twelve hundred dollar shoes aside. "Unless you came here to discuss a new recording contract, I'd rather not—"

"Wharton Brothers has decided to push for damages. They're moving forward with the lawsuit."

"You said they were blowing smoke."

"I called their bluff. I was wrong."

"I'm not giving up my advance."

"You haven't heard what I came to tell you."

Melissa drew a deep breath and exhaled harshly. "I'll counter-sue. They never delivered the marketing campaign they promised for my last album. My tour never got off the ground."

"They'll claim your accident was the reason your album tanked."

"It wasn't my fault."

"They'll argue it impacted your ability to fulfill your contract."

"My accident has nothing to do with their incompetence."

"They hold all the cards on this one, Melissa. And the house always wins."

Melissa reached for her purse on the table to retrieve her prescription. She unscrewed the top and dispensed a pill in her hand.

"You said you were done with those."

Melissa swallowed the OxyContin tablet. "Last refill."

Sid opened his briefcase on the coffee table. He gave Melissa a file folder with her name. "I had my accountant audit your books. I'm not an expert with numbers, but I could tell something was way off. The CPA you hired was skimming from your investments. You're six months behind on your mortgage, and your retirement savings have been substantially depleted."

Melissa slowly teetered side to side, lucid but light-headed. "How much is left?"

"I don't recall the exact figures."

"How much?"

"About one point five."

"Are you for real?"

"I'm sorry."

"We need to contact the police."

"I already have. They served a search warrant this morning on your accountant's residence, but the house was empty."

Melissa rubbed her temples. "I don't understand. He worked for a reputable firm. He came highly recommended to me."

"His credentials were fake. The police ran a background check. His real name is Steven Harper. He has outstanding warrants for fraud and embezzlement in three states. You're not the first mark he's targeted."

"Doesn't make me feel any better."

"The FBI's involved as well."

Melissa cupped her hand on her stomach, both sick and angry at the same time. "How deep does it cut?"

Sid picked up the folder and scanned the figures. "Drawing interest and dividends only, without touching principal, factoring your current royalty payments—"

"Bottom line, Sid."

"About seventy grand a year. Assuming you sell the house and make good on your mortgage debt. And assuming you cut staff completely, you could stretch your income by another—"

"I can't live on seventy thousand a year! I'm not selling this house, and I'm sure as hell not cutting the only staff I have left. Tomás is family."

"Your finances are completely broken, Melissa. You're bleeding cash. If you don't stop spending—"

"What if I sell the house?"

"You mean *when* you sell the house. With the market way down like it is, you're probably looking at a short sale, assuming the bank approves. You'll lose the mortgage debt, but you'll also come away with nothing."

"Then find me another way out of this."

"I'm working every angle."

"Well work harder!"

"The police are doing everything they can."

"I'm not talking about the stupid cops. If my accountant left the state, they'll be as useless as tits on a bull. I need a new recording contract."

"That's the least of your problems right now."

"No new contract, no new money, Sid. How else am I supposed to recover from a loss like this?"

Sid checked his phone when a text came in. "I get it, but you're cold product. A few nibbles here and there, but no one's biting. No major label will touch you until you settle your contract dispute with Wharton Brothers."

"You're an attorney. Can't you make this go away?"

"Not without more legal help. Wharton Brothers will roll out the big guns soon. I can't take on their litigation army alone. I have other clients to support as well."

"Your other clients weren't raped by my accountant!"

"I get that you're frustrated."

"I passed frustration twenty mile markers back. I'm fucking furious, Sid! I shouldn't have to bear the burden for someone else's criminal act."

"You're apples and oranges, Melissa. As crooked as your accountant was, he has nothing to do with your album sales or your label demanding their money back."

"You're not helping."

"I booked you for a summer festival tour."

"Sid—"

"It will give you some exposure. Maybe generate some air time, not to mention extra income."

"Forget it."

"You have to connect with your audience on a local level. Boost your credibility with the industry. Show that you can still rock a country ballad."

"The money sucks."

"There's more at stake here than money. I've been your agent, your manager, and your friend a long time now. I've always done right by you."

"Give me something on a national scale."

"Give me something I can sell."

Melissa spied her boys eavesdropping at the top of the stairs and lowered her voice. "I've made you a lot of money in fourteen years. I've had two number one hits. Five singles in the top ten. Album of the year—"

"A decade ago. You can't live in the past."

"You think I'm damaged goods."

"I think you have to be honest with yourself. The fickle nature of this business doesn't lend itself to the way things used to be. At the end of the day, the bean counters call the shots. Think it over. And one more thing…Mayor Dean's hosting a charity event the day after tomorrow at his home in Antioch. Your invitation's in the mail."

"I hate charity events."

"Only when you're not hosting them. It's a good opportunity. A chance to mingle with some power players. Besides, I hear he serves great hors d'oeuvres."

"Who's going to be there?"

"I'll find out."

"I can't deal with another social event right now. Not until the cops track down my stolen money."

"They're doing everything they can. You need to focus on something positive. I'll let you know as soon as I hear any news."

Melissa opened the liquor cabinet to pour herself a drink. "This better be worth my time."

"I'm in your corner on this one, Melissa."

"I hope so. Because our future depends on it."

CHAPTER 19

L eland finished his third cup of coffee alone at the kitchen table, staring at unopened moving boxes piled inside the modest single story rambler. The house felt empty and alone without Nicole. From his perspective, Nicole's revelation about a new man in her life explained her odd behavior in recent weeks. He understood her frustration with his obsession for music and her need for more attention than he could spare. But what he couldn't grasp was her decision to leave so abruptly, as if their relationship meant nothing. Nicole's infidelity aside, he harbored strong feelings for her. He saw a future with her and a stable companion in Abby's life. Unlike so many who'd come before her, Nicole had an honest presence about her. Or so he thought.

He dumped his coffee in the sink and packed a leftover turkey sandwich in his lunch cooler while Abby's cat jumped on the microwave and started purring for food. "I'm leaving," he called out, gently scooping the tiger-striped tabby in the air. "We had a deal," he whispered to the cat. "You're not supposed to be up here. I'm supposed to squirt you with the water bottle when you are." He lowered the cat to the floor when Abby emerged from the hallway in short-shorts and a tube top exposing her midriff. "What are you wearing?"

Abby tugged on her shorts. "I've worn these before."

"In a Beyoncé video?"

"Dad…"

"They're too short. I can see your…You just…You need to change. Top and bottom."

"Everyone wears these."

"Everyone but you."

"I'm not changing."

Leland dropped a water bottle in his lunch cooler. "Yes, you are."

"Fine. Then I'll stay home."

"Wrong answer."

"You're so mean!"

"I don't have time to argue."

Abby stomped back to her room and changed clothes. "These make me look fat."

"They make you look respectable."

"Who's going to take me to school?"

"The bus."

"I'm not riding the bus."

"Then you can walk."

"It's like ten miles."

"Then I would go with the bus."

"Where's Nicole?"

"She doesn't live here anymore."

"Since when?"

"Don't worry about it."

Abby twirled her hair. "Did she dump you?"

"She didn't dump me. We decided we're not compatible anymore."

Abby sighed. "She dumped you." She grabbed a strawberry Nutri-Grain from the pantry. "She always hated me."

"Nicole never hated you."

"Then why did you break up?"

"I broke up with her, not the other way around."

"Guys always say that."

Leland rinsed the coffee pot. "I'll pick you up after school."

"I have detention."

"Again? What did you do this time?"

"Nothing. My principal is a wench. She's trying to make sure the crippled girl gets the same punishment as everyone else."

"Abby—"

"Why can't you drop me off?"

"Because I'm already late, and school doesn't start for another hour."

"So drop me early."

"There's nowhere to drop you. I'm not leaving you outside the building by yourself."

"It wouldn't be the first time."

Leland fished his keys from his pocket. "Make sure you lock up when you leave. And take your umbrella. They're calling for more rain today."

Abby held her position in the bus line behind a column of geeks and freaks, waiting for the jackknife doors to open. She could see the other students on the bus looking down at her from their window seats while the line in front of her moved ahead single file. She tugged on her backpack strap as she climbed aboard and scoped out a seat several rows from the back. The bus smelled like dirty socks and warm vinyl mixed with sweat and body spray. A soiled placard above the driver read *no food, no drink, no talking*.

She wanted to strangle her dad for making her ride the bus. Part of her missed Nicole, not only for the morning transportation, but because Nicole made her dad happy.

She claimed the last seat—the dreaded aisle seat on the left, which meant her bad arm was in full view of everyone behind her. She also hated people bumping her when they passed. She thought about detention and whether her dad would show up on time after school. She missed her friends in Tulsa. Fingers crossed, she would stay in the same zip code long enough to finish middle school in one place without transferring for the third time in three years.

She touched her neck when something buzzed past her ear. She cocked her head to see everyone facing forward with the same subdued expression. She kept her backpack between her legs, her knees almost touching the seat in front of her. When the bus accelerated, she felt something smack her hair and reached up to pick a wet spitball from behind her ear.

She spun around and made an angry face. "Who did that?" she yelled, observing her peers one by one to spot a guilty flinch. She quickly focused her attention on the two boys seated opposite from one another in the last row. She recognized the one with long hair and zits from her homeroom—a friend of the girl who'd knocked her arm off and humiliated her in class.

Abby faced forward again, recalling her dad's lecture about making better choices. Then another spit ball hit the back of her neck.

This time she whipped around and caught the boy with long hair and zits, cupping the straw in his hands.

The back of the bus erupted in laugher.

"You try that again," Abby focused her rage at the guilty party nearly twice her size, "and I'll shove that straw up your nose."

The boy looked away and fist-bumped his friend.

Abby unzipped her backpack to retrieve her keychain. When another spit ball smacked her hair, she stood up in the aisle. No one had the right to disrespect her. Not at home. Not in class. And certainly not on the damn bus.

"I know it was you," she confronted the bully at a distance. She held the backrest from the seat in front of her while the bus hung a left through a busy intersection.

The boy laughed at her. "No standing while the bus is in motion."

"You think this is funny?"

"I think *you're* funny."

Abby charged toward the back of the bus until she came within a few feet of her target and raised her key chain mace to spray the spitball jester between the eyes.

CHAPTER 20

Principal Hendrix settled her full-figured frame behind the desk in her office and looked across at the student she'd summoned to appear. She had enough on her plate to keep her buried in paperwork for weeks without the added aggravation from Abigail Presley's flagrant breach of conduct. Always the optimist, she saw potential in every student, no matter how dim the light shined at first.

She fanned herself with a stack of papers and made a note to contact facilities about the air conditioning. In all her years with Davidson County, including her tenure as a local church member and an advocate for children's services, she'd never met a young woman like Abigail Presley. The girl's school records revealed only a portion of the story behind the whimsical and highly precocious seventh grader. This morning, she hoped to glean the rest. "I assume you know why you're here."

"It wasn't my fault," Abby started from her seat with her arm in her lap.

"Where did you get the pepper spray?"

"My backpack."

"Who gave it to you?"

"My dad's girlfriend."

"Does your father's girlfriend realize pepper spray is illegal for a minor to possess?"

"I didn't ask her. I borrowed it from her purse."

Principal Hendrix folded her hands on her desk. "Possession of any weapon on school property is an egregious offense."

"I wasn't on school property," Abby retorted. She leaned forward in her chair. "And pepper spray is not a weapon."

"Don't argue with me, Miss Presley. The student you attacked spent two hours in the nurse's office this morning."

Abby pointed to her prosthesis on top of the cabinet. "At least I didn't hit him with my fake arm."

"You could have seriously injured him or another student."

"I wasn't aiming at other students. He was the one shooting spitballs at me."

"Doesn't justify your actions."

"My action should have been a fist in his face. He's lucky he has all his teeth."

"You should have waited until the bus arrived at school and notified myself or someone in my office."

"He's the bully. Why are you taking his side on this?"

"No one's taking sides, Miss Presley, but the fact is you exercised poor judgment."

"This is about money, isn't it? His parents have more than mine, so he becomes the victim and I get in trouble."

"This has nothing to do with money. You assaulted another student. As your principal, I bear the responsibility for the safety of every student in this school. By law, I'm required to file a report with the superintendent. At a minimum, this incident will go on your permanent record. You could be facing expulsion."

"That's not fair!"

"I don't author the rules and regulations, Miss Presley. I simply enforce them."

"What about the bully who shot spitballs at me?"

"The students I spoke with from the bus corroborated his version of events. You got out of your seat and attacked him with pepper spray."

"He was shooting spitballs at my head! Everyone saw what happened. They're just too chicken-shit to tell the truth. I hate you, and I hate this school! You're all a bunch of liars!"

"This is a serious infraction."

"So is shooting spitballs at me. I think a one-armed girl defending herself against a bully twice her size would make for good news coverage."

"Miss Presley—"

"And don't think I won't do it. My dad knows people."

"Your first day of school you attacked a girl with your prosthetic arm."

"Because she broke it off!"

"It was an accident."

"So was her conception."

Principal Hendrix leaned way back in her chair and contemplated a different conversation with Abby. One laced with less hostility, geared more toward understanding and less about casting blame. The more she emphasized the grave consequences of Abby's negligent actions, the more Abby pushed back with sarcasm and insult. "Tell me about your parents."

"What about them?" Abby shot back.

"Do you spend time with them?"

"My mother's dead, so that's a no. My dad and I get along."

"What does your dad do for a living?"

"He's a carpenter and a musician. He sings in bars mostly."

"Does he spend time with you?"

"Sure."

"Do any other children live with you?"

"Not unless you count his ex-girlfriend. But she doesn't really live with us anymore."

"I'd like to schedule a conference with your dad."

"To talk about me?"

"To talk about a lot of things."

"My dad already knows I'm in detention."

"Abby, this issue with the pepper spray notwithstanding, I'm less concerned about where you've been and more concerned about where you're headed."

"You mean my next school?"

"I mean with life in general. I'm here to enforce the rules, but that doesn't mean I'm the bad guy all the time. I was your age once. I remember the challenges. I want to see you succeed."

"Can I have my pepper spray back?"

Principal Hendrix opened her desk drawer to retrieve a handful of plastic cockroaches and a rubber rat. "What can you tell me about these?"

"They look fake."

"My cafeteria staff thought they were real. I nearly shut down the lunch preparations and called an exterminator. You're not the only one who's served detention recently. I don't believe you left these behind, but I suspect you know who did."

"I'm not a rat."

Principal Hendrix squeezed the rubber rodent and pondered the irony. "No need to get theatrical with me. I'm simply asking for a name."

"Why don't you ask the students on my bus? They seem to know everything."

CHAPTER 21

Leland drove his antique Dodge pickup through the open gate at Melissa's Belle Meade estate, where a Sotheby's "For Sale" sign directed buyers to an open house event under overcast skies and the threat of more rain. He followed the long, swooping driveway along the lushly landscaped setting to the front of the majestic property and parked between an Indian red Porsche 911 Turbo and an arctic white Rolls Royce Phantom.

He carried his guitar from his truck and hummed a melody from a song in his head. When he reached the front door, he greeted a tall brunette in beige slacks and a matching blazer with a Sotheby's stick pin on her lapel. "My name's Leland Presley. Mrs. Hamilton is expecting me."

"Were you here for the open house?" the agent inquired.

"No ma'am," Leland answered. He took off his hat and raised his guitar case. "I'm here for a lesson."

The realtor blushed at Leland's handsome features. "Are you the teacher or the student?" she asked before she disappeared inside the residence to find Melissa.

Leland waited in the foyer, enamored by the autographed head shots of famous country singers centered on one wall. He also noticed framed photos of Melissa Hamilton riding horseback in equestrian apparel. He stepped away when he heard the sound of high heels clicking on marble floor and saw Melissa with her hair in a pony bun. Thick eye liner gave her eyes a smoky draw. A pair of white diamond earrings sizzled under halogen lights. "Bad time?"

"What can I do for you, Mr. Presley?"

Leland pointed to the equestrian photos. "Do you compete?"

"Not anymore."

"You have a beautiful horse."

Melissa checked the time. "Is there something I can do for you, Mr. Presley?"

"I brought my guitar."

"I see that."

"I have a voice lesson today."

"I can't right now."

Leland smiled wryly. "I showered this time."

"Good to know, Mr. Presley. Let's reschedule for next week."

Leland tightened his grip on the guitar case handle. Lean muscle flexed inside his tattooed forearm. "I left work early and gave up two hours pay to arrive on time. And gas isn't getting any cheaper."

"If you're asking for recompense—"

"I'm asking for you to honor our appointment. I also brought the part for your toilet."

Melissa motioned for Leland to follow her. "Can you look at my hot water heater?"

Leland set the guitar case down. "I'll get my tools."

Melissa showed her agent to the driveway. Underwhelmed by the names in her visitor's log, she fought the urge to call her nosey neighbors and patronize them for snooping with no intention to buy. The six hour event sent droves of foot traffic through her spotless home, but yielded zero offers—in spite of listing the property well below market value.

She found Leland in the back of the four-car garage, peeking under a tarp draped over a Ranger bass boat on a single-axle trailer. "You find what you're looking for?"

Leland let go of the tarp. "I was curious."

"It was Martin's toy. My ex...He rarely used it. It's for sale, if you're interested."

"Not right now. Won't fit in my new place."

"New house?"

"New adventure. We haven't finished unpacking yet." Leland diverted his attention to the hot water heater, where a puddle gathered on the floor beneath the base of the eighty-gallon tank. He cut off the water supply line and inspected the pressure relief valve.

Melissa kept her distance. "Can you fix it?"

"I need to figure out what's wrong first."

"It leaks."

Leland examined the copper plumbing for faulty welds, a bad connection, or a crack in the tubing. "How long has it been leaking?"

"A few days. My agent's home inspector found the problem."

"I think you're going to need a new tank."

"How long will that take?"

"A couple hours with the right tools. And a new tank."

"Is this something you can handle?"

Leland washed his hands at the utility sink. "I'm a musician who does carpentry. This type of work is not exactly in my wheelhouse."

Melissa escorted him to the formal living area. "Explains why my toilet still runs," she murmured under her breath. She poured herself a whiskey from the crystal decanter behind the wet bar beside the wood-burning fireplace and offered Leland a glass.

"I'm good," Leland politely declined. He scanned the framed family photos propped on the wood beam mantel centered on the stone chimney.

"How old are you, Mr. Presley?"

"Thirty-eight."

"You understand the average age of an up-and-coming singer in this town is barely a day over twenty."

"You're saying I'm too old?"

"I'm saying your age won't do you any favors."

"You seem to be doing fine," said Leland. "I mean, career wise. Not on account of your age."

Melissa adjusted a crooked picture frame. "According to the Internet, I'm only thirty-two in biological years. Calendar years don't tell the whole story. Scientific research supports it."

"You look great for your age. I mean, not that you're old."

Melissa rolled her eyes. "Quit while you're ahead, Mr. Presley. I lost the baby fat when George W. was in office, but my ass won a second term." She sipped her single malt scotch. "Why are you here?"

"What do you mean?"

"It's not a trick question, Mr. Presley. You clearly know how to sing. I assume you're no stranger to guitar."

"One can always improve."

"True. But if you think vocal lessons will open doors—"

"It can't hurt."

"It won't help, either. This town doesn't care about your vocal chops or how well you can play guitar. Half the guys pumping gas can sing as well as most male vocalists on the charts."

"Yes ma'am."

Melissa sipped her drink. "Where did you go to school?"

"Vanderbilt."

"You think that makes you a better musician?"

"Not necessarily. A lot of successful artists never studied in college. Clint Black, Chet Atkins, Christina Aguilera, Bryan Adams, Taylor Swift…"

Melissa set her glass down. "Anyone with a mouth and two good ears can learn to sing and play guitar. It's what you bring to the table. How you stand out from the pack that matters."

"You sound like someone else I know." Leland opened his guitar case and lifted his acoustic Gibson. "My mother gave me this when I was young. She saved her pennies waiting tables."

"Does she play?"

"She used to. Before she died."

"I'm sorry…"

"She always loved music. Said I should follow my dreams no matter how crazy. The whole *life is too short* thing."

"What about your dad?"

Leland adjusted the A string to sharpen the note. He strummed through a simple chord and heard the tone resonate. Then he played scales with a classical arpeggio style, his callused fingertips effortlessly transitioning from string to string and fret to fret. "He encouraged me to do what I love."

Melissa glanced at his empty wedding finger. "Are you married?"

Leland stopped playing. "Never met the right one."

"Girlfriend?"

Leland looked up at Melissa. "Not anymore."

"Sounds like she ripped the Band-Aid off."

"Something like that."

"What do you do for fun?"

"I play music."

"I meant besides music."

"I write songs."

"That's still music."

"Music is my life. When I sing, everything sort of falls into place."

Melissa finished her whiskey and opened the double glass doors to her private recording studio. She dimmed the recessed lighting and sat down at the grand piano. "Play something."

Leland carried his guitar and tapped the microphone. He heard *thump, thump* from the speakers. "Anything?"

"You didn't come here to dance."

Leland thought a moment and cleared his throat. He strummed the guitar with a slow tempo rhythm. "Nothing's easy anymore," he whispered into the microphone.

I've been up all night alone
Facing troubles on my mind
What I would give to kiss your lips
And feel you close to me, this time...

But nothing's easy anymore
I got heartache on my mind
I never felt this way before
I guess a part of me resigned
'Cause nothing's easy anymore...

There doesn't have to be a reason
Time will sort the truth from lies
I want to fall in love again
Throw away this damn disguise

But nothing's easy anymore
I'll let you see a better man
You're the one who I adore
Sometimes you have to take a stand
'Cause nothing's easy anymore...

My father died alone
A good man gone astray
Left my family feeling empty
Before he finally slipped away

'Cause nothing's easy anymore
You have to fight for what you need
Pick the pieces off the floor
It ain't easy to succeed

'Cause nothing's easy anymore!

Melissa clapped. "Breathe from your diaphragm. And don't put your mouth so close to the microphone. It distorts the sound. And don't stand like a mannequin. Move around."

Leland tuned the strings. "How'bout this one?" He tapped his boot on the floor to keep the beat. "Love is a state of mind."

It's about time…
It's about space…
It's a memory…I can't erase

It's about then…
It's about now…
It's a way to win you back, somehow

So don't leave…me now
Some doors are meant to stay open
A heart can't be loved if it's broken
Don't be afraid, to look inside
You might, be, surprised to find

Love is a state of mind
Love is a state of mind

It's a new path…
An about face…
Emotions that we can't replace

It's about us…
It's about them…
It's about how we start this over again

So don't leave…me now
There's only so far you can see
Trust in your heart to be free
But don't be afraid to give in sometimes

You might be, surprised, to find...

Love is a state of mind
Love is a state of mind

You should try it from time to time...

Love is a state of mind...
Love is a state of mind...
Love is a state of mind...

Melissa rested her hands on the piano bench. "You hold a lot of resentment. She must have been someone special."

"I play how I feel it."

"Work on something more upbeat. Something with a positive vibe. A song to show off your range."

"I have one in mind."

"Do you dance?"

Leland grinned. "Are you asking me to prom?"

Melissa avoided eye contact with the handsome stranger who reminded her of a boyfriend she had in college. "Mayor Dean is hosting a charity event." She read Leland's curious expression. "Our Nashville mayor."

"I knew that," Leland said sheepishly.

"I hate going to these things alone. I'm not asking for a date. Just thought you might want to tag along. Big names will be there."

"I appreciate the invite, but I told my daughter I'd take her fishing."

"The forecast is calling for rain again."

Leland reached in his pocket when his cell phone rang. He cringed when he heard Abby's principal on the other end. "I'm sorry," he told Melissa. "I need to get my daughter from school before she earns another merit badge for detention."

CHAPTER 22

Leland drove Abby home in silence. Upset by his own decision to force her on the bus to school, he found it hard to discipline her for an act of self-defense. He needed a woman's perspective on his daughter and her teenage mindset—someone to help him crack the code on what to say and when to say it without igniting a firestorm of raw emotions strong enough to make an exorcism feel like a trip to Disney World. "Your principal wants a conference with me," he said softly, his eyes focused on the road ahead.

"Fine," said Abby, staring out her window at the traffic beside her.

"She also wants you to apologize to the student you hurt."

"Not going to happen. I didn't *hurt* anyone. I taught him a lesson. If anyone deserves an apology, it's me."

"It could have gone a lot worse."

"Would you rather me get hurt?"

"Of course not. I'd rather you not get expelled from school. What were you thinking?"

"He attacked me!"

"You shouldn't have brought the pepper spray on the bus. Never mind that you stole it from Nicole."

"I was only borrowing it. Nicole said cops use it all the time."

"You're not a cop."

"And you're not listening to me. This kid was shooting spitballs in my hair! And he was huge. He would have crushed me in a fight."

I doubt that, Leland thought as he navigated around slower moving traffic. "Did you tell him to stop?"

"Yes."

"Did you tell the driver?"

"The driver barely speaks English."

"You could have gone to the principal when you got to school."

"You didn't see the way they looked at me. Like I'm some kind of freak."

"No one thinks you're a freak. Now your principal's threatening to expel you."

"She's bluffing."

Leland flashed his high beams at the slower car in front of him. "This isn't a game, Abby. This is real life. You could end up in serious trouble."

"Thanks for taking my side," Abby said sarcastically. "I just want a normal life in a normal school with normal people. Like our old neighborhood."

"I know."

"No, you don't."

"I'm trying, Abby. Real hard. But you don't make it easy for me."

"Why can't we move back to Tulsa?"

"Because our old house isn't there to go back to."

"The bank took it, didn't they."

"What are you talking about?"

"Nicole told me."

Leland traveled down a side street and drove into the driveway. "I did the best I could with what I had. Unfortunately, it wasn't enough."

"Are we going to lose our new house too?"

"Absolutely not."

"Nicole said—"

"Forget about Nicole. Okay…She's not part of our lives anymore, and I wouldn't trust everything she told you." Leland waited for Abby to climb out of the truck before a Toyota Prius rolled up to his driveway. "I'm sorry we had to move," he told Abby while a young woman with dark hair and professional attire approached him from the late model hybrid. "Whatever you're selling, I'm not interested."

"Are you Leland Presley?"

"Yes."

The woman handed Leland a sealed envelope.

"What is this?"

"You've been served."

Leland opened the envelop and unfolded the legal document inside to read the heading, *Petition for Joint Custody*.

CHAPTER 23

Melissa waited in line at her Belle Meade pharmacy an hour before the store closed. She stood behind an elderly man dressed in polyester pants and a wrinkled Hawaiian shirt with a straw Fedora on his bald head and his right arm cradled in a sling.

She clutched her hands and shifted from side to side in Prada wedge sandals, her mood bouncing from impatient to vexatious with the onset of her nagging back pain. She'd challenged herself to stop the prescription pills, but the chronic muscle aches, insomnia, and increasing irritability overpowered her will to quit. Despite mixed results from two surgeries and the best chiropractic therapy in Nashville, she needed the meds to cope.

She retrieved the empty prescription bottle from her purse while the customer in front of her painstakingly scrolled his name on the signature pad. When the counter finally cleared, she gave her prescription to the young man in a white lab coat and glasses.

The pharmacist read the label for the 30mg OxyContin tablets. "Your date of birth?" he asked Melissa.

"December seventh, nineteen-sixty."

The pharmacist typed Melissa's information in the system. "This prescription's expired."

"Not for two more months."

"The prescription's only authorized for three refills. This would be number four."

"It can't be."

"You'll need a new prescription or an authorization from your doctor to extend another refill."

"My doctor's on vacation."

"He can phone it in."

"From Australia? I don't even know what day it is over there, let alone what time zone they're on."

The pharmacist put the bottle on the counter. "I'm sorry."

"I want to speak to your supervisor."

"He's not here right now."

"Then I want the store manager."

"He's going to tell you the same thing I've already explained. This is a controlled substance. I can't legally refill a non-refillable prescription."

"I'll pay you double."

The pharmacist gave a disconcerting look.

"Triple? Cash."

"We sell over-the-counter medications. I recommend you try one of those."

Melissa snatched the empty prescription bottle. "If that shit really worked, I wouldn't need these!" She looked away, then snapped her head back. "Do you know who I am?"

The pharmacist glanced at the monitor and read the name in a monotone voice. "Melissa Hamilton?"

Melissa retreated in disgust. She knew people who knew people with the right connections to procure marijuana, molly, cocaine, heroin, or any other hard-core substance. But she had control of her meds, not the other way around. Her lower back hurt, but the chronic pain and insomnia she experienced when she stopped taking oxy, hurt worse. She simply needed her little blue pill and all would be right with the world.

She charged toward the front of the store, searching through her phone's contact list, almost oblivious to the elderly man passing in front of her with his arm in a sling. At the last second, she turned sideways to avoid a full-on collision but bumped the man against a magazine shelf, causing him to drop his shopping basket and spill his sundry items—including a Percocet refill. "I'm so sorry," she apologized vehemently when she saw the man adjust his glasses to view his essentials scattered across the floor. "I didn't see you." She knelt down to help him retrieve his goods, and in a moment of weakness, palmed the Percocet refill in her purse.

Tomás advanced his king two spaces on the chess board at the dining room table. "The key is controlling the center of the board," he told Jonathan, who sat directly across from him.

Jonathan advanced his solid ebony pawn one space. "Why is Mom selling the house?"

"You'll have to ask her."

"I did. She just ignores me."

Tomás advanced his king pawn. He could hear Adam wailing on his electric guitar upstairs. "Your mother has a lot on her plate."

Jonathan took out his iPhone and read an incoming text from Abby. He sent her a short reply. "What happens if Mom sells the house?"

"We move."

"But I don't want to."

"Does your girlfriend know you're about to lose a game you barely started?"

"She's not my girlfriend," Jonathan replied and put his phone away. He studied the chess board.

Tomás waited for Jonathan's move before he made his final advance. "I may be an old buffoon, but there is nothing you haven't seen or done that I have not already tried before. The virtue of age is wisdom and the impediment of youth is inexperience."

"What does that mean?"

"Checkmate."

"No way. How did you—"

"Fool's mate. Look it up."

"You moved your queen," Jonathan surmised. "I should have seen it."

"Sí. You took your eyes off the game."

Jonathan toppled his chess pieces. "I don't want to play anymore."

Tomás leaned forward in his chair and put his hands together on the table. "I know you and your brother have dealt with a lot of change recently. Change can be a good thing, but sometimes, too much change does harm."

"This is *our* house. I'm not leaving here."

"Everything will work out. It always does in the end."

"Why does Mom get to decide everything?"

"Because she pays the bills."

"What if Adam and I hire you to work for *us* instead?"

"I don't think so."

"Why not?"

Tomás grinned. He reached out to ruffle Jonathan's hair. "Mucho dinero. You can't afford me."

Jonathan's expression went solemn. "What do you know about girls?"

"What is it you want to know?"

"Everything."

Tomás lowered his head slowly. "Lo siento. No man knows everything about a woman. They are complex creatures."

"But you were married."

"Sí. Forty years."

"So you know things."

"Not so much a matter of what you know or don't know. Women are more about how you feel to them."

"I met this girl at school, and I don't know how to talk to her. She's different, but in a good way."

"More important you listen than speak. You'll know what to say when the time comes to say it."

Jonathan heard his mom return. "What took so long?" he asked when she approached with bags of groceries.

"A little help," Melissa encouraged him. She brought the bags to the kitchen counter. "I got stuck in traffic." She looked out at Tomás in the other room. "I hope the boys weren't too much trouble."

"Never," Tomás replied.

Melissa pointed to Jonathan. "Once you get this stuff put away, you and your brother should get ready for bed."

"One more hour."

"Your hour was up sixty minutes ago." She waited for Jonathan to leave the room before she asked Tomás, "Were they good for you, or were you trying to be nice?"

Tomás folded the chess board. "Your boys would be lost without you."

"Family is everything to me, and you will always be part of ours. Now, I have a favor to ask."

PART II

Storm of the Century

May 1-10, 2010

CHAPTER 24

Leland admired his blue western shirt in front of the bathroom mirror. Dressed for success in new Wranglers and a pair of black Python Laredos he'd snagged for cheap money at Ross, he applied enough Chrome cologne to smell nice without overachieving. Outside the house, heavy rain splashed at windows while rushing water gurgled furiously through aluminum downspouts. "I'll be back this afternoon," he called out to Abby as he entered the living room to find her snooping behind piles of opened boxes. "There's fresh bread for sandwiches and a new milk in the fridge. Leave your phone on and keep the doors locked until I get home."

Abby shoved a box against the wall. "I can't find Tiger."

"He's around here somewhere."

"I've looked everywhere."

"Did you check all the closets?"

"I already did. And under my bed."

"He probably found somewhere new to hide."

"What if he snuck outside in the rain?"

Leland opened the kitchen pantry and checked the bottom shelf. "He's not in your room?"

"He slept on my bed last night, but when I woke up, he was gone."

"Open a can of food. He'll come out when he hears you pop the lid."

"I tried that already. I think the storm scared him off."

"The storm will be over soon. He'll come out when the thunder stops."

Abby marched through the house, inspecting the same hiding spots she'd checked before. She left her phone on the kitchen counter unplugged from the charging cord. "Why do you have to be at the mayor's house?"

Leland hunted for his umbrella. "Because I was invited."

"When are you coming back?"

"This afternoon."

"You said you'd take me fishing today."

"It's supposed to rain all day."

"It might stop."

"We'll go tomorrow if it clears up."

"Can you drop me off at the mall?"

"I don't have time."

"My friends can bring me home."

"Do I know them?"

"They go to my school."

Leland fumbled with the broken release mechanism on the golf umbrella he found sandwiched between a stack of moving boxes. "Not today," he concluded with an apologetic tone.

"Why not?"

"Because I don't want you out with people I don't know."

"Then take me with you."

"I can't. This isn't a family event."

"So I'm supposed to sit here all day and do nothing?"

"I'll be back in a few hours. You can finish your homework while I'm gone."

"I don't have any."

"Then play Xbox."

"I don't remember where we packed it."

"Look in the living room boxes. I thought we put it with the DVD player."

"I don't know how to hook it up."

Leland grabbed his keys from the counter. "I have to go."

"What if something happens while you're gone?"

"Nothing's going to happen." Leland opened the front door to face the rainstorm in his driveway and saw the cat scamper inside between his legs. "I promise."

Melissa touched up her makeup in the mirror and puckered her lips painted with Chanel rouge allure velvet alluminous matte. Dressed to the nines in her strapless Jovani and heels, she hoped to draw attention from the stuffy social circle at Mayor Dean's charity event.

She stuffed her compact in her purse and made her way toward the front of the house to find Tomás on the living room sofa with her boys engaged in a video game battle depicted on the giant flat screen against the wall. "I'll be back in a few hours," she said when she noticed Leland's pickup truck on the property surveillance monitor. She used her smart phone to open the gate and took a pair of crisp hundred dollar bills from her purse. She folded the money and laid it on the sofa beside Tomás. "For lunch and whatever you all decide to do."

Tomás stood up to follow her to the door. "Gracias."

Melissa touched his arm. "Thank *you*." She waved at Adam on the sofa, momentarily disrupting his concentration.

"Mom!" both boys yelled at once. "We're in the middle of a game."

"You boys listen to Tomás," Melissa lectured. "He's in charge while I'm gone." She checked the front windows and sent Leland a text message when she saw his truck outside the house. *We'll take my car.*

Melissa kept both hands on the wheel of her Mercedes coupe with ample distance between herself and the van in front of her while relentless rain pounded the highway along I-24 near Antioch. "They're calling for two to three inches today."

"I believe it," said Leland. He adjusted the power seat to give his legs more room. "Have you ever been to the mayor's house before?"

"Once. A few years ago."

Leland viewed the slower-moving traffic in adjacent lanes. "That's more than me."

"Where's your daughter?"

"With friends." Leland kept a straight face to conceal the fib. The last thing he needed was another woman judging him without seeing the big picture. Between a construction job with no health care, playing small-time gigs at night, a girlfriend who dumped him without leaving her share of the rent, and a crazy wife suing him for partial custody of a daughter she tried to drown, he needed a win. His audition with Capital Country Records was a step up to bat, but any groundwork he could lay beforehand would only help his chances of securing a record deal. "I like your car," he said to continue the small talk with a woman he barely knew.

"Thanks."

"Any offers on your house?"

"Not yet."

"Are you moving locally or out of town?"

"I haven't decided."

Leland noticed the way Melissa's hair caressed her shoulders; the way her lips went crooked when she smiled; the way she talked with her hands.

"Is there something on my face?" Melissa asked after several seconds of awkward silence.

"Nice earrings."

Melissa touched one of her diamond studs. "They're from Tiffany's. My ex gave them to me the first year we were married. The only jewelry he ever bought me—aside from my engagement ring."

"They look nice on you."

Melissa shifted in her seat. She touched her hair and adjusted the air vent. Her thoughts vacillated between her stolen savings and her former accountant. "This isn't a date or anything."

"No worries. Just point me in the right direction when we get there, and I'll stay out of your way."

"I'll find you when it's time to scoot."

"You don't sound enthused."

"I don't know the mayor's friends very well."

"Me neither," Leland said wryly.

"I'm trying to record a new album, and I need all the buzz I can get to help promote it."

"Do you write your own music?"

Melissa focused on the road, where significant accumulation pooled along the interstate and gusting winds drove the rain horizontal at times. "On occasion. What about you?"

"I like to play my own material."

"What inspires you to write music?"

"People."

"What do you mean?"

Leland thought about the question. "I'm a people watcher. Life is about relationships. With ourselves. With others."

"How can you have a relationship with yourself?"

"A relationship doesn't have to involve two people."

"I think a lot of couples would disagree."

"Doesn't change how I see things."

"So what is it about people that inspires you?"

Leland rubbed his hand on his arm above his treble clef tattoo. "Their emotions, mostly."

"But what *inspires* you to write about their emotions?"

"People are afraid to admit what they're thinking. What they're feeling. How life affects them day to day. Music has a way of evoking emotions people are afraid to acknowledge."

Melissa changed lanes. "So…if you believe you can have a relationship with yourself, then you're saying you write about feelings you're unwilling or afraid to acknowledge yourself?"

"Sometimes."

"How can you write about something you can't acknowledge? That's contradictory."

"That's life. Music is art expressed in song. It doesn't have to involve a logical sequence of events." Leland watched the rain fall in sheets. "Music is about escape. When I sing, everything in the world makes sense to me. I find solace when I play guitar."

"You sound like you know what you're doing."

"My daughter would disagree." Leland laughed to himself. "What inspires you to sing?"

Melissa veered into the far right lane and slowed behind stalled traffic. "Shit…"

"What's wrong?"

Melissa bit her lip. "I think I drove past our exit."

CHAPTER 25

Melissa tapped her brakes in the stop-and-go traffic crawling south along Antioch Pike off I-24. Runoff water from massive rainfall swelled the normally benign Mill Creek that ran parallel to her location on the jam-packed route outside the rural Nashville suburb. Her navigation display showed less than three miles to the mayor's residence. "There must be an accident up ahead."

"Where's your radio?" Leland asked, pointing at the center console.

Melissa tapped the touchscreen for an AM station and adjusted the volume.

...our weekend forecast calls for heavy rain with two to four inches of accumulation expected by this afternoon over the entire Nashville metropolitan area. The result of unseasonably deep storms originating from the Pacific Northwest and tracking eastward through central portions of Mississippi, Kentucky, Tennessee, and the Cumberland River Valleys. The powerful system brings a low pressure center in the central plains combined with a cold front trailing southward toward the Rio Grande. Expect continued rainfall throughout the day and into tomorrow morning...

Melissa reached for the Percocet prescription in her purse. She opened the lid with the label facing away from Leland and quickly dispensed a pill.

"We'll get there eventually," said Leland.

"Sometime today would be nice. We haven't moved a quarter mile in an hour."

"No worries."

Melissa ran her hand through her reddish-brown hair. The pain in her lower back had worsened since she left the house. "For you. I've got an album to finish and a tour to plan. This trip is a bust."

Leland checked his phone for messages and replied to a text from Abby. "I hear teenage boys are easier to raise than girls."

Melissa cracked a smile. "Did you read that in *Men's Health*?"

"*Playboy*," Leland confessed with a straight face.

"I'm sure your daughter's an angel."

"I love her, but she tries my patience at times."

"You don't strike me as an impatient man."

"You've never met Abby."

Melissa checked her blind spot and signaled to enter the adjacent lane. "My boys fight all the time."

"How old are they, again?"

"Twelve and eleven. Irish twins born ten months apart. I always dreamed of having girls."

"Not too late."

"It is for me. I shut the factory down when my youngest son, Adam, was born." Melissa tapped the brake to slow with traffic along the road submerged more than three inches deep. "How do you feel about having more children?"

"Is that a question or an offer?"

Melissa blushed.

"One is enough for me," said Leland.

"What about your ex-wife? Did she ever remarry?"

"Not yet."

"My ex graduated from the Bill Clinton school of monogamy. Apparently, commitment was a four-letter word in our marriage. Deep down, all men are the same. No offense."

Leland shifted in his seat. "You just haven't met the right man."

Melissa inched forward in traffic. "How long were you married?"

"A few years."

"A short timer…I guess marriage didn't agree with you."

"We weren't good together," Leland said with a note of disdain.

Melissa honked her horn in frustration. She steered toward the center line and crept ahead for a better view of the traffic spread in front of her. "This is ridiculous." She touched the steering wheel controls to surf the stations and stopped on an old Randy Travis hit. "Sorry I dragged you out here on your Saturday."

Leland liked the way Melissa looked at him when she spoke. The way her eyebrows arched when she emphasized her point of view. The way her lips pursed slightly when she listened. The way her hair caressed her face. "At least we don't have to worry about a drought."

"No kidding."

Leland tuned out the thrum of steady rain and the metronomic rhythm from the windshield wipers. "What inspires you to sing?"

"What do you mean?"

"You never answered my question."

"What inspires *me* to sing?" Melissa smiled broadly. "Getting paid." She gave Leland a sidelong glance. "What? Like you haven't thought about the money you could make in this business."

"Money pays the bills," Leland relented.

"My dad wanted me to go to law school."

"But you wanted to be a singer?"

"I wanted to be successful at something I was good at. Singing came naturally to me. School, not so much."

"What did your dad think about you not going to law school?"

"My mom warmed up to it. My dad was always pissed. He thought I was throwing my life away."

"You would have made a good attorney."

"Hardly. What about you?"

"Music is all I ever wanted to do. Sounds cliché, I know. But it's the truth."

"Nashville can be a lonely place," Melissa proffered. "It's all about whom you know and who wants to know you. Speaking of which, how did you hook up with Sid?"

Leland thought to himself. "Long story."

Melissa motioned at the standstill traffic outside the car. "I've got nowhere to be."

Leland nodded. "He heard me play a small gig in Tulsa a few years back. Thought I could use someone to further my career."

"Just like that?" Melissa asked incredulously.

"Just like that."

"Did you grow up in Tulsa?"

"I grew up all over. My parents moved a lot when I was young."

"What brought you to Nashville? Never mind…I think that's obvious." Melissa looked away for a moment, then she cast the gaze from her probing brown eyes on Leland. "I've known Sid a long time. I know most of the acts he represents. Funny he never mentioned you before."

Leland shrugged off the comment. "What was life like on the road? When you were touring with a band."

"Exciting. Monotonous. Lonely. But I miss it. You know? The energy. The sound of screaming fans who paid to see me. It's hard to describe. There's no feeling like it."

"You must have a lot of stories."

"A few."

"Who was the most interesting person you ever met?"

"Tim McGraw. He was the most genuine, down-to-earth person I ever worked with. Not to mention super sexy. He would walk out on stage and draw everyone's attention to him immediately. One time he told me he never made music for critics. He simply made the record he heard in his head."

"Did you ever sing with him on stage?"

"No, but I wanted to! I got to meet a lot of incredible people on his team."

"Maybe I'll meet some of them today," Leland said with an optimistic tone, punctuated by a loud thunder clap.

"Maybe…" Melissa stretched in her seat. "If this storm keeps up, we might get there faster by boat."

CHAPTER 26

Tomás drove the Lincoln Town Car through torrential rain outside the Regal Cinema at Opry Mills Mall and parked near the theater entrance. He left the motor running and twisted in the driver's seat to face the boys, and Abby, in the back. "Call me when the movie gets out."

"We will," Jonathan answered.

Tomás looked directly at Adam. "Adiós."

Adam rested his elbow on the armrest and propped his chin in his hand. "I don't want to see this movie."

"You sure?"

"I can't eat popcorn with braces."

"We'll tell you how it ends," said Jonathan, who climbed out with Abby before his brother could change his mind.

Tomás glanced in the rear view mirror to see Jonathan and Abby enter the mall together. "Last chance," he told Adam.

"Can I play Xbox when we get home?"

Tomás sighed and drove away. "Sí." He set his wipers on high when the downpour intensified. He drove slowly toward the exit at the back of the mall along Opry Mills Drive and the rapidly rising Cumberland River. The front tires dipped inside a cavernous pothole, launching an arc of muddy brown water across the front of an oncoming car.

"Will you play Halo with me?"

Tomás slowed behind a dump truck with missing mud flaps and a broken tail light. "That game hurts my head. I can't figure out how to work the controls."

"I'll show you."

"These games are for younger minds and smaller hands. Why don't we play chess? I'll teach you how to beat your brother."

"Jonathan pretends to like chess because you let him stay up later."

Tomás adjusted the rear view mirror. "Does he pretend to like movies too?" He followed the dump truck to the left around two state police cruisers blocking an accident scene that diverted traffic to the northbound entrance for Briley Parkway. He drove slowly with his hazard lights on while the monsoon rain transformed the northbound lanes into shallow rivers. Battered sign posts twisted in the wind as flash flood conditions scoured new channels in low-lying areas inundated by the slow-moving storm.

He thought about circling back for Jonathan and Abby, but he'd driven through harsh conditions before without incident.

He flashed his high beams in a futile effort to improve the limited visibility. "You still awake?" he asked Adam.

"I'm hungry."

"We just ate lunch."

"Can we stop at McDonalds?"

Tomás followed the parkway heading west above Pennington Bend Road and slowed in advance of the bridge up ahead. "I can make you a sandwich at home."

"I'd rather eat McDonalds. Or Wendy's if you find one first."

Tomás squinted at the windshield. Something felt wrong about the bridge in the rain—a peculiar subtlety his eyes failed to recognize but his primitive survival instincts acknowledged to command his foot on the brake immediately.

"How much longer?" asked Adam, his chest pressed against the shoulder belt when the Town Car slowed abruptly.

"Not now!" Tomás responded in a harsh tone of voice reserved for the rare occasion when something made him angry—or scared. Thunder exploded outside the car close enough to straighten the hair on his arms. He took his foot off the brake and let the car creep forward toward the bridge extending over the swollen river below.

Without warning, the Town Car's front end dip precariously as the road caved in beneath the wheels, exposing a large section of corrugated drain pipe protruding through the jagged cavity in the washed-out embankment. Outside the car, steel guard rail posts wobbled like loose teeth above the eroded terrain.

Tomás heard Adam scream as the flooded road engulfed the stranded sedan. He unbuckled his seat belt and reached for the boy with both arms. "Vámonos!"

Adam climbed toward the front of the car, his eyes wide with fear.

Tomás shoved his weight against the door but couldn't overcome the force of rushing water as the chassis slid nose down inside the mammoth sinkhole. He dug frantically for his utility knife and opened the blade with his thumbnail. He jabbed the tip at the window, cracking the glass on impact. The window imploded with the surge of cold, murky water.

"Ándale!" Tomás shouted as he reached for Adam's arm.

But Adam recoiled in fear, anchored to the steering wheel with a death grip while gushing water quickly filled the front cabin space.

In the distance, traffic came to a standstill on the northbound lanes, where drivers stopped short of the bridge, oblivious to the stranded Town Car or the occupants trapped inside.

CHAPTER 27

Melissa shifted awkwardly in the driver's seat. They'd been stuck in traffic for hours, and her bladder swelled like a water balloon while the incessant drone of pounding rain exacerbated the discomfort. "Any luck?" she asked Leland, who held his phone to his ear.

"It went to voice mail again."

"She's probably gabbing with her friends."

Leland tucked his flip phone away and pointed to the dashboard's GPS display. "Can this thing find us a detour?"

Melissa poked at the touch screen. "I hope so. I need to find a restroom, stat!"

"How's your gas?"

"Excuse me?"

"Your fuel."

"Half a tank."

Leland rubbed a clean spot on his window and noticed the water level rising in relation to the tires on the cars stuck in traffic beside him. "The road's really starting to flood." He changed the radio station to find a weather update. "We should get to higher ground."

"This is crazy," Melissa grumbled to herself.

...heavy rains continue to pound the Nashville metropolitan area, triggering flash flood conditions in certain low-lying portions of Davidson County as more thundershowers move in from the west. Standing water on Interstates sixty-five and forty have brought traffic to a halt with more than six inches of rainfall already reported by the National Weather Service. A dynamic jet stream moving in from the Gulf of Alaska southward into central Mexico and then northward through the Mississippi Valley region continues to drive widespread thunderstorms and heavy rainfall over the mid-Mississippi, Tennessee, and Cumberland River Valleys. Forecasters predict another four to five inches over the next thirty-six hours as a string of thunderstorms continue to siphon warm air from the Gulf of Mexico. Dozens of road closures have been reported in Bellevue, Franklin, and Antioch as water continues to rise.

Melissa tried Jonathan's cell phone. When the call dropped, she tried Adam's and left a message. She tried Tomás but kept getting a busy signal. "I can't get through."

Leland tried Abby's phone again and heard an *out of service* prompt. "Me neither."

Melissa forced her knees together and rubbed her legs to suppress her swollen bladder. "If I were a man I could stick my junk out the window and pee."

"I suppose a penis has its advantages," Leland offered with a straight face.

Melissa grinned demurely. "Should I be worried about my boys?"

"I'm sure they're fine. This storm will let up soon."

Melissa tapped her fingers on the steering wheel and tried her phone again. She needed her boys to tell her they were okay; to make her feel guilty for worrying about nothing. But she had reason to worry and reason to accept what her intuition kept telling her. The storm was not a passing front or a run-of-the-mill disturbance dumping water for a couple hours. It was a living, breathing beast with its teeth sunk in and no intention of letting go. "What if we can't reach anyone?"

"We keep trying until we do."

Melissa laid on the horn to prompt the driver in front of her to move up. Then she pulled a U-turn, clipping the car's back bumper.

Leland stiff-armed the dashboard and braced himself against the passenger door. "What are you doing?"

"Getting the hell out of here."

"You just hit that car!"

Melissa drove on the shoulder to pass the stalled traffic that extended for miles along I-24. Deep water splashed inside the wheel wells. "Desperate times. Desperate measures." She accelerated to thirty miles an hour, and for the moment, the urge to pee subsided.

CHAPTER 28

◆

Jonathan kept his phone tucked away with the ringer off while the action movie *Losers* played on the big screen in front of him. Seated near the back of the packed theater with Abby on his right side and a large Dr. Pepper in the cup holder on his left, he found it awkward to hold the popcorn bag for a girl with one arm—on account of her having to reach across her own body from right to left every time she had the munchies. To complicate matters, he couldn't put his right arm around her shoulder without having to hold the popcorn bag with his left, which seemed like no big deal at first until his nerves got the better of him. He thought about switching seats, but that proved difficult as well. First base never seemed so far away.

Abby didn't just look different from other girls. She *was* different, and in a good way. He could tell she liked him as a friend. He hoped she liked him as something more.

He sipped his drink and kept the popcorn bag in Abby's reach. Even with all the gratuitous violence unfolding on the screen, Abby held his undivided attention.

If he sat on her other side, he could reach for her hand. A task less daunting than trying to swing his arm around her shoulder and look cool in the process. *Does she want me to? Will she care if I do? Will she be mad if I don't?*

The situation seemed overly complicated, and the more he thought about it, the more he second-guessed every move. No matter how hard he tried to convince himself to make the move, his arm failed to budge, which left him holding the popcorn bag. Tomás warned him girls were complicated.

He leaned in closer to Abby. He wanted to touch her leg in lieu of a left arm that wasn't there, but he knew better. At least he thought he did. If her arm was there, he'd touch her hand. Nothing wrong with starting slow. What he gained in desire, he lacked in confidence. If he got up and moved to her right side, problem solved. Then again, she might wonder what he was doing in the middle of the movie.

He thought about excusing himself to use the restroom and then returning down the opposite aisle. Seemed simple enough. Yet even the simplest approach brought major trepidation. If he couldn't bring himself to put his arm around her, he had no hope of trying to kiss her. Unless she tried to kiss him first, which never seemed to happen in the real world.

Don't over-think it, Tomás would tell him. *Girls know when a boy is interested in them. They have a sixth sense about such things. If she likes you, you'll know it.*

But how? he wondered. Abby wasn't holding flashcards with "kiss me" written on them or sending text messages with instructions. Practically everyone in school had a girlfriend they made out with in the hall between classes. Everyone except Jonathan Hamilton.

He sipped his Dr. Pepper, preoccupied by his own shenanigans when Abby reached across for the bag of popcorn and parked it between her legs. Now he didn't dare touch the bag. Just when he thought he had the inside track, Abby changed the rules again.

Then genius struck him.

He could lean a little closer when she wasn't looking and gradually bring his cheek toward her face. He would ask for the popcorn and startle her. She would turn her head and brush her lips against his cheek. If she liked him, she could kiss him on purpose. If not, no harm, no foul. The plan seemed easy enough, assuming he could get close enough without looking lame.

He let her chew for a moment, timing his move during an action-packed scene. He had his mind made up with no intention of backing down—until the soundtrack stopped abruptly and the image on the screen disappeared.

Emergency lights came on, followed by a collective moan from the audience who furthered their disapproval when the manager entered the theater to announce the power was out.

CHAPTER 29

Adam clung to the branch of an uprooted oak tree splayed across a rain-swollen tributary, his eyes transfixed on the washed-out bridge torn asunder from the powerful flood dislodging chunks of pavement from the road. The distant wail of rescue sirens vanished in the roar of wind and rain above the tumultuous stream rife with sodden refuse, raw sewage, and oil residue.

He tried to pull himself closer to the tree trunk, tilted and skewed on its side from the locomotive force of rushing water, but his arms grew heavy from exertion, his strength depleted from the chill of persistent showers lashing his body mercilessly while he fought to hold on. Above him, a loud pop from a seven-thousand volt transformer mounted to a crooked utility pole met with sparks and a short burst of smoke. Seconds later, a power line broke free and dropped toward the water below, its energized core snapping and sparking like a Frankenstein whip as the pole's foundation receded beneath the raging torrent.

The branch slipped through Adam's raw, swollen hands, casting him to the mercy of the fuming Cumberland that swept him away, his small frame dipping and rolling in a corkscrew motion toward a sharp bend, where a maelstrom of floating debris intersected his path. He bobbed up and down, coughing and gagging, uncertain if his next breath would be his last before a hand grabbed his forearm with a vice-like grip and hoisted him onto land. "*I got you!*" he heard Tomás exclaim as he clawed his way up the precipitous slope and collapsed on a patch of marshy soil. He wiped the mud from his eyes to see a blurry image of Tomás standing over him with his arm outstretched.

Lightning crackled. Thunder boomed like a bass drum between his ears. When he blinked, Tomás was gone. And for a fleeting moment, he wondered if the brutal storm would ever end and whether he would live to see his family again.

CHAPTER 30

Leland twisted the turquoise spinner ring on his right index finger. After more than five hours stuck in gridlocked traffic on I-24 outside of Nashville, he had concerns of his own. "At least we won't have to water the grass," he said to add some measure of levity to the stressful situation.

Melissa patted her hair with a handful of glove box napkins. Drenched from her desperate jaunt outside the car to relieve herself behind a barricade of trees, she wiped her face and recoiled at her image in the vanity mirror. "I look like the swamp thing."

"You look fine," Leland offered.

"I can't believe I just did that. I'm soaking wet. My hair's a mess, and my new shoes are ruined."

"Shoes are replaceable, but you're stuck with the hair," Leland teased.

Melissa adjusted the A/C. "And you're stuck with me in this mess. I'm sorry I ruined your Saturday."

"No worries. It's not a great day to fish anyhow." Leland gazed out the passenger window. "Do you fish?"

"Only from the seafood department."

"What about your boys?"

"Their father used to take them."

"Abby loves it."

"How does she deal with the whole hook in mouth thing?"

Leland thought about the question. "Very carefully."

Melissa kept her foot on the brake and blew her nose in a napkin. "Sorry. Next time you'll think twice about a road trip with me."

"The storm will pass. We can crash the mayor's house another time."

Melissa discretely stuffed the used napkin in her door compartment. "Can I ask you a personal question?"

"How personal?"

"Do you believe in soul mates?"

"I thought this wasn't a date?"

Melissa rolled her eyes. She inched the Mercedes forward when the traffic started crawling again in the southbound lanes. "I'm not talking about us."

Leland adjusted his power seat. "Do I believe in soul mates? I believe in love. I think sometimes people chase what they think they want without taking the time to figure out what it is they really need."

"Your girlfriend hurt you, didn't she."

"Life goes on."

Melissa viewed the mess outside her window. In spite of the horrid weather and the ridiculous amount of time stuck in the car together, she gleaned a genuine warmth from Leland Presley; a man without a hidden agenda, who sacrificed quality time with his daughter to spend half a day socializing with a woman he barely knew. "My record label's suing me," she confessed. "I don't know why I'm telling you this."

"What happened?"

"My last album didn't live up to the hype—or the cash advance they fronted me for my tour."

"Ouch…"

"Be careful what you wish for in this business. You might get it."

"Things will turn around. They always do. Tonight the sun will set. Tomorrow it will rise again."

"Do you always see the positive side of everything?"

"It beats the alternative."

"Where does Abby go to school?"

"Parkview Middle."

"My boys just transferred there."

"Do they like it?"

"When they're not in detention." Melissa wiped her face with another napkin. "Have you ever sang professionally? And I don't mean some vomit-through-the-nose honky-tonk. I'm talking about vocal sessions in a studio or background vocals on tour."

"I've done some studio work, but I've never been on tour."

"But you want to?"

"Absolutely."

Melissa took her eyes off the road and tried Sid's number. "I think it's ringing!"

"Mel?" came a muted reply from the car's Bluetooth system.

"Sid?"

"Hello?"

"Can you hear me?"

"Barely," Sid's voice broke through, hollow and distant. *"Where are you?"*

"I'm still on the interstate," Melissa spoke loudly at the phone.

"Roads are closed. Bridges are washed out."

"I can't reach Tomás or the boys. Can you go by the house and check on them?" Melissa heard the connection go silent. "Sid? Are you there?" She redialed his number and got a busy signal. "I had him," she told Leland, who acknowledged her frustration with a knowing glance.

Leland tried his phone again. "I still can't reach Abby."

"No connection?"

"It goes straight to voice mail."

"I'm sure she's fine. Probably still on the phone with her friends."

Leland wanted to believe Melissa. He *needed* to believe her. "Can I try your phone?"

Melissa cut the wheel and rolled toward the car in front of her. "Sure, but I can't get a signal either." She gave Leland her phone. "Am I clear on your side?"

"You're jammed in. The right lane's barely moving."

Melissa waited for an opening and gunned the engine, spinning the rear wheels momentarily before she reached the severely flooded shoulder and proceeded cautiously with her hazard lights flashing. She wanted dry clothes, a hot shower, and food. More than anything, she wanted confirmation that her boys were safe. "I haven't seen a single cop since we left my house this morning."

"They're probably stuck in traffic." Leland stared through the windshield at the blinding rain. He pointed to a spot in the distance. "Look…"

"I don't see anything but rain."

"Exactly."

Melissa stiffened in her seat, mesmerized by a portable classroom drifting into rows of stalled traffic across the interstate. "Oh my God…This is worse than I imagined!"

CHAPTER 31

Jonathan and Abby stood beneath an awning outside Opry Mills Mall, facing the flooded parking lot where shoppers scurried between cars with inverted umbrellas destroyed by the powerful winds. Towering clouds filled dark skies punctuated by arcs of lightning in a dazzling display of lethal current.

"He still doesn't answer," Jonathan complained when his call to Tomás went straight to voice mail again.

Abby gawked at the mass exodus outside the mall. "Maybe he's on his way?"

"He doesn't know the power went out. The movie's not supposed to end for another hour."

Abby tried her phone again. "My battery's dead."

Jonathan poked at his phone in frustration. "I can't get a signal anymore."

"My dad's going to kill me if I don't get home before he does."

"Maybe we should go back inside."

"We can't. There's like a million people leaving here. The mall is closing."

Jonathan took Abby's hand and weaved through the crowd toward the food court entrance. "Not all of it."

* * *

Inside the mall, a security officer with receding hair and a thick mustache approached Jonathan and Abby with a black flashlight and a walkie-talkie. "Sorry guys. You can't be in here. We're shutting down."

"Told you," Abby said to Jonathan.

Jonathan ignored the comment. "We're waiting for our ride," he explained to the officer, hoping the conversation would end.

"You can't stay here," the officer declared.

"Where are we supposed to go?" asked Abby.

"You'll have to wait outside."

"It's pouring rain," Jonathan argued.

"If it were up to me, I'd let you stay. But the power is out."

Jonathan glanced at his phone. "Just another hour. Until our ride gets here."

"Did you call someone?"

"We can't get through. But our ride will be here."

"Can you take us home?" Abby asked with a hint of desperation in her voice.

The officer rubbed the base of his walkie-talkie against his head. "I can't leave my station until the mall's secure, but there's a bus shelter across the parking lot. Runs every half hour. If you hurry, you might catch the next one."

Jonathan looked at Abby, wishing he'd done more to persuade the officer to let them stay. "Thanks for nothing," he said with an apathetic tone and left the food court with Abby. "We'll go out the way we came and come back through one of the big stores. We can hide in there before they close and use their phone to call Tomás."

Abby pushed her way outside and saw the officer keeping tabs on them. "He's still staring at us."

"He'll walk away in a second."

"Maybe we should take the bus," Abby cautioned. "I really need to get home before my dad."

"I've never ridden the bus before."

"Ever?" Abby scrutinized the flooded parking lot, her field of view obstructed by the rain. "It's no big deal."

"I think we should wait."

"I think we should go. Your driver will be late in this storm, if he gets here at all."

Jonathan debated his options, none of which seemed reasonable—especially the idea of riding public transportation with a bunch of soaking wet strangers who couldn't afford their own cars.

"I see it!" Abby shouted. "Hurry up!"

Jonathan ran through the storm with Abby, chasing the metro bus around the parking lot perimeter. Puddles mimicked small ravines. Flooded storm drains spilled over long stretches of pavement brimming with runoff water. In the bleary sky, an enormous apparition took form as the congregation of warm air met with the cold air inside the turbulent frontal boundary. The cauliflower-shaped supercell morphed into a greenish hue, spitting lightning as warm air rose up while cold air descended, cycling frozen droplets into hailstones. In the upper atmosphere, gale force winds clashed in opposite directions, spinning the rogue formation counter-clockwise.

Jonathan and Abby boarded the bus before the driver closed the folding doors. Hail pounded the metal roof like marbles falling from the sky.

"Look!" Jonathan exclaimed when Abby claimed the seat beside him.

The bus swung away from the mall along Opry Mills Drive, heading south along the rising Cumberland toward the exit for Briley Parkway.

"What is it?"

Jonathan rubbed the greasy window for a better view. Spellbound by the sight of the rotating funnel cloud, he held his breath when the narrow vortex touched down near the wooded edge of the mall parking lot, uprooting trees and sign posts in its path. "Tornado!"

Abby trembled beside Jonathan, awestruck at the mass destruction she'd previously only gleaned from the pages of a library book. She gripped the back of the seat in front of her and screamed at the sight of towering trees bent parallel to the ground.

Jonathan remained transfixed by the twister's awesome display of power, engrossed by the spectacle of broken tree limbs churning in a mass of whirling rubble. The piercing, jet engine sound of high speed winds continued as the revolving formation effortlessly hurled metal dumpsters like cardboard boxes.

The bus accelerated toward the edge of the parking lot, pursued by a sinister force powerful enough to peel slabs of pavement like skin from a raw potato.

The tornado intensified, promptly dislodging light posts from their concrete foundations; lifting cars on their noses before dropping them in crumpled heaps. Across the street, a shuttle bus levitated fifty feet in the air and imploded like an eggshell. Mud, grass, and landscape shrubbery dissolved inside the raging leviathan skirting the mall perimeter. Tempest winds tore outer walls away, exposing the interior of an anchor store showroom, consuming dry wall panels, roofing shingles, and sheet metal siding inside the twister's upward spiral.

"Drive faster," Jonathan mumbled to himself in an almost catatonic state, vaguely aware of Abby clutching his side while he watched the juggernaut obliterate a construction trailer along a path of destruction more than a football field wide. Telephone poles snapped in half, blasting the airwaves like cannon fire while boulder-size chunks of broken concrete centrifuged in the cyclone's lower half, demolishing everything, living or inanimate, in its path.

Jonathan fell against Abby as the bus made a hard turn. He tumbled forward and collided with another rider when the bus stopped abruptly to avoid the impact from flying debris. He gathered himself and reached for Abby, his face the color of alabaster as he confronted his own mortality.

A monotonous roar stifled the sound of screaming passengers and distant sirens. Then every window imploded at once, launching a salvo of shattered glass as the twelve-ton bus rose up and teetered in the air like a marionette before crashing near the overflowed banks of the Cumberland River.

CHAPTER 32

Sid plowed his black Escalade through eight inches of standing water at the gated entrance to Melissa's Belle Meade estate. His headlights illuminated the warped "For Sale" sign bent backwards from the unrelenting wind.

He powered his window down and pressed the intercom. When no one responded, he waved at the surveillance camera and shouted to no avail. He searched his phone for Melissa's access code and entered it on the keypad to open the gate himself.

He charged up the sloping driveway, displacing waves of water accumulation under the beefy SUV tires. The house looked dim from the outside, with few lights on in the main living area. He saw Leland's truck out front; the Town Car oddly absent. Standing water covered the brick paver sidewalk leading up to the front door. He held the horn for several seconds, hoping Tomás had parked inside the garage.

When no one appeared, he considered his options before he shifted the Escalade into park and got out to find the house key Melissa hid inside a fake rock beneath the mulch bed bordered by a train of red brick pavers.

He entered the house dripping wet and punched the code to deactivate the alarm. Dirty boot prints trailed behind him. The storm persisted outside, but the house remained relatively quiet without the boys running wild or Melissa tapping melodies on her grand piano.

He searched the first floor and checked the empty garage. In the kitchen, he found a realtor's portfolio on the counter along with several business cards, a half glass of milk, and a video game controller. Concerned for Tomás and the boys, he powered on the flat screen television in the living room to see a news reporter in a yellow rain parka standing on a flooded curb outside a Nashville pub. He recognized the young brunette from a local news station. A Davidson County tornado warning flashed on the bottom of the screen while he listened to the live update about record-breaking rainfall and flooded waterways with more precipitation expected throughout the evening. Parts of Interstates 40, 24, and 65 were closed. Portions of Middle Tennessee had lost power. Dozens of people were missing with at least two confirmed deaths.

He powered off the TV and found a notepad on the coffee table. A deep pen impression read, OM Regal 2:25.

Opry Mills?

He thought about the mall and remembered the Regal theater. The 2:25 had to be a movie time.

He jingled his keys in his pocket. His Rolex read 19:15. A 2:25 show would have ended hours ago unless they chose a later time or stayed to hang out at the mall.

He flicked the porch lights on and reset the alarm on his way out. Inside the Escalade, he wiped the rain off his face and thought for a while. He had no conclusive knowledge that Tomás or the boys were anywhere near Opry Mills Mall, and driving twenty miles to get there in severe weather, on a hunch, seemed foolhardy at best. He worked in the entertainment industry, not search and rescue operations. But as much as he tried to persuade himself otherwise, he couldn't ignore his gut feeling that something was terribly wrong.

He tried Melissa's phone again and drove away from the empty house. He'd take the back way through Chickering

Road and Harding Place to hit Route 431 heading north to
Route 155. Then head east toward Briley Parkway and
Opry Mills Drive. God willing, he would find Tomás and
the boys.

CHAPTER 33

Adam heard his mom calling him from outside the house. When he came to the window in his room and looked down on the snowy field behind the driveway, he found her in a coat and gloves, waving a snow shovel above her head. He had no desire to leave the cozy confines of his room to go outside. Let alone to shovel snow.

He cracked the window. Freezing air pierced his pajama top; a prelude to a loud sneeze. "I'm tired," he shouted down.

"*I need your help,*" he heard his mom reply.

"Ask Jonathan."

"*Jonathan's not home.*"

Adam shut the window. The cold draft followed him to his brother's empty room. He checked the bathroom and the guest rooms. He checked the wrapping paper room Mom reserved for hiding Christmas gifts.

He ran downstairs to find Tomás asleep on the sofa in front of the big screen television, his head lolled to one side. Through the windows behind the sofa, he could see the snow shovel protruding from a deep embankment. A wintery mix of sleet and wet powder obscured his view. The room grew colder. Water dripped from the ceiling.

He dragged Tomás off the sofa and heard his head hit the floor. The sickening crack of bone on Spanish tile snapped him out of his dream state and back to reality. When he opened his eyes, he found himself huddled on a wooden picnic table beneath a park pavilion surrounded by water on all sides. A virtual island unto himself.

"Help!" he cried above the roar of ceaseless rain, punctuated with the harsh report of thunder echoing off the pavilion's concrete walls and the eerie sound of howling wind. He dug his nails into the wood when a lightning flash exposed acres of standing water. He gripped the slat-board table in a spread-eagle pose, afraid the flood waters might carry him away. Then he craned his neck to look up at the empty rafters and cried for help again. Desperate to quench his insatiable thirst, he crawled along the table toward a water fountain against the wall. "Who's there?" he called out when he thought he heard footsteps splashing.

He stood up on the table and scanned the darkness engulfing him. Leery of who or what lurked beyond the shadows, he saw a tall figure in a green, hooded jacket appear like an apparition inside a flat-bottom boat with a passenger on board.

"*Over here,*" Adam heard a deep voice reply. "*Looks like we got us another straggler.*"

CHAPTER 34

Towering cumulonimbus clouds filtered moonlight from the upper atmosphere, illuminating the flood of biblical proportions that stranded motorists along the east Nashville stretch of I-24, where Leland and Melissa waded through hip-deep waters near the overflowed Harpeth River to board the Metro Fire Department's twenty-eight foot rapid-response boat. A half mile away, the abandoned Mercedes remained completely submerged in the lower-lying region. To the north, the Cumberland River crested above flood stage, forcing thousands of homeowners to evacuate from nearby Bellevue, Franklin, and Antioch.

Leland steadied his hand on the bow rail to help Melissa board while the other refugees huddled in close proximity on the center console boat, their faces painted from a palette of shock, disbelief, frustration, and fear. "You okay?" he asked Melissa above the noise from the twin outboard engines.

"I hope my car has flood insurance," Melissa answered whimsically, clutching her soaking wet purse.

"We made it this far."

"I'm not worried about *us*."

Leland held her closer. He could feel her shivering. "How bad is it?" he asked the firefighter standing beside them.

"Nothing's burning at the moment. Never seen anything like this in my life."

"We need to contact our kids," Leland urged.

"Power's out everywhere. Cell towers have been up and down. Calls are spotty at best."

"How many people have you found?"

"Too many to count. Harpeth River is almost five feet above flood level in Franklin. The Cumberland is worse. Too many roads underwater. Most are impassable. There's storm damage six counties wide. People are hurting everywhere."

"Where are you taking us?"

"Red Cross shelter at McGavock High School."

"What about Belle Meade?" Melissa asked the firefighter.

"The golf course is underwater. Old Harding Pike is flooded. Richland Creek looks like the Colorado River. St. George's church was flooded. Been reports of broken gas mains and fallen power lines. The Harrington water treatment plant is shut down from flooding. Nothing but bad news all around."

Water lapped at Jonathan's feet. Dazed and confused, he bled from a gash on his forehead. Above him, a dome light flickered on and off, revealing rows of vacant seats and blown-out windows. Toward the front of the bus, the sides caved to a v-shaped point as if a giant clever had dropped from above and nearly severed the bus in half. He could move his arms and legs, but the effort to stand met with pain along his side. He touched his head and winced from the sting of an open wound. He called out for Abby as he climbed over several seats toward an outstretched arm to find a lifeless body with a face lacerated by flying glass.

* * *

Melissa charged through the Red Cross shelter lined with folding cots along McGavock High School's gymnasium floor. "I have to find my boys," she yelled at the first volunteer she could find while Leland followed her inside.

"Slow down," the Red Cross worker acknowledged in a calm, yet deliberate tone. She maintained eye contact with Melissa. "We're doing everything we can."

"Who's your supervisor?"

"He's been deployed to the shelter in Murfreesboro."

"Do you know who I am?"

"Local law enforcement is working with fire rescue personnel and the National Guard. This is the safest place for you to be right now."

Melissa looked at Leland with a pained expression. "Not without my boys."

"How old are they?"

"Eleven and twelve."

"Are they alone?"

"They're with my driver."

"Then I'm sure they're safe. Once the storm is over—"

"I need to find them now! I need a car or a truck. Anything you can spare to get us out of here."

"I can't help you."

"Then what are you doing here?"

"Thank you," Leland offered in an overt attempt to diffuse the situation and let the woman do her job. He steered Melissa away from the entrance, where hundreds of evacuees arrived by bus from the flooded Opryland Hotel and Convention Center.

"I need a drink," Melissa announced.

"There's bottled water."

"I mean a real drink."

Leland retrieved two bottles from a case stacked against the wall.

Melissa opened her purse for the Percocet prescription and swallowed two pills. "I'm not sitting around this place waiting for a Christmas miracle. We need to get out of here and find our kids."

Leland gave her a water bottle and a chewy granola bar. "You should eat something."

"I'm not hungry."

"You're dehydrated."

Melissa unscrewed the cap on the water. "I'm frustrated." She drank half the bottle and stopped when her cell phone rang. "It's Sid…" She tapped the screen to answer. "Where the hell have you been?"

"I've been trying to reach you," Sid replied.

"Did you check on the boys?"

"No one home. I think they…"

She pressed the phone to her ear. "I can barely hear you."

"House was empty when I got there. Roads are impassable."

"Have you seen the boys?"

"No."

"What about Tomás?"

"I think they might be at the mall."

"Where are you now?"

"About ten miles from Opry Mills. Traffic's stopped in high water. Haven't seen anything like this since the flood of seventy-five."

"What about—" Melissa checked her phone's signal strength when the call dropped out. "I lost him," she told Leland.

"Keep trying. We need all the help we can get."

Jonathan climbed over the lifeless body and advanced several seats to find Abby with her leg caught underwater in the twisted wreckage. An oily sheen floated on the water's surface. "Can you move?"

"I'm stuck," Abby pleaded, her ashen face a portrait of fear as the water level continued to rise inside the bus. "You're bleeding."

Jonathan pushed on the seat behind Abby to try and bend it away from her leg. "I'm fine."

"My foot's caught on something. I can't see what it is, but it hurts when I move it."

Jonathan stuck his head below the surface but couldn't see his own hand in front of his face. "It's too dark," he said when he came up for air. "Try to turn your foot or something."

"I am."

Jonathan crawled around Abby to get a better look as the bus wreckage slid along the steep embankment and sank deeper along the edge of the flooded river. "Can you move your leg at all?"

"My ankle's stuck!"

Jonathan reached underwater to feel Abby's ankle wedged between twisted metal. "I won't leave you."

"What if I can't get out?"

"You will."

Abby shivered in place. Her eyes darted wildly back and forth. "The water's getting higher…"

"I'll get you out."

"How?"

"I don't know yet! Just give me a second to think!"

CHAPTER 35

A dam winced at the slashing rain, his gaze transfixed on the endless expanse of flooded field under siege from the powerful storm. Hunched in the center of a twelve-foot Jon Boat, he covered himself with a plastic tarp while a frail-looking man in glasses and a hooded windbreaker operated the small outboard at the stern. Near the bow, a bald man with a ragged beard and crooked teeth baled water with a plastic bucket.

"We have to keep looking," Adam pleaded. "Tomás needs our help."

The bald man signaled for the driver to circle the pavilion one more time. "The rain's too heavy," he said, scooping the plastic bucket at his feet.

"Tomás!" Adam shouted when the first sign of daybreak cast a faint glow on the horizon. Trees swayed violently as heavy winds and rain continued to carve an indelible mark on the storm-ravaged region. "TOMÁS!"

"We need to find your parents."

"Not without Tomás." Adam's voice started cracking. "I saw him standing over me."

The boat slowed to idle speed and continued trolling the area around the park.

The bald man lifted the tarp off Adam's head to see the boy's face. "You'll catch your death in this rain."

"My brother's at a movie in the mall. Tomás was supposed to pick him up."

"We can't get there from here in this boat."

"What about Tomás?"

"We need to find your folks."

"We have to find Tomás!"

The man looked over Adam's shoulder toward his driver at the stern and signaled to end the search. "We'll keep looking after we take you back. Chances are, your friend's already home."

Leland paced around the school gymnasium and tried Nicole's number again. "Can you hear me?" he asked loudly when the call finally went through.

"Leland?"

"I'm here."

"Where are you?" Nicole asked, her voice distorted by the weak connection. *"I can't believe how much rain—"*

"Is Abby with you?"

"What?"

"Is Abby with you?"

"I'm in Georgia."

"So she's not with you?"

"Why would she be with me?"

"Has she called you? Do you know where she is?"

"I haven't talked to her."

"If she calls you, tell her to call me immediately."

"Of course."

"Just tell her to call me," Leland stated again emphatically. "I need to know she's okay." He ended the call and gave Melissa's phone back.

"No news?"

"She hasn't seen Abby, either. I have no idea where my daughter is."

"I'm sure she's fine. She's probably glued to the TV playing Xbox Live."

"What about your boys?"

"Sid's still looking for them. They're not answering their phones."

Leland took Melissa's hand and approached another Red Cross volunteer. "Excuse me," he said to the sleep-deprived woman in a wet poncho. "Is there any kind of truck or van we can borrow?"

"I'll be with you in one second," the volunteer acknowledged Leland and redirected her attention to the family of four circling to claim an empty cot in the crowded gym.

"We need transportation right away."

"The roads are closed," the woman replied tersely. She wiped a strand of wet hair from her face. "We've got busloads of people coming in. This is the safest place for you to be right now."

"What about the rescue team who brought us here?" asked Melissa.

"They're on another run."

"When will they be back?"

"Whenever they get back."

"Please! My daughter's missing."

Melissa tugged at Leland's arm. "Forget it…"

Leland walked away.

"Wait," the woman replied. She produced a Ford key from her pocket. "I'm an empty nester. My van's a beater but it runs. Chances are, you won't make it very far in this storm."

"How much?" Melissa asked.

"I can't take your money."

"I'm good for it. My name's Melissa Ham—"

"I know who you are. I recognized you when I saw you come in. My son was in love with you."

Melissa reached inside her purse and fetched a soggy hundred dollar bill. "This is all I have on me. Call it a down payment or donation. Name your price, and I'll send you the difference."

* * *

Melissa plodded with Leland through shin-deep water in the parking lot outside as swirling winds blew heavy rain across blinking yellow traffic lights that rocked back and forth above the flooded street beyond the high school. "Over here." She directed him to the Ford Aerostar with faded paint and missing hubcaps.

Leland unlocked the van for Melissa and got in.

Melissa whisked the water off her sleeves and fastened her seatbelt. "I can't see anything…"

Leland started the van and put the wipers on high. He scanned the radio for weather updates and drove slowly toward the main road, where high water engulfed smaller cars. In the distance, a pair of kayakers paddled toward a bucket truck stranded near a concrete culvert.

Leland cranked up the volume. The van's speakers crackled and hummed.

The National Weather Service has issued several tornado warnings for parts of Middle and Western Tennessee, including Davidson, Williamson, Sumner, and Rutherford Counties. Police are advising everyone to stay home while emergency officials continue to evacuate residents from the hardest hit areas in southeast Nashville as substantial flooding continues to engulf low-lying homes, churches, schools, apartment buildings, and small business centers impacted by more than twelve inches of accumulation since yesterday. So far, eight deaths have been reported since the flooding started while dozens of local Davidson County residents remain missing. Officials are preparing for more rain as the Cumberland and Harpeth Rivers continue to crest above flood stage. Portions of I-24 remain closed in Antioch. I-40 remains closed near mile marker one-eighty. I-65 remains closed in Franklin. Members of the Red Cross, National Guard, Salvation Army, and local law enforcement have staffed more than twenty shelters in Davidson County. More than thirty thousand Nashville Electric Service customers remain without power. We'll have more at the top of the hour as we continue to monitor

*this unprecedented weather phenomenon some are calling
the storm of the century...*

Melissa answered Sid's incoming call with a terse,
"Where are you?"

"Traffic is completely gridlocked. I can't get through."

Melissa tapped Leland's shoulder and put the call on
speakerphone. "Did you find the boys?"

"Not yet."

"I can barely hear you."

"Reception...spotty."

Melissa's phone signaled another call from a number she
didn't recognize. "Hold on," she told Sid and switched
callers. "Hello?"

*"Mrs. Hamilton? This is Sergeant Nichols with the
Nashville Metro Police Department."*

Melissa sank in her seat from the tone of the officer's
voice, afraid the next words would shatter her world.

"Are you there?"

"Yes…"

*"We've been trying to reach you. Your son Adam was
admitted to Vanderbilt Children's Hospital."*

"Is he okay?"

"He's got some bumps and bruises—"

"Can I talk to him?"

"He's with the ER doctor at the moment."

"Is his brother with him?"

"No ma'am, but we're still searching. Your son made
reference to his brother and a girlfriend at a movie in Opry
Mills."

"You have to find them!"

"We're doing everything we can."

"What about my driver, Tomás? I haven't heard from
him since yesterday. My boys were with him."

Melissa heard the call drop out and redialed to hear an
out of service message. She looked at Leland, who kept his
focus on the road barely visible in the violent rain. "I'm
worried about Jonathan and Tomás."

Leland slowed at an intersection with flashing red lights. "The police will track them down, assuming Sid doesn't find them first." He waited for a tractor trailer to cross in front of him and thought back to his last words with Abby before he left her at home alone. She'd argued with him to take her to the mall. She'd practically begged him to let her go.

He looked both ways and headed south toward Belle Meade. "We need to get to Opry Mills!"

"Opry Mills is north of here," Melissa corrected him. "You're going the wrong way."

"We'll never get there by car."

"We need a boat," Melissa grumbled.

Leland put his hand on hers and said, "I know where we can find one."

CHAPTER 36

Assaulted by the pungent odor of diesel fuel and death, Abby coughed inside the mangled bus along the overflowed Cumberland. Her body shivered in the chest-deep water that continued to rise within the sinking wreckage. "My leg's still stuck!"

"I'm trying," Jonathan replied. He held his breath and dunked his head underwater to grapple with the twisted metal trapping Abby's ankle. When he came up for air, he fanned his hand along the surface to catch a clump of floating trash and snagged a lid from a fast food cup. He removed the fat straw and gave it to Abby. "Hold onto this. You can breathe through it if the water goes over your head."

Abby held the flimsy plastic in her trembling hand and asked, "What if the water goes over the straw?"

Leland parked the van in Melissa's flooded driveway and followed her through the deluge outside. "I'll back my truck to the garage," he shouted over the perpetual noise from the storm. He commandeered his faithful pickup while Melissa opened the four-car garage. He wiped his face and backed the tailgate toward the twenty-foot bass boat. With the truck hitch centered under the raised trailer tongue, he jumped out and pulled the boat cover off. He secured the drain plugs at the stern and unplugged the battery tender. "Are you sure it runs?" he asked Melissa.

Melissa rubbed her wet arms vigorously for warmth. "Tomás took care of it."

Leland stepped on the trailer fender and swung his leg up. He found the key inside the ignition with a foam rubber key fob attached. He switched the battery to the "ON" position and ran the outboard in neutral a couple seconds before he powered the motor off. "We're good."

"What if we don't find them?"

Leland retrieved four life vests and a telescoping boat hook from the bow locker. "We will. Right now we need to find rope and flashlights."

Melissa scavenged a garage shelf with a cooler and a pair of boat fenders. She grabbed a lantern flashlight and several lengths of nylon dock line and handed them up to Leland.

Leland tied the dock lines together and secured one end to a stanchion near the helm. "Is this all the rope?"

"It's all I could find."

Leland jumped down and cranked the trailer's jack stand to lower the tongue onto the hitch ball. "Abby begged me to take her to the mall this morning. She said friends could bring her home."

"We don't even know for sure if she and Jonathan are still at the mall. Tomás could have picked them up. The police could have found them. They could be stranded somewhere. They could be—"

"We'll find them," Leland tried to reassure her. He sensed Melissa's apprehension. "Sid will keep looking. The police will keep looking. We have to do our part, and right now, my gut says our kids are hunkered down, waiting for their ride."

Abby gripped the arm rest in front of her while Jonathan struggled to free her leg. Numb to the cold, murky flood water eroding her body's core temperature, her teeth chattered uncontrollably as water slowly rose to her neckline. She clutched the straw in her hand, afraid to use it and afraid to let it go. Despite Jonathan's valiant efforts, her hope diminished with prayers gone unanswered. Impaired by her daunting circumstances, a memory sequestered in the recess of her subconscious mind resurfaced to ignite the terrifying moment when she crashed into the windshield of her mother's car. Caught in limbo between the present and the past, she held her nose and put the straw in her mouth before Jonathan resurfaced, gasping for air with a length of bent metal tubing clutched triumphantly in his hand.

Leland detoured in heavy traffic off Route 70, west of I-440 and the Nashville International Airport less than five miles from the Opry Mills Mall. "We're getting closer…"

Melissa pressed her forehead to the window. "I think I see something." She rubbed the back of her hand on the glass and tried to make out the image concealed by thrashing rain.

"What is it?"

"I can't tell."

Leland moved over at the sight of flashing lights and rescue vehicles blocking traffic from a wreck up ahead. He pressed the cab light to illuminate the damp street map in his hand. "We launch from here."

"Are you sure?"

"The water's too deep to drive further."

"What if we don't find them?"

"Then we keep searching until we do."

Melissa reached for Leland's hand and squeezed. "Thank you for doing this."

Leland positioned his truck to back the boat into deeper water as rescue workers passed in a rigid hull inflatable with a blue strobe light mounted above a center console. "Thank me when we find our kids." He unhooked the winch in the driving rain and slid the boat off the padded trailer bunks. He pointed to a crooked sign post that read, Browns Creek. "This inlet runs north toward the Cumberland. We'll follow the river to the mall." He started the outboard. Then he grabbed a pair of life vests and the boat hook from the bow storage locker.

Melissa climbed on board and buckled an orange life vest at her chest. She hunkered down in the bucket seat beside the helm's offset console while Leland nudged the throttle forward.

The boat gathered speed in the pale moonlight and pushed its way through the creek off plane.

"The inlet's too narrow," Melissa shouted above the engine noise.

Leland kept the boat centered with the prop set high to avoid submerged obstructions. "Hang on!" he shouted as he navigated a sharp bend before the creek opened up. He followed the overflowed river northeasterly along a parallel path to Briley Parkway dotted with distant headlights from stranded cars.

When the river widened, he shoved the throttle forward to bring the boat on plane and headed toward Opry Mills Drive. The fiberglass hull carved a shallow bow wave as the bass boat passed Mills Creek and approached the bikeway bridge extending over the Cumberland toward Two River's Parkway and Gaylord Drive.

Minutes dragged into hours of endless searching in the dark along the river littered with pulverized landscape outside the mall. Impeded by strong winds and continuous rain, Leland circled through the vacant parking area that resembled a war zone with dozens of fallen trees and overturned vehicles scattered in random formations. Afraid to search in one place for too long, he traversed the mall perimeter, his spirit beaten but not broken as he refused to relinquish his faith despite the dire circumstances.

Melissa pointed to a large obstruction protruding from the river's edge. "Over there!"

Leland eased the throttle back and guided the boat toward floating garbage bags and a swarm of rusted paint cans bobbing on the surface near sheets of Styrofoam, a propane tank, and an animal carcass. Fighting the wind and current, he worked the steering wheel and throttle simultaneously to navigate safe passage. "What is it?"

"I see something!" Melissa cried out. She pointed to the starboard side.

Leland skirted along the riverbank. "Aim the light."

Melissa panned the lantern flashlight at the murky water with one hand clasped on the bow rail.

Leland cut the throttle abruptly. "Listen…"

"What is it?"

Leland took the flashlight from her and scanned the flooded embankment as the boat drifted aimlessly in the absence of forward propulsion. Thunder boomed. "Did you hear that?" He gave the flashlight back and worked the throttle to control the boat's direction of travel.

Melissa panned the beam toward a large box-shaped enclosure in the water. When the sound of thunder dissipated, she heard a cry for help and yelled, "Over there!"

Leland maneuvered the boat to find Jonathan and Abby clinging to the top of a bus protruding from the surface. "Take the wheel!" he shouted while he reached for the telescoping boat hook and leaned over the grab rail to snag a section of the crumpled bus frame.

"Get on!" Melissa screamed at Jonathan, who helped her lift Abby on board. "Are you hurt?"

"I'm okay," Jonathan replied in a raspy voice. "But I think something's wrong with Abby."

CHAPTER 37

Paula Presley surfed the television news from the recreation room of the Tennessee Mental Health Institute. Every local channel showed the same footage of a city decimated by what some were calling the worst storm in Tennessee history.

Safe inside the confines of her secure facility, she paused on the last station with a young female news reporter dressed in hip waders and a yellow rain coat, standing in a flooded parking lot with a yard stick at her side to emphasize the obvious, as if the bevy of submersed vehicles behind her didn't give away the whole story. "Have you seen this?" she asked the attorney in the chair beside her—a svelte gentleman with neatly combed hair and a flashy gold pen beside the visitor's badge clipped to his breast pocket.

"Who hasn't?" the public defender replied without looking up from the last page in his black binder. "Sign here," he instructed Paula. He pointed to the underlined section below the last paragraph and gave her his shiny gold pen under the vigilant eye of a super-sized orderly who monitored the room of permanent residents dressed in white pajamas.

"This it?" Paula asked.

"Almost."

Paula signed the page and gave the pen back. She changed channels, hoping to find anything but more news about the storm and the impact on the local economy. "They said the Cumberland rose to fifty-two feet."

"Uh huh…"

"That's the highest water mark since 1937."

The attorney reached into his leather attaché case and replaced the signed paperwork with another legal folder.

"The first water treatment plant is still shut down," Paula continued. "They're saying the second one might close too. And there's still nine thousand people without power." She scratched behind her ear and looked at her attorney. She could see the concentration on his face while he reviewed the next page. "Do you have family here?"

"Vermont," the attorney replied, after pausing to reread the last paragraph.

"My husband, if you can call him that, and my daughter, are all I have. Family is everything."

"I suppose."

"Do you have children?" Paula asked.

"No."

"Are you married?"

"Divorced."

"If you do find yourself with children one day, tell them the story of this hundred year flood. There's no life without water, but this kind of water isn't natural. Someone pissed off Mother Nature awful bad. All these carbon emissions people talk about. And global warming. Not to mention all those experiments they keep doing in space. I've always said it's a matter of time before we do something bad we can't take back." She changed channels to find another news reporter commenting about the Grand Ole Opry, the Country Music Hall of Fame, the Schermerhorn Symphony Center, and other Nashville landmarks impacted by the storm. "How long do you think it will take for all this water to subside?"

The attorney shrugged his shoulders and marked a small 'x' on the bottom of the page where he wanted his client to sign.

"A few days? A week?"

"I couldn't say."

"Take a guess," Paula urged him.

"I'm sure it will clear up soon."

"*Clear up soon?* You sound like you're talking about a late spring shower. This is cataclysmic. Half the city is underwater."

The attorney made eye contact with the orderly to signal he was ready to leave. "We're almost done here."

"I hope my daughter's safe."

"I'm sure she's fine."

"I heard the storm's claimed ten lives already. I'd be careful if I were you." Paula pointed to the television screen, where news footage showed water rushing into ground floor apartments while residents looked on from second-story balconies. In another segment, firefighters waded hip-deep to rescue a drowning dog before the camera cut back to show hundreds of people stranded in overcrowded shelters.

"Read this last page carefully before you sign."

Paula took the leather binder from her attorney and skimmed the first few sentences of legal jargon. "You sound so gloomy. This is supposed to be a good thing."

"The judge still has to approve it."

"The judge is more worried about getting his car towed out of the drink."

"Once you sign the papers, I'll submit the application to the courthouse."

"How long will it take for the court to decide?"

"Depends on the case load."

Paula slammed the notepad against her lap, drawing unwanted attention from the orderly who approached to put his hand on her back. "Then give me a ballpark figure." She flinched when she felt the orderly's meaty paw on her shoulder.

"Several days at least. Could be weeks, maybe months."

"Months?"

"I don't control the schedule. I'm just a servant of the court."

"I still don't like it."

"I never said it would take months, I said it *could* take months. There are lots of variables."

Paula muted the television with the remote. "You don't think I have a shot at leaving here?"

"I never said that."

"But you're thinking it."

"I'm late for my next appointment. If you don't mind—"

"I imagine you don't like me very much. What with everything I've done and all. But I'm not the same person I was ten years ago. Remember this before you go marching off to your next appointment in your fancy suit with your fancy pen. I'm a good person. A good mom. I deserve to have what any good mother has."

"I'm not here to assess you, Mrs. Presley."

"Do you think I'm crazy?"

"I think you've made a lot of progress in recent years."

"That's exactly what I told my husband. He doesn't believe me." Paula eyeballed her attorney without blinking. "But you believe me?"

"I think you have good intentions."

Paula broke eye contact and focused on the legal paper in her lap. "I get it. I'm not asking for redemption. Just a chance to make things right." She muddled through the legal gibberish, tuning out the screaming tantrum emanating from the room next door; the sound of knuckles tapping on a window; random babble from a new patient who'd arrived the day before; the pervasive humming from the guy in the corner conducting his own symphony. She'd made mistakes, no doubt. But after years of psychiatric treatment, she'd come to terms with her transgressions and saw her future in a different light.

The attorney pointed to the signature line at the bottom of the page. "Are you sure about this? If you leave here, you're on your own."

Paula reached for the pen and signed her name. "I've never been more certain about anything in my life."

CHAPTER 38

L eland approached Abby's bedside in the shared intensive care suite. A curtain partitioned the room down the middle with a clock, a calendar, and a tack board along one wall. He held her hand and saw her chest rise and fall out of sync with the metrical beep from the heart rate monitor. A bank of medical equipment monitored her vital signs. A respirator fed air to her lungs through a breathing tube while an IV drip supplied medication to her system.

He hadn't eaten. He hadn't slept. His emotions ran the gamut from anger to despair, reliving the last forty-eight hours in his mind. Nothing made sense, especially his decision to leave his daughter home alone. He'd snatched her from certain death, only to find her fighting for her life again, as if God gave her a second chance only to take it away.

"You should go home," he heard someone whisper before he realized the nurse had reentered the room.

"I can't leave her."

"We'll contact you if her condition changes."

Leland let go of Abby's hand. "She needs me here," he told the nurse in clogs and green scrubs with hints of grey in her raven-black hair.

The nurse checked the readings on the monitor attached to a vertical column of critical care outlets for power, data, medical gas, and vacuum. "No rush, but there's someone waiting outside to see you."

Melissa greeted Leland with a hug when he emerged from Abby's room. "They wouldn't let me come up here at first."

Leland reciprocated with a tentative embrace. "I'm glad they did."

"How is she?"

"The doctor says the hypothermia affected her system. She just...shut down. I don't know what to do."

"They're doing everything they can."

"I should have never left her by herself."

"No one knew the storm would hit so hard."

"What about your boys?"

"Adam's downstairs with Sid, complaining the Wi-Fi doesn't work. They're keeping Jonathan overnight for observation. He's been asking about Abby."

"I'm grateful your son was with her."

"You made a lasting impression on him. And me."

Leland's cheeks grew warm. "Anyone else would have done the same."

Melissa shook her head. "Our kids are alive because of you." She glanced away for a moment, then refocused her curious expression at Leland. "How did you know how to navigate the river so well?"

"I think God had a hand in it," Leland answered. He followed Melissa to a vending machine. "Any news about your driver?"

"Tomás is still missing. The police are looking for him. Adam is convinced he was with him the whole time, but he can't remember where he saw him last." She pushed four quarters in the coin slot and selected a black coffee with sugar. The machine dispensed the steaming beverage in a paper cup.

"He's probably stuck in a shelter somewhere," Leland reasoned.

"It's been two days." Melissa retrieved her coffee from the small enclosure and blew across the top. "I'm worried."

"He'll be okay."

Melissa held the cup with both hands. "Adam insists he's going to find Tomás himself. He thinks I know more than I'm telling him, but I don't know what to say."

"Tell him the truth."

"I am. Tomás could be standing on the roof of someone's house or stranded on the side of the road."

Leland gave a sympathetic nod. "Let me know how I can help."

"You've done more than enough already."

"What about your car?"

"Sid's working it. I'm just grateful to have my boys back. If there's anything I can do for you—"

"I'm good."

Melissa touched his arm. "Abby's a fighter. She'll pull through."

"She's all I have."

Melissa looked away to hide her pain. "You should go home and get some sleep." She walked toward the elevator by the nurse's station and glanced at a copy of the Monday morning paper. The headline read: OVERWHELMED. "I heard they evacuated five hundred people from Metro Center because they're afraid the levy won't hold. A lot of folks are hurting right now."

Leland thought about the lyrics to a song he'd started and heard the melody play out in his mind so clearly he knew which chords would bring the music to life. The last thing he wanted to think about was writing music, but in a strange way, the *only* thing he could focus on was the song he heard over and over in his head. "I need to hang around awhile longer. Check on Abby some more."

Melissa pressed the elevator button. "I should get back to my boys." She acknowledged a nurse who passed her in the hall and exchanged a knowing glance toward the stoic father determined not to leave his daughter's side.

CHAPTER 39

"I don't have time for this," Melissa complained to Sid, who paced inside her living room, talking on his cell phone. "I'm worried sick about Tomás. He should have been back by now."

Sid raised his hand to wave her off.

"What are they saying?" Melissa pressed him.

Sid ended the call. "Nothing. Metro police are doing everything they can. A lot of people are still missing. Tomás is one of them."

"How many men are looking for him?"

"They didn't say."

"Did you ask?"

"They're doing everything they can."

"Did you tell them to search the mall?"

Sid drew a deep breath. "They're searching county-wide. They have his photo, the Town Car's description, and the license plate."

"What if they can't find him?"

"They found Adam. They'll find Tomás."

Melissa wanted to believe what Sid was telling her. She needed to believe him for her own sanity. *Hope for the best and prepare for the worst,* she told herself, convinced the storm must have carried Tomás four counties away. "This house is a mess. The yard's a swimming pool. My car's totaled—"

"At least the storm subsided. You still have power and no flood damage to the house."

"Adam won't come out of his room. He's worried sick about Tomás."

Sid approached the burled walnut liquor cabinet along the wall. "I need a drink."

"Make mine a double."

Sid poured two tumblers from a crystal decanter. "How's your back?"

Melissa took the double shot and downed it. She craved the slow burn from the balanced scotch. "Better, now. Any news on my money or the miscreant who stole it?"

"The investigation's ongoing."

"I doubt that. Not with this weather."

"The FBI's involved. They'll track him down eventually."

"And my money?"

Sid sipped his bourbon. "When they find the man, they'll find your money."

"How can you be certain?"

"I can't. There are no certainties in this life. You need to hold it together, for your sake and your boys'."

Melissa rolled her eyes. "Tell me something I don't know."

"I heard piranhas are loose in Opry Mills Mall."

"That's absurd."

"At this point, nothing surprises me anymore."

Melissa set her glass down and entered her music studio. She let her fingers caress the piano keys.

Sid followed her. "I like where that's going."

"I'm not finished."

"I know a song writer who could help."

"Forget it."

"He worked with Mariah Carey and Whitney Houston. If you're serious about—"

"Miles Steinard is a pervert who likes to show off his Ferrari. I don't want my name associated with him or his sleazy reputation. Period. I write my own material now."

"The music, sure. But the lyrics…"

"What about them?"

"The market's changing. What worked ten years ago doesn't have the same pull anymore."

"What are you saying?"

Sid finished his bourbon. "Focus on your strengths."

"As opposed to what? My inept record label who couldn't find a hit song if it sat on their face?"

"I'm talking as your agent now."

"A turd dipped in sugar still tastes like shit. You want me to be like every other starlet with bubblegum lyrics and candy corn rhythms a toddler could bang out on a ten dollar Casio. You want me to play it safe."

"I want you to play what your audience wants to hear. Miles Steinard has a penchant for writing songs. Half of them are hits before their albums even drop. At least commit to lunch with him."

"Not interested."

"What have you got to lose?"

Melissa played the next few bars. "My reputation, for starters. Not to mention my time."

"All the melodies you write won't sell concert tickets without the words to go with them."

"Who says I don't have the words? I'm a singer, aren't I?" She put her lips near the microphone suspended from the ceiling. She had nothing original in her repertoire anymore, and trying to convince Sid otherwise was futile. "I should check on the boys."

Sid took the hint and followed Melissa to the foyer. "How's Abby?"

"You didn't see her yourself?"

Sid shrugged. "It didn't feel right."

"You should check on her and Leland. I think he stayed the night at the hospital."

"That was quite a stunt with your boat."

"Leland saved Jonathan's life."

"Indeed." Sid moved toward the door to let himself out. "Call me if you need anything. And let me know if you change your mind about Miles."

Melissa walked Sid to his Escalade. The grounds were soaked but not flooded on the hillside location. "Thank you for helping me find my boys."

"I was useless. Leland did all the heavy lifting." Sid hugged her. "I'll call you if I hear anything about Tomás."

Melissa watched Sid drive away. She wanted another drink but settled for a glass of water and the last two Percocet pills in her possession. She dialed Tomás's cell phone and masked her fear with anger. Had he left the state? Did he leave the country? If he were stuck at a shelter, why didn't he borrow a phone and call? If he cared about her boys at all, why would he suddenly renounce them?

She wanted answers. And she wanted her life the way it was: the life of a country music superstar, where all the pieces fit together and a legion of fans adored her; where every station played her music, and everyone in Nashville knew her voice, her face, and her name. Now, she barely recognized herself—a shell of the woman she once was, transformed by a cheating husband, a corrupt accountant, stalled record sales, and the pitfalls of age in an industry that lauded young celebrities and discarded the rest like the morning paper.

CHAPTER 40

Leland awoke in his bed to find Abby's cat vigorously licking his forehead. He threw the blanket off and rolled over to check the time on his alarm clock while the orange tabby remained strategically perched on a queen-size pillow. Dressed in the same clothes from the night before, he dragged himself to the kitchen and fed his furry companion a can of leftover *Fancy Feast*. Then he powered on the TV to catch the morning news.

In the wake of record-breaking flood conditions, muddy waters continue to spill over the rising Cumberland River, flooding Lower Broadway along First and Second Avenue, engulfing warehouse spaces and destroying millions of dollars in music equipment, including a sixty-foot-wide video screen assembled for Brad Paisley's upcoming tour. In other areas, floodwater inside the Gaylord Opryland Resort caused substantial damage with more than two thousand rooms decommissioned indefinitely. This comes at the height of tourist season as local businesses continue reeling from the lingering effects of this unprecedented storm. The downtown Nashville Hilton accumulated ten feet of water inside its underground garage, but no rooms were impacted, and hotel management has made rooms available for guests evacuated from the Opryland Hotel.

The Hard Rock on Second Avenue will be closed for several days due to basement flooding that destroyed most of their produce and dry goods. And in some residential communities, hundreds of families are finding water, food, and gas in scarce supply due in part to weekend power outages. So far, nine people have perished with at least two thousand homes destroyed or damaged by the flood. City officials peg damage estimates above the one billion dollar mark. Meanwhile, President Obama has declared the four-county region a natural disaster area and has unlocked federal money through FEMA. While county officials stress the fresh water supply is safe, they are urging people to limit unnecessary water usage and avoid traveling, if possible. With flood waters now receding, recovery and clean up efforts have begun as county officials and municipal workers focus on high priority tasks like power restoration and sanitation issues. Nashville Mayor, Karl Dean, announced that much of city government would reopen by Thursday and that every effort was being made to restore city bus services. We'll keep you posted as we learn more...

Leland rinsed a coffee cup in the sink and poured a shot of Jim Beam. He ran his hand through his matted hair and went outside to find his newspaper floating in a plastic bag at the edge of the driveway. He carried the soggy edition to the house, pausing to inspect several saturated cardboard boxes on the wet garage floor. The Tuesday paper's front page headline read: SWAMPED.

A quick shower and shave restored his energy before he left the house with his keys and guitar.

The drive to the hospital seemed like an eternity, fraught with winding detours punctuated by standing water, broken roads, downed power lines, and fallen trees. Police managed roadblocks city-wide while the persistent buzz of chainsaws filled the airwaves. On some streets, kayaks, canoes, and inflatable boats outnumbered cars. In other neighborhoods, displaced homeowners used shovels and rakes to clear rubbish left behind in the wake of the devastating flood.

Leland found an open space in the hospital parking lot and carried his guitar inside. He took the elevator to Abby's room and found her sleeping on her back while a ventilator pumped oxygen through her endotracheal tube. Flower bouquets scented the room with the blinds closed to block the morning sun.

"How is she?" he asked the first nurse who entered the room.

"She's stable."

"Is she getting better?"

"We'd like to get her off the ventilator."

"Where's her doctor?"

"He's on rounds, but I'll let him know you're here."

Leland touched Abby's hair. He kissed her cheek and parked a chair beside her. He missed the sound of her voice and her guarded smile.

He took his guitar from the case and softly strummed a few chords. He tightened the D and G strings to sharpen the notes, vaguely aware of the empty bed behind the curtain bisecting the room.

He'd played the same song over and over in his mind the night before; every word and every note, painting his emotions on a lyrical canvas. Now, his callused fingertips caressed the strings along the guitar neck while his right hand slowly danced above the rosewood sound hole until he found the strength to sing…

> *I've been trying to find*
> *A way to convey, I love you*
> *But the higher I climb, the further I fall away*
> *Now every note I send you, comes out wrong…*
>
> *You are my song!*
> *My soph-is-ti-cated, four part har-mony…*
> *A twelve-note composition*
> *A Beethoven symphony…*

A soothing voice, to carry me along
You are my song...

I've been try'n to ignore
What my life would become, without you
But the harder I try, the greater the weight of it all
Now every word I write you, comes out wrong...

You are my song!
A sentimental five chord melody...
A twelve-note composition
A Schubert symphony...
A soothing voice, to carry me along
You are my song...

Remember this My Love, before you're gone...
The notes I tried to find for you
Were right here all along...

You are my song...
My soph-is-ti-cated, four part har-mony...
A soothing voice, to carry me along
You are my song
You are my...song

Leland kept strumming the acoustic Gibson until he heard someone enter the room. The doctor, he presumed, but when he looked up, the person he found in front of him was the last one he expected to see.

Nicole stepped around Abby's bed to touch her hand. "I heard about what happened. I got here as soon as I could. After you called me, I started thinking…"

"I thought you were on tour."

"Me too," Nicole professed. "He dumped me for some skank he met at the bar."

"I'm sorry."

"Don't be. He was a loser. I'm the one who should be sorry." She watched Leland gently rest his guitar in the case. "Don't stop on my account."

"Abby's probably too old for my singing, anyhow."

Nicole moved around Abby's bed to get closer to Leland. "A girl's never too old to hear her father sing to her." She put her arm around him and kissed his face.

"Good to know."

"I just wanted to stop by and check on Abby. I'm staying with my sister until I get a few things squared away."

"How's she doing?"

"Better, now that the rain finally stopped. Her yard got flooded, but her house was spared."

"She's lucky."

"Not as lucky as Abby is to have a father like you."

"That means a lot."

Nicole squeezed Leland's arm. "She'll pull through."

"She doesn't give up easy."

Nicole gave Leland a gentle hug. "Neither do I."

CHAPTER 41

A dam rolled over in bed wide awake, his heart pounding in anticipation. The alarm clock on his dresser showed 4:30 a.m. He got dressed in the pale glow from a night light beside his bureau and packed a duffle bag with a map, a flashlight, and his Swiss Army knife. He added three bottles of water and an assortment of snacks he'd squirreled away.

He'd gone days without sleep, and yet sleep was the last thing he needed. No one listened. No one cared. If anyone was going to find Tomás, it would be him. Tomás needed more than phone calls and prayers. He needed someone to help him. If the police cared about Tomás, they would have found him already.

He made his bed with the pillows shoved under his comforter and stuffed several twenty dollar bills in his pocket—the last of his birthday cash he'd saved for a pellet rifle his mom refused to buy him.

The house was quiet when he crept down the sweeping staircase. He knew the code to deactivate the alarm and how to open the gated entrance. He'd left his bike outside behind the bushes the night before.

At the bottom of the stairs, he moved quietly toward the alarm panel on the wall in the foyer. He paused when he heard a noise in the kitchen and saw his brother staring back at him from across the house like a soldier on the opposite side of a demilitarized zone. "What are you doing down here?" he whispered to Jonathan, hoping his brother was merely an illusion.

The kitchen lights came on.

"Turn 'em off," Adam whispered tersely.

Jonathan lifted a milk jug from the fridge and unscrewed the cap. "I can't see."

"You'll wake Mom up."

"Where are you going?"

Adam backtracked to kill the lights. "Don't worry about it."

Jonathan drank from the milk jug and wiped his mouth with his hand. "You picked a bad time to run away."

"I'm not running away."

"Then go back upstairs before I tell Mom."

Adam set his duffle bag down to rest his arm. "Why are you up?"

"I was thirsty."

"Don't tell Mom you saw me."

"Not unless you tell me where you're going."

"I have to find Tomás."

"By yourself? Half the world's looking for him."

"They're not doing a very good job."

Jonathan put the milk back and rubbed his eyes. "You have no idea where he is."

"I know where he *was*. I remember the road from the mall. The car fell in a giant hole."

"The police will find him."

Adam lowered his head. "Maybe." He picked up his duffel bag and headed toward the foyer.

"How are you going to get there?" Jonathan pried. "The roads are still flooded."

"I'll ride my bike."

"That's dumb. You can't ride a bike through a storm."

"The storm is over."

"What if you get stuck somewhere?"

"I'll call the police for help."

Jonathan looked upstairs when he heard his mom's cell phone ring. "Mom will be mad."

"I don't care. Someone has to find Tomás."

"They will." Jonathan followed Adam to the other room. "You'll get in trouble."

"I don't care."

"What am I supposed to tell Mom when she finds out you're gone?"

"Tell her I went to clean the stables."

"We don't have horses anymore. It might sound more believable if I told her you went to Paris."

Adam touched the control panel on the wall to deactivate the house alarm. "Tell her whatever you want. I'm leaving."

"Maybe Mom fired Tomás like everyone else. She just hasn't told us."

"She didn't fire Tomás. She wouldn't do that."

"How do you know?" Jonathan posed.

"Because I know."

"Think about it. Mom made us change schools. She canceled vacation. She fired Yolanda and the pool guy. She sold the Bentley. She sold the horses. Now she's trying to sell the house."

Adam thought about his brother's logic. "Tell her—" he started before the upstairs lights came on.

Melissa held the guardrail with a firm grip. The weight of the phone conversation with police made her queasy from the news she'd prayed would never come. "Why are you boys up?" she asked at the bottom of the stairs. Tears slid down her face like rain drops on a window pane. "You two should be in bed."

"I'm leaving to find Tomás," Adam stated decisively.

Melissa wiped the corner of one eye with her hand. "No, Honey…"

"We have to find him!" Adam pleaded. He looked at his brother for support, sensing Mom had news no one wanted to hear.

Melissa held her arms out. "Come here."

"I'm leaving."

"Where is he?" asked Jonathan.

Melissa hugged her oldest son. "I love you." She held her other arm out for Adam. "Come here…"

"I have to find Tomás!" Adam resisted.

"The police already found him."

"Where?" Adam dropped his duffle bag and approached his mom. "When is he coming home?"

Melissa reached out for Adam. "Tomás loved you both very much."

"But when—"

"Honey…I'm so sorry. The police said Tomás died in the flood."

CHAPTER 42

Leland sipped black coffee in the hospital cafeteria with the morning paper open in front of him. Familiar headlines cited widespread devastation across middle and western parts of Tennessee. Photos showed desperate homeowners plucked from their roofs by helicopter and a pregnant woman airlifted from the highway. Another story covered a Belle Meade police officer swept away in his patrol car. More photos showed ravaged neighborhoods lined with mounds of damaged goods piled high along the curb.

Leland flipped the page to see the image of a house torn away from its foundation with the entire basement contents visibly destroyed by the flood. Another home marked with a giant "X" reminded rescue workers to check for bodies. Downtown, the Schermerhorn Symphony Center suffered $40 million in damages to property, concert grand pianos, and numerous orchestral instruments trapped inside their flooded basement. Statewide, various shelters gave storm victims safe haven from thousands of evacuated homes and apartments.

Leland analyzed the news. The catastrophic damage and the city leaders' pledge to rebuild notwithstanding, the impact from the meteorological anomaly seemed almost insignificant from his perspective. The more he fought the urge to compose new music, the faster the words poured forth—as if the greater the tragedy in life, the more focused his creative mind became. So many lyrics came to pass, mostly junk he threw away until he found the right words to continue.

He sipped his coffee and folded the newspaper in half. "You sure you don't want something to eat?" he asked Nicole when she returned from her car.

Nicole hung her purse on the chair and slid a house key across the table. "I meant to give you this."

"No worries."

Nicole rubbed Leland's forearm. "Abby will wake up when she's ready."

"I hope so," Leland mumbled, his head low with his eyes focused on the silver house key. "When do you need to be at work?"

"No rush. I'm sort of in between jobs at the moment."

"You should have kept the one you had."

Nicole slid her hand away. "We were good together."

"Yes, we *were*."

"I liked the song you wrote for me."

"I write a lot of songs."

Nicole crossed her arms. "I should have been home with Abby when you were gone. If I hadn't bailed on you, she wouldn't be in this hospital."

"Not your fault."

"Then why do I feel so bad?"

"Because you care for her." Leland twirled the key on the table. "I can't think about us right now."

Nicole opened the newspaper and scanned the employment section. "Does her mom know about her condition?"

"Abby's not her concern."

"You have to tell her. She's Abby's mother. She has a right to know."

"She gave up that right a long time ago."

"People make mistakes, Leland. You can't hold it against her forever." Nicole shied away, debating her willingness to confess a truth she should have expressed weeks ago. "My mother died from breast cancer."

"I know."

Nicole let out a deep breath. "What you didn't know is that I thought I had it too."

Leland moved closer to his side of the table and leaned forward. "What are you talking about?"

"I should have told you before. When I left. I was in a bad way. I found a lump in my right breast."

"I didn't know."

"My doctor kept running tests. I thought for sure I had cancer."

"But you don't?"

"No."

"Why didn't you tell me?"

"I was scared. Confused. I didn't want to become another statistic."

Leland sat back in his seat. "I could have helped you."

Nicole toyed with a napkin on the table. "There was nothing you could do."

"I would have listened."

"I'm sorry. I'm not sure why I'm even telling you this right now. I know you have a lot on your mind." Nicole skimmed the employment section. "This is all minimum wage crap."

"Maybe you should look out of state."

"Do you want me to leave?"

"I want you to have a job." Leland finished his coffee. His flip phone rang on the table with Sid's name in the small display. "Hey," he answered in a scratchy, sleep-deprived voice.

"How's Abby?"

"The same."

"How are you holding up?"

Leland switched the phone to his other ear. "Like ten pounds of shit in a five pound sack."

"I got a call from Brad Siegel at Capital Country Records. He wants to meet with you tomorrow morning."

"I can't."

"I know the timing sucks."

"Abby's still in the hospital."

"Where she's going to recover. Brad wants you in his studio by ten. Bring your guitar."

"Tell him I need to reschedule."

"There is no reschedule, Leland. You won't get another chance like this with Brad."

"Then I'll take a chance with someone else."

"I'm well aware of Abby's condition. I feel for you and for her. But you have to put things in perspective."

"That's your job," Leland mumbled into the phone. He looked at Nicole when he talked. "Mine is taking care of my daughter."

"You'll be gone a couple hours. Abby would understand."

"Abby needs me. The last time I left her alone—"

"But she's not alone. She's the reason you're committed to this."

Leland laid his head in his hand and rubbed his temples. "I'll think about it," he said before he ended the call.

"Who was that?" asked Nicole.

"No one."

"I can stay here with Abby if you need me to."

"What I need is for my daughter to wake up and start her life again."

"She will. But you can't stop living yours."

"Abby *is* my life."

Nicole leaned over to touch Leland's arm. "You're not alone in this. I hope you know that."

Leland forced a smile. Nicole's hand felt warm. Soothing. He focused on the good memories, and any notion of a meaningful future he might construct with her. But despite her comfort in a time of grief and uncertainty, his attention remained focused elsewhere.

* * *

Leland paced inside the hospital, deep in thought about Abby and oblivious to his surroundings or the entrance to the children's chapel he'd passed three times already on the second floor. The marvels of modern medicine aside, Abby's fate came down to waiting and hoping for the best.

He wandered back to her room with his guitar, the same music playing over and over in his head; a sad melody he'd conjured the night after he hauled Abby from the shadows of the briny deep.

He opened his guitar case on the chair beside her hospital bed and whispered, "I'm proud of you." Then he took the guitar out and slung the strap over his shoulder. He strummed slowly and said, "I know you can't hear me, but I wanted to play another song for you."

> *So many years have come and gone*
> *Harder to tell where I went wrong*
> *Caught in the fear of the great, be-yond*
>
> *Now I can't bear, to see, your pain*
> *My life will never be the same*
> *If I could change, one, thing*
> *What I would give for one more day*
>
> *One more day...*
> *To hold you in my arms*
> *One more day...*
> *To wrap my heart around you*
> *One more day...*
> *To find our way, back, home*
> *One more day...*
> *Please don't leave me all alone...*
>
> *All I want...is you, to know, I love you...*
> *And I will always be, at, your side*
> *So close your eyes*
> *While I bow my head and pray*

Please, Lord, let me hold her one more day

One more day...
To take away the fear
One more day...
To find our way, back, home
One more day...
To show you what tomorrow, will bring

Please, Lord, let me hold her one more day
Don't take my girl away
I need her with me...one more day...
One more day...

Leland kissed Abby's forehead. Then he set his guitar in the case and wiped his eye. He left the room for a drink at the water fountain. Sunlight shined through a bank of windows in the multicolored pediatric critical care ward overlooking the city vista.

He sipped from the stainless steel faucet and thought about his conversation with Nicole. He could have done more for her had he known about her cancer scare. But his life always centered around his music. And his relationship with Nicole—like so many before her—always ended in a state of denial and regret. Disavowing his own shortcomings made it easy to cast blame on his partner. But music wasn't something he produced out of obligation; it was the center of his life. Only Melissa understood his deep reverence. She, more than anyone he'd ever met, had achieved enormous success in a business where most people fell short. Now he questioned if his connection with Melissa was rooted in something deeper or whether he wanted a future in music at all anymore.

He loped to the end of the hall away from a group of medical students flocking room to room under a doctor's supervision and dialed Sid's phone. "It's Leland," he said as soon as he heard the connection go through.

"Can I count on you tomorrow?"

"I appreciate everything you've done for me, but I'm going to pass."

"Did something happen? Is Abby—"

"Her condition is the same."

"I know you're dealing with a lot right now. But you're making a huge mistake. Brad Siegel's offering you a once-in-a-lifetime opportunity. You need this Leland. More than you know."

"I need my daughter, Sid. That's what I know. If she dies, my life dies with her. All the music in the world can't fix what's happened."

"Record companies sell the dream. They never talk about the struggle. I know you. And I know you've struggled. You need to get right with this and push beyond the pain. If you don't, you will live to regret your decision."

"I gotta go," Leland said when he saw Abby's nurse rushing toward him from down the hall. He stuffed his phone in his pocket. "Sorry if I was playing too loud again."

"I need you to come with me," the nurse explained.

"What's wrong?"

"Your daughter regained consciousness. She's breathing on her own."

Leland entered Abby's hospital room with mild trepidation. He'd been strong for days, but now his false bravado vanished. "I knew you'd come back to me," he said, standing over Abby's bed with his arms at his side.

"How long have I been here?" Abby asked. Her voice cracked when she spoke.

"A couple days."

"What happened?"

Leland ran his hand through her hair. "You're safe now."

"I remember a storm."

"It's over."

Abby coughed. "Where's Jonathan?" she asked, her voice scratchy and hoarse.

"At home with his mom and brother."

"What day is it?"

"Wednesday."

"I have detention…"

"Shhhh."

"I saw a tornado. So loud. My leg was stuck." Abby pointed to her dad's guitar case. "I heard singing."

"You were dreaming."

Abby swallowed dryly. "Nice try. At least you didn't bring the ukulele."

CHAPTER 43

Melissa slowed her rented Mercedes SUV outside the gated entrance to Sid's condominium and powered her window down. She pressed the call button on the access control system and waited beneath a star-filled sky.

"*Who is it?*" Sid's groggy voice replied through the intercom.

"Melissa. I need to talk to you."

"*Now?*"

"Tomás died in the flood."

The steel gate opened.

Melissa parked crooked and staggered into the building. She rode the elevator to the top floor and found Sid outside his condo in a robe and slippers, his hair in disarray. She held her hand up and said, "Five minutes."

"You could have called."

"Would you have answered?"

Sid scratched his hair and maintained a perfunctory silence.

Melissa followed him inside his condo. "I want Tomás buried in our family plot. I want a nice casket. The price is irrelevant. And I want the funeral director to oversee the burial personally."

"Slow down. What happened?"

"The police called this morning. They asked me to identify the body." Melissa broke down. "It was Tomás."

Sid closed his eyes for a second. "Sweet Jesus…I'm so sorry." He hugged Melissa and kissed her head.

"They said he drowned in the flood. You told me the police were looking for him."

"I'm sure they did everything they could."

"Well it wasn't good enough!"

"I'm sorry. Sometimes these things happen."

"Not to me. I'm a goddamned Hamilton! Tomás was family. He didn't deserve to die this way."

"He saved Adam's life."

"Why couldn't someone save his?"

Sid brought her to the sofa and dimmed the overhead lights. "Why are you really here?"

"The boys are fine. Thanks for asking." Melissa opened her purse for the empty Percocet prescription. "I'm out."

"You told me you were done with those."

"My back's not done with me."

"You need to see your doctor."

"I don't need my doctor. I need one more refill."

"You've had one more refill every month since the accident."

"I'm in pain."

"Physical or emotional?"

"What does it matter?"

"Maybe you should think about getting help."

"That's why I'm here."

"For your addiction…"

"I'm not addicted, Sid. I had a broken back."

"I'm not a drug dealer."

"And I'm not a junkie. I don't take these to get high."

Sid paced uncomfortably, half awake from the first salvageable night's rest in days. "I can't just grab my phone and order refills like Chinese takeout."

"Then reach out to someone who can. I'm not asking for a rock of crack cocaine. My doctor's half way around the world on vacation. My old connections won't return my calls."

"Will you leave if I tell you I'll try?"

"I need something now."

Sid opened his liquor cabinet and poured a scotch. "This will take the edge off."

"I hit my limit already."

Sid downed the shot and winced. "I wasn't talking about you."

Melissa nudged her fist in the small of her back. "I can't finish an album like this or even think about a tour on the Hee Haw circuit."

"Maybe you should slow down. Spend some time with your boys."

"Don't piss on my leg and tell me it's raining. I need this album, Sid."

"There's not going to be a new album. Not with the lawsuit pending. No label's going to help you produce new material while Wharton Brothers drags you to court."

"You said you had this shit under control."

"I'm working on it. Go home. Be with your boys. I'll reach out for the meds."

"How long have we worked together?"

"A long time."

"Fourteen years, Sid. My career made your career. My sales paid big dividends for you, not to mention the attention it threw your way. I'm not asking for a hand-out. I want this album to happen."

Sid glanced toward his bedroom when he heard the door open far enough to momentarily reveal a strikingly handsome gentleman in a black, silk robe. "I'll be there in a minute."

Melissa stepped aside to glean a better look at Sid's guest. "You didn't tell me you had company."

"None of your business. And frankly, I'd like to get back to bed."

"Why are the best-looking men always gay?"

"Ask Wikipedia."

"You've been holding out on me."

"I've been busy."

"I can see that. He looks ten years younger than you."

"Twelve."

"He's too clean cut for a musician. An attorney? A music producer? Does he have connections?"

"I'll call you a cab," Sid proposed. "The roads are dangerous enough to drive sober, let alone in your condition."

Melissa touched her finger to the tip of Sid's nose. "Call me whatever you want. Just don't call me late for dinner." She rocked on her back foot. Her eyes glazed over from the liter of red wine coursing through her system. "When are you going to come out of the closet? And don't tell me it's none of my business. You're my agent. I have a right to know."

Sid ventured to another room and dismissed the random babble. He returned with a pillow and a blanket to find Melissa sprawled lengthwise on the leather sofa, her arm dangling off the cushion with her head tilted back. He spread the blanket over her and wedged the pillow by her head. "Life only comes around once," he whispered. "I suggest you make the most of it. Get out of this business while you can."

CHAPTER 44

Leland woke up beside Abby's hospital bed, tired and sore from another night on the torture rack disguised as a chair. "Was I snoring?" he asked when he noticed Abby staring at him with her arm across her forehead and a look of exasperation on her face.

"Does a bear shit in the woods?"

"Abigail…"

"People say it all the time."

"Did you sleep?"

Abby sat up and leaned over to touch her ankle. "Barely. You sounded like you were trying to suck marbles through your nose."

"I was tired."

"When can I go home?"

Leland stood up and stretched. He moved his head side to side to relieve the tension in his neck muscles. His entire upper body felt riga mortis stiff like he'd crawled four laps through the ceiling jungle gym at Chuck E. Cheese. "We'll ask the doctor."

Abby rubbed her taped ankle. "What if I'd died?"

"Don't say that."

"Who would take care of you?"

"*I* would take care of me."

Abby rolled her eyes. "Good luck with that."

Leland put his Stetson on. "I have an audition with Capital Country Records this afternoon. I'll be back as soon as I'm done."

"Does this mean you have to travel more?"

"Right now it doesn't mean anything."

"What are you going to sing?"

"I haven't decided." Leland opened the blinds to let more light in the room. In truth, he'd thought long and hard about what he should sing to impress the executive audience. Sid had his opinions. Nicole had hers. In a perfect world, he'd showcase several songs to demonstrate his range and his proficiency on guitar. But in the real world, in the music world, where he'd groveled for stage time at some of the seediest bars in Nashville, he needed to grab Capital Country's attention in a big way.

Somewhere between talent and perseverance, luck factored into the equation. He'd heard better voices than his and seen his share of standing ovations for no-name singers who blew the doors off packed roadhouses—only to find themselves at square one with a bad hangover and the sound of amplifiers ringing in their ears without a contract or so much as an honorable mention for delivering a world-class performance.

"It's too bright in here," Abby complained. She motioned for her dad to come closer. When he did, she hugged him tight and gave him a peck on the cheek.

"What was that for?"

"I love you. Now tell me what you're going to sing."

Leland drove through the heart of Music City, tracking random detours around deserted store fronts still reeling from the flood's aftermath. He parked several blocks from the Capital Country building near Music Row and carried his guitar inside to find Melissa waiting in the hall. "What are you doing here?"

"Sid told me you'd be here. I wanted to thank you, again, for everything."

"No worries. Sid told me about Tomás. I'm very sorry. I hope your boys are okay."

Melissa bowed her head slightly and winced before the words came through. "His funeral's tomorrow. You're welcome to attend, but please don't feel obligated."

"I appreciate the invitation. If there's anything I can do…"

"How's Abby?"

"She goes home tomorrow."

"That's fantastic! Are you ready for today?"

Leland carried his guitar toward the music studio and found an empty recording booth with a window looking inward on a standing microphone. "I'm good."

"Nervous?"

"Never," Leland lied to carry the conversation. "If this song doesn't light their fire, their wood's wet." Leland rubbed a sweaty hand on his jeans. His throat was dry and scratchy. His heart pounded in his chest. Hovering over the precipice of the biggest opportunity in his life, he couldn't take his mind off Abby's recovery and the thought of almost losing her. "You don't have to stick around," he told Melissa, hoping she would answer to the contrary.

"I'm not going anywhere."

Leland noticed a tall, lithe gentleman approach from a separate hallway in a Brooks Brothers dress shirt and lambs-wool trousers. Track lighting reflected off his partially bald head with thinning strands of dark hair combed back behind his ears. Wooly eyebrows grew together haphazardly in contrast to his impeccably-groomed ducktail beard.

"Brad Siegel," the Capital Country executive introduced himself to Leland and Melissa with a certain savoir faire. He shook Leland's hand and winked at Melissa.

"Leland Presley. This is Melissa—"

"We've met before," said Brad. He smiled at the former acquaintance and opened the recording studio. "Whenever you're ready."

"Now?"

"Time is money, Mr. Presley. Let's not waste both."

Leland nudged his way inside and laid his guitar case on the floor. He opened the lid to expose the scent of red spruce and Honduran mahogany from the vintage Gibson.

He took a seat on a padded stool and slipped his arm through the shoulder strap. He strummed an open chord and loosened the B string with the tuner. He tightened the E string and strummed again, this time working his fingertips through the frets along the fingerboard. "*Any time, Mr. Presley...*" he heard Brad Siegel's voice through the control booth speaker. He glanced at Melissa behind the viewing area and cleared his throat while he strummed an up-tempo beat.

You had a hard...time
In a house, without, a home
You came out, all...right...
When the storm had come and gone

The year was nineteen, ninety-five
And for the first time in your life

You found American Pride!
Girl...
Now you don't have to hide
Your American Pride
Girl...
Take those reins and ride
Your American Pride...

She knows your voice when you call her name
Deep brown eyes and velvet mane
She's every-thing you dreamed of
And now the life you know
May ne-ver, be, the, same...

She's your American Pride!

Girl…
She makes you come a-live
With your American Pride
Girl…
Saddle up and ride
Your American Pride…

You always lived your life alone
But now you have a friend, to call, your own…

She's your American Pride!
Girl…
There ain't nothin' like that ride
On your American Pride…
Girl…

Ain't nothin' you won't do
For your American Pride…
All your dreams come true
On your American Pride…
Nothing else will do
But your American Pride!

Leland stepped back from the microphone and looked through the control room window. "*Was that a song about lesbian rights?*" he heard Brad Siegel through the intercom speaker.

"It's a song about a horse," Leland spoke into the microphone. "I can play something else if you want."

"*That won't be necessary,*" Brad replied.

"What did you think?"

"*We'll be in touch.*"

CHAPTER 45

Melissa sat at her grand piano and played a melody she'd written for Tomás. The words never came together, but the notes touched her soul. She missed him deeply, especially his presence with her boys, who dragged through the morning head down and heavy-hearted, unwilling to accept Tomás was gone.

She'd spared no expense with the funeral arrangements, prodding Sid to pitch in for the more expensive casket and a marble headstone. Money would come back to her. Tomás was gone forever.

She tapped the keyboard with her pinky and held the foot pedal down to let the last note sustain. Then she closed the cover and ventured to the war zone in her living room, where her boys argued over which shoes to wear. "Enough!" she blurted when their ongoing dispute dissolved her veil of serenity.

"Adam won't give my shoes back," Jonathan complained with his black Ralph Lauren dress shirt opened at the neck.

"Mine don't fit anymore," Adam fired back. "Jonathan has three other pairs he can wear."

"It's not my fault you have big feet," Jonathan retorted.

"At least I don't have your pea brain."

Melissa grabbed the brown loafers from Adam. "These shoes belong to Jonathan. Pick out a pair of your own."

"They don't fit."

"They can't *all* not fit."

Adam sighed. "I don't have brown shoes to wear. I need brown shoes to match my belt."

"Then wear a black belt instead."

Adam thought for a moment. "A black belt doesn't go with my socks."

"Then change your socks."

"I told him the same thing," said Jonathan.

Melissa gave the brown loafers to Jonathan. "Put these on."

"What about me?" Adam complained.

"Pick out a different pair and get dressed. You two sound like girls fighting over the same dress for prom. Brown shoes, black shoes, it doesn't matter. At this point, I don't care if you wear any shoes at all. Just don't make us late."

"Do I have to go?" asked Adam.

"Tomás would want you there."

"Is he going to be all swollen and gross like a floating body in the river?"

Melissa looked at Jonathan. "What did you tell him?"

"Nothing!" Jonathan insisted. He looked at his brother then back at his mom. "I didn't say anything. Adam's seen too many CSI reruns."

"I don't want to hear it," Melissa said sternly. "I want you both ready in five minutes. Teeth brushed. Hair combed. You boys are growing into young men. It's time you started acting like it."

Leland took the lid off the cat's litter box and dumped the contents in a plastic grocery bag. He replaced the old newspaper with the legal custody papers from Paula's attorney. With Abby coming home and a mountain of hospital bills, he needed all the help he could get without adding Paula's legal wrangling to the mix. Paula deserved to spend the rest of her life involuntarily committed. She'd brought her own damnation upon herself. No court would see it otherwise. At least he tried to convince himself of such assumptions. The way he'd convinced himself he would never see Paula again, and yet, there she was, back in his life like nothing ever happened. As Abby's mother, she retained a biological connection to her offspring regardless of her mental deficiencies—a fact any good family lawyer with questionable integrity would exploit. On the other hand, she was bat shit crazy—a fact no court would overlook. With Abby's health returning, he had much to be grateful for, and no reason to spend a second thought on Paula's delusional machinations. Now he faced a funeral he'd rather do without, but the notion of seeing Melissa again stoked a hunger he wanted to explore.

CHAPTER 46

Melissa adjusted a framed picture of Tomás on her wall while her doleful guests hovered around her home. "I still can't accept what happened," she confided to Sid while she claimed her third glass of Chardonnay from the catering tray. "I feel like I'm stuck in a bad dream."

Sid put his hand on her shoulder. He wore a dark blue blazer with a solid red tie, and an aura of genuine sadness about him. "Sometimes bad things happen to good people. Tomás deserved better."

"What about my boys? How are they supposed to forget Tomás is gone?"

Sid stepped aside for a guest to pass through. "It's not about forgetting as much as learning to accept what happened and move on."

"The boys don't want me to sell the house."

"Your boys don't pay the bills. You're doing the right thing."

"Then why do I feel so bad?"

"You buried a best friend today. No one's judging you."

Melissa sipped her wine. She acknowledged the familiar faces in her formal living area. "What would Tomás have wanted?"

"In terms of what?"

"Everything. This funeral. My boys' future. This house." Melissa tried to smile through her barren expression but couldn't tap any positive vibes. "I miss him so much." She finished her drink and passed the empty goblet to Sid when the doorbell chimed. "I'll get it," she said as she moved toward the open foyer to greet Leland in his black Wranglers and a wide collar cowboy shirt with the sleeves rolled up. She glanced over her shoulder to see a dozen women intrigued by the tall, rugged gentleman with a Stetson in his hand and their undivided attention. "I didn't think you would come."

"I wanted to be here."

Melissa motioned for him to leave the foyer and the bevy of prying eyes.

Leland followed Melissa to an adjoining room partitioned behind French doors. Autographed photos of celebrity singers lined the walls. A French country sofa with exposed wooden feet and padded arms anchored the other end of the room. "I'm sorry for your loss."

"I'm sorry you had to drive all the way out here. I know the roads are still a mess."

"I can't stay long." Leland stood hat in hand, squeezing the brim between his fingers. "If there's anything I can do to help you with the house."

"You already have. I'm sure Tomás is delighted you're here." She lifted her head slightly and caught a whiff of Leland's enticing cologne. "Any word from Brad Siegel?"

Leland motioned with his hat. "Sid knows more than I do."

"Would you like a drink?"

"I'm good." Leland cleared his throat. "How are your boys?"

Melissa aired a mischievous smile. "I sent them outside to burn off energy. They're probably setting something on fire."

"Have you seen the news lately?"

Melissa toyed with her hair, her smile morphing into a serious, introspective stare. "I haven't, but from what I keep hearing, we're the best kept secret. The national news has mostly ignored us. The media's more concerned about the Gulf oil spill and some New York City car bomber than they are about our natural disaster."

"I suspect that will change."

"Do you really think so?" Melissa challenged him. "People are hurting. They need to know they're not alone in all this mess, even if they really are. If that makes sense."

"I heard Anderson Cooper's in town today with his crew."

"Don't tell Sid. He's had a crush on that man forever."

Leland grinned. "The city will pull together."

Melissa opened a portable liquor cabinet and fetched a thirty-year-old bottle of Highland Park. "You sure I can't get you a drink?" She poured two glasses. "Don't tell Sid I hide the good stuff in here." She offered one to Leland.

"No thanks."

"You shouldn't let a woman drink alone."

Leland took the glass and sniffed the single malt scotch, the bottle of which cost more than his rent. "You always get what you want?"

"Depends on who I want."

Leland swallowed his first sip. The warm burn lingered at the base of his throat. "You have good taste."

Melissa followed Leland to the sofa, her eyes heavy from the wine and a restless night. "I liked the song you did for Brad. You sing from the heart."

"I sing what I feel."

"And what do you feel right now?"

"Like I should probably be on my way."

Melissa leaned against the sofa's padded arm rest. "If you're worried about Abby, I'm sure she's in good hands." She downed her scotch and set the empty glass on the window ledge. "I came by the hospital the other day. You were singing about a four-part harmony, comparing your daughter to a Beethoven symphony." Melissa looked away.

"Might have been one of the most beautiful songs I've ever heard. I saw a woman with you and Abby. Your ex-wife?"

"My ex-girlfriend."

"Does she know that?"

"It's late," Leland proffered, instead of fumbling with a complicated answer to a very simple question.

"It's seven thirty."

"I hate to wear out my welcome."

"The only thing you're going to wear out is me."

Leland choked on the scotch, coughing with his hand on his mouth. "Wrong pipe," he said nonchalantly, convinced he'd misinterpreted the flippant comment; although he wondered if Melissa was naked under her curve-fitting dress. "I just came to pay respects," he said without thinking before he spoke. Torn between dismissing himself again or advancing on an overt invitation, he played his best poker face in a room alone with a beautiful woman who stoked a fire within him.

Melissa slipped off her heels and locked the French doors with a flourish. "People die every day. Doesn't mean we stop living our lives."

"I think I should—"

"Don't think. Feel. Like you do when you sing."

"You seem, vulnerable."

Melissa reached behind her back and unzipped her dress. "Like you've never taken advantage of a vulnerable woman before?" She moved slowly toward Leland while she unfastened her bra. "Do you think I'm attractive?"

Leland set his hat down and cupped his hands to her hips with his arms bent in a futile effort to keep her away. "Very much."

Melissa stepped back and peeled down the top of her dress to expose her bare breasts—firm, yet supple and inviting. "I find you very attractive, Mr. Presley. In more ways than you can begin to imagine."

Leland moved closer and raised his hand to frame her face, his thumb caressing her soft facial features. He found her intoxicating. "What are we doing?"

"Whatever we want," Melissa whispered demurely.

Leland kissed her softly on the mouth. When her breasts pressed against him, he dismissed any reason he should leave.

Melissa broke off the kiss and stepped out of her dress altogether. "How does this look to you?"

Leland kissed her passionately this time. Then he gently bent her over the sofa arm and slid his hands along her hips to feel her quiver from his touch. He opened his pants and penetrated her slowly from behind.

Melissa gasped between short breaths, indulging her fervent desire.

Leland kept an eye on the door, certain one of Melissa's guests would burst in at any moment and find their host in flagrante delicto.

CHAPTER 47

Abby packed her clothes and a small stuffed animal in a pink suitcase on her hospital bed. "Where were you last night?" she asked her dad, who hovered about the room with his cell phone in his hand. "I woke up and you were gone."

Leland checked his phone for messages. "I got here late."

"How late?"

"Late. You were out cold."

Abby limped on her sore ankle, afraid to put too much pressure on her foot and unwilling to use the crutch the nurse gave her. "Jonathan sent me a text about Tomás. He said you went to his funeral yesterday." She reached for a dirty shirt on the chair beside her and stuffed it in the suitcase. "I could have gone with you."

"The doctor wanted you to stay here one more night."

"What did you do after the funeral?"

"I paid my respects to the family."

"But you never knew Tomás."

"Doesn't matter."

"Why were you gone so long?"

Leland tried Sid's number and hung up when the call went to voice mail again. "There were a lot of people there."

"Jonathan said you like his mom."

"Abby…"

"I'm just saying. Jonathan said you were there until midnight."

"Jonathan needs to worry about himself. His mom teaches vocal lessons. I'm a student of hers."

"Since when do you need voice lessons?"

"Everyone has something to improve."

"Are you dating her?"

Leland grabbed the crutch and a cluster of *Get Well* balloons. "Get your stuff together."

"Can I keep the flowers?"

"Yes."

"What about the flat screen?" Abby asked.

"That stays."

"I want a cheeseburger, and not the kind Nicole used to bring home. I want a big fat one with pickles and ketchup and mustard. And I want a chocolate shake."

"Anything else, Your Highness?"

Abby looked away from her dad for a moment. "I don't ever want to ride a bus again. And I miss my cat."

"He misses you."

Abby grabbed the flower vase while her dad carried her luggage and her cluster of colored balloons. "Some woman came to see me yesterday while you were gone."

"A nurse?"

"She wasn't dressed like one. I never saw her before."

"What did she want?"

Abby shrugged. "She didn't say anything. She just came in and stood here for a second."

"Did you call for help?"

"She didn't bother me. I think she was lost."

"What did she look like?" Leland asked, his suspicions leaning toward the improbable, yet unnerving possibility, Paula had been there.

"Old. Probably in her thirties. She was tall, and she had super short hair."

"What did she say?"

"Nothing."

"How did she get in here?"

"She opened the door," Abby said flippantly.

"You can't just let people wander in your room."

"I didn't *let* her do anything. She walked in when I was sleeping. I heard the door open and woke up. I thought it was you at first."

Leland gently moved Abby aside when a nurse brought a wheelchair to the room.

The nurse locked the wheelchair brakes and looked at Leland. "Someone from accounting will go over the paperwork with you downstairs."

Leland ushered Abby toward the wheelchair. "Let's blow this joint and grab a burger," he said when his phone rang. "I'll catch up in a second…"

He waited for the nurse to help Abby. Then he set the suitcase down and leaned the crutch against the wall. "I left you three messages," he told Sid on the incoming call.

"You got the gig."

"You're kidding?" Leland lowered the phone from his ear and did a fist pump with his other hand.

"I just got off the phone with Brad Siegel. Capital Country wants to make you an offer."

"Thank you!"

"Don't thank me yet. We haven't heard their offer. Besides, you did all the heavy lifting."

"What did he say about my song?"

"He said he liked the way you played."

"What else?"

"They're a major record label, Leland. Who cares? You sold Brad Siegel on your talent."

Leland ended the call in a state of disbelief. When he caught up to Abby, he commandeered the wheelchair from the nurse and popped a wheelie. "Capital Country Records wants to sign me!"

"Let me down before we crash!" Abby screamed with *joie de vivre*.

Leland lowered the front wheels. "Can you believe this is happening?"

Abby tilted her head back to see her dad's beaming smile. "I never had any doubt!"

CHAPTER 48

$\blacktriangleright \blacklozenge \blacktriangleleft$

Melissa stepped out of her shower, jostled by the sound of shattered glass, followed by quiet contemplation of the pending catastrophe from her unattended offspring downstairs. Her back pain had subsided, but a lingering hangover reminded her why she never mixed whiskey with wine.

"What are you doing?" she yelled from her room upstairs loud enough for her boys to hear.

"*Nothing Mom!*" she heard Adam reply. "*We can fix it.*"

Melissa dried off with a plush bath towel and imagined Leland's hands on her bare skin; his lips on her mouth.

"*Mom!*" Jonathan shouted from downstairs. "*We can't find the vacuum.*"

Melissa threw her clothes on and ran a brush through her hair. "For the love of God," she mumbled under her breath, convinced a boarding school might be in order after all; although she knew in her heart she could never send her boys away while her personal life spiraled out of control. She'd gone too far with Leland. A mistake, no doubt, but one she'd hoped to repeat again. She craved his voice; his smell; the way his touch made her melt in his hands. Real or imagined, her physical pain seemed to lessen in his presence.

She advanced downstairs to confront her boys head on and found Adam carrying a dust pan full of broken glass while Jonathan held a shattered picture frame with an autographed head shot of Kenny Chesney. "How many times have I told you not to throw stuff in the house?"

"It was an accident," said Adam.

Jonathan dangled the frame over an empty box to shake out loose fragments. "We can't find the Super Glue."

"How 'bout I super glue you both to the wall?"

"We're sorry," the boys acknowledged in unison.

"How did this happen?"

The boys looked at each other.

"I don't know," said Jonathan.

"It just fell off the wall," said Adam.

"You boys were throwing that damn ball around, weren't you?"

"We wanted to surprise you," Jonathan confessed. "We were cleaning the house. I accidentally bumped the picture with the mop handle and knocked it off the wall. The glass broke when it fell."

Melissa inspected the other rooms and grimaced inwardly at her own short-temperedness. "Thank you. I'm sorry I yelled."

"Your phone rang while you were sleeping," said Jonathan.

Melissa unplugged her phone from the charger on the kitchen counter. She read a text message from Leland and parted a strand of hair from her eyes. A voice mail from the realtor instilled a sense of urgency. "We need to leave for awhile. Someone's coming to look at the house."

"Are they going to buy it?" asked Adam.

"I don't know."

"I don't want to move," Jonathan complained.

Adam looked at his brother, then shifted his attention to his mom. "Will we get to keep our stuff when we move?"

"Of course," said Melissa.

"But we sold the horses."

"We had to."

"What about Dad's boat?" asked Jonathan.

"We'll see."

"What about Tomás's stuff?"

Melissa thought about the honest question. She'd been inside the guest house twice since the night she learned Tomás's fate. She'd left the room unaltered with his personal belongings on the bureau and his clothes hung neatly in the closet.

"You told us things would get better," Jonathan fumed.

"They will, Sweetheart. I promise."

CHAPTER 49

Leland rode the elevator to Sid's third floor office overlooking Music Row's tree-lined streets dotted by quaint houses with wood-planked verandas, where record companies, recording studios, and public relations firms shared the same patch of modest Nashville real estate. He brought Abby with him, ignoring an inner voice contesting his decision. Business was business and no place for young ears to absorb conversations regarding money or Sid's war stories about the perils of the music industry. Signing a contract with a major record label meant his life was about to change in a very big way. Twenty years of playing honky-tonks for petty cash was about to end. He would cut his first album within a year and promote a debut single before he started his tour with a headline act.

"How long is this going to take?" Abby asked when the elevator opened.

"Not long."

"Does this mean we're going to be rich?"

"It's not about the money," Leland answered. He brought Abby inside the window office suites at the end of the hall and found Sid crouching with his hands in the air in front of him, left palm at his chin facing down with his forearm perpendicular, right palm facing up underneath his left arm as if holding an invisible beach ball between his hands. "What are you doing?"

Sid maintained his posture and released a slow breath from his abdomen. "T'ai Chi."

"God bless you."

Sid ignored Leland's overt attempt at humor and resumed a normal stance. "I see you brought the hired gun."

"My best negotiator."

Sid bumped fists with Abby. "Glad to see you on your feet again."

"Are you going to make my dad rich?"

Sid faced Leland with a stolid expression. "You weren't kidding."

Leland ruffled Abby's hair. "Why don't you find something to do in the other room."

"No thank you."

"I wasn't asking," Leland gently asserted.

Abby put her hand on her hip. "Why can't I stay with you?"

"Because I need to talk with Sid alone."

"Who's going to stay with me when you're on tour?"

"We'll figure it out."

Abby limped to the water cooler. "My ankle hurts."

"I offered to bring the crutch, but you didn't want it." Leland waited for Sid to return from an adjacent conference room. "It will take the weight off your ankle."

"It makes me look like a nerd."

Sid offered his iPad to Abby. "We have Wi-Fi in the building. Why don't you take this to the other room."

"Can I download an R rated movie?" Abby asked her dad.

"No violence. No nudity. No language."

"No fun," said Abby. She took the iPad from Sid and thanked him. "When you're done, we're going fishing," she told her dad. "That deal is nonnegotiable."

"She's a good kid," Sid told Leland behind closed doors. "Have a seat."

Leland plopped himself on a plush caramel-colored leather sofa. "She has her moments."

"I had a niece like her once. Used to drive her dad crazy when her parents got divorced."

"What happened?"

Sid maneuvered himself behind his desk with an iMac and a bronze pineapple lamp. A framed quote on the wall behind him read, *Teamwork makes the dream work.* "Her dad sent her to live with her mom." He typed his password to unlock the screen. "How's the voice?"

"Good."

"You were flat on your audition."

"I had a lot on my mind."

Sid tapped the mouse to open his email. "I spoke with Brad again."

"Great. What sort of deal are we talking about? You know I write my own music. I'm willing to collaborate, but I'm not pulling lyrics from a catalogue."

"Let's back up a second..." Sid printed the short email and gave Leland a copy. "Why don't you read this first? Brad sent it, along with a contract for you to sign."

Leland sat forward on the sofa and skimmed the text. "Where's the rest?"

"The offer's fair."

"Compared to what? Laying asphalt for the county. Is this a joke?" Leland read the email again more closely. "This doesn't say anything about a recording contract. He's asking me to play backup guitar for a band I've never heard of. I'm a singer, not some Guitar Hero for hire."

Sid leaned back in his chair. "This is your ticket to bigger things."

"What kind of money are we talking about?"

"Around four hundred."

"A day?"

"A week," Sid corrected him.

Leland sank into the sofa cushion, completely flabbergasted by the offer. "Are you high? My girlfriend made more money in fast food."

"It's an entry point."

"It's poverty."

"You've never been about the money."

"I have to put bread on the table."

"And you can do that pounding nails for a living."

Leland pushed the paper across Sid's desk and swallowed dryly. He rubbed his forehead, mad at himself for believing the impossible was possible. "Let me play for Brad again. Something more contemporary. Something to show off my range."

"You know the drill. You had your shot. Right now Brad's deal is the only offer on the table."

"This is bullshit in a caviar cup."

"This is reality, Leland. What were you expecting?"

"To quit my day job, for starters. At a minimum, my own recording contract."

"Take the deal. When Capital Country sees your full potential, we'll renegotiate. Four hundred a week could turn into four thousand very fast."

"How fast?"

"Depends. Brad's a gambler, but you're still unproven talent. He's offering you a predevelopment deal. Something you can build on over time."

Leland saw beyond Sid's salesmanship, but as much as he hated to admit it, Sid made a valid point. "I'm not saying no, but I'm not excited about this either."

"No one cares if this deal perks your panties. Brad can always find someone else."

"Good for him."

"He wants a decision by tomorrow morning. Capital Country has a lot invested in this startup band. They need a strong guitarist to replace the one who broke his wrist in a motorcycle accident. Someone who can play well and sing background vocals."

"Is this band even signed?"

"Not yet, but Brad's agreed to sponsor them for the Nashville benefit concert. Tim McGraw and Faith Hill are producing it. If this gig does well, the band will likely sign with Capital Country, and you'll be one step closer to your own recording contract. This is real, Leland. A legitimate path to more lucrative opportunities down the road."

"What do you know about the band?"

"They play mostly country-rock. They're green, but they have a small following on YouTube. Brad sees potential in them. And in you."

Leland scoffed at Sid's attempt at flattery, a quirk he'd learned to accept from a man who could sell sand to a Sheik. "What about my own music?"

"What about it?"

"If I sign up for this, I want—"

"Brad calls the shots on this one. He decides who plays what and when."

"I'm talking about studio time."

"The band writes their own material. Their lead singer, Jimmie Lockhorn, fronts most of the lyrics himself. You play what they tell you, when they tell you, but whatever you pay to produce on your own dime would be yours exclusively."

"What about their guy with the broken wrist? What happens when he comes back?"

"I can't predict the future."

"Then give me your best guess."

Sid let out a long sigh. "Best case, you outshine him and take his place, permanently. Worst case, you find another gig."

"I don't know…"

"Is this a deal of a lifetime? No. Are you going to get rich quick? No. But you will have on-air exposure when this benefit concert goes live. Not in front of a dozen drunken fools in some dive bar—but in front of millions at home, including other studio executives in Nashville."

Leland glanced around the room, contemplating his next move. "This is not how I pictured it."

"Picture this… No travel. Indoor work. A steady paycheck from a major studio. The prospect for a better deal down the road. Any musician worth his salt would jump at the opportunity."

"Would you?"

Sid put both hands on his desk. "You and I share a lot in common. We're also cut from a different cloth. If I were you, I'd sign the damn papers and spend some quality time with my daughter instead of sitting in this man cave listening to me flap my gums." He clicked the mouse and printed a copy of the contract for Leland. "Take this home and think about it. Then sign it in the morning and don't look back."

CHAPTER 50

Nicole examined her bare chest in the bathroom mirror, cupping both breasts in her hands to inspect the soft tissue. She stood askew and scrutinized her figure. She had a clean bill of health and no reason to dispute her tests results.

This time.

Given her family history, she worried about her future as a single woman in a new town without family or friends and an ex-boyfriend who seemed distant and unwilling to reconcile their relationship. *People die alone every day*, she told herself. *I don't want to be one of them.*

Part of her wanted a fresh start, someplace new and exciting like Atlanta, D.C., or New York. But not without Leland in her life.

A knock at her apartment door prompted her to throw a shirt on. She checked the peephole and saw a woman in business attire with a buzz haircut and a badge hanging from a lanyard around her neck. "Whatever you're selling," Nicole spoke loudly through the door. "I'm not interested."

She watched the woman hold up a plastic badge holder with a name imprinted beneath a bar code. "It's upside down," she said behind the door with growing trepidation toward the unexpected visitor. She grabbed her purse and discovered her pepper spray was missing.

"My name is Rhonda Towson. I work for the Department of Children's Services. I'm sorry to bother you at home, but I need to ask you a few questions."

Nicole unlocked the deadbolt and cautiously opened her apartment. "I don't have any children," she said, confused by the social worker's request, not to mention her awkward demeanor, which suggested something off about her but not enough to be overly concerned. She scrutinized the photo ID sandwiched between the plastic laminate and read the name Rhonda Towson. "What is this about?"

"Are you Nicole Mason?"

"Yes."

"Is this your primary residence?"

"Yes."

"May I come in?"

"My roommate will be home any second. I'm not sure—"

"It won't take long."

Nicole hesitated before she let Rhonda in her apartment. "I'm not sure how I can help you."

Rhonda stepped into the small foyer with an empty coat rack and a floating shelf on the adjoining wall. "I need to ask you a few questions about Abigail Presley."

"Is she okay?"

"As far as we know."

"Then what is this about?"

"I've been assigned to conduct a follow-up investigation."

Nicole stuffed her hands in her pockets. "Of what?"

"Routine procedure when a complaint is filed."

"A complaint? What does this have to do with me?"

Rhonda produced a pen and a memo pad from her purse. "Do you know Leland Presley?"

"He's my boyfriend. What complaint are you talking about?"

"The details are confidential."

"Does Leland know you're here?" Nicole asked, still puzzled about the true nature of Rhonda Towson's visit.

"Does he live with you?"

"He has his own place. Why are you asking—"

"But you did live together at one time? With his daughter Abigail."

"Is this because he left her home alone during the flood?"

"What can you tell me about that?"

"Leland told her to stay home. Abby snuck out with friends and got caught in the storm. Leland's not in trouble, is he?"

Rhonda scrawled in her note pad. "How long was Abigail left alone?"

"Leland worships Abby. He's torn up about what happened. If he'd known a flood was coming, he never would have left her home."

"Does he often leave her home alone?"

"He's a single dad. A musician. He plays gigs at night. But he's one of the good guys."

"Does Abigail go to school?"

"Of course."

"Which one?"

"Parkview Middle School, I think. She's in seventh grade this year."

"Have you seen her recently?"

"Not for a few days."

Rhonda chewed the end of her pen. "Do you know where she is now?"

"Probably with her dad."

"Or home alone by herself again?"

Nicole motioned toward the door. "I think you should leave now."

Rhonda Towson gave Nicole an apathetic stare. "How long did you and Leland live together?"

"I don't see how that's any of your concern."

"I'm trying to understand Mr. Presley's level of commitment to his daughter."

"He's the most committed father I've ever known."

"Has he ever hit his daughter?"

"Of course not!"

"Has he ever exhibited lewd or obnoxious behavior?"

"No."

"Has he ever raised his voice to her?"

"Sure, sometimes. All parents do."

"Does he drink alcohol?"

"Sometimes."

"How often?"

"He's not an alcoholic, if that's what you're asking."

"Does he smoke?"

"No."

"Use drugs?"

"Hell no!"

Rhonda looked up from her notes. "How can you be certain?"

"Because I lived with him for nine months. I dated him for a year and a half."

"You mentioned Abigail attends Parkview. Does she ride the bus?"

"Sometimes. And sometimes Leland picks her up after school. Why?"

"Has Leland ever forgotten to pick her up?"

Nicole looked up at the ceiling for a moment and wiped a strand of hair from her eyes. "No."

"Are you sure?"

"It happened once, but it was no big deal. I came and got her."

"Does Mr. Presley live with anyone else besides his daughter?"

"I don't think so."

"So what happens when he forgets to pick her up again?"

"He has my number," Nicole replied hotly. "I really think you should leave."

Rhonda flipped through her notes. "How well do you know Abigail?"

"She's not my daughter."

"Do you know how she lost her arm?"

"Some sort of accident when she was little."

"Did she ever talk about it?"

"Not to me."

"Did she talk about her mother?"

"She never knew her mom."

Rhonda stopped writing. "Any problems in school?"

"No more than any other teenage girl."

"Can you be more specific?"

"She's a good kid. Sometimes she earns detention."

"Why?"

"Why do you think? People tease her. She fights back."

"Does she have behavioral issues at home?"

Nicole motioned toward the door. "I'm not answering any more questions. If you want to know about Abby, I suggest you talk to her father."

"Would you be willing to sign a statement?"

"I'm not signing anything. Now get out of my apartment before I call the police."

CHAPTER 51

Leland hooked his guitar over his shoulder and flicked the lights on and off in Abby's room. "Rise and shine porcupine."

Abby rolled over and covered her face with her pillow. "I'm not going back to school."

"You like school."

"I hate school," Abby mumbled through her pillow.

"I made waffles."

"I don't like the frozen kind."

Leland strummed his guitar slowly. Then he erupted with a mariachi rhythm. "You've got five minutes before I come back and start singing Elvis."

"Dad!" Abby groaned. She took the pillow away. "You're not funny in the morning."

"My jokes get better as the day goes on."

"No. They don't. I just got out of the hospital. I shouldn't have to go back to school already."

Leland stopped playing. "Your doctor said you're good to go."

"I don't want to go back to school."

"It will be good for you."

"There's only two weeks left."

"The time will go by quickly." Leland plucked the strings. "Your food is getting cold."

"It was frozen to begin with."

"There's always summer school," Leland offered as he walked away. He heard a pillow hit the wall, followed by loud stomping. He rested his guitar on the stand in his room and proceeded with his shower and shave. He gave Abby's cat some attention while he waited for Abby to get ready. Then he ushered Sleeping Beauty to his truck.

"At least I get to see my friends again," Abby contemplated with her backpack on the truck's floorboard. She wore her favorite top with her low cut jean shorts.

"What happened to your other shorts?" Leland asked as he backed out of the driveway.

"Which ones?"

"The ones that cover your legs."

Abby put her hand on her thigh. "What's wrong with my legs?"

"Nothing. I think they're perfect, but the world doesn't need to see so much of them. You look great in longer shorts."

"Longer shorts are boring. Besides, you bought these for me."

"I did?"

"And you still owe me three weeks allowance."

Leland advanced through the winding neighborhood and merged onto an open lane. "I know."

"Jonathan saved my life," Abby said in a monotone voice. "I wouldn't be here if he hadn't freed me from the bus."

Leland put his right arm around her shoulder. "You like him."

"I do, but it's not like we're having sex."

Leland tightened his grip on the truck's steering wheel. "Good to know."

"Would you rather we were having sex?"

"No."

"Relax, Dad. He's like a big brother to me. I think Adam's cool too."

Leland slowed at the next intersection and drove right to follow the winding detour toward Abby's middle school. "Don't forget to clean your room and Tiger's litter box."

"My ankle's still sore."

"Then use your arm to scoop the litter."

"Dad…"

"It won't take you very long. You need to finish unpacking your room, too."

"I want a raise."

Leland laughed out loud. "You can't negotiate a raise by complaining about the work you haven't done yet."

"We should talk about birth control."

"Jesus Abby…you're killing me here. You're only thirteen. And we already had this discussion."

"Would you rather I get pregnant?"

"I'd rather you not think about sex at all. At least not until you're…forty."

"Does sex make you nervous?"

"No. Yes. Why are we even having this conversation?" Leland twisted uncomfortably in the driver's seat. A few days ago, he wasn't certain if Abby would ever recover. Now he couldn't find a way to turn her off.

"Let me out here," Abby ordered when her dad drove closer to the school property.

"I can pull around the bus line and bring you up front."

"Please don't. I can walk from here."

Leland stopped the truck. "You don't have to."

Abby gathered her backpack. "Don't be late when you pick me up."

"I love you too."

Abby opened the door to get out. "And don't wave when you drive off. Someone might see."

Leland kept his hands on the wheel while Abby trekked toward the crowd of students congregating out front. He slowly accelerated and made a U-turn when he saw Melissa drop her boys off. He followed the Mercedes SUV through the busy parking lot and rolled up on the passenger side with his window down. He bumped the horn. "Nice wheels," he said when Melissa lowered her window.

"It's a rental."

"Can I buy you a cup of coffee?"

"My schedule's packed this morning."

"I know a place near here."

"I'm really busy."

Leland waved his arm out the window. "Follow me."

Melissa followed the rickety pickup toward a busy intersection outside an older shopping plaza, while her inner voice kept telling her to turn around. She had her hair in a bun with her cheap clothes on and a pair of sneakers without socks—and now of all places—she found herself outside a Waffle House restaurant. "I've never been to one of these," she said when she got out to meet Leland in the parking lot.

"It survived the flood."

"So did Noah's Ark. Doesn't mean I want to eat there."

Leland held the door for her and claimed a table in the back by the window. Bacon sizzled on the grill, adding to the aroma of fresh coffee, warm hash browns, and buttered toast.

Melissa used a napkin to wipe her seat. "Do you take all your girlfriends here?"

"Only the ones I want to impress," Leland said with a smirk. "I left a message on your phone."

Melissa took her seat and squeezed a dollop of hand sanitizer from her purse. She offered some to Leland. "About the other night…"

"No worries."

"I was drunk and upset, and I should have known better. I shouldn't have put you in an awkward situation."

"It wasn't awkward for me," Leland reassured her. He flagged the waitress coming toward them and ordered two coffees. One with cream and one with sugar. "I think about you."

Melissa blushed. "I heard you joined a new band," she said in an obvious attempt to redirect the conversation.

"More like Brad Siegel's pet project. The band's a short term gig. They needed a warm body to play guitar."

"They're lucky to have you."

Leland reached across the table to touch Melissa's hand.

Melissa moved her arm away when her coffee arrived. "Life is crazy for me right now."

"Me too."

"I'm not sure I have time to be involved in a new relationship."

"I hear you," Leland offered. "I wrote a new song."

"Where do you find the time?"

"The song found me. I need to work out the melody, but the lyrics are there. Like they were waiting to be discovered all along."

Melissa sipped her coffee. "Please don't tell me I inspired you."

"And what if you had?"

Melissa glanced out the window to see a biker with a chain wallet dismount a matte black Harley and amble toward the restaurant. "How's Abby?"

"She's not thrilled about going back to school."

Melissa slid forward on the bench seat to open her prescription under the table. "I'll trade you my boys for Abby."

Leland sipped his coffee, ignoring the ambient chatter from the patrons in the booth behind him. "Careful what you wish for. I might take you up on that offer."

Melissa pinched the pain medication between her thumb and index finger. When she brought it to her mouth, she pretended to pick a tooth before she sipped her coffee again. "You must have someone in your life vying for your attention."

"I like you," Leland started. "You don't pull punches. You're not afraid to speak your mind."

"And you don't know when to quit."

Leland focused on Melissa. "I know when someone's worth fighting for."

"I'm older than you. Ten years from now, you won't give me a second glance."

"Ten years from now, we could be having a very different conversation. I think you underestimate yourself."

"Says Doctor Phil…"

Leland reached across the table to touch her hand again. "Let me take you out tonight."

"On a date?"

"Call it what you want."

"I have my boys."

"So get a sitter."

"She's out of town."

"I know a mutual friend…"

"I'm not leaving my boys with Sid."

"Why not?"

"Because he's Sid. He'd have them drinking malt liquor and surfing porn."

"I'm sure he's seen your boys before."

"Only when I'm home," Melissa pushed back gently. She liked the touch from Leland's hand. "I'm not sure this is a good idea."

"I want to know you better."

"I'd say you know me pretty well."

Leland persisted. "You want the same from me. You're just afraid to admit it."

"Are you always this arrogant?"

"Don't mistake confidence for arrogance."

Melissa wanted to kiss him, but she liked to see him squirm. "I don't know."

"One dinner. Somewhere quiet, where we can talk."

"One condition," Melissa relented. "I get to choose where we eat."

CHAPTER 52

Jonathan parked himself near the back of his algebra class with his notebook open and his focus on anything but the math in front of him. While the teacher droned on about the quadratic equation at the chalk board, his attention span meandered between Abby, who sat two rows ahead, and the dark clouds hovering outside the windows.

He could still hear people screaming when he closed his eyes, followed by haunting images burned into his memory. No matter how hard he tried to forget, he couldn't shake the unending replay of events or convince himself a tornado would never find him again. He'd witnessed Mother Nature's fury up close and experienced life and death in a way he could have never imagined. The storm had been a nightmare come true for him, compared to Abby who seemed lost somewhere between content and bored.

When the bell rang, he remained in his seat, confounded by his indecision to attend next period or skip the rest of the day. "*Will you walk with me?*" he heard Abby ask before he realized she was standing in front of him. He couldn't remember if the bell rang two seconds, or two minutes, prior. More importantly, he didn't care.

* * *

Abby waved her hand in front of Jonathan's face. "Are you okay?"

"I'm fine," Jonathan replied, his demeanor almost catatonic when he got up and slid his algebra textbook off his desk.

"What do you have next period?"

"I'm not going to next period."

Abby followed him past the cafeteria and down the hall toward the gym exit that opened to the rear parking area. She knew the right thing to do, but she chose the wrong path instead. "Wait up," she said, limping as she tried to keep stride. "My ankle still hurts."

She followed Jonathan toward a park pavilion with wooden picnic tables behind the soccer fields along the school property. "I sent you a bunch of texts."

"I know," Jonathan acknowledged without looking up from the ground.

"You never replied."

"I've been busy."

Abby caught up. "I'm sorry about Tomás."

"Sucks to be him."

"At least your mom and brother are okay."

"Adam still thinks Tomás is missing. He thinks the police found the wrong body."

Abby climbed up on a table and rubbed the side of her ankle. "What do you think?"

"I think Adam is a moron. Tomás is dead. Our mom went to see for herself."

"Did she tell you what happened?"

"She just said Tomás died in the flood." Jonathan rubbed his eye, fighting to maintain his composure. "Your dad seems pretty cool."

"I'll keep him."

"My dad's never around anymore," Jonathan groused.

"At least you have a brother."

"It's not the same."

"I always wanted a brother."

Jonathan propped himself on the bench seat beside the table. "I'll let you have mine if you can get him to stay out of my room." He scratched his fingernails against the wood. Dark clouds moved eastward above the school. "Did the flood scare you?"

Abby looked up at the same patch of clouds drawing Jonathan's attention elsewhere. "I thought we were going to die. But God gave us a second chance."

"Do you believe in God?"

"Usually."

"What do you mean? You either do or you don't."

Abby remained on the table, slightly elevated from Jonathan's position on the bench beneath her. "If he does exist, why do so many bad things always happen? On the other hand, if he doesn't exist, how did we survive the flood? I should have drowned. I should have died in the hospital. But I didn't. I think God saved me for a reason."

"Or you just got lucky."

"If I was lucky, I'd have both arms. I think God has a bigger plan for me."

"When did you get so holy?"

"It's not a matter of holy or unholy but how you choose to live your life."

"What if I don't have a choice?"

"You always have a choice. You're here aren't you? Instead of sitting in class where you're supposed to be."

"True."

"How long have you lived in Tennessee?"

Jonathan moved closer to Abby. "My whole life."

"Your mom is like some kind of famous singer."

"She used to be."

"How long has your dad been gone?"

Jonathan glanced at the spider webs in the rafter corners. "A long time."

Abby spotted her gym class on the basketball courts across from the weed-infested soccer field. "What do you want to be when you grow up?"

"A lead guitarist in a band."

"My dad loves music. He'd play guitar all day and night if he could."

"What about you?" Jonathan inquired.

"A juggler," Abby said with a straight face. She punched Jonathan's shoulder and checked her phone when she felt it vibrate. "My dad's picking me up after school."

"What about detention?"

"NMP."

"What?"

"Not my problem."

"That doesn't make sense."

"Life is what you make of it. No one said it had to make sense!"

CHAPTER 53

Leland sat in his truck with the headlights on and the engine running outside the familiar Belle Meade address, where he spied the Sotheby's "SOLD" sign posted on the sprawling estate. *The Thunder Rolls* played from a local station airing Garth Brooks' favorite hits. As the song continued, Leland wondered what his future held with Melissa, a country music diva who could have any man she wanted, yet decided to be with him instead.

He killed the motor and checked himself in the vanity mirror to inspect his blue denim shirt unbuttoned far enough to expose his gold cross necklace. A pink rose occupied the seat beside him, the flower's natural fragrance muted in the presence of his Chrome cologne.

He left his truck and approached the house to see Melissa appear in heels and designer jeans with a form-fitting top to accentuate her figure. "You look amazing," he said sincerely.

Melissa adjusted her top. "Are your contacts dirty?"

Leland offered the pink rose. "This is for you."

"I'm allergic."

"I didn't know," Leland said with an apologetic tone.

"Just kidding…" Melissa kissed him on the cheek and took the rose. "You're too easy, but thank you. How did you know pink was my favorite color?"

"Abby told me."

"Smart girl."

Leland escorted her to his truck and opened her door to help her up before he came around the driver's side. He secured his seatbelt and twisted the key in the ignition. The motor cranked but wouldn't fire. "This never happens," he said, baffled by the unexpected result.

Melissa smiled. "That's what they all say."

Leland pumped the pedal and tried the ignition again. This time the engine fired.

"Let's go MacGyver. I'm starved!"

Leland backed away from the house and drove down the long, sloping driveway toward the gate. He liked the scent of Melissa's perfume, sweet and delicate, yet alluring. He also admired the way her shoulder-length hair complemented her face. "You find a sitter for your boys?"

"They're at a sleepover with friends."

"What did they think about going back to school?"

Melissa held her rose by the stem and sniffed the petals. "They're not thrilled, but considering everything that's happened, a familiar routine will be good for them. What about Abby?"

"The principal caught her skipping class again."

"Seriously?" Melissa adjusted her seatbelt. "The gate will open by itself," she said when they reached the end of the driveway. "Hendrix has been nagging me to meet with her since my boys transferred there. That woman has a rattlesnake temper."

Leland nodded. "I did my time with her already."

"For skipping class?"

Leland winced. "Not exactly."

"Is Abby home?"

"I dropped her off at Sid's. Figured that was punishment enough. Sometimes I feel like I'm not connecting with her anymore."

"Give her some space. She's been through a lot. More than most kids would see in a lifetime."

Leland waited for the big gate to open and headed east toward downtown Nashville. He liked the way Melissa laughed at his jokes, or at least pretended to be amused by them. The more time he spent with her, the more he enjoyed their time together. He wanted to kiss her but decided to wait for a more opportunistic moment to present itself.

He drove slowly through the moderate traffic, amazed by the magnitude of the ongoing cleanup effort. Determined to give back what the city had given him, he had plans to volunteer his time and effort in support of the marathon recovery the city would undertake in the coming months and years. But tonight was his to own in pursuit of a new relationship with a woman he'd hoped to impress. "I'm glad you're here," he said when he reached his destination downtown and found a parking space. "I thought we'd catch some live music and grab a bite, but not necessarily in that order." He got out to feed the parking meter and opened Melissa's door.

"You're such a gentleman," Melissa offered with a hint of sarcasm in her voice.

"You don't know me well enough."

Melissa sniffed her rose again. "How did Abby know pink was my favorite color?"

Leland walked her to the entrance of Robert's Western World. "Lucky guess." He put his hand on Melissa's lower back and gently led her inside.

Melissa scoped out the bar. "What happened to me deciding where we eat?"

Leland shrugged his shoulders and grinned. "The man always decides on the first date."

"Is that so?"

"It's man code."

"Does the man hope to see a second date?"

Leland scratched his sideburn. "Point taken. We can go somewhere else if you like."

Melissa brushed her rose petals against his chin. "I thought the flood wiped out this hillbilly diner."

"Not yet. Still the best cheeseburger on Broadway." Leland bumped fists with a bartender who gestured toward an empty table near the back.

"Do you know everyone in here?" Melissa asked.

"I've played a few gigs," Leland offered. He pulled a chair out for Melissa and ignored the tall, blonde waitress who immediately recognized him. "She's just a friend."

Melissa took her seat. "You seem to have lots of friends for someone who moved to Nashville recently."

"I'm a people person," Leland said blithely.

"So I gathered."

"It's not like that."

Melissa winked at him. She nudged his leg with her foot under the table. "How's the band treating you?"

"I have my first rehearsal with them tomorrow. Brad Siegel's going to be there."

"Are you excited?"

"I'm playing rhythm guitar for a bunch of country-rock wannabes and singing background vocals on lyrics a Girl Scout could write."

"I was a Girl Scout!"

"Did you hustle cookies door to door?"

"I sold my share."

When the waitress arrived, Leland ordered a Coors Light for himself and a glass of Chardonnay for Melissa. "The band's a short term gig."

"It's good exposure."

"Are you done with your album?"

Melissa thought carefully before she answered. She wanted to come clean on a few things, but she couldn't bring herself to go there. "Not yet."

"I saw the sign in your yard. Your place sold quickly."

"A cash buyer from out of state made an offer. He's flying in to close the deal."

"You don't sound enthused."

"I'm bitter sweet. My boys grew up in Belle Meade. It's all they know."

Leland reached for his beer when the waitress backtracked toward the table with her shirt unbuttoned to expose her cleavage. "If you need help moving, I know a guy with a truck."

Melissa reached for her wine. "If you could date anyone in the world, past or present, who would it be and why?"

"Isn't that obvious?"

Melissa blushed. "I'm serious. You must be crushing on someone."

"Maybe Wonder Woman. I always liked Linda Carter. She wore that stars and stripes outfit with her magic lasso and red boots."

"You must have been like five when her show came out."

"I was old enough to appreciate her…accessories."

Melissa sipped her wine. "Ed Ames."

Leland laughed beer through his nose. "The Jimmy Crocket guy?"

"Daniel Boone. He played Mingo, a Cherokee Indian."

"So you're into Native Americans?"

"My great grandfather was Native American Cherokee. They dressed him for the part on the show."

"Your great grandfather?"

"Stop…" Melissa smirked. "Ed Ames. His voice always struck me. So soothing and powerful. I grew up listening to him on the radio. My mother liked to play his RCA records." Melissa sipped her wine and studied Leland's expression. "You probably don't remember those. The big plastic discs you had to drop on a rotating platter."

Leland kept his attention on Melissa. "I have some vinyl of my own. Mostly classic rock I listened to in high school. Some of the jackets got flooded in my garage." He sipped his beer, casually admiring Melissa's soft facial features with every passing glance.

"What are you thinking?" Melissa asked. She crossed her legs at the knee and put her hand on Leland's arm.

"Nothing."

"You have any hobbies?"

"Between work and music and Abby, I don't have much free time. What about you?"

"Just two: peace and quiet."

"I can relate."

Melissa traced her finger along the cross tattoo on Leland's arm. "You ever think about acting?"

"I have a face for radio."

"I think the waitress with her tits spilling out of her shirt would disagree." Melissa sipped her wine. "A lot of singers got into acting. David Bowie, Harry Connick, Jr., Justin Timberlake, Tim McGraw."

"I can't see myself in movies."

"Think about it."

"Maybe after I win male vocalist of the year."

Melissa tapped Leland's hand. "And you're modest, too."

"Do you like to cook?"

"I can think of better things to do in the kitchen." Melissa blushed. She gulped her wine. "Forget what I said. Sometimes I speak before I think."

"I like that in a woman."

"What about kids? You ever consider having more?"

"One teenage daughter is enough for me. Speaking of which, Vanderbilt told me her bill was covered."

"You must have good insurance."

"I don't have any insurance."

Melissa looked away to avoid Leland's probing stare. "Maybe there was a clerical error. I won't tell if you don't."

"For fifty thousand dollars?"

"Sometimes good things happen to good people."

"I'm going to repay you. Every penny."

Melissa reached into her purse for her pain medication. "You don't owe me anything. And don't read too much into it." She fumbled for the prescription in her purse, unable to unscrew the top one-handed. In her haste, she dropped the bottle on the floor.

"I got it," Leland offered before Melissa could reach it. He glimpsed the label.

"It's not what you think," Melissa explained.

Leland gave her the meds. "None of my business."

"I have back pain."

"I'm not judging."

"But you're curious?"

"I didn't say anything."

"It's what you're *not* saying."

Leland lowered his voice. "Did I say something wrong?"

Melissa unscrewed the lid and took two pills out. She gave the hovering waitress an evil eye and swallowed the black market tablets with the ice water on the table. "A few years ago, my tour bus was hit by a tractor trailer as we were coming off the interstate. The driver was speeding and didn't slow down in time. When he hit the back of the bus, I went flying and slammed into a table. The impact ruptured two discs in my lower back. Six months and three surgeries later, I could finally walk without a cane. They replaced the damaged discs with synthetic ones, but my lower back still hurts. My doctor says the pain is psychosomatic."

"What do you think?"

"It didn't help my career. My driver died in the accident. One of my backup singers suffered a permanent neck injury. I had to cancel the tour. My album tanked. I've tried to put it behind me, but it's hard sometimes. On a good day I can touch my toes. Other days, it hurts to get out of bed."

"I never realized."

Melissa finished her wine. "To be honest…it's been a rough ride for me the last few years. Since the accident, I haven't exactly been at the top of my game. I've had to make some lifestyle adjustments, as Sid would say. Sold my horses. Let go of most of my staff at home, and put my boys in public school. No offense."

"No worries. I'm sure those weren't easy decisions."

"On top of that, Sid discovered my accountant was stealing from me. The bastard took most of my life savings."

"I'm really sorry."

Melissa frowned. "I should have been more careful. I was so hell-bent on rebuilding my career, I took my hands off the wheel. I trusted him."

"You're human…"

"My new album is more of a fantasy than anything I expect to finish, let alone promote on tour." Melissa pinched her wine glass stem and tipped her drink back. "Sorry. Bet you didn't see this coming. I guess I'm not really the woman you thought I was."

"On the contrary," Leland reassured her. "I think you're amazing."

Melissa circled her finger along the rim of her empty glass. "Let's get out of here."

"We haven't eaten."

"I'm not hungry anymore."

Melissa rode home in Leland's truck, lost in her thoughts about what she should have said but didn't say as the night went on. She'd taken Leland country dancing and saw how God never meant for him to dance. She'd seen him eat meat on a stick from a roadside vendor. He had to eat, she'd reconciled, feeling guilty for depriving him from the cheeseburger he'd ordered from his favorite dive bar. Aside from his rugged good looks and his southern charm, she found something undeniable about his character and his family bond. Moreover, he'd risked his own life to save her son, and for that, she would always be grateful. He accepted her for who she was: a washed-out vocalist whose spotlight faded years ago in a town full of singers half her age and twice her talent.

She held the rose on her lap, diverting her eyes from oncoming headlights and the reassuring smiles Leland cast upon her. She knew he liked her. That much was obvious. What she didn't know was where she wanted the evening to go. And as she rode through her gated entrance along the winding driveway toward her soon to be vacated property, she wanted the evening to end without an awkward goodbye.

"Thank you for driving," she offered when Leland rolled up to her house.

"Thank you for a wonderful evening," Leland replied. "I enjoyed spending time with you."

"Ditto."

Leland put his arm around her and leaned closer for a kiss.

Melissa shied away. "I had a nice time tonight. I hope I didn't say anything to offend you."

"Aside from stepping on my toes when we danced the promenade—"

"I did not!" Melissa retorted. "You were the one dancing like a donkey in heat." She laughed at her own analogy. "I didn't mean the way it sounded."

"So now you're calling me an ass?" Leland needled her.

"Are you sure you're safe to drive?"

"I'm good."

Melissa held up her pink rose. "I should get going." She touched the door latch. "Would you like to come inside? I make a mean cup of coffee."

Leland rested his arm on the steering wheel. "I should probably head home."

"Just for a few minutes? I have something I want to show you in my studio. And don't get any ideas. This is not an invitation to sex."

"Yes ma'am."

Melissa entered the kitchen and filled a twelve-cup carafe with tap water. "I'll start the coffee."

"Can I help?"

"I'm pouring water, not serving a five course meal." Melissa powered the Cuisinart Grind & Brew and poked her head around the corner to see Leland venture toward her music studio. With his attention focused elsewhere, she ran upstairs to retrieve a small guitar case from her closet. When she carried it back to her studio, she found Leland at the piano. "A band member gave this to me as a gift." She placed the case on the floor to open it. "A nineteen sixty-seven—"

"Daniel Friedrich," Leland finished her sentence. "Very nice."

"How did you know? Never mind. I thought you might like to play it."

Leland took the guitar and rested it on his knee. He brushed the strings with his fingertips and played several bars of Rodrigo's Concierto de Aranjuez, the sound warm and lush with every note from the elegant guitar made of European spruce. "Thank you very much. How long have you had it?"

"Almost ten years."

"It's beautiful."

"I thought of all people, you would appreciate it the most."

Leland gave the guitar back and diverted his attention to the grand piano. He played chopsticks while Melissa put the vintage instrument away. "I learned this when I was five." He tapped the keys until Melissa parked herself beside him.

"Cute. Maybe you should stick with guitar."

Leland paused to crack his knuckles. Then he let his fingers fly across the keyboard. "Remember this one?"

"Only the Good Die Young!" Melissa blurted, flabbergasted by Leland's ability to pump the piano like Jerry Lee. "I love Billy Joel!"

Leland played several bars then stopped to think of a different tune. This time, he played "Walking in Memphis."

"I met Marc Cohn by accident in a New York City diner," Melissa recalled. "He's a very handsome man."

Leland worked the foot pedals and slowed the tempo to play a different tune, a slow, methodic melody in F minor. "I can't compete with Marc Cohn or Billy Joel, but this one belongs to me. Sort of a work in progress."

There was a time in my life
When I thought I held all the answers...
What happened to love?
What happened to reason?
And where do we go from here?

One heart breaks and one heart mends
Where new love starts and old love ends, in a moment
of time...
Along a nebulous line, somewhere
Between lovers and friends...

You tell me to stay but you want me to go
You can't decide...
Make up your mind
Or let it ride, and take it slow...

One heart breaks and one heart mends
Where new love starts and old love ends, in a moment
of time...
Along a nebulous line, somewhere
Between lovers and friends...

We're flyin' blind without a net
To live our lives and not forget
The long goodbyes and no regrets
Somewhere between...lovers and friends
A stiff lip breaks, a soft one bends
When you blur the line between...
Lovers and friends
Between lovers and friends
Lovers...and, friends...

Melissa slipped her heels off and lifted her sundress over her head. She unfastened her white lace bra and laid it on top of the piano in stark contrast to the black lacquer finish.

She shimmied her panties to her ankles and stepped out of her French-cut lace. Completely naked, she moved slowly and deliberately onto Leland's lap, straddling him face to face. She kissed him softly on the mouth and whispered, "I dare you to play it again."

PART III

Checkmate

May 11–August 6, 2010

CHAPTER 54

Sid inspected the plants inside his downtown office. Some looked lifeless; others showed signs of life renewed—much like his clients' careers. He'd managed his share of worthy players and struggling artists who faced the same gauntlet of music moguls hungry to score their next Top 40 hit with a contract heavily slated in the studio's favor. But now, for the first time in his career, he began to question his involvement with two very different artists who shared a passion for their craft and a stubborn propensity for refusing to accept the realities of the rabid music industry.

"I'm not here," he told Melissa when she entered his office unannounced. He added water to the English Ivy and Wandering Jew without looking up.

"You said you'd be in today," Melissa reminded him.

"Physically, yes. Mentally, I'm taking a leave of absence." He added extra water to the English Ivy. "Half of these damn plants keep dying."

Melissa dropped her keys in her purse. "Maybe you should stop mixing bourbon in the water."

"That was an accident."

Melissa smiled broadly, basking in the afterglow from her date with Leland the night before. "Leland told me you kept Abby for him last night."

"Now you know why I drink so much."

"Leland says she's an angel."

"With the devil's tongue. That girl can flap her gums. She nearly talked me into a coma."

"Not funny."

"Not joking."

Melissa adjusted a crooked picture frame with an autographed photo of Kenny Rogers. "I changed my mind about selling the house."

"You don't have a choice."

"I always have a choice, Sid. I didn't work this hard to give up everything I've worked for."

"You're not *giving* anything away. You have a cash offer for six million dollars and a chance to get your finances back on track."

"My boys need this home. So do I."

"Your boys need their mother. Belle Meade is a temple, not a home."

"Belle Meade is worth twice what he's offering."

"Not in this market."

Melissa gazed out the window overlooking the assortment of converted houses and post-modern buildings unscathed by the prodigious flooding. "Tell me how someone like me ends up in a predicament like this."

"You still owe your label and the IRS."

"Screw the IRS."

"They could seize your assets."

"Then handle it!"

"I'm trying, but you've got to meet me half way."

"What about my stolen savings? I feel like the perpetrator, not the victim."

"The police are doing everything they can."

"Then convey that to the IRS. If I had the money I would pay them. It's not my fault I got embezzled."

"I get it, but Uncle Sam doesn't care."

"What about my new record deal?"

"I'm working every angle I can. At the moment, there is no deal."

"Just more excuses…"

"I appreciate your frustration, but as your friend—"

"I don't need you to be my friend, Sid. I need you to manage my career, or at least what's left of it."

"Miles Steinard wants to work with you."

"You know how I feel about him."

"I know you could work with him if you tried. As your manager, and not your friend, this might be the last option you have. I strongly suggest you reconsider."

Melissa gave Sid a scathing glance. A flushing toilet in the private bathroom outside his office steered her attention away. "Who else is here?"

"I wasn't expecting you to drop by."

"Sid…"

"Your buyer flew in this morning." Sid grabbed his iPhone off his desk when the restroom door opened. "I left something in my car," he said, promptly dismissing himself.

Melissa did a double take when her ex-husband, Martin, entered the office. "What the hell are you doing here?"

Martin Hamilton put his hands up. "I come in peace," he said, his lanky, six-foot frame dressed in Chino's and a light gray shirt a shade darker than his sandy blond hair.

"What is this?"

Martin proceeded with caution. "Sid never mentioned you'd be here. I was planning to call you first."

"What for?"

Martin nudged his Hugo Boss glasses on his prominent nose. "I'm here about the house."

Melissa saw the pieces come together. She stood transfixed and somewhat dumbfounded by Martin's unexpected appearance. "You're the buyer from California?"

"My offer is legit."

"I should have known…I don't want your money, Martin."

Martin leaned against the edge of Sid's desk, his manicured fingers interlaced in front of him. "I heard about the flood. And I heard about Tomás. I'm sorry on both accounts."

"For what?"

"For everything. I've made a lot of mistakes."

"I don't have time for this."

"Hear me out. I rode the redeye from LAX to get here."

"With your tramp?"

"We broke up six months ago." Martin held his hands out, palms open. "I miss you. I miss our boys."

"They don't miss you."

"I know…I own that. I was a different man. I'm not asking you to forgive me. At least not yet. I just want you to know I'm here to help."

Melissa kept her legs planted wide. Her nostrils flared. "You can help by getting on the next plane home."

"This is my home."

"Not anymore. You made your decision when you bailed on us. Tomás was more of a father to our boys than you could ever hope to be."

"Tomás never loved the boys the way I do."

"You're a disgrace to his name and to our family. The boys don't want anything to do with you."

"I'm their father."

"*Were,* their father. You gave up your right the minute you walked out on us."

Martin bowed his head. "I hurt you, and I own that, but don't deny our sons the chance to know me."

Melissa arched her eyebrows. "And you reached this epiphany when? When your little tart finally left you? When you realized you're too old to chase women half your age?"

"Sid told me about what happened in the flood. Our boys could have died."

"Go home Martin."

"Please…"

"There's nothing here for you."

"I didn't fly three thousand miles to turn around and go back. I'm moving my practice to Nashville. A fresh start for me. For all of us. I promise things will be different this time."

"Are you finished? I don't want you here. The boys don't want you here. As far as I'm concerned, the house is off the market. Whatever delusions you're clinging to about reconciliation—"

"I deserve a second chance. I care about you. I'm not asking for forgiveness. I'm asking for a chance to make amends."

Melissa told herself to breathe. She wasn't the one responsible for spousal conduct unbecoming. She wanted to lash out at Martin, but deep down inside, she had no response. Martin was extinct to her, but he was still her boys' father.

Martin withdrew a business card from his wallet and laid it on Sid's desk. "My new cell phone number's on the back. My offer on the house still stands. When you're ready to talk, I'm ready to listen."

CHAPTER 55

Leland stood in front of a microphone inside a studio booth with a bearded drummer, a bass player with a nose ring, and a lead guitarist who shared an uncanny resemblance to Sting. He could see Brad Siegel arguing behind the control room window with the band's lead singer, Jimmie Lockhorn. He couldn't lip read the conversation, but the angry facial expressions and flagrant hand gestures telegraphed the verbal exchange.

He tuned the D and G strings on the cheap Kramer electric. He had as much respect for the band's lead singer as he did for the karaoke crooners off Broadway.

He strummed the guitar and rehearsed his own song in his mind. Then he lost himself in the thought of seeing Melissa again. He felt good with her. Content. Curious. Aroused. She stirred a passion inside him the way no woman ever had before. He wanted more of her in his life.

He stopped playing when Jimmie Lockhorn reemerged from his spat with Brad Siegel and reclaimed his post at the front microphone, where he directed the band to press on.

Leland played the rhythm piece from heart. A simple chord progression that repeated itself over and over throughout the song.

Jimmie Lockhorn stepped away from his microphone and signaled for the band to stop. "No, no, no!" the angry frontman complained to Leland. "Play the notes the way they're written."

"I am."

"Which ones?"

Leland ignored the smartass comment from the volatile prima donna in a muscle shirt with a poorly drawn heart tattoo on his shoulder and pierced ear plugs wide enough to fit a broomstick handle. "All of them."

"You keep playing the song the way you want it to sound, not the way I wrote it. You *can* read music?"

"No worries."

"No, you sound like shit," Jimmie pressed him. "We go live in three days. Play it the way I wrote it or find another gig."

Leland ignored the caustic remark. He'd dealt with guys like Jimmie before. Untalented fools with the right connections and the wrong approach to everything. "Maybe we should take a break?"

"Keep it tight, Presley. A monkey could play this piece."

Leland played the next few notes. "Is this not what you wrote?"

"Your rhythm is way off."

Leland gave him the guitar. "You play it for me."

"I'm a singer."

"If that's what you call it," Leland mumbled under his breath.

"What was that?"

"I said you're a dick."

Jimmie made a fist but lacked the nerve to use it. "There's a hundred musicians who would kill to take your place. I could bounce you off this gig…" He stopped when Brad Siegel entered the studio. "I've got this," he told Brad.

Brad pointed at Leland. "Let's talk for a second."

* * *

Leland followed Brad to the control room like a student to the principal's office. "If you've got a problem with me," he started.

"It's not you," Brad explained. "Jimmie's been under his ex-wife's thumb more than usual, and he likes to spread the misery. He can be an asshole, but as far as this band's concerned, he's the leader. What he lacks in people skills, he makes up for with raw talent. He's a prick who can sing."

"Are we talking about the same guy?"

Brad stepped into Leland's personal space. His breath smelled like sushi and cigarettes. "My people want to see this work as much as you do. But you need to find a way to get along or *get along*. You follow me?"

"Play it the way it's written," said Leland.

"Eighty people applied for this gig. I entertained three. Sid convinced me you're the man. I didn't care for your pony song, but you've got skills. Don't make me regret my decision." Brad patted Leland on the back and gave him a pair of backstage passes for the benefit concert. "Bring a date, or two. Girls love this shit."

Leland wanted to lash out, but he'd worked too hard and sacrificed too much to squander the opportunity with Capital Country Records, no matter how menial the role. He played the music note for note in the mundane order they were written. Truth was, he didn't care much for playing in a band at all, even one with a solid drummer and a lead guitarist who could play like Clapton.

CHAPTER 56

Leland strummed his acoustic Gibson with a fury, indulging one of his favorite riffs from ELO's "Fire on High." Originally recorded on a twelve string guitar, he hammered the instrumental piece on his vintage axe and let the last note ring when Abby appeared outside his room in her pajamas and tousled hair. "You almost ready?"

"Do I look like I'm ready?" Abby mumbled through a yawn. "I'm too tired to go to school."

Leland set his guitar in the stand. "I need to leave soon."

Abby bent down to pet her cat, who vigorously rubbed his face against her leg. "Did you feed Tiger?"

"He's your cat."

"I have to get ready."

"Then you better hustle. This train leaves the station in twenty minutes."

"Twenty minutes! Why didn't you get me up sooner?"

"I've been trying for half an hour."

"Where did you put my phone?"

"I didn't touch it."

"I left it on the kitchen table with the charger plugged in, and now it's gone."

"Check your room."

"I did."

"Check it again."

Abby sulked back to her bedroom, toting her cat sprawled over her shoulder in a helpless pose. "Don't leave without me."

Leland skimmed the newspaper on the table and poured himself a glass of OJ while Abby got ready for school. He read a back page story about volunteers feeding the hungry. The article highlighted four high school students who delivered warm meals to random homeless families still reeling from the lingering effects of the city's flood. He flipped to the last page in the lifestyle section to read the concluding paragraphs. When his doorbell rang, he opened the house to find Paula outside. "What the?"

"Where were you?"

Leland looked back to check on Abby and lowered his voice. "What are you talking about? Why are you here?"

"You were supposed to be in court yesterday."

"How did you get here?"

"I've been released. I'm a free bird now."

Leland rubbed the side of his neck and grimaced. "How?"

"New meds and a better lawyer."

"You shouldn't be here."

"Is Abby home?"

"She's at school."

"Her school doesn't start for an hour."

"How do you know?"

"She's my daughter. I have a right to be involved in her life."

Leland started to shut the door. "You should leave."

Paula blocked the door with her foot. "I'm not going anywhere. I tried to call, but your phone kept going to voice mail."

Leland reached in his pocket for his phone. "You need to leave."

"I have a right to see my daughter. I know she's here."

"Get off my property!"

"Abigail!" Paula screamed through the partially open door. "I'm your mother!"

Leland dialed 911 as Abby emerged from the other room. "Dad?"

"Get back in your room," Leland ordered Abby. "I'm calling the police."

Paula scowled at Leland and stepped away from the house. "This isn't over."

"What's going on?" Abby persisted.

Leland ended the 911 call. "Get ready for school," he said as he shut the door on Paula.

"She called me Abigail. No one calls me Abigail but you."

"We're late."

"Why did she say she's my mom?"

"She's confused."

"Who is she?"

"Never mind."

"Why did she come here?"

"Is your backpack ready?"

Abby touched her stomach with a shaky hand. "You're scaring me."

"Everything's fine."

"Then why were you calling the police?"

"You need to get ready for school."

"You need to tell me the truth."

"There's nothing to tell right now."

"I don't believe you. Why are you lying to me?"

Leland put his phone in his pocket. He knew the day would come sooner or later, with Abby too young to understand but mature enough to question. "You know I love you very much."

"I know you love me. Tell me who that woman was. Why did she say she's my mother?"

"Abby…"

"Is she?"

Leland braced for impact. "Biologically speaking…" He took a deep breath. "She's your mother."

"You said Mom died in the accident."

"I was trying to protect you."

"By lying to me?"

Leland reached out. "By keeping you safe. There's a lot you don't know."

"Why did you lie to me?"

"Abby…"

"Does Nicole know about my mom?"

"Nicole's not important."

"She does, doesn't she? You told her, but you never told me."

"Nicole's an adult." Leland shrank from his own reply, wishing he could take the words back before Abby came unglued.

"Where has Mom been?"

"A mental health hospital."

"Why?"

"Your mother needed help."

"What for?"

"Abby…"

"Tell me!"

Leland ran his hand through his hair. "Your mother tried to drown you in a lake when you were young. She crashed her car on purpose. She never buckled you in your car seat."

Abby faced her dad with a wounded look in her eyes. "I remembered the accident. On the bus, when I thought I was going to drown. I remember it happened so fast."

"You were thrown into the windshield. Your arm saved your face, but the cuts on your arm were deep. Doctors tried to save it, but they couldn't."

"It was an accident."

"Your mother never fastened the car seat."

"Maybe she forgot to."

"Maybe."

"Why didn't you tell me?"

"I was waiting until you were older."

"I am older."

Leland followed Abby to her room. "She's never been part of your life."

"Because you never let her."

"Your mother's sick. The court placed her in a psychiatric hospital because that's where she belongs."

"She got better."

"We don't know that."

"She's still my mother."

"She tried to kill you, Abby. I'm sorry. I know that sounds awful to hear. But it's the truth."

"I don't believe you. The crash was an accident." Abby snatched a pillow from her bed and cried into it. "Why would she do this to me?"

"I don't know, Baby. Only your mom can answer that."

CHAPTER 57

Principal Hendrix escorted Melissa to her office, traversing packs of frenzied middle school students racing to beat the morning bell. "Thank you for meeting me," she offered before she closed the door and positioned herself behind her desk. She reached for the files on the Hamilton boys and sipped a mug of hot tea.

"I only have a few minutes," Melissa replied curtly.

"This won't take long. I think your boys have great potential, Mrs. Hamilton. They're both very bright students. Their transcripts highlight their previous academic achievements."

"Is this about the plastic cockroaches? I got your messages, but with everything that's happened—"

"We're way beyond fake insects, Mrs. Hamilton."

Melissa leaned forward in her seat and put her phone away. "What happened this time?"

"Do your boys talk about school?"

"Sometimes. Not always."

"I learned they no longer ride the bus."

"They don't have to. I drop them off and pick them up. What is this about?"

Principal Hendrix slid Jonathan's interim report card across her desk. "Jonathan is failing three of his classes.

The rest he's barely making 'Cs.' Your son was an 'A' student before he transferred here." She seized another page from Jonathan's file. "Your son's English teacher gave me a copy of a recent homework assignment. Students were asked to list their three favorite authors and write a paragraph about each one. Your son wrote about Mike Hock, C. Dees Nuts, and M. Astor Bator." She gave the notebook page to Melissa. "This is obviously not the work of an 'A' student."

Melissa skimmed the homework assignment. "Why am I seeing this for the first time?"

"I left you several messages, Mrs. Hamilton."

"So this is my fault now?"

"I'm not laying accusations. I'm trying to help you help your son."

"Jonathan's been under a lot of stress."

"He's also been cutting classes."

"Jonathan wouldn't do that."

"Truancy is a serious offense, Mrs. Hamilton."

"You're blowing things way out of proportion. So what if he skipped a couple classes? He nearly died in the flood. He's had more important things to deal with than school."

Principal Hendrix sipped her tea. She could relate to Mrs. Hamilton's denial. A smart woman with a successful career; a good mother; an honest citizen; a disillusioned parent. "I'm not here to berate your son. I'm here to enlighten you about his behavior. I've been a single mother of three boys. I know how hard it can be at times." She reached around her desk to retrieve the prosthetic arm with three fingers and the thumb bent down, leaving the middle finger extended up. "This was your son's handiwork."

"I've never seen it before."

"The prosthesis belongs to a classmate of his. A young woman he shares homeroom with. You can see why she doesn't want it back."

"Do I need a lawyer?"

"You're missing the point, Mrs. Hamilton. Your son needs his parents."

"I'll talk to Jonathan again."

"I hope so," Principal Hendrix continued. She opened Adam's file and shared her notes with Melissa. "Were you aware that Adam was caught pulling the fire alarm? Twice."

"Adam?"

"A classmate caught him the first time. Our security guard caught him the second. I can live with fake roaches in detention, but tampering with the fire alarm is a criminal offense."

"When did this happen?"

"A few weeks ago. Before the flood. I tried to contact you."

Melissa sunk back in her chair. "I've been busy."

"I'm not trying to tell you how to raise your family, but this is a partnership, Mrs. Hamilton, between yourself and my school. It only works if both sides put forth the effort."

"My boys are coping with a lot right now."

"All the more reason they would benefit from professional help."

"My boys don't need a shrink."

"They need someone to talk to, Mrs. Hamilton. Yourself, your husband—"

"Ex-husband. Their father's out of the picture."

"How long?"

"A few years."

"Is he involved at all with your boys?"

"Not anymore."

"He should be. Seventy-one percent of high school dropouts lack a male role model at home. Sixty-three percent of youth suicides stem from fatherless homes. Eighty-five percent of all youths in prison come from fatherless homes."

"Are you trying to scare me?"

"I'm trying to educate you."

"My boys aren't *fatherless*, they just have a deadbeat dad who worships his penis more than his family." Melissa noticed the photos on the principal's desk. None showed a man in the picture. "What about your husband?"

"He found a similar calling," Principal Hendrix conveyed in a slightly disgusted tone. "I'm not saying it's easy. Lord knows if that were true we'd all sleep better at night. And I'm not telling you how to raise your children. But I am strongly encouraging you to get help for them." She opened her desk drawer and retrieved a business card for a behavioral health specialist.

Melissa took the card and read the doctor's name. "I'm not sure this is a good idea."

"It's not about you."

"My boys don't open up to strangers."

"Don't give them a choice. They can come to terms with their personal issues and experience a normal, healthy life. Or they can squander their youth on a path of self-destruction."

"How well do you know this psychiatrist?"

"Well enough to know I wouldn't recommend him if I didn't believe he could help." Principal Hendrix leaned across her desk. "Talk to your boys. Make an appointment. The longer you put this off, the more problems you're going to face down the road."

Melissa slid the card in her purse. "How long have you been a principal?"

"Too long. But don't tell my superintendent."

Melissa gathered her purse and stood up. "I'll talk to my boys."

"Tell them I might be old, but I know everything that goes on in this school."

"What about your boys?"

Principal Hendrix looked at Melissa with a vacant stare and lowered her voice. "My oldest has two years left on his parole, and my middle son works the night shift at Walgreens. My youngest is dead."

"I'm sorry."

"Don't be. They had an absentee father as well."

CHAPTER 58

Leland knocked gently on Abby's bedroom door. He'd given her space and let her blow off school for the day. Against his better judgment, he'd called in sick for work and spent the morning on the phone with Sid, venting over Paula's unannounced visit and her preposterous assertion of custody rights. No matter how many ways he sliced it, he kept coming back to Paula's state of mental health and the chance she still posed a danger to Abby.

He tried the doorknob and found it locked. "We should talk about this."

"*I hate you!*" came the stern reply from inside the room.

"No you don't."

"*Yes, I do.*"

"Then can you hate me out here so we can talk face to face?" He put his ear to the door and listened for signs of life—or at least demonic voices he could reason with. He empathized with her frustration, but a bad reply was better than no reply at all. "I was trying to protect you."

"*I don't need you to protect me.*"

Leland put his hand against the wall. He touched his gold cross necklace with the other. Abby would have to leave her room eventually, he reasoned. "I thought we had a deal. No more shut-ins when things got tough."

"The deal is void."

"Since when?"

"Since you lied to me."

"This isn't how adults communicate."

"I know. They keep secrets instead."

Leland went back to his room for his guitar. He knew better than to try and sing his way out of the dog house, but he needed something to focus on. "You're right. No more secrets. I promise." He strummed the guitar with a lazy hand and asked, "Can you please open the door?"

"Did my mom try to kill me because I was bad?"

"Absolutely not. Don't ever think that. You had nothing to do with what happened."

"Then why did she come here?"

Leland rested the guitar against the wall. He wanted to play something, anything, but the mood didn't feel right. "She believes she's better now and wants to be part of your life."

"Then why did she try to hurt me?"

"I don't know."

"Do you trust her?"

"No."

"Am I safe here?"

"Absolutely."

"How do you know for sure?"

"Because I know your mother doesn't want to hurt you."

"You just said you don't trust her. You said she tried to kill me."

"It's hard to explain through the door."

"Nice try, Dad, but I'm not coming out."

"You have to eat eventually. And you *will* be going to school tomorrow." Leland let his words sink in before he retreated to the other room with his guitar. He understood Abby's point of view, but he couldn't fathom her stubborn nature, the root of which had kept her alive in the storm. He thought about calling Melissa but hesitated to involve her in his family affairs. His issues were his alone to deal with. Abby would come out eventually. Life would continue.

Default reset to normal, whatever normal had become anymore.

He set the guitar in its case when he heard the doorbell ring. He counted twelve dollars and loose change from his pocket for a pizza he'd ordered an hour ago. But instead of a delivery driver, he found Nicole on his welcome mat. "What are you doing here?"

Nicole waved at Leland. Her clothes were frumpled. Her hair and makeup were a mess. "Can I come in?"

"Now's not a good time."

"I wanted to grab a few things. I would have called, but I wasn't sure you would answer."

Leland stepped back to let her in. "Real quick…"

"Is Abby home?"

"She's in her room."

"How is she?"

"Her ankle's still sore, but it's manageable."

"That's not what I meant."

"She's gone through a lot. We take it day by day."

"I miss you," Nicole said in passing, almost as if she were talking to herself.

Leland walked back toward the living room, where he kept a box with Nicole's name on it.

Nicole followed closely. "A social worker came to my apartment the other night, asking about Abby."

"A social worker? What did she want?"

"She wanted to know where Abby went to school. She asked me how long we lived together."

"Why?"

Nicole shrugged. "She said something about a complaint being filed. It was weird. I felt like she knew me. She kept asking questions about us."

"What did she look like?"

"I don't remember exactly. White. She had a buzz haircut."

"What was her name?"

"Rhonda something…"

Leland knew better than to trust Nicole, but he believed her. He also imagined Paula pretending to be someone she's not; a woman who would sell her soul for a chance to reinsert herself in Abby's life. He showed Nicole the box with her name on it. "What else did she say?"

"Nothing. She kept asking questions." Nicole pushed the box aside. "Is this everything?"

"I think so."

"I miss being here, with you."

Leland backed away. "I think you might have stuff in the garage, but a lot of boxes on the floor got wet."

"I remember the song you wrote for me."

"The one I sang before you dumped me?"

"I didn't dump you, Leland. I was scared. I told you what happened."

Leland shoved his hands in his pockets and straightened his arms. "I know."

"I miss waking up with you. I miss seeing you with Abby. I miss everything about *us*."

"Don't go there…"

"I need you in my life, Leland. I want us to be a couple again."

"If you want, I can mail the rest of your stuff to you."

Nicole blocked Leland's path when he tried to step around her. "I don't care about my useless junk. I came here to see you. I'm not the same person without you."

Leland took his hands out and pushed her gently, but firmly, away. "I can't do this."

"Are you seeing someone else?"

"I don't love you anymore."

"You don't mean that."

"I care about you. So does Abby. But you and I are in different places, and I've got a huge gig coming up with this benefit concert."

"When did this happen?"

Leland looked away from Nicole when his phone vibrated in his pocket. He dug it out and heard, "*Where are you?*" from Sid's voice on the other end.

"At home. Now's not a good—"

"Melissa collapsed an hour ago. She's at Vanderbilt hospital right now."

Leland gaped in stunned silence. "What happened?"

"I think she had a heart attack."

"Oh my God…"

"I'll meet you there."

"I'm on my way!"

CHAPTER 59

Leland met up with Sid in the emergency room at Vanderbilt Hospital. Slightly winded from his jaunt through the parking garage, Leland caught his breath and asked, "How is she?"

Sid motioned for Leland to follow him. "This way."

"What happened?"

"The doctor said Melissa suffered a small myocardial infarction."

"How?"

Sid moved aside for a team of paramedics to wheel a gurney past him. "They're running tests."

"What about her boys?"

"They're with her now. She's been asking for you."

"Is she okay?"

"She's stable."

"Thank God."

"Thank Adam. He found her on the floor at home and called for help."

Leland rubbed a knot in his shoulder. He could only imagine what Melissa's boys were going through. "This is crazy."

"She's behind the last curtain on the left. Go see her. I have another call to make."

Leland stood alone for a moment to compose himself before he ventured through the ER and opened the privacy curtain to find Melissa's boys half asleep standing up. He gave a curious nod to the tall, slender man with sandy blond hair and glasses who stood between them. He approached Melissa slowly. "Sid told me you were here."

Melissa touched her face. "I look like crap."

"I got here as soon as I could."

"No worries," Melissa assured him. She laid on her back with her head propped up on pillows. A bevy of medical equipment monitored her heart rate and pulse oximetry. "Where's Abby?"

"At home with a friend."

Melissa pointed to the man with her boys. "This is Martin. The boys' father."

Leland extended a handshake and received a vice grip from Martin's bear paw in return. "Leland Presley."

"Martin Hamilton, the Third." He gripped Leland's hand for several seconds before he finally let go.

"Good to meet you," Leland offered.

"Likewise. What brings you here?"

"Why don't you take the boys for a soda," Melissa intervened.

"You sure?" asked Martin.

"It's okay."

Martin looked at Leland through pinched eyes. "I appreciate what you did for my boy. Mel told me what happened in the storm."

"It was nothing."

"I'm glad my boat was there to help."

"Me too."

"I heard you went to Vanderbilt?"

"Long time ago."

"So did I," Martin added. "What year did you graduate?"

"Ninety-eight."

"What was your major?"

"Music."

"Same here. You ever have Doctor Blackman?"

"I don't recall."

"You don't remember your professors?"

"It was a long time ago."

Martin nudged his glasses on his nose. "So you said."

"Give us a minute," Melissa prompted.

Martin diverted his attention from Leland in the three-way conversation. "I'll take the boys to the cafeteria."

Leland waited for the room to clear before he leaned over to kiss Melissa's head. "I was worried about you."

"Don't be. I'm fine."

"You had a heart attack."

"More like bad indigestion."

"Sid told me you passed out."

"For a couple seconds. No big deal. Sid exaggerates."

"What happened?"

"Nothing." Melissa swallowed. "My prescription ran out for my pain meds. My doctor wouldn't sign another refill, so I had Sid explore alternative options."

"You could have died."

"But I didn't." Melissa reached for the pink water pitcher by her bed. "I'm out of here tomorrow morning."

"Let's see what your doctor says."

"I have a hair appointment."

"Your hair can wait."

"You're sweet. No guitar?"

"Not this time."

"I was hoping you might play for me," Melissa quipped, her sense of humor tapered by the buprenorphine in her system. She held Leland's hand for comfort. "Thank you for coming. It means a lot to me. *You* mean a lot to me."

"Wait 'till the drugs wear off."

"I'm not delusional, Leland Presley. I know exactly how I feel." She kissed his hand. "Do I scare you?"

"I see I've got some competition."

"Martin is an ass. I'm sorry you had to meet him like this."

"Don't be. He's part of your life."

"*Was* part of my life. He wants to buy my house."

"Why?"

"Martin doesn't know how to live alone. His girlfriend left him, so he's decided he misses his boys." Melissa let go of Leland's hand and brushed her hair back with her fingers. "My boys barely know him anymore. He was a very different man before I married him. Before he went to law school and decided music wasn't his thing anymore."

"Does he play?"

"He used to play guitar. At least he thought he did. He was never much of a singer. Tried to start his own band."

"What happened?"

"He bombed." Melissa sipped water from her plastic cup. "I don't regret my boys for one second, but if I could do it over again, I would." She touched her hair again. "I didn't want you to see me like this, but I'm glad you're here."

Leland helped her adjust a pillow. "I think you're an amazing woman."

"Your concert's coming up."

"Three days."

"Are you ready?"

"I'm good."

"What about the band?"

"Brad Siegel has a lot of faith in them."

"Well I have a lot of faith in you! This is a great opportunity."

"I suppose."

"What does Abby think about you singing live in front of millions?"

"She doesn't know yet."

"Why not?"

"She never asked."

"She's your daughter."

"She's driving me nuts."

"She's a teenager girl. That's part of her job description." Leland refilled her water cup. "Does your back hurt?"

"I'll deal. I'm not spending the night in here. This place is a germ factory."

Leland studied her expression. He could tell something bothered her, a deeper pain, more emotional than physical. "Are you sure you're okay?"

Melissa glanced at Martin when he entered the room. "I'm tired."

Leland acknowledged the boys' father again. "It was nice to meet you."

Martin typed a message on his phone. "Likewise," he said without looking up.

"Take good care of her."

"I will."

CHAPTER 60

M artin smoked a menthol-flavored Kool outside the hospital, where he contemplated his options with Melissa and the house. He needed time to reconnect with the life he'd left behind; a life with a thriving practice and a family he sorely missed.

He blew smoke when an ambulance approached in the distance, lights flashing, siren wailing. He could feel the sense of urgency as the ride drew closer, an almost mild euphoria he attributed to the blended tobacco and his instincts as a highly successful personal injury attorney. The same instincts that told him when something, or *someone*, didn't feel right.

He flicked his ash at the sidewalk and checked his messages. His last settlement from a wrongful death suit would keep him flush long enough to rebuild his Nashville practice. With the right contacts in a city nearly crippled by historic flooding, new clients would present themselves in short order.

He dropped his cigarette butt inside the smokers' receptacle and went back inside to catch Sid and the boys. "You headed home?" he asked Sid who shuffled through the waiting area with Jonathan and Adam by his side.

"We'll be back in the morning."

"I can take the boys with me."

Sid looked at Jonathan and Adam. "Melissa asked me to take the boys tonight."

"You're her agent, not her babysitter. The boys should crash with me and spend some time with their old man."

Sid ushered the boys toward the parking garage. He had no one to blame but himself. He should have forced Melissa into rehab, or at the very least, stopped supporting her addiction. He'd given her what she wanted instead of what she needed. Now her boys needed a father, not their dad.

Martin followed them. "My car's not far."

"Unless Melissa says otherwise, her sons are staying with me."

"I'm not the bad guy here."

"We'll be back tomorrow morning. You can see the boys then."

"What time?"

"Early."

"What about school?"

"I'll drop them off late." Sid clenched the car keys in his pocket while Martin lingered like a bad cough. "What exactly is your end game?"

"My family."

Sid brought the boys to his black Escalade. "Good night, Martin." He unlocked the doors to let the boys climb inside and put their headphones on.

"Mel needs me."

"That's for her to decide."

Martin waved at his boys through the tinted windows. "Is she still using? I can have the hospital send me her lab results. I'd be willing to bet you supply her with more than career advice."

Sid moved away from his SUV and stood toe-to-toe with Martin. "She's still in pain."

"She seemed cozy with Mr. Presley."

"He's a friend."

"He's been tapping her, hasn't he."

"Melissa's personal life is none of my concern—or yours."

"And yet my sons are going home with you."

Sid looked back at the boys through the Escalade windows. "I think we're done here."

Martin stood his ground. "No, we're just getting started. My sons nearly died in the flood. Mel's broke. Her career is over. I know about her label's lawsuit and the IRS vultures circling over her waning assets. What I don't know is why she's with that cowboy circus act."

"Leland saved Jonathan's life."

"Jonathan should have never been put in that situation to begin with. Tomás was irresponsible."

"Tomás is dead."

Martin reached for his cigarettes. "Despite what you think of me, I'm still the boys' father."

Sid opened the driver's door. "Only on paper," he said before he climbed inside his luxury SUV and drove off.

Martin lit up and blew smoke. He wanted his old life back. A fresh start. A clean slate. An opportunity to undo the mess he'd made with his family. He couldn't change the past, but he could bury it and build a future. His boys would come around eventually. He could see it in their eyes. Melissa would prove the greater challenge.

He inhaled a long drag and shuffled toward his black BMW 850i parked near the back of the garage. He'd ordered flowers for Melissa's room with a box of her favorite chocolates. He had time on his side, and he had the law.

He drove from the hospital to his hotel, pursuing the same detour he'd traveled the night before. A hot shower and a meal at the onsite restaurant revived him before he caught the local news coverage of the ongoing flood relief efforts. "One second," he said inside his top floor suite when he heard the expected knock from his associate.

He powered off the flat screen and opened his room to a man in jeans and a brown leather jacket. "You dyed your hair."

The man entered the room. When the door closed behind him, he handed Martin a cash-filled envelop. "I need to stay under the radar."

"Anyone see you come up?"

"I waited in the car for awhile and came through the side entrance. No one saw me."

Martin counted the money. "I trust everything's in order?"

"The cops think I split town. How's the Mrs.?"

"You tell me."

"I did some digging like you asked. She's got money troubles for sure. The bank wants the house. Her record label has a law suit pending for breach of contract. She's sold a lot of property recently and several horses. The IRS is pressing her for back taxes."

Martin continued counting the large denomination bills. "What else?"

"The Mercedes was totaled in the flood. The house suffered some minor roof damage but nothing serious."

"What do you know about Leland Presley?"

"Who?"

"Some musician she's been seeing. I don't like the guy getting close to my boys."

"I can dig into him."

Martin peeled off several hundred dollars from the crumpled envelope and extended the cash. "For your time…Pull everything you can on Leland Presley. I want to know his life inside and out."

"What are you looking for?"

"Anything I can use."

CHAPTER 61

Leland woke up with Abby standing beside his bed. Still groggy, he rolled over to see his alarm clock flashing 12:00. "What time is it?"

"It's after 7:30," Abby informed him in her baggy shorts and a wrinkled T-shirt from the dryer. She wore her hair in a ponytail. "I'm going to be late for school."

"I thought you hated school?"

"I don't hate school. I hate being late for school."

"Why didn't you wake me up sooner?"

"I thought you were getting ready."

Leland threw the covers off and reached for his jeans on the chair beside the bed. "Geez Louise, the power must have gone out again."

"No kidding."

"I need five minutes."

"You've got two," said Abby, holding up two fingers in the air as she left with the cat galloping ahead of her.

Leland rubbed his eyes and stretched his arms above his head. He put his clothes on and splashed cold water on his face at the bathroom sink. He brushed his teeth in rapid fashion and found Abby in the living room petting her cat on the floor. "I'm ready."

Abby scratched her tabby's chin. "Why don't you get an alarm clock with a battery?"

"Because the one I have still works." He could hear the cat purring loudly.

"Newsflash, Dad. The Civil War called. They want their clock back."

"Very funny."

"Why don't you use the alarm on your phone?"

Leland looked at his flip phone. "What alarm?"

"Are you serious?"

Leland hugged his arm around Abby and kissed her forehead. "Are we good?"

"I talked to Nicole about Mom when you went to the hospital to see Mrs. Hamilton. Nicole agreed you should have told me about Mom sooner, but she also helped me see the issue from your perspective."

"As opposed to hearing my perspective from *me*?"

Abby gathered her backpack. "Nicole's smarter than I gave her credit for. She thinks you have real potential."

Leland couldn't decide if he wanted to thank Nicole or chastise her for inserting herself into his personal life again. "What else did Nicole tell you?"

"She thinks my mom has a right to see me despite what happened."

Leland grabbed his keys and brought Abby outside to his truck. "Nicole should worry about her own problems."

"I asked her what she thought. She gave me an honest answer."

"You're too young to have this sort of conversation with her."

"She told me you would say that."

Leland started the motor and backed out of the driveway. "Did she tell you how much I love you?"

Abby checked her makeup in the mirror. "Don't be cheesy."

"What's on your face?"

"Blush. Nicole gave me some of her makeup before she left. I like black eye liner too."

"You don't need makeup."

"I do if I don't want to look like a thirteen-year-old girl."

Leland drove through a yellow light up ahead. "You *are* a thirteen-year-old girl."

"You know what I mean."

"I think you're perfect the way God made you."

"When do you think I can see my mom?"

Leland bristled at the comment. "I'm not sure."

Abby leaned back in the truck's bench seat and zipped her lip gloss in her backpack. "Maybe she can have dinner with us sometime?"

"I'm not sure that's a good idea."

"Why not?"

"Because I don't want her around you."

"Are you telling me I can't see her?"

"I worry about you."

"That's not an answer."

"I think you need to move slowly. That's all I'm saying." Leland kept both hands on the wheel and drove in silence for the last few miles. He'd been hard on Abby about her mom and about her challenges at school. Probably too hard at times. He wanted the best for his only child. He wanted her to be safe and protected at all times. He also wanted her to accept herself for who she was and be happy with the life she had.

"I want a horse," Abby announced.

"Save your allowance."

"I'm serious."

"Me too."

Abby's eyes narrowed. "You still owe me like four week's worth."

"I know."

"Jonathan and Adam had a horse, but their mom sold it. I told them they should get a job and buy it back."

"Horses are expensive."

"So are big houses and fancy cars. You don't hear me asking for one of those."

"Not yet. Wait 'til you get your driver's license."

"I don't care about cars."

"Then you'll be happy to drive this truck."

Abby looked away and twirled her hair.

Leland drove around a section of damaged roadway under repair. FEMA trailers occupied a parking lot across the street. "I can drop you in front of the school."

"I'll walk."

"What about your ankle?"

"It's fine."

"What time should I pick you up from detention?"

"Detention's over."

"Your principal doesn't think so."

"My principal hates my guts. She wanted to throw me in jail for macing that bully on the bus."

Leland slowed at the next intersection. "She thinks you have great potential."

"What do you think?"

"I think you better hustle, or you're going to be late again." Leland eased along the curb and stopped.

Abby got out and slung her backpack on her shoulder. She gave her dad a fleeting wave good bye.

Leland drove slow enough to track Abby's progress in his side view mirror. Regardless of the tragic events in recent past, he'd finally achieved some balance in his life. With the benefit concert looming and the promise of better things to come, he had momentum in his career—and new love in his sights.

CHAPTER 62

Melissa gathered her personal belongings from her hospital room and stuffed them in her Gucci bag while her boys looked on. "This is ridiculous," she told the nurse who arrived with a wheelchair. "My boys can help me out."

"Hospital policy," the nurse replied.

"We'll manage," Melissa snapped. She rubbed her lower back, tired and sore from a sleepless night fed by an intravenous cocktail of buprenorphine and Motrin to counter her withdrawal symptoms.

"I'll push you," Jonathan offered.

"I'll do it," Adam argued.

Melissa sat in the wheelchair with her bag on her lap and her feet in the metal footrests. She touched her hair, anxious to leave the premises before the paparazzi caught up with her. "Let's go," she told her boys who pushed the chair with one hand on each handle bar. "Not too fast!" she scolded them. "This isn't a roller derby." She checked her phone for messages. "Where's Sid?"

"He left after he dropped us off," said Jonathan, who helped his brother push his mom inside the open elevator. "He said he had shit to do."

Melissa ignored her son's colorful recollection of Sid's agenda and rode the elevator to the ground floor. She apologized for snapping at them and blamed her bad mood on the withdrawal suppression meds.

Outside, she ditched the wheelchair and walked to her rented Mercedes SUV while her boys carried her bags.

"Can I drive?" asked Jonathan.

"Do you have your license?"

"No."

"Then stop asking me."

"Dad said he would teach me."

Melissa climbed inside and adjusted the power lumbar support. "You don't even have your learner's permit."

"Is Dad going to live with us again?" asked Adam.

Melissa started the motor and shifted the SUV in reverse. "What did he tell you?"

"Nothing."

"Your dad's in town to see a client."

"Is he going back to California?" asked Jonathan.

As much as I can help it, Melissa thought to herself. She drove out of the parking lot and made her way toward home. "Your dad's only here temporarily."

"Why can't he stay?" Adam persisted.

"Because he lives in California."

"What if he moves back to Tennessee?"

"Do you want him to?" Melissa glanced in the rear view mirror to see Adam turn away. She recalled her conversation with Principal Hendrix and her lecture on father figures. The woman had no business poking at her personal affairs, but she preached a hell of a sermon.

"Why do you hate him so much?" asked Jonathan.

"I don't hate your father. I disapprove of his actions."

"Because he moved away from us?"

"Because of a lot of things."

"He said he could take us to school tomorrow. It's our last day."

"We'll see."

"I'm not taking the bus," Jonathan stated flatly.

"I'll drop you off."

"Why can't Dad?" Jonathan persisted.

"Because I don't think it's a good idea."

"Why not?"

Melissa gripped the steering wheel, her frustration escalating with her pulse. "Jonathan, please! Enough! Either I take you, or you ride the bus. End of discussion." She reached in her purse out of habit. Now the prescription that nearly destroyed her was gone, along with her desire to continue down a path of substance abuse disguised as self medication. The mild heart attack had been a rude awakening for her. A potent reminder of life's frailty. The thought of here today, gone forever had rocked her world and forced an immediate course correction. More than anything, she missed Leland's touch, the way his hands caressed her skin. The way he looked at her. And his voice…

She cursed under her breath when she reached the gated entrance to her estate to find Martin standing beside his car in the driveway.

"Dad's here!" Jonathan announced.

Melissa parked the SUV and shut the motor off. "I want you guys to go inside and start your homework."

"We don't have any."

Melissa gave Jonathan her keys. "Then play a video game or something."

"What about Dad?"

"He's not staying," Melissa said emphatically. She waited for her boys to enter the house and took a second to collect herself. "You shouldn't be here!" she demanded when Martin approached her and dropped his cigarette butt on the ground.

"No love from my boys?"

"I sent them inside."

Martin put his arms out for a hug. "I called the hospital. They said they released you today. I would have come by to get you…"

Melissa rebuffed his advance. "I can manage on my own."

"And our boys?"

"The boys are fine."

"I asked your real estate agent to draw up the papers on the house."

"It's not for sale anymore."

"Don't do this, Mel. I'm throwing you a life line here."

"I don't need your help."

Martin produced a folded envelop from his pocket. "This came today."

"Are you going through my mail?"

"Both our names were on the address. Back taxes are killing you. The IRS could seize your property."

"Are you finished?"

Martin gestured toward the house. "You can't ignore the situation. The government will come down on you. Hard."

"I'll handle it."

"How?"

"None of your business."

"It is when my boys are living here. What's going to happen to them when you're homeless?"

"Don't be so melodramatic. Nothing's going to happen to them."

"My offer on the house is fair. You won't get a better price in this market."

Melissa put her hands on her hips. She could see the boys spying through the drapes in the living room. "Not interested."

"I can stall the IRS for you. I know a colleague who specializes in tax fraud evasion."

"I'm not evading anything. I'll pay what I owe."

"When?"

"When I have the money."

"You're broke, Mel. If the IRS doesn't take your property, the bank will." Martin put his hands up in a defensive posture. "All I'm saying...I think you're in over your head. Our boys need me in their lives. You can hate me all you want, but don't let it spill onto them."

"Spare me the *Mea Culpa*. You had your chance to make right by us, and you spit in our face. I've moved on with my life. Our boys have too."

"And how does Leland Presley fit in?"

"Wherever he wants to." Melissa saw Martin's expression change abruptly when the words hit home. "Stay away from me. And stay away from our boys."

CHAPTER 63

Leland softly strummed his acoustic Gibson to produce the melody he'd written the day before. He closed his eyes and imagined Melissa's image, her very essence captured in the lyrics he'd penned before he set the words to music and brought a new song to life while Abby's cat howled outside his door. Unfazed by the feline accompaniment, he stopped playing when he heard Abby scream, "*DAD!*"

"It's late," he called out from the makeshift studio he'd assembled in his room.

"Come here..."

Leland rested his guitar in its stand. "Hold on."

Abby stood in the hall and pointed at her room. "I heard a noise."

"What kind of noise?"

"I think there's a bug in my room. A cricket or one of those flying cicada bugs."

"Abby…"

"I'm serious. You know I hate those."

Leland scooped the orange tabby and rubbed his fur. "I'll throw Tiger in there and let him find it."

"I don't want him to eat it."

"Then you won't have the bug anymore."

"What if Tiger gets sick?"

"What if you let this go and try to get some sleep?"

"Nicole let me stay up until eleven."

"Nicole's not here anymore." Leland felt his phone vibrate in his pocket. He set the cat down and read a text message from Melissa.

"Who's that from?"

"Don't worry about it."

"Jonathan said his mom came home from the hospital."

"Good to know."

Leland's phone buzzed again. "You need to get back in bed."

"I'm not tired."

"You will be when you close your eyes."

"What about the bug?"

Leland gave her room a cursory inspection. "Do you want me to sing tonight?"

"Dad…"

"I'll break out the ukulele."

"To scare the bug away?"

Leland tugged the lamp chain on Abby's nightstand. "You want your door open or closed?"

"Leave it open so Tiger can get in."

"I think the bug's outside your window."

"It sounded louder a minute ago."

Leland stayed by the door. "Good night, Abby."

Abby called the orange tabby, who purred loudly with his tail in the air. "Dad," she said in a quiet voice. "I liked the song you were playing."

"I didn't know you were listening."

"I'm always listening."

Leland closed the door gently and flipped open his phone to re-read Melissa's invitation for an impromptu rendezvous. The timing was bad, but he wanted to see her again.

He scrolled through the names in his contact list until he came across Nicole's. He hesitated before he made the call, contemplating his half-baked plan before he made his decision and pressed the phone to his ear. When he heard Nicole reply, he asked, "Could you watch Abby for me tonight?"

Melissa kicked at a clump of hay inside her empty barn, contemplating Martin's offer on the house. She missed Tomás, and she missed her horses. So much had changed in recent weeks with her life turned inside out. But she had her boys, and she had an amazing man in her life who made her feel like anything was possible. *Dream big or go home,* she told herself, staring through the open barn door at the star-filled sky. She slid her hand in the back pocket of her favorite skinny jeans—the ones she wore without underwear—and a form-fitting blouse unbuttoned lower than she'd dare to wear in public.

Headlights approached from the access road adjacent to the edge of her property. Desire swelled within her when she recognized Leland's ride. "Sanford and Son called," she said when Leland jumped out to greet her. "They want their truck back."

Leland bent down to kiss her. "I got here as soon as I could."

"I missed you. I wasn't sure if you'd be able to come at all."

"I found someone to stay with Abby."

"I assume this *someone* knows you're taken." Melissa brought him toward the barn with a blanket spread over fresh hay. "I hope you don't mind the accommodations. My boys are in the house with Sid."

Leland scanned the empty barn with clean floors and new lumber to replace the rotten wood. "I like what you did with the place."

Melissa kissed him on the mouth more vigorously this time. Then she removed her top to reveal her naked breasts. "Did you miss me?"

"More than you know."

Melissa felt Leland's hands on her hips, sliding south in a hurry to help unveil her from her jeans. She unbuckled his belt and unzipped his pants.

Leland kissed her passionately, cupping his hands along the side of her face. He sank with her to the padded blanket and caressed her body.

Melissa felt his arm beneath her and leaned in for another kiss, trembling with every uneven breath as Leland's warmth pressed against her, then within her. She looked up at his soothing green eyes with her hands on his shoulders, pulling him closer until everything about her life made sense again.

Leland pondered the stars through an opening in the rafters above while Melissa rested hear head on his chest, her naked body nestled against him. "What are you thinking?"

"I want you to spend the night with me."

"In the barn?"

Melissa rubbed her hand on his chest. "I didn't hear you complaining."

"What about your boys?"

"They're fine," she said, enjoying the afterglow. "I love my boys, but I need a break from it all."

"I missed you."

Melissa raised her head. "I missed *us*."

"No more hospital adventures."

"No more pills," Melissa added.

"Are you in pain?"

"Not with you here."

"Any offers on your house?"

"My ex-husband still wants to buy it. He couldn't leave fast enough five years ago. Now he pops up like nothing happened. Thinks he can turn his life around and make up for lost time. He doesn't deserve me or our boys."

"How do your boys feel about him?"

"Jonathan's indifferent. Adam craves the attention. Ever since Tomás died, Adam hasn't been himself."

Leland caressed her backside with his fingertips. "Do you think we'll recover from the flood?"

"Nashville is a strong city. Things will get better. What about your concert? Are you ready to command the stage?"

Leland lowered his hand to the small of her back. "I'm good."

"What does Sid think about it?"

"He thinks I should join The Wiggles."

Melissa tapped his chest. "He does not!"

"What about your album?"

"I'm still trying to line up the right connections. I'm not exactly Carrie Underwood."

"She's not exactly Melissa Hamilton."

Melissa rolled on top of him with her hips firmly planted on his pelvis. Beads of perspiration damped her forehead. "Good answer."

CHAPTER 64

Martin followed his GPS directions on I-40 heading east toward a Cracker Barrel exit. He drove through heavy traffic, glancing at the notes in his Steno Book as he made his way toward a low-rent apartment complex nestled behind a Food Lion. He followed the road beyond the leasing office to a shaded, brick-front building with faded white balconies overlooking a picnic area with graffiti-carved tables and a public grill.

He parked in a handicap zone and climbed to the second floor with his black attaché case. He knocked on Paula Presley's apartment and introduced himself as Martin Hamilton, attorney at law.

"Do I know you?" Paula asked through the gap in the partially open door, where she eyed the lawyer in a double-breasted jacket with wavy blond hair and glasses.

"Is your husband Leland Presley?"

"Yes. What do you want?"

"I'd like to talk with you about him if you don't mind."

"What for?"

"May I come in?"

Paula clutched the aluminum baseball bat hidden from Martin's view behind the door. "How did you find me?"

"My associate contacted someone at your former residence at the hospital."

"You mean the psyche ward." Paula opened the door as far as the chain lock allowed. She kept the bat at her side, just in case. "Who sent you?"

Martin pointed inside the apartment. "If I may?"

Paula gripped the bat tighter. She sized up Martin's stature with his fancy clothes and polite demeanor. Then she slid the chain lock free and opened her apartment. "Just for a second. I have errands to run."

Martin noticed the bat and moved slowly. He rested his attaché case on a pine coffee table centered with faux flowers in a glass bead vase. "This won't take long." He popped the latches and retrieved a folder with copies of legal documents inside. "I'm aware you've filed for joint custody of your daughter, Abigail Presley."

Paula leaned the bat against the wall. "Why do you care?"

"Because I think we can help each other."

"How?"

"I've reached out to your attorney, and he's verbally agreed to enlist my help as co-counsel in your custody case. I need your signature to formally authorize my participation."

"My lawyer never mentioned you."

"He's been tied up in court." Martin handed her the co-counsel agreement. "I understand you had some issues in your past." He glanced about the sparsely furnished room and noticed the lack of any family photos.

"I tried to kill myself when my daughter was eighteen months old. I never meant to hurt her. I had some problems, but they're behind me now." She reviewed the pages of legal jargon while she paced inside the small apartment. "I can't afford to pay another lawyer."

"My time would be gratis."

"Gratis?"

"Without charge. Free."

"Nothing in life comes free, Mr. Hamilton." She scrutinized the legal paperwork, oblivious to the carefully embedded language acknowledging her consent to release Abby's medical records. "I can read, but I can't make heads or tails of what this paper says. I'm not about to sign—"

"It's a standard co-counsel agreement. Basically, it states you would now have two attorneys working together on your behalf instead of one. I can email the signed copy to your attorney this afternoon." He analyzed Paula's body language and the strange way she counted on her fingers while she reviewed the legal documents. "Do you have regular contact with your husband?"

"Only when I have to."

"I would keep it that way. The less Leland knows about our conversation, the better."

"And you're certain you can help me with my daughter?"

"There are no certainties with the law, Mrs. Presley, but the odds are in your favor."

Paula discretely slid a forged ID badge off the counter and secured it in a drawer. "And what about my past?"

"We can't ignore it, but I don't believe it will be the deciding factor."

"How do you know?"

Martin ignored the smart phone vibrating in his pocket. "I've practiced law for a long time now. Your case is not unique. People are human. They make mistakes."

Paula settled on the fabric loveseat across from Martin. An argument erupted in the apartment upstairs, followed by loud stomping on the ceiling. "When the accident happened, I told myself it was God's will."

"Maybe. But I suspect the devil had a hand in it."

"I had no intention of drowning my daughter. Munchausen by Proxy, the doctors called it."

"I believe you."

Paula shifted her position on the loveseat with the legal paperwork on her lap. "Do you have children, Mr. Hamilton?"

"Two boys."

"You seem like a decent man."

"I try to do what's right."

"Amen to that." Paula reached for a pen to sign the papers and gave them back. "What's in this for you?"

"A chance to help someone who deserves a fresh start."

"But why me? How did you even know about my case?"

"Serendipity, Mrs. Presley. Sometimes people cross paths for a reason."

"I suppose you're right."

Martin closed his attaché case and stood up. "Thank you for your time," he said as he let himself out. He descended the stairs to the parking lot and found a blob of white bird shit on the roof of his gleaming BMW. He cursed out loud and tried to clean it with a tissue from his pocket, but the effort only made it worse.

He dropped the tissue on the ground and opened the car to settle in the driver's seat. He checked his voice mail. Then he left the apartment complex and headed for Music Row to meet the infamous Brad Siegel in person.

CHAPTER 65

Leland drove to Sid's office with Abby and found his daughter's usual strong-willed banter replaced by a more subdued teenage girl—one who obviously had something on her mind but wasn't prepared to talk about it. In contrast, Sid's request for a face-to-face meeting in his office implied one of two things: Sid had bad news to share, or Sid had *very* bad news to share.

Leland knew the record deal was short term. He also knew Brad Siegel didn't take kindly to casting unsigned musicians for his boy band experiment, no matter how much clout he leveraged to ensure the band's successful debut at the benefit concert.

He kept his focus on the road without acknowledging the random sighs from Abby texting with her phone in her lap. "This shouldn't take long," he said, hoping to infiltrate Abby's invisible cone of silence. "Sid probably needs me to sign some papers."

Abby looked up from her phone. "I hope you're not getting fired."

Leland hung a left on a green arrow. "Why would you think that?"

"If Sid called with good news, you'd be in a better mood."

"I'm in a great mood. I'm just thinking about the concert."

Abby read an incoming text from Jonathan. "You haven't said two words since you dragged me out of the house."

Leland squeezed the wheel. "I didn't *drag* you anywhere."

"Then why couldn't I stay home?"

"Because there's no one to watch you."

"You could take me to Jonathan's house."

"His mom just left the hospital. She doesn't need another body to manage."

"You think I'm hard to manage?"

"I didn't say that."

"But you were thinking it."

"Abby…"

"You told me we were going fishing today."

"I know, but it's been a crazy day. I wasn't planning to meet with Sid."

Abby replied to Jonathan's text with a sad emoji at the end of her message. "What am I going to do all summer?"

"Let's focus on today."

"Nicole still loves you."

"What are you talking about?"

"She told me. I hope you know what you're doing."

"You let me worry about my personal life."

"Why can't we buy a new truck?"

"Because there's nothing wrong with the one we have."

"Everything's wrong with the one we have."

"It has character."

"It's embarrassing."

"Not for me."

"Because you're old."

Leland laughed. "I'll tell you what," he said with an upbeat tone, "I'll buy a new truck when you graduate from college."

"I can't go to college."

"Sure you can."

"Not with only one hand to type."

"You don't have to type at all to go to college."

"You do if you want to graduate and get a job."

"Says who?"

"Everybody at school."

Leland parked in front of Sid's office building. "Define *everybody*."

"Whatever…"

Leland cupped Abby's chin in his hand and squared her face with his. "Look at me. You have two eyes, two ears, a tremendous brain, and a big heart. You have everything to succeed in this life and more. Don't ever let anyone tell you different."

Abby blinked, somewhat startled by her dad's evangelistic tone. "What happens if you lose this gig?"

"I'll work construction until the next one comes along."

"Will we have to move again?"

"I don't know."

"I hate moving."

Leland climbed out of the truck and walked around to open Abby's door. "Me too."

Sid admired the autographed head shot of George Straight on the wall in his office. He had Brad Siegel on speakerphone, contemplating a risky proposition to a problem neither party expected to address.

"*You still there?*" Brad Siegel's voice boomed from the phone on Sid's desk.

Sid poured himself a double bourbon. "I'm here."

"*Alone?*"

"Do we have a deal or not?"

"*I don't like it.*"

"It's not our first rodeo."

"*My ass is on the line, Sid. This band goes live in three days. I need assurances. If this goes south—*"

"I'll save you a spot in the unemployment line."

"*The contract stands as is. I'm not budging on the fee.*"

"Sure you are," Sid countered assertively. "We're the only play you've got."

"I can have a second option in my office in an hour."

"If that were true, you wouldn't still be on the phone with me." Sid swirled the bourbon in his tumbler. "Do we have a deal or not?"

"Fine," Brad continued after a long silence. "Does your boy even know what's happening?"

Sid peered out his office window to see Leland's truck out front. "I'll explain the situation."

"Don't make me regret this."

"You won't," Sid declared. He ended the call and finished his drink, quietly contemplating the new deal with Brad. When he heard the elevator, he greeted Leland and Abby outside his office. "Perfect timing," he told Leland. Then he shifted his attention to Abby and said, "I'm going to let you wait in the other room while your dad and I talk in here."

"I go where he goes," Abby declared.

Sid took out his wallet and gave Abby twenty dollars. "This won't take long."

"Deal."

Leland followed Sid inside his office. "Sorry about that. Abby can be a little headstrong at times."

Sid shut the door and settled behind his desk. "She's going to put me out of a job."

"Say what you need to say," Leland blurted in a slightly defeated tone.

"There's been a change in plans."

"Then I want severance pay. Brad Siegel can't replace me last second without—"

"No one's replacing you," Sid interjected. "Jimmie Lockhorn came down with laryngitis."

"Since when?"

"This morning. He's been fighting it for a couple days, but his voice can't take the strain anymore. That's why your last rehearsal was canceled."

"Where does this leave me?"

"Center stage."

"What do you mean?"

"Brad's got a guitarist lined up to replace you. You're going to replace Jimmie on lead vocals."

"Me?"

"You know the music and the lyrics. Brad's heard you sing before."

"I've rehearsed on rhythm guitar. I never memorized the lyrics."

"Then I suggest you start."

"Now?"

"It's one song."

"It's not about regurgitating words. There has to be emotion. A personal connection to the song. I didn't write this music. If I can't get people to believe in me, I might as well lip sync the show."

"I'm not asking you to win a Grammy."

"But you're asking me to lead someone else's band on the biggest stage I've ever played."

"The same band you've been rehearsing with for days."

"On rhythm guitar."

"You could do this in your sleep."

"If I had a week to practice."

"You trying to talk yourself out of this gig?"

"I'm trying to be realistic."

Sid slammed his empty glass on the desk. "You don't get to pick and choose opportunities like this. I sold Brad Siegel on you, a musician of relative obscurity, not a seasoned artist I could have plucked from my A-list catalogue and negotiated twice the fee. This is your opportunity, Leland. I suggest you think long and hard about the direction you want your career to go. Stop trying to bend the bow backwards. You've been fighting for your shot. You better step up and take it."

CHAPTER 66

Melissa grabbed a bottle of maple syrup from the pantry and gave it to her boys at the dining table. She poured herself a cup of coffee and skimmed the front page of the morning paper to read about the city's recovery effort. "I'm leaving in ten minutes!"

Jonathan poked his fork at the waffle on his plate. "This syrup tastes funny."

"It's the same one I always buy."

"I like the other brand better."

"They didn't have the other brand. They all taste the same."

"The other one tastes sweeter."

"You'll survive."

"My waffle's cold in the middle," Adam whined.

Melissa skimmed the front page. "Then put it in the microwave."

"The microwave makes it soggy."

Melissa put down the paper, exasperated, and snatched Adam's waffle from his plate. She dropped it in the toaster for another cycle and said, "You boys have eight minutes."

Jonathan cut his waffle with his fork and mopped the bite size portion through the puddle of maple syrup on his plate. He read a text message on his phone and sent a short reply. "Can I stay at Abby's house tonight?"

"No," Melissa answered. "Now finish up and brush your teeth."

"Why not?"

"Because it's a school night. And you're not spending the night at a girl's house."

"We're just friends. And today's the last day of school."

"I don't care."

"Her dad said it's okay."

Melissa rolled her eyes. "Her dad's delusional. Now finish your breakfast." She slipped her fingers through her coffee mug handle and carried her drink with her phone to the other room. She craved a conversation with Leland as soon as she had five minutes to spare.

"*Mom!*" she heard Jonathan groan from the kitchen. "The dishwasher's still full of clean dishes."

"Then empty it!"

"Where do the clean dishes go?"

Melissa stuffed her phone in her purse and grabbed her car keys from the glass bowl in the foyer. She felt alone in the house with her boys, who had good intentions, but no direction. With Tomás gone, they were lost. They needed a solid role model as much as she needed someone kind and thoughtful. Loyal. Honest. Caring. A man with strong morals and a positive attitude toward life. These things she needed to feel whole again; to know her future held more than a series of risqué encounters with a handsome man who stole her heart and played with her emotions like a concert pianist. Music had always been at the center of her life. Now a stronger need emerged. The need to love and be loved. To give freely and unconditionally of herself, and in return, to feel cherished as an equal partner in an honest relationship rooted by friendship and trust. Lofty expectations, perhaps, but she deserved at least as much. Her boys deserved it too.

* * *

Leland dropped Abby at school and followed the Audi A6 in front of him. He drove to an upscale café where eggs and toast would set him back twenty bucks without a drink or tip. Melissa always offered to pay. He always firmly declined. This morning, he left his appetite at home, more consumed by the pressure of his upcoming performance than his need for sustenance.

He arrived at the swanky bistro a few minutes early and claimed a table in the art-lined setting with real linens and high-back chairs. He'd trade the food and drink for Waffle House any day, but the place made Melissa happy.

He ordered water for himself and checked his phone. And then, almost as if on cue, Melissa appeared and promptly made her way toward him. He greeted her with open arms. "I got here early."

Melissa kissed him. She rubbed her hands on his forearms. "I missed you."

"I missed you too."

"Did you order yet?"

"I wanted to wait for you."

Melissa took her seat across from Leland and helped herself to his ice water. "Today's my treat."

"Not this time," Leland vetoed.

"I have good news!"

Leland's eyes lit up with excitement and curiosity. "Tell me."

"My label dropped the lawsuit."

"That's fantastic! What happened?"

Melissa laid her arms on the table and reached out to hold Leland's hands. "Sid worked it out with Wharton Brothers. Don't ask me how. One minute they're threatening to sue me, and the next thing I know, they drop the case and make an offer to promote my music."

Leland kissed her hand and let go. "I told you everything would work out."

"Now I can move forward with the festival tour. A lot of big names are headlining this year. It's an ensemble group and a chance to reestablish my career."

"When does the tour kick off?"

"Not for a few weeks, but they want me involved sooner. I want you to come with me."

Leland twisted the spinner ring on his finger. "How would that work?"

"I'm not sure exactly. We can figure it out as we go."

"What about Abby?"

"What about her? She would come with you, of course."

"What about your new album?"

"I'll finish it on the road."

Leland acknowledged the waitress who approached the table in a short skirt and bobbed hairstyle. "We're good," he said, not wanting to disrupt his conversation for the sake of ordering food. "What about your boys?"

"They would love it." Melissa smiled. "Think about it."

"I will."

"What about your big news? I've been running my mouth non-stop since I got here."

"It's no big deal."

"What's so important you couldn't tell me on the phone?"

"Jimmie Lockhorn came down with laryngitis. Brad Siegel wants me to take his place and lead the band."

Melissa cupped a hand over her mouth. "Wow! That's great! When did this happen?"

"Last night."

"You must be thrilled."

"I'm still trying to wrap my head around it."

"Brad Siegel's a jerk, but he's smart. Capital Country Records would eat their young before they'd take a chance on someone they don't believe in. You're an asset to their label, and they know it. Don't underestimate yourself."

"You're starting to sound like Sid."

"Maybe he knows what he's doing after all?" Melissa let a short laugh escape. "What does Abby think?"

"I haven't told her yet."

"Why not?"

"I don't want to disappoint her."

Melissa leaned over the table and kissed him. "You're a sweet man, Leland Presley. You could never disappoint your daughter."

CHAPTER 67

Martin lowered his window in the car loop line outside Parkview Middle School and flicked his cigarette to the curb as the final bell rang. He had plans for the future and every intention of achieving his goals in light of a few unexpected setbacks along the way. He liked the boys' school, although he preferred them to have a private education—an issue he would broach with Melissa before the next school year. He wanted the best for his boys, which meant injecting himself in their lives as a positive role model. He was, after all, their flesh and blood. His boys needed a real man in their lives, someone with the means to provide for them and their mother.

He got out of his BMW and looked back at the school to see Jonathan and Adam emerge from a crowd of students making their way toward the parking lot. He put two fingers in his mouth and whistled loudly to draw the boys' attention.

"Where's mom?" Jonathan asked when he and Adam approached their dad.

"She's busy."

"Does she know you're here?" asked Adam.

Martin opened the trunk with his key fob. "She sent me to pick you up. Drop your bags. We gotta go."

The boys put their bags in the trunk and settled in the back seat.

"We should send her a text," said Adam when his dad got behind the wheel.

"And spoil the surprise?"

"What surprise?" asked Jonathan. He stretched his shoulder belt across his chest and buckled the latch.

Martin cut the wheel and pulled out of the car loop line. He accelerated briskly across the school property and merged with traffic heading east outside the city. "You guys will like it. Your mom will too."

"Mom doesn't like surprises," said Jonathan.

"She'll like this one."

Jonathan looked at his dad. "Why does Mom hate you?"

"Your mom doesn't hate me. She's just confused. Women get that way sometimes."

"All women?" asked Adam.

"Pretty much."

"Are you going to live with us again?"

Martin glanced at Adam in the rear view mirror. "I'm not going anywhere."

"You were gone a long time."

"I didn't mean to. My work sort of got in the way."

"Mom told us another woman got in the way," said Jonathan.

"Your mom and I don't always agree on everything, but we both want what's best for you and your brother."

"Mom says you're moving back to California," said Adam.

"I'm not moving back to California."

"Where is this surprise?" asked Jonathan.

"You'll see."

"Give us a hint."

"It's bigger than you expect."

"Is it money?"

"No."

"Is it a new Bentley?"

"No."

"Is it a new house?"

Martin continued out of town toward more rural countryside. He cracked his window and lit a cigarette. "If I told you what it was, it wouldn't be a surprise."

"Were you here for the flood?"

"I was in California. But I heard about it. I'm really sorry it happened."

"Tomás died in the storm," Adam muttered somberly.

"I know…"

"Mr. Presley rescued Jonathan."

"Your mom told me."

"I wish someone had rescued Tomás."

Martin took a long drag on his cigarette and drove faster when the traffic thinned out. "Tomás was a good chauffeur. I feel bad about what happened."

Adam grabbed the headrest in front of him and leaned forward. "Why didn't you come to his funeral?"

"I was in California."

"Why did you move there in the first place?"

Martin blew smoke at the open window and pondered Adam's question. "Maybe we can get out the bats and balls this summer."

"We don't play baseball anymore," Jonathan replied before his brother could answer.

"Since when?"

"We outgrew it."

"You never outgrow baseball."

"Mom takes us to the country club. They have a nice pool there."

Martin slowed off the highway and hung a left at a four-way stop. He drove until he reached a gravel driveway and followed the entrance to an old farm house situated on several acres of open land surrounded by triple-rail fence.

"Where are we?" asked Adam.

"We're here…"

"Is this our surprise?" the boys asked together.

"You'll see." Martin parked the BMW outside the farm house with faded shutters and a wraparound porch with a self-supporting hammock and a roof with missing shingles. He got out with the boys and approached the property when the screen door opened to a bearded man in overalls and rubber boots.

"You're right on time," the man announced.

"Mr. Cooper," said Martin, shaking hands with the property owner. "Good to see you again."

"You brought the whole crew this time."

Martin gestured toward his boys. "These are my sons, Jonathan and Adam."

Mr. Cooper shook hands with the boys. "Jim Cooper. Nice to meet you both." He redirected his attention to Martin. "Do they know?"

"Not yet."

"You wanna take them out or should I?"

"Your property."

"She's your animal."

Martin followed Mr. Cooper around the back of the house with Jonathan and Adam trailing behind. "I appreciate your time."

"I appreciate your offer. I served the Army for twenty-seven years. Now I serve this farm. My nephew helps out from time to time. Don't get many folks out here anymore, beyond neighbors and family."

Martin stopped at the fence line and pointed toward the center of the grassy flatland near a pond, where a black Tennessee mare pawed at the dirt and faced the group. He noticed his sons' expressions change from bored to bewildered to elated. "Does she look familiar?"

"Sabrina?" asked Jonathan.

"Call her name, son. She's waiting for you."

Jonathan looked at Adam in disbelief. "I thought Mom sold her?"

"She did," said Martin. "I bought her back."

"Can we keep her this time?" Jonathan asked on the verge of tears while his brother waved his arm to draw the horse's attention.

"She's your horse. She belongs with you."

"I thought you bought us a pig or something!" Adam exclaimed. "This is awesome!"

"You deserve to have her," Martin told his youngest son. Then he looked back at Mr. Cooper. "I hate to ask, but could I borrow your trailer?"

Mr. Cooper pointed to the Chevy Silverado out front. "Leave your car and take my truck. I'm already hitched."

CHAPTER 68

Martin towed the horse trailer through the open gate at the entrance to Melissa's estate. "I'll need you to help me unload her," he told Jonathan and Adam in the Silverado's crew cab.

"No problem," said Jonathan from behind the driver's seat, engaged in a text message dialogue with Abby.

"Me too," Adam chimed in, peering over the front headrest to see his mom outside the house. "What about your car?"

"I'll get it when I take the truck back."

Adam shifted in his seat to view the horse trailer in tow. "I thought we'd never see her again."

Martin glanced up at the rear view mirror. "She's a beautiful animal. You do right by her, and she'll do right by you."

"Mom's going to be surprised!" said Adam.

Martin slowed when Melissa stormed toward the truck. He waved his hand from the top of the steering wheel and braced for the verbal assault.

"What the hell is going on?" Melissa fumed the instant Martin stepped out. "Where the hell have you been? I called the boys. I called your cell. No one answered. Not even a text message."

"Everything's fine."

"When I got to their school, the principal told me you picked up the boys. I never authorized you to take them. I was worried something happened."

"Don't blame the boys."

"I'm blaming you! I've been trying to reach you for hours!"

"We were busy."

"I called the police. Twice."

"We brought Sabrina home!" Adam interrupted.

Melissa charged toward the back of the trailer. "I can't believe you did this," she said to Martin who followed close behind.

"Sabrina belongs to the boys."

Melissa made a sweeping arm gesture to emphasize her point. "You had no right."

"I thought you'd be happy. The boys need a win. They've been through a lot lately."

"Are you delusional? You have no idea what our boys have been through. The fact that you kidnapped them to buy a horse I sold to someone else only makes things worse."

Martin ran his hand through his hair. "I didn't kidnap them. They're my sons too. This horse belongs to them."

"You should have consulted me first."

"Not my style."

"You mean, not your problem. Who's going to take care of this animal when I go on tour? I can't afford to board a horse. Why do you think I sold her in the first place?"

"We'll work something out."

Melissa stomped away from the trailer out of earshot from her boys and waited for Martin to catch up. "There is nothing to work out. We're not keeping this horse."

Martin lit a cigarette and blew smoke through his nose. "Relax. The boys can muck a stall as well as anyone."

"The boys are going on tour with me."

Martin drew a long breath through the filtered Kool and grimaced. "We never talked about this."

"There is no *we*. This whole thing, this, mess you keep stirring up. This damn horse. This was never a mutual decision. This is you doing something foolish because it makes you feel good."

Martin flicked ash at the ground while his boys interacted with Sabrina in the trailer. "You and the boys have lost so much."

"The boys have everything they need."

"I just want to help."

"We don't need your help, and we don't need your charity."

"The boys deserve more."

"The boys deserve *better*. I know what you're trying to do. I think it's pathetic."

"Mel…"

"Don't call me that. I hate it when you call me that."

Martin blew smoke as the boys approached. "What do you want me to do?"

"Take her back."

"She's not a puppy I picked up from the pound. I can't just turn around and take her back."

"Sure you can."

"I made a deal."

"Not my problem."

"We can't take her back!" Jonathan exclaimed.

"We have to keep her!" said Adam. "She belongs to us!"

"Your dad made a mistake."

"Please!" both boys exclaimed. "We'll take good care of her."

Melissa pointed toward the house. "Go inside."

"Sabrina wants to live here."

"Sabrina already has a new home. Your dad's going to return her there."

"Dad?" Jonathan pleaded.

Martin looked away. "I'm sorry."

"Please!"

"Get inside," Melissa ordered.

"This isn't fair," said Jonathan.

Melissa held her ground and kept her anger in check. "We're not keeping the horse."

Jonathan stomped toward the house. "I hate you!"

"Same here!" said Adam, who followed his brother in disgust.

Martin dropped his cigarette butt and crushed it under his shoe. "Not too late to change your mind," he told Melissa.

"What you did was wrong."

"I disagree."

Melissa pointed to the truck. "Get out of here. You've done enough damage already."

Martin climbed inside the cab and gave Melissa a token wave. Then he mumbled to himself, "Checkmate."

CHAPTER 69

Melissa settled into a booth by herself in the downstairs bar at Robert's Western World, a place she wouldn't typically frequent, if not for Leland and the lasting impression he'd made on her.

Live music filled the air from young musicians on upright bass and steel guitar in the self-proclaimed home of traditional country music. The tang of cheap beer, fried bologna, and sweet potato fries barely moved the needle on her appetite, but she wasn't there for midnight snacks or live music. She wanted the one person she could open up to about anything, without remorse or second-guessing her intentions; a man she experienced an almost soul-mate connection with. Leland Presley brought her joy, and for the first time in many years, she found herself falling in love again.

She flagged a waiter and ordered a drink. When she saw Leland enter the bar, she stood up and received him with an assertive kiss. "What took you so long?"

Leland dragged a chair beside her and settled in. He held Melissa's hand on the table, ignoring the drunk patron playing grab-ass with the waitress at the booth beside him. "Since when do you hang out at hillbilly diners?"

"Best cheeseburger on Broadway."

"And the prettiest woman in Nashville."

Melissa grinned. Her brown eyes danced in the warmth of Leland's affection. "You mean, Tennessee."

Leland kissed her. "Yes ma'am."

"Thank you for meeting me so late. I didn't think you'd be able to get away. Where's Abby?"

"At home with a sitter."

"How'd you manage that at this hour?"

"I tip well."

"I bet you do," Melissa baited him. "Sid came to my house to check on me, so I left the boys with him." She laughed quietly. "Does that make me a bad person? I needed a break, and I wanted time alone with you." She nestled against Leland's arm. "Sometimes I wish Martin was the one who drowned in the flood. I know that's a terrible thing to say, but he can be such a bastard at times."

"What happened?"

"Nothing. It's not worth your time."

"I'm here with you. My time is yours."

Melissa rubbed his arm. "He bought the boys' horse, Sabrina, from the man I sold her to and towed her back to my house."

"When?"

"Today."

"Did your boys know?"

"They were with him. He picked them up from school without my permission. I made him take the horse back. The boys are devastated. Now they hate me, which is exactly what he wanted all along."

"They don't hate you."

Melissa accepted her bourbon from the waiter. "I know, but now I look like the bad guy. Again. I sold Sabrina and the other horses because I can't afford to keep them anymore. Now I've let my boys down twice."

"They're strong boys. They'll understand."

"And to think I married Martin in the first place."

"How long did you know him before you were married?"

"We met in college. I know it sounds cliché. He was a music major. You believe that? We both dropped out to chase the same dream. I wanted to be a singer. He wanted to start a band."

"What happened?"

"My career took off. His didn't. He was never cut out for the life. He went back to school when Jonathan was born and changed majors to study history. He started law school a year after Adam was born. He wanted one of us to have a stable career, which was ironic because I was the one supporting our family while he was neck deep in school work. Eventually, I discovered I wasn't the only woman in his life. I divorced him when he chased his paralegal to California."

Leland rubbed her hand. "You've been through a lot."

"Nothing I can't handle. I know this sounds crazy, but I'm thinking I should sell the house to Martin after all. School is over. I can take the boys on the road with me for the summer."

"You'll still need a place to come home to."

Melissa kissed him tenderly. "As long as I have you to come home to…"

"I'm not going anywhere."

"You have a big concert coming up. I shouldn't be distracting you like this."

"Sid thinks the concert will open doors."

"He believes in you. And so do I."

"I'm worried about Abby. She keeps pressing me to spend time with her mother."

"What did you tell her?"

Leland looked up at the ceiling and across the room before he refocused his attention on Melissa. "I told her the truth."

"Then you did the right thing."

"Abby doesn't understand."

"She was too young to know what happened. She sees her mom in a different light. Give her space. You can still protect her, but she's not a baby anymore. At some point, she's going to know her mom whether you want her to or not."

"What if I don't want her to?"

"It's not about you, Babe."

"But I'm all she has right now."

"My boys still wake up from nightmares about the flood. I think they're terrified of water. They keep asking about their dad. How long is he staying? Is he going to live with us again? I don't want to hurt their feelings, but I can't stomach three minutes alone with their father."

Leland gave a sympathetic nod. "How do you feel, physically?"

"I'm good. Some days have been better than others. Sometimes I can't sleep, but I blame my insomnia on you." She smiled warmly. "I love you Leland Presley. I think I have from the first time I met you. I was just afraid to admit it."

"I have this affect on women."

Melissa gently bit her lip. "Do I scare you?"

Leland kissed her softly on the lips and wrapped his arm around her. "I love you too. I can't imagine my life without you."

"Come home with me."

"I can't stay long."

"I want you to stay the night." Melissa kissed him again. "I want to wake up and feel you beside me. Can you do this for me?"

"You make a convincing argument."

"Have you thought about traveling on tour with me?"

Leland gently pulled his hand away and sat upright in his seat to acknowledge Martin suddenly standing at the table. "I think we have company."

Melissa moved her chair. "You've got to be kidding me." She could tell by Martin's appearance, he'd been drinking. "What are you doing here?"

"I was in the neighborhood."

"You shouldn't be here."

"If you're still mad about the horse—"

"I'm not having this conversation with you."

Martin gestured toward Leland. "I can see you're with company." He mimed the action of tipping an imaginary hat. "I bid you, good evening Mrs. Hamilton and Mr. Presley. Or should I say Mr. Blankenbaum? Mr. Peter Blankenbaum."

Leland kept his arm around Melissa.

"Well…" Martin continued. "Which is it? Presley or Blankenbaum."

"The name is Presley," Leland emphasized. He caught Melissa's head nod in his peripheral vision.

Melissa laid her head on Leland's shoulder. "Go home, Martin. I'm too tired for your bullshit."

Martin stepped back and threw his arms up. "Why don't you ask him yourself? His birth certificate says Peter Blankenbaum. If it were me, I'd have to wonder why someone with a birth name would go around pretending to be someone else?"

"You're drunk, Martin. And you're embarrassing me. Leave us alone, or I'll have you thrown out."

"You're not the one who should be embarrassed. Peter Ryan Blankenbaum. Born December twelfth, nineteen seventy-five. Parents, Lucinda and Ryan Blankenbaum. Both currently residents of Illinois' Menard Correctional Center. Both convicted for the manufacture and distribution of methamphetamine. Should I go on?"

Melissa lifted her head from Leland's shoulder. "I thought you said your mom died?"

Leland looked at Melissa. "My foster mom died from breast cancer. I never knew my biological parents."

"So are you Leland Presley or not?"

"I took Leland Presley for my stage name. I legally changed it ten years ago. Always thought it sounded better than the one on my birth certificate. My father was never around. I had no reason to carry his family name."

Melissa put her hands on the table and drew a deep breath. "So you lied to me?"

"I never use my former name. It has no meaning to me. No connection to who I really am."

"And who are you? *Really?*"

"The man you know. The same man I've always been."

"You said your mother encouraged you to follow your heart and pursue your dream."

"My foster mother. She was all I knew growing up."

"In Nashville?"

"I grew up in Oklahoma City."

"You told me you grew up outside Nashville."

"I did, at one time. After I left foster care. I got married and had Abby. When she was born, we moved back to Tulsa to be closer to her mother's family."

"He never went to Vanderbilt," Martin added. "I checked. There's no record he was ever enrolled."

Melissa leaned away from Leland. "Did you ever study there?"

"No. But I know more about music than any worthless degree could grant me. No one learns to sing from a book."

"Then why lie about it?"

"I wanted to impress you. To find some common ground. A connection. My feelings for you are genuine."

Melissa glared at Martin in disgust. He'd done a bad thing in a bad way, but he spoke the truth; a truth she wanted to believe was a lie. For the man she'd fallen in love with would have never invented himself and carried such a ruse for so long.

"Ask him about his wife," Martin gloated. "Go on…"

Melissa touched Leland's arm. "You mean, ex-wife?" she asked rhetorically.

"Technically, I'm still legally married," Leland confessed. "But I can explain—"

"Save it," Melissa cut him off. She stood up from the table and pushed Martin aside. "I knew it when I saw that woman with you and Abby at the hospital. I should have trusted my instincts."

"That was Nicole."

"So you've been two-timing me with your girlfriend *and* your wife?"

"That's not what I meant."

Melissa bristled. "You're quite the gigolo."

"Wait," Leland pleaded.

"You've been lying to me all along."

"I was going to tell you. When the time was right."

"That time has come and gone. I trusted you. I shared things with you."

Leland fought the urge to throw a fist Martin's way, but refrained from a course of violence. "I know…And you have every right to be mad at me. I never meant to hurt you. I've been chasing the same dream for so long, I failed to realize what I wanted most in life was staring right back at me."

"Really?" Melissa stammered. "Then maybe you should stop staring in the mirror."

CHAPTER 70

Melissa charged inside her foyer to find Sid playing Mozart on the grand piano in her music studio. She dropped her purse on the marble end table and yanked off her heels. Out of tissues and out of patience, she wiped her eyes with the back of her hands and disrupted Sid's live performance with a firm, "Get out!"

Sid ended the concerto abruptly. "I take it your night didn't end well."

"How long have you known?"

Sid closed the lid over the piano keys. "What are you talking about?"

"Leland Presley is a fake."

"How much have you been drinking?"

"Not enough."

Sid got up and checked the time on his Rolex. "Why don't you rewind the tape for me."

"Where are the boys?"

"Sleeping. Or at least pretending to be."

"I can't believe he lied to me."

"Who?"

"Leland. Peter…Blankenpoop or whatever the hell his real name is or was. And don't tell me you didn't know about his past."

Sid left the studio to pour two glasses of scotch from the crystal decanter in the antique cabinet outside the formal dining room.

Melissa cupped the tumbler in her hand and downed the contents in one motion. The burn took the edge off her heightened anxiety. "Leland Presley is a hoax."

"I've known Leland for years."

"Did you know he's not from Nashville?"

"Neither are most of your peers."

"He never graduated from Vanderbilt."

"Neither did you."

"I'm saying he never *went* to Vanderbilt. I don't believe he ever went to college, period. He invented his past to get close to me."

"So do most of the people in this business."

"I don't have sex with most people in this business!"

Sid sipped his drink. He kept his voice down when he spoke. "You're upset. I get that. But from Leland's perspective—"

Melissa slammed her empty drink on the counter. Her smeared mascara gave her raccoon eyes. "Whose side are you on?"

"I'm not taking sides. I'm trying to be objective."

"Screw objective. You have a counterfeit artist about to go live in front of millions, and you don't seem the least concerned."

"The man can sing, Melissa. And he's a guitar virtuoso."

"So you knew about his past?"

Sid finished his drink and poured himself another. "What I know and what I believe to be important are mutually exclusive."

"You sound like a politician."

"I'm a talent agent, not a private investigator."

"How did you find Leland, let alone agree to represent him?"

Sid brought his glass to his lips. This time he lowered it without drinking and paused to recite a Native American parable. "There's a story about an old Cherokee grandfather who was talking with his grandson. The Indian grandfather tells the boy, 'There is a battle between two wolves inside us all. One is Evil. It is anger, jealousy, greed, resentment, inferiority, lies, and ego. The other is Good. It is joy, love, hope, humility, kindness, empathy, and truth.' The boy ponders his grandfather's words for a moment. Then he asks him, 'Which wolf wins?' To which the grandfather calmly replies, 'The one you feed.'"

"And what does that have to do with anything?"

Sid knocked back his drink and winced. "Leland's been through some difficult times. Before, and after, his daughter was born. He chose the path of joy, love, and hope, when so many of us would rather feed our anger and resentment."

"You never answered my question. Of all the starving artists this town devours, why do you represent him?"

"The same reason I represent you. I see the good. I see the potential. I first met Leland at a songwriters show in Memphis. When I heard him play guitar, I knew he had something special."

"So you knew about his past?"

"Not at first. I left the bar when his set was finished. Leland was rushing to catch a bus. There was this barefoot Vietnam veteran begging for spare change outside the club. He looked ravaged like he'd been on the streets a long time. He wore one of those old Army jackets covered in patches. Probably served multiple tours. I heard Leland tell him he was broke and that he barely had bus fare to get home. I believed him."

"So what?"

"Leland thanked the man for his service to our country and told him he had never walked a day in his shoes. Then he took off his own boots and gave them to the man right then and there. Leland told him, 'The least I can do is let you walk in mine.'"

"Doesn't change what he did," Melissa protested. "Leland lied to me."

"I'm not saying I condone his actions. I'm saying, what we do in this life defines us more than the words we speak—or the words we don't."

"Actions speak louder than words…I get it."

"I'm not sure you do." Sid followed Melissa back to her music studio. "From your perspective, I get the hell hath no fury part. But you have to understand—"

"Understand what, Sid? How the man I thought I knew has been living a lie all along? How I trusted him with my life? With my son's life?"

"Don't dismiss him on account of his past. Leland is a good man."

"Stop calling him Leland. His name's Peter Blankenbump from bumfuck Illinois. Both parents are still in prison, and you're about to put him on stage for a benefit concert he has no business performing in."

"One thing's got nothing to do with the other."

"Like hell it doesn't. Leland Presley is a sham."

"He doesn't sing like one. And right now, he has the biggest gig of his life coming up. I pulled a lot of strings to make this happen. Called in a lot of favors from people who would rather see someone else get this shot."

"So he's all about the money for you. Is that it?"

"And my reputation in this business. And this is a *business*, Melissa. I know how you feel right now. I've been there."

"You can't begin to know how I feel."

"I suppose you're right. I've never been in love with another man before. I've been with them, but I haven't loved them. Not the way I love this business."

Melissa covered her face, her anger morphing into despair. An overwhelming sadness she couldn't dismiss. "I don't even know who he is. I feel betrayed. And lost. Where am I supposed to go from here?"

"Wherever you want. Whenever you want." Sid hugged her. "Focus on your boys and your career."

"He should have been honest with me."

"People from all walks of life flock to Nashville to reinvent themselves. Most are honest, hardworking folk chasing a dream few will ever achieve. It takes a lot more than flair to carve your name in this city. Leland's trying to do whatever he can with what he has."

Melissa reached in her pocket for a leftover tissue to blow her nose. "You're taking his side again."

"Leland did what most men do when they're scared."

"Scared of what?"

"Commitment. Rejection. Losing you. I'm not saying he shouldn't have told you about his past. But you have to see it from his perspective."

"I'm not sure I can do that."

"Then you have to let him go."

"I'm not sure I can do that either."

"Then sleep on it. You might see things differently in the morning."

Melissa rubbed her eyes. "I miss Tomás so much. He would have seen this coming. I should have been more careful."

"Don't do this to yourself."

"Leland was everything I've ever wanted. A polar opposite of Martin, at least I thought so." She craved another drink, but more alcohol wouldn't cure what ailed her. "I must look bat shit crazy right now. I know I sound it."

Sid returned to the piano and played something soothing. "You're a beautiful, intelligent woman."

"Not today."

"I can stay if you want me to."

"I don't know what I want anymore."

Sid stopped playing. He sat up straight and rested his hands on his legs. "It's been a long night. I should probably get going."

"Thank you."

"For what?"

"For listening. For putting up with me all these years. For keeping me from coming unglued. I still wish you'd told me about Leland, though."

"There's nothing to tell. He's still the same man inside. The same man you fell in love with."

"Love is a heavy word. I'm not sure I can carry the weight anymore."

Sid left the piano to offer Melissa a parting hug. "Your festival tour starts soon. Life on the road always brings a new perspective. Everything will come together in time."

CHAPTER 71

Leland rehearsed the tired lyrics he'd crooned over and over inside the Capital Country studio with the band he would lead at the benefit concert. He played the same notes systematically without passion, his thoughts scattered aimlessly while he sang into the microphone.

When the song concluded, he rested the Kramer six-string on its stand and snatched his bottled water off the floor. He owed Melissa the apology of a lifetime for destroying her trust in him, but he had no idea how to pull it off without pushing her further away.

"What are you doing?" Brad Siegel's voice bellowed through the intercom from the engineer's control room.

Leland finished his water. "I need a break."

"Play it again."

"We've played it enough," Leland replied. His band members concurred with subtle nods and drawn faces.

"One more time," Brad insisted.

Leland picked up the guitar and tuned the A string. "You heard the man," he told the band. "From the top."

The drummer rapped his sticks together as Leland counted, "One, two…one two three four." And off he went, strumming the guitar as he leaned toward the ribbon microphone and belted the first line.

"*STOP!*" Brad's voice boomed through the intercom speaker.

Leland signaled the band. "Now what?"

"*I don't like what I'm hearing.*"

"Maybe you should have your ears checked," Leland mumbled to himself.

"*I heard that!*"

Leland rolled his shoulders and craned his neck to relieve the tension in his upper back. The room was hot. The guitar felt heavy. "Let's go again," he told the rhythm guitarist who stood beside the curvy keyboard player and the Sting doppelganger on bass.

Leland played the song as written note for note without zeal, his own indifference spilling out of him with every verse he projected in the studio. He perceived the band's trepidation toward his troubled demeanor, and despite Brad Siegel's leering gaze, he continued to the end with a rousing guitar solo along the way.

"*Take five,*" Brad announced through the speaker.

The band cleared the room when Brad made his presence known. "My late grandmother could sing better than you today."

Leland propped the guitar on its stand. "Then why don't you invite her to join us?"

"Live is one thing. This studio is another. I need a track I can push on the radio. We've got thirty-six hours until the ball drops on this gig. Get your head in the game!"

Leland gestured at the control room. "My guitar sounds like shit."

Brad pointed in the opposite direction. "The exit's over there. If you're not up to the challenge—"

"I'm good."

"You don't sound like it. And you sure as hell aren't playing like it."

Leland contemplated the invitation to leave and pursue a path of mutually assured destruction. "I just need some time."

"That's a luxury you don't have."

"I get it."

"I'm not sure you do."

Leland shifted his attention away from Brad when he caught Melissa's image on a video monitor linked to a camera outside the control room. "I'll be back in a second."

Leland found Melissa in the hallway outside and stood for a moment in an awkward pose, not sure if he should reach out to her or play it safe and keep his distance. "I'm glad to see you."

"Bad time?" Melissa asked.

"I think Brad needs a diaper change. Seriously, I've been thinking about you. About us."

Melissa lowered her voice. "Can we go somewhere private?"

Leland motioned toward an isolation booth with a drum kit inside. He closed the door behind them. "I miss you."

Melissa put her hands on his chest and gently pushed herself away. "I haven't slept. I can't eat. I feel like I owe you an apology for the way I acted the other night."

"It's not you who should be apologizing."

"Martin can be a real jerk sometimes. I'm not sure why he did what he did, but I have my suspicions."

Leland moved closer. "I should have been up front with you from the start. I should have never kept my past from you. I wasn't looking for a relationship, but I never imagined how I would feel about you."

Melissa smiled curtly. "I have this affect on men."

"If I could rewind everything, I would," Leland offered sincerely.

"Me too, which is what makes this so hard for me."

"What are you saying?"

"I can't see you anymore. I get why you kept your past from me. And I'm grateful to you for saving my son's life. For inspiring me to ignore my critics and believe in myself. I think you are an amazing man with a God-given voice. You are a wonderful father, and Abby is so blessed to have you in her life."

"I'm blessed to have *you* in my life as well."

"You're very sweet, but we're very different people."

"Which is why we complement each other." Leland touched her arm. "We see things from different perspectives, but we make a great team."

"You should have been up front with me. Your words, not mine. And I need to focus on my tour."

"I don't want our relationship to end."

Melissa took a small step back and touched her hand to the side of her neck. "I'm sorry. The last thing I want to do is hurt you. I came here to tell you in person because I didn't like how we left things between us."

"After everything we've been through—"

"*Because* of everything we've been through, Leland. We're stronger now than we were when we met."

"Stronger together than we are apart."

"You'll understand, eventually."

"You're wrong," Leland countered.

"It's not about right or wrong anymore. I have to see things for what they are, Peter Blankenbaum. I know who I am in my world. I think you still need time to sort yours out. You keep running from the past. I need to focus on the future."

"So do I."

"Says the married man."

"Only on paper. My marriage ended a long time ago." He reached for Melissa. "Rehearsal's almost finished. We could go somewhere else and talk."

"I can't. But I'll be at the concert tomorrow night to support the city."

"Don't leave."

"I'm sorry, Leland. Or Peter. Or whatever your real name is."

Leland followed her out of the isolation booth with his head down and mumbled to himself, "Look who's running now."

CHAPTER 72

Leland parked his truck beside the familiar Nissan in his darkened driveway. He kept the engine running. No matter how many times he tried to brave a new path, and no matter which direction he traveled, he found himself at the same precipice he'd worked so hard to avoid. The more he struggled to distance himself from his past, the more he relived the same memories of the people he'd hurt and the love he'd squandered. Melissa wasn't any woman. She was *the* woman. The one who opened his heart and his eyes to a love so strong he found it hard to contain his emotions in her presence.

When he entered the house, he found Nicole alone on the sofa watching television in the dark. "Where's Abby?"

Nicole changed the channel. "In her room." She pointed to the kitchen table with an empty plate. "She was mad you didn't come home for dinner. She made spaghetti all by herself."

Leland stepped out of his boots and set them in the hallway. "I'll talk to her."

"Everything all right?"

"I'm good."

"How did rehearsal go?"

"It went." Leland took out his leather billfold and pinched a twenty dollar bill. "Thanks for watching her again."

Nicole took the cash. "She kept asking me about your concert tomorrow night. That's all she talked about."

"She can catch it on cable."

"She wants to be there to see you on stage."

Leland stuffed his wallet in his pocket. "And I'd like to win a Grammy, but since neither of those things is going to happen, I'm hoping you can stay with her again tomorrow night. If not—"

"I can be here. But we should talk…"

"Not now."

Nicole moved closer to him. "The more I'm around, the more Abby questions our status."

"We're just friends."

"I get it. Abby doesn't. She sees me come and go. She asks a lot of questions about her mom, most of which I can't answer."

"I'll talk to her."

Nicole crossed her arms in a sullen pose. "What about me?"

Leland reflected on his conversation with Melissa in the isolation booth. He could still smell her perfume on his shirt. "I'm involved with someone else."

"Is it serious?"

"I care about you."

Nicole gathered her purse for her car keys. "You don't have to explain."

Leland followed her outside to her car. "I appreciate everything you've done for Abby. I'd be in a jam without your help right now."

Nicole touched the side of his face. "Good luck tomorrow night. I hope you steal the show."

Abby closed her blinds when she saw her dad walk back toward the house. She waited for the inevitable knock at her door, followed by a clumsy apology. Her dad would pursue a lame analogy about something she didn't understand. She would remind him how he was wrong. He would try to console her. And so on and so forth.

But this time, the knock never came. Instead, she heard the familiar guitar play a melody she didn't recognize, followed by a long pause, then a short riff, and then nothing. As if he'd forgotten which note to play.

Had he forgotten about her? Did he know she was waiting for him to apologize for being late?

She put her ear to the door and heard nothing. More concerned than angry, she ventured outside her room to find her dad in a corner with his guitar—his eyes red and puffy the way she remembered when she woke up in the hospital and found him in the chair beside her. "What's wrong?"

Leland strummed the guitar. "You shouldn't be up."

"There's dinner in the fridge."

"Thank you."

Abby picked up her cat and hoisted him on her shoulder with his paws dangling against her back. "What time do you go on stage tomorrow?"

"Eight thirty. I need to be at Bridgestone Arena by four. Nicole's coming back to stay with you."

"I wish I could come with you."

"I won't be on stage very long."

"But a lot of famous people will be there. I read Carrie Underwood, Blake Shelton, Taylor Swift—"

"Not everyone is who they pretend to be."

"Could you get me Taylor's autograph?"

"I doubt I'll even see her, but I'll try."

"Who goes up before you?"

"Blake Shelton, I think. Or Brooks & Dunn. I can't remember. It doesn't matter."

Abby let the cat down. "Those are big acts," she said with her hand on her face to muffle a sneeze.

"Bless you."

"It's okay to be scared," Abby continued, "as long as you control the fear and not let the fear control you."

"Who told you that?"

"You did."

Leland adjusted the strings. "I'm not scared."

"Either way, I believe in you."

"That makes one of us."

Abby saw the sadness in her dad's eyes. "Did I do something wrong?"

"No, of course not."

"What happens after tomorrow night?"

Leland put his guitar away and grabbed a notepad from the kitchen junk drawer. "I come home." He tore the first page away and crumpled it into a ball.

"I meant with your band."

"They're not my band, Abby. I'm just filling in for someone else."

"Will you have to travel?"

"Maybe."

"When?"

"I don't know."

"For how long?"

Leland tossed the paper in the trash. "I said I DON'T KNOW!"

Abby recoiled from the sudden backlash.

"I'm sorry," Leland gushed. "I didn't mean to raise my voice at you. I'm just...I can only focus on one thing at a time right now."

"Nicole said you might sign a record deal."

Leland rubbed his arm. "I doubt most of the country even knows this concert exists."

"You're going to be famous."

"Abby, this gig's not about me. The city needs money and hope. With any luck, the concert will generate both."

"What about Mrs. Hamilton? Is she going with you?"

Leland scratched the stubble on his face. "She'll be there, but not with me."

"That's why you're sad, isn't it? You're not worried about the concert at all."

"Good night, Abby."

"I know you don't sleep with Nicole anymore."

"Abby…"

"And I know you like Mrs. Hamilton." She noticed her dad's expression change. "Do you love her?"

"I miss her."

"Did you tell her how you feel?"

"I tried to."

"That's the problem. Girls don't want to be told how you feel. They want you to show them."

"And how am I supposed to do that?"

Abby hugged him. "The best way you know how."

Leland rolled on his stomach in bed with one eye on the clock by his nightstand. Midnight gave way to 1:30 with his mind wide awake; his heart pounding in his chest as he thought about one person, the only person who defined true love for him in a way he'd never known before. He recalled every detail of Melissa's face, as if she were standing in front of him; her voice crystal clear.

Half this town can sing well enough to play in most honky-tonks. You have to be great to stand out.

Be careful what you wish for in this business. You might get it.

Desperate times. Desperate measures.

The only thing you're going to wear out is me.

You're not a very good liar.

I'd say you know me pretty well.

Leland rolled over on his back. He wanted what he couldn't touch; needed what he couldn't have; longed for what he hoped would be, until his restless urge forced him out of bed and prompted him to pour his thoughts on paper.

CHAPTER 73

Leland sat on the end of a metal bench near the back of the men's locker room in the basement of the Bridgestone Arena. The spartan confines provided a place of solitude to ponder his own fate while big name acts ran sound checks with their equipment and the venue's sound system before the sold-out show went live.

Dressed in black jeans and a long-sleeve western shirt, he tapped his polished boots to the beat of a familiar song and rubbed his hands together. He looked good. He smelled good. But most of all, he was confident he would sound good, despite a restless night and a nervous twinge in the back of his throat. Hours away from taking the Nashville stage in front of twenty-thousand country music fans and millions of viewers at home, he felt insignificant in a venue occupied by highly acclaimed artists.

He raised his head when he heard someone enter and saw Sid approach with a black T-shirt folded over his arm. Laminated credentials hung from the lanyard around his neck. "Did you get my text?"

Leland dug his phone out of his pocket. "I never got it."

"Must be the walls in here. The band's warming up. Brad Siegel wants to see you."

"Tell him to get in line."

"Are you good?"

"Like solid gold."

Sid put his hand on Leland's shoulder. "Take a breath. You look as nervous as a long-tailed cat in a room full of rocking chairs."

"Big night."

"Lots of headline acts in the house."

Leland pushed his phone in his pocket. "Very small fish. Very big pond."

"You're a piranha on guitar, and you've got the vocal chops. You'll do great." Sid smiled wryly. "It's not like you'll be swinging a hammer for the rest of your life if you screw this up."

Leland cocked his right ear toward his shoulder to stretch his neck muscles. He took a deep breath to practice a consistent exhale. "Don't you have somewhere else to be?"

Sid ignored the question and unfolded the black concert shirt off his arm. "I brought you this. A souvenir from our friends at Capital Country Records."

Leland took the shirt. He trilled his lips as he exhaled and pressed his tongue to the roof of his mouth. "Brad Siegel never wanted me on stage. You know it. I know it. So does every record label in this city."

"Don't be so grim. You earned this shot. And if there's one thing I've learned after thirty years in this business, it's never underestimate the power of perseverance."

"Have you seen Melissa?"

"Not yet."

"She won't return my calls," Leland added with a somber voice.

"Give her time. Women tend to work through issues at their own pace."

"Did Abby tell you that?"

Sid dabbed the perspiration on his forehead with a tissue. "I read it in *GQ*."

"What else did you find?"

"Nothing I don't already know. Keep your head in the game tonight. You've got a band to lead, and a record executive about to shit himself if you don't tag up with him soon."

Melissa entered a private changing room reserved for VIPs, her reflection captured in the wall-mounted mirror behind a mobile wardrobe station and a Hollywood-fashioned makeup booth. Dressed in her favorite jeans with Jimmy Choo pumps the color of candy red, she wore her hair in a layered bob with a diamond necklace resting on her red silk top. A French manicure highlighted her hands with a gleaming crescent of white nail polish.

She took a packet of pills from her clutch and set it on the rollaway cart. *Let it go,* she told herself, fighting the urge to succumb to old habits, knowing one pill would lead to five and then to ten with no relief from the real pain she held inside.

She checked her phone for messages and pinched a single tablet, oblivious to the knock at the door muted by an electric guitar riff during the live sound check. Her love life had come full circle, leaving her desperate for the man she wanted but couldn't bring herself to have.

She brought the pill to her mouth and caught Sid's reflection in the mirror. "How did you get in here?" she asked harshly, startled by his sudden appearance. She palmed the black market tablet when she faced her unexpected visitor.

"I've been looking for you," Sid announced in a voice loud enough to overcome the live guitar on stage.

"Don't you knock anymore?"

"You can't be in here," Sid warned. "This room's reserved."

"I need a minute."

Sid noticed the pills on the rollaway cart. "You won't solve anything with those."

"I'm not trying to solve anything. I'm trying to get on with my life. This city is family to me. I'm here to support it."

Sid snatched the meds. "By taking these?"

"My issue. Not yours."

"This issue almost cost you your life."

"Sometimes I wish it had."

"No you don't."

"You think you know how I feel?" Melissa opened her hand to slap him and saw the pill fall away. She bent over to find it and bumped her head on the rollaway cart. "Leave me alone," she snapped when she stood up and rubbed her forehead.

"Leland asks about you."

"I can't do this, Sid."

"Listen to your heart."

"What if I don't like what I'm hearing?"

"Then get a second opinion." Sid put his hand on her shoulder. "Ask yourself if you'll feel better with him or without him."

"I still love him, but I can't let go of who he really is."

"Who he is or who he was?"

"They're one in the same to me. I don't know where the lies end or the truth begins."

"Then talk to him."

Melissa gathered her clutch and wiped her eyes with a tissue. "I think we're past that point already."

Sid slipped the meds in his pocket. "You can't stop the waves, but you can learn to surf. Stop trying to manipulate what you can't control and learn to live with what you can."

"I hear you, but deceit is still a deal breaker for me."

Brad Siegel glanced at the monitors in the Bridgestone Arena's master control room while the sound checks proceeded on schedule. Charity event or not, he treated the rehearsal preparations as thoroughly as he would for any concert—especially a major event less than two hours away from kickoff on live television. With the sound dialed in to the venue's acoustic proclivities, he adjusted the lighting and camera angles above and below center stage. Huge advertising dollars would boost the concert's payout, but all eyes from the upper echelons of Music Row would be centered on his start-up studio and the wide-scale launch of a new band eager to carve a name for themselves and the label poised to bankroll their success. His reputation aside, he had a hefty portion of his own money invested in the band's success and the future of Capital Country Records.

He panned the remote camera and zoomed in to see a stage hand appear on the Jumbotron. He snatched a Motorola radio from the charging station as Martin Hamilton entered the room. "You shouldn't be up here."

Martin nudged his glasses on his nose. "I wanted to see where the sausage gets made."

Brad squeezed the talk button and brought the unit toward his head. "Check camera eight," he told the stage hand. "And don't pick your nose when the whole world's tuned in." He set the radio down and ushered Martin away from the master control panel. "The field trip's over. I've got four hours worth of work and ninety minutes to get it done."

"For a benefit concert?"

"This is the fucking Super Bowl of advertising."

Martin stood next to Brad in front of the master control panel. "You were smart to convince Wharton Brothers to drop the lawsuit."

"Depends on how much longer your ex can sing."

"Doesn't matter. It's the sizzle not the steak. Her face will sell tickets."

"I hope you're right."

"I rewrote her contract. The majority of her tour earnings will flow back to Wharton Brothers, minus your cut, of course."

"And what about you?"

Martin forced a crooked smile. "I get to catch her when she falls."

Nicole inched her way through the traffic congestion leading up to the Bridgestone Arena. She could see the arena in the distance but couldn't move any faster than the cars in front of her allowed.

She checked her hair in the Sentra's vanity mirror. She needed her split ends trimmed, but she looked good enough to attract the right attention—the kind with deep pockets and a taste for local groupies. "We should have left earlier," she told Abby.

Abby noticed a billboard advertising the Predators hockey team. "What if my dad already sang?"

"The concert's just starting. All the big acts go first."

Abby scanned the radio stations. "I can't believe how many people are here."

Nicole put her turn signal on and changed lanes abruptly. If Leland couldn't appreciate her, she would find someone who would. "We need to find a place to park."

"I've never been inside the Bridgestone before."

"Never?"

"My dad was going to take me to a concert, but we never got to go."

"This show could open a lot of doors for him."

Abby glanced at the shiny black Cadillac limousine beside her. "I'm not sure I like what's behind them."

"You want your dad to be happy."

"What if he chokes tonight?"

"He won't. There's too much money at stake."

"Music's never been about the money for him."

Nicole tapped her brakes. "No one likes to play for free."

"My dad doesn't play for money. He says food can feed the body, but only music can nourish the soul."

CHAPTER 74

Crammed in the last row of the standing-room-only section reserved for VIP guests, Melissa maneuvered around a pair of taller gentlemen gazing at the Jumbotron and the swooping television cameras above the sold-out space inside the Bridgestone Arena, where thousands of delirious, screaming fans enjoyed another Brooks & Dunn ballad. Caught in the rapture of live music, her life made sense again. She had her boys. She had an agent who supported her decisions, and she had her career on track for the first time in years. Her carte blanche pass to the best show of 2010 notwithstanding, she embraced the action off stage, an anonymous observer lost in the crowd, adrift in her indecision about the man who stole her heart.

Sid put his hand on Leland's shoulder. "You're on in ten minutes," he shouted backstage above the sound of live music.

Leland picked at the strings on his unplugged guitar while the rest of his band huddled in the staging area amongst the entourage of country acts waiting to grab the spotlight. "I think I'm going to be sick."

"No you're not. You were born for this."

"I've got a big act to follow."

"In ten minutes, you won't remember who played before you."

Leland shoved his hand in his pocket when his phone vibrated. His heart sank when he read the message from his wireless carrier, prompting him to enroll in paperless billing. "I'm not sure I can do this…"

"Yes you can. Your whole life has brought you to this moment. Right here. Right now. You pull this off, and your career will explode in ways you never dreamed of."

Leland looked at Sid through sad eyes. "In some ways it already has."

Sid acknowledged the stage hand who gave the *one minute* warning. "You're almost up. Whatever feelings you have for her, you need to put them on hold."

"What if there's more to life than music?"

"Music is your life."

Leland heard the audience erupt when Brooks & Dunn finished their set. "Maybe I've been pretending to be someone else for so long I can't remember who I really am anymore."

"You need to focus on the here and now. Put your feelings aside. Think about your future. This is *your* night, Leland."

"Maybe, but I'd give anything to have Melissa in my life again."

Brad Siegel studied Leland from the bank of video monitors inside the master control room. Behind him, a sound technician stepped over coax cables protruding from a wall-mounted patch panel. Production assistants and television executives lined the perimeter segregated by racks of equipment, camera control units, video servers, digital effects computers, and other electronic apparatus for the concert.

"He sounds flat," Brad announced with his eyes on Leland and his band on stage. He pressed a single headphone speaker to his ear to hear the stage manager barking about bad lighting.

"We're live," a production assistant commented from across the room. "No one will hear the difference."

Brad pointed to one of the video operators. "Switch to camera number five."

The assistant manned the controls for the pan-tilt-zoom heads mounted along the catwalk near the ceiling. "Switching to number five."

Brad pointed to the video monitor that showed a woman and a girl with an amputated arm standing in the right wing. "Who are they, and what the hell are they doing back there?"

Leland played through the song without incident, well aware of the crowd's tepid response to the music he'd rather forget than have to play again. Undistracted by the glare from infernal sidelights and the high intensity arc lamps above him, he finished the song note for note with the band he'd inherited from Brad Siegel and the major record label vying for their share of future spoils. When the token applause ensued, he looked out at the sea of bodies packed inside the largest venue he'd ever played, perhaps the only major venue he would ever play. For now, the next few minutes were his to own; a decision he'd made the night before; a decision he hoped would change his life forever.

Brad hovered over a soundboard. He watched Leland slip off his guitar and step toward the piano at the back of the stage while the band made their exit. "What is he doing?"

"Don't know," the production assistant replied. "He's gone off script."

Brad slid his hand down his face. "Patch me in. I wanna talk to him now!"

"I can't."

"Why not?"

"He took his ear bud out."

"Then kill his microphone."

"I can't."

"Then go to commercial!"

"We're not scheduled for another—"

"I don't give a shit! I want him off the air!"

Leland sat at the grand piano and adjusted the gooseneck microphone in front of him. His heart pounded in his chest. "I wrote this song for someone very special," his amplified voice boomed through the concert hall. "Someone who means the world to me. If you're here tonight, you know who you are. I realize I can't change the past, but I'm hoping this will show you what I've been trying to say."

He played a melodic intro in E flat major, letting his fingers caress the keys before he took a deep breath and started to sing…

I close my eyes and feel your smile
Hoping that you'll stay awhile, and share your thoughts
In my life I've known true love
But still I find I'm thinking of, something more
Something I cannot ignore
I hold your hand and kiss your lips
If only I could make you see…

A man like me
Could fill your heart and soul, with all the love you need
A man like me
Could help you live your life, beyond the walls, of recent memories
A man like me…

I hear your voice inside my mind
And then I find
An empty space has filled this place and left me here without you
I know our time has come to pass

On faded lines of moon-lit paths
That lead us back to what we had
Reflections, of the time we shared, and thoughts of
what could be...

A man like me
To help you live your life, beyond the walls, of recent
memories
A man like me
To hold you close at night
And never let you go
A man, like, me...

The past is gone, tomorrow's now
But in my heart I know somehow
I need to set you free
Still, I hope one day, you'll find a way, to open up and
see

A man like me
Would lift you up and fill your heart, with all the love
you ever need
A man like me
Would help you rise above this barricade of recent
memories
A man like me...
A man like, me!

CHAPTER 75

Leland rose from the piano to acknowledge the cheering audience in the Bridgestone Arena. Blinded by the stage lights, he stared out at the legion of concert fans, searching for a single face among the thousands caught up in the country music madness.

When the lights dimmed, he left the stage to confront Sid. "Have you seen Melissa?" he shouted above the ringing in his ears.

Sid paced like an animal in a cage. "Brad Siegel is looking for you! He's hot as a pistol about this little stunt you carried out."

Leland pushed through the backstage fracas among performers and production crew. "I have to find her."

"Brad wants you upstairs, pronto. If he doesn't tan your hide, I will. What in God's name were you thinking?"

"She said she would be here."

Sid snapped his fingers in front of Leland's face. "Are you hearing me? You need to get your ass upstairs."

Leland focused his attention on the melee backstage. "Have you seen her or not?"

"You just threw away your music career!"

"I never had it to begin with," Leland countered. He followed Sid toward a troupe of backup singers, convinced he saw Melissa among them, only to be disappointed when the woman he chased down was someone else. "She's not coming, is she?"

"What did you expect?"

"A second chance."

Sid rubbed his hands together. "This isn't Love Connection. This was your moment. Your shot with a major record label. Do you have any idea how much Capital Country invested in you?"

"I love music, but I love her more."

Sid pawed at the back of his neck, his expression a mixture of grief and anger. He knew when to push and when to fold. "I saw her this morning in one of the VIP dressing rooms." He pointed in the opposite direction toward the rehearsal staging area and marched off to find Brad Siegel.

"Are you sure?" Leland stopped in his tracks when he felt a tap on his shoulder and spun around to see Nicole and Abby with all-access passes around their necks.

"I was looking for you!" Nicole exclaimed. She wrapped her arms around Leland in a long embrace.

"What are you doing here?" Leland asked, dumfounded.

"We came to see you!" Abby shouted above the noise.

Leland looked at Abby and gently pushed Nicole away. "You're supposed to be at home."

"Not on the biggest night of your life," said Nicole.

Leland touched her backstage pass. "How'd you get this?"

"You know me. I know people who know people." She kissed his cheek. "That might be the most beautiful song I've ever heard. I had no idea you felt that way. Don't be mad at Abby. I couldn't leave her home alone."

Abby touched Leland's arm. "We wanted to see you on stage."

"I'm not mad," Leland reassured her. "Did you like the band?"

"I loved your song."

Leland checked his voice mail but found a dozen incoming texts from Brad Siegel instead.

"What's wrong?" asked Abby.

"Nothing. I'm just surprised to see you here."

Nicole put her arm around Leland. "Let's go somewhere and celebrate!"

Leland ushered Nicole and Abby toward the exit when a man in a tie approached him.

"Leland Presley?" the man asked.

"Yes," Leland replied. He patted his shirt for an autograph pen. "I don't have anything to sign with."

The man handed Leland a sealed envelop. "You've been served."

Leland took the envelop and opened it to read the folded page inside. The contents hit him like a sucker punch.

"What is it?" asked Nicole.

Leland dropped the page and looked up. "Paula's suing me for full custody. She's trying to take Abby away."

CHAPTER 76

Melissa paced inside the private conference room of a reputable title company in Nashville. Dull clouds covered the skyline outside the windows overlooking the retail space next door. "What the hell were you thinking?" she grilled Martin, who sat quietly at a long office table with a stack of mortgage papers and a pen.

"I wanted to see the live show."

"I told you to keep an eye on the boys. After everything they've been through—"

"I was only gone a few hours. They were fine when you got home."

"No, they weren't. Adam thought something happened to you. Jonathan sent me a text and asked if you were ever coming back."

"I'm sorry."

"Sorry is forgetting to put the toilet seat down. I should have never trusted you. I asked you to stay with them for a few hours, not abandon them."

Martin clicked the cheap ball point pen on the table. "The boys are fine. Nothing happened."

"I missed half the concert."

"There wasn't much to miss."

"That's not the point."

"You're making a big deal about nothing."

Melissa sent another text to her realtor. "I can't believe I'm doing this."

"My offer's fair."

"I don't care about the money. I care about my boys' future."

Martin put his hands on the table and laced his fingers. "So do I. And I'm sorry about the horse. I should have consulted you first."

"The boys always want what they can't have."

"They deserve a better life. So do you."

Melissa paced in front of the window. "What's taking so long? We should have been done an hour ago."

Martin parted his hands and leaned back in his chair. "Sit down and relax. Stress will age you faster."

"This is the dumbest thing I've ever done in my life."

"And yet, you're still here."

"Like I have a choice." Melissa stepped away from the window and read her realtor's reply: *running late.*

"You're making the right decision," Martin reassured her.

"It doesn't feel that way."

"You'll be square with the IRS. And you won't have to defend a foreclosure."

"I just want to get this over with."

"You don't have to move out right away."

"I'm sending the movers tomorrow. I want my stuff in storage while I'm on tour."

"What about the boys?"

Melissa read a text message from Sid asking if she saw the concert. "They're coming with me."

"What about school?"

"School's over."

"Until next fall."

"I can homeschool the boys on the road."

"If you call that rolling coffin a home."

"They'll be fine. What happened on my last tour was a fluke. It won't happen again."

Martin leaned forward in his chair and got up. "I think it's a bad idea."

"Says the man who left his family to chase his secretary across the country. You couldn't take responsibility to tend our boys for one night."

"*Paralegal.* And I told the boys I would be home before ten."

Melissa rolled her eyes. "Whatever…"

Martin took his reading glasses off and pinched the bridge of his nose. "Their principal wants them to see a shrink."

"When did you talk to her?"

"Doesn't matter. I share her concerns. Our boys are twisted up inside. They need someone to talk to."

"They have me," Melissa stipulated.

"They need their father."

Melissa looked away. "Their principal needs to stay out of our lives."

"She cares about our boys. She wants what's best for them."

"I'll decide what's best."

"They're my sons too. Don't act like I don't care about them."

"It takes more than sperm to be a father."

Martin took out his cigarettes. "That's low, Mel. Even for you."

"Don't call me that. And don't light up in here."

"How long will you be on tour?"

"Not long enough."

"The boys could stay in the house with me. I could fly them out to see you."

Melissa read another text from Sid. "Never going to happen."

"Jesus, Mel. I figured you might be more amenable by now."

"You figured wrong."

"I could take you to court and fight for partial custody. I could block you from taking our sons outside the state without my written consent."

"You try that, and you'll never see them again."

Martin raised his hands in a defensive pose. "I don't want to argue about our boys. If you think a life on the road is best for them, I defer to your judgment."

Melissa threw him a steely gaze. She knew better than to trust a man whose moral fabric held water like torn pantyhose. Martin had something to hide. She could smell it on him, but at the moment, she didn't care. She wanted her old life back and her boys in her purview. She thought of Leland for a moment and then quickly dismissed any notion of a reconciliation. He had his life. She had hers. "This is taking way too long."

"You got somewhere else to be?"

"Anywhere but here."

CHAPTER 77

Leland pushed his way through a downtown bistro's lively dinner crowd to find Sid by himself at a table against the wall with a half eaten cobb salad and a double bourbon. "I got your message."

"I recommend the shrimp scampi."

"I've eaten."

Sid poked his fork at the chopped greens and pierced a tomato wedge. "Where's your sidekick?"

"At home with Nicole."

Sid chewed the tomato doused in salad dressing. "I can't figure out what makes their red wine vinaigrette so tangy. They must age their dressing in oak barrels."

Leland moved a chair and parked himself across from his agent and long-time friend. "Did you look at the papers I sent you?"

"Let's kick the can on that one for a second. Brad Siegel's decided to postpone the band's debut album until Jimmie Lockhorn recovers."

"I'm not surprised."

"You grabbed the tiger by the tale. I had to peel Brad off the ceiling. At one point, I thought he was going to spontaneously combust. He's threatening to sue you for damages."

"What damages?"

"Relax…I told him you can't put the toothpaste back in the tube. I convinced him to terminate your contract instead."

"You told him to fire me?"

Sid skewered a piece of roasted chicken and hard-boiled egg, maintaining his stony expression with Leland. "I saved your ass."

"What about my next gig?"

"There is no next gig. Reputation is everything in this town. You can't fart in the shower without someone hearing about it. And you went rogue on live television in front of ten million people. You might as well have dropped your pants and mooned Brad Siegel on stage. You're a honky-tonk bull in a China shop. No one in this city's going to touch you."

"Have you seen Melissa? Have you talked to her?"

"Melissa has her own problems."

"She won't return my calls."

"I can't help you there." Sid poked his fingernail at a piece of bacon wedged between his teeth. "I'm dropping you from my agency."

"Why?"

"This is a business decision. You made yours on stage in front of a televised audience. I like you, Leland. I always have. But I need to cut my losses and move on."

"I'm sorry about the concert."

"Son, you pissed off all the wrong people when you went off script. You should have kept me in the loop."

"You would have tried to talk me out of it."

"I would have saved your career. Now you'll be lucky to land a gig in some backwoods pub in Arkansas."

Leland waited for Sid to chew his food. "What about my custody case?"

Sid pushed his plate aside and reached for a folder on the chair beside him. He shared the contents with Leland and waved off the waitress who buzzed the table with a water refill. "I'll represent you. You're a tough act to manage, but you're a good father. You deserve good representation."

"I appreciate your help."

"Don't thank me yet. I reviewed the motions. Your wife is making child abuse allegations."

"That's bullshit! I would never hurt Abby."

"I know. That's why I'm taking your case pro bono."

"There is no case. Paula tried to drown her! She's been institutionalized for over a decade, and now she's out here throwing lies around."

"In custody cases, the truth is often irrelevant. What matters is what her attorney can convince the court to believe."

"But she's deranged."

"Not anymore. At least according to her psychiatric profile. She's claiming you left Abby home alone, unsupervised, which placed her in grave danger during the flood. Her lawyer's subpoenaed the hospital for Abby's medical records as evidence."

"She was hypothermic."

"She was unconscious for two days."

Leland fiddled with the turquoise spinner ring on his right index finger. "Abby wouldn't be here at all if I hadn't found her."

"And Paula wouldn't have as much leverage if you'd stayed home with Abby in the first place."

"Can't you make this go away?"

"I'm your attorney, Leland, not your fairy godmother. You have to face the facts. Your wife's lawyer will do everything he can to discredit you and cast doubt on your ability to maintain a stable home and provide for Abby's wellbeing."

"You make this sound like I'm the bad guy here."

Sid followed the waitress with his gaze. "I'll get you a drink."

"I'm fine," Leland lied. "Just tell me what I need to do."

"I'm afraid it's not that simple."

Leland moved his chair closer to the table. "Why not?"

"Abby doesn't share your DNA."

Leland propped his arms on the table and leaned toward Sid. "What are you saying?"

"Biologically speaking, she's not your daughter."

"Like hell she's not my daughter! She was born when I was married. I've raised her since she was a baby."

"But you're not her biological father. I reviewed the DNA results myself. Abuse allegations aside, Paula's lawyer is going to argue that you have no custody rights. By law, Paula is Abby's sole guardian."

Leland slumped back in his chair, deflated. "You can't be serious. The test results must be wrong. A lab mix up or something."

"The odds are miniscule."

Leland put his head in his hands. "This is ludicrous. I'm her father. I've always been her father. I can't believe this is happening."

"We'll get through it."

"How?"

"You do your job. I'll do mine."

"Meaning, what, exactly?"

Sid wiped his mouth with a napkin. "I'll dig into Paula's case some more. You need to stay gainfully employed. And avoid all contact with Paula or her attorney until I get this mess sorted out."

CHAPTER 78

Leland started his morning shower with his arms above his head, palms pressed flat against the tile above the faucet handle. Hot water sprayed his head and back, cascading down his lean torso and legs toward the gurgling drain at his feet. He lost track of how long he'd been standing in the steady stream, only knew that the water soothed his body and mind. He felt numb inside, a hollow shell nearly void of emotion, unable to process the truth Sid had conveyed to him. This time, no lyrics came to mind; no melody sad enough to follow him along his uncharted path.

He wanted someone to lean on. A partner who knew him better than he knew himself. Someone who could help him make sense of where his life was headed. "*You want some company?*" he heard Nicole ask outside the bathroom. Before he could answer, he found her naked in the water beside him with a washcloth in her hand. "It's tight in here," he complained, hoping she would dismiss herself and leave him to his solitary burden.

"Tight works for me. I'll wash your back."

"I'm good."

Nicole poured shower gel on the wet washcloth and lathered Leland's shoulders. "I couldn't sleep."

Leland dipped his head in the faucet stream when Nicole's touch awakened his senses. "Me neither."

"What did Sid have to say last night?"

"Not much."

Nicole washed Leland's lower back at the point right above his firm buttocks. "You'll feel better if you talk about it."

"I don't feel like talking right now."

"Then turn around so I can wash your front."

Leland maneuvered to let the shower spray his backside. "I can't do this," he said when Nicole touched his penis.

"Not all of you agrees."

Leland cupped her breast and kissed her, an impulsive reaction to a stimulating moment. But this time, he experienced nothing beyond his involuntary physical response. "I'm sorry." He parried her hand and opened the sliding stall door to grab a towel from the rack beside the shower. Steam covered the vanity mirror above the sink.

"What's the problem?"

Leland dried himself with a towel. "I'm not in the mood."

"I thought you'd be happy to see me."

"I have a lot on my mind."

"What does that mean?"

"It means what it means. Paula's trying to take Abby from me. My record label kicked me to the curb. Sid thinks I'll never play a gig in Nashville again." He put his jeans on and slipped a clean shirt over his head.

Nicole stopped the shower and got out to wrap a towel around herself. "What about your record deal?"

"My contract's been terminated. There is no record deal."

"They can't do that."

"They already have."

"Then sign with someone else."

"It's not that simple."

"You've paid your dues."

"The record label owns the band. I was only along for the ride."

"Then talk to Sid."

"I already have." Leland opened the bathroom door to let the steam escape. "He's dropping me too."

"He can't do that!" Nicole draped her towel over the rack and slipped her bra and panties on. "What are you going to do?"

"Fight for custody of Abby."

"What about your record deal?"

"I don't care."

"You can't just throw your life away."

"I'm not throwing anything away."

"Then fight for this, Leland. No one's going to hand you a better deal unless you get out there and press for it. If Sid won't help you, then find an agent who will."

"When the time is right."

Nicole followed him around the bedroom and put her clothes on. "The time is now! You'll never be happy swinging a hammer for ten bucks an hour."

"Twelve-fifty. Plus overtime when I can get it."

"You can barely make rent."

"I'll figure it out."

Nicole snatched her bracelet from the dresser. "So that's your master plan? Spend the rest of your life playing dirty honky-tonks for free pretzels and beer while some lowlife singer steals your slot with the band."

"It was never my band to begin with."

"You're right," Nicole said in a sarcastic tone. "I forgot. You gave it away when you blew your shot on a song you weren't supposed to sing. And don't tell me you wrote it for me."

"I never said I did," Leland replied, immune to Nicole's mean-spirited response.

"You're still in love with her."

"What do you want me to say? Life isn't some fairytale. You and I live on two different sides of the coin."

Nicole grabbed her purse. "What happened to the man I used to know?"

"You don't have to leave."

"But you don't want me to stay…"

Leland heard the front door slam. Instead of chasing Nicole, he retreated to his room and picked up his guitar. He played a melody to an instrumental piece he'd written while he ventured through the house to hear the way the notes sounded when they bounced off different walls. Eventually, he stopped outside Abby's room to listen for signs of movement. "Are you up?" he asked through the door. He tried the knob and felt it turn in his hand. "It's almost time," he said before he entered her room and rested the guitar at the foot of her bed.

"I'm not going to camp today," Abby mumbled with her face in her pillow. Across the room, her orange tabby stretched inside the open dresser drawer.

Leland leaned over the edge of the bed. "I have to be at work in a hour."

Abby rolled over and brought her covers to her chin. "Why can't I stay home with Nicole?"

"Nicole had to leave."

"When is she coming back?"

"I'm not sure."

"I heard you arguing with her."

"I thought you were sleeping."

Abby's expression went solemn. "Why is Mom trying to take me away from you?"

"Don't worry about it."

"Is it true?"

"No one's going to take you away from me."

"Promise?"

Leland hesitated for a moment. "Promise." He left the room and returned with a long cardboard tube. He opened one end and extracted a poster. "Check this out," he said, unrolling the glossy photo of Taylor Swift on stage in concert. He smiled at Abby's reaction when she read the autograph in the corner.

Abby hugged her arm around him and squeezed. "I thought you forgot!"

"I wanted to surprise you."

"Thank you! You're the best dad in the world!"

CHAPTER 79

Leland drove to Belle Meade to confront the only woman he'd ever truly loved—convinced that if she loved him back, she would give him another chance to explain. He owed her more than a heartfelt apology. He owed her a glimpse into his past, a snapshot of his life before he'd met her. He'd kept from her what he'd withheld from so many friends along his journey as a single father and a struggling artist trying to balance his obligations with his music dream. He wrote songs to touch lives and bring people closer together. Not tear them apart.

He rolled his window down when he found himself at the gate to Melissa's property and reached his arm out to press the keypad on the access control system. He hesitated with his finger an inch away from the box. Was he chasing something better left alone? Should he turn around and leave his past behind or confront his fear head on?

He punched the code Sid gave him and waited for the iron gate to open inward and grant him access to the long, swooping driveway with a "SOLD" sign prominently displayed in the lawn.

When he reached the house, he parked beside a black BMW and got out to see Martin advancing toward him, his aggressive posture loaded for bear. "I need to speak with Melissa."

"You're trespassing on private property," Martin asserted himself before Leland could take another step.

"Then who opened the gate?"

"Mel's not here."

"When will she be back?"

"This property belongs to me now."

Leland scanned the windows on the front of the house. "Where is she? I've been trying to call her—"

"You should leave now," Martin dictated as Paula emerged from the house barefoot in a T-shirt and shorts.

"What are you doing here?" Leland directed his angst at Paula.

Paula shuffled toward him. "The second flood is coming. Only I can save our daughter."

"What are you talking about?"

"Abby needs her mother. You can't be with her anymore."

"Her mother needs to take her medication."

Paula avoided eye contact with one arm bent behind her back. "You can't be seen with her," she said in a monotone voice. "You think you have all the answers, prancing around like some kind of God, Mr. big shot rock star. They canceled you like a bad check. You aren't fit to be her father."

"You need help, Paula. Taking Abby away from me won't solve your problems."

Paula remained expressionless; her face an empty page. "I'm not the problem, and you're not the father."

Leland followed Martin toward the house. "What did you do to her?"

"I'm her attorney. Anything you need from Paula, you go through me first."

"She's not right in the head."

"Get off my property."

"Where's Melissa?"

Martin pointed toward the driveway. "You've got one minute before I have you arrested for trespassing."

Leland climbed in his truck and dialed Sid's number. "We need to talk," he started when Sid answered.

"Where are you?"

"Belle Meade."

"You need to pick up Abby."

"Is she all right?"

"Paula's attorney filed a motion for an emergency custody order."

"He can't do that!"

"The judge granted the order to have Abby removed from your care. Children's services sent an officer to your house. The state is planning to take temporary custody of Abby, today."

CHAPTER 80

Melissa locked herself in her tour bus, physically depleted from the rigors of endless preparations and daily rehearsal schedules at the start of her East Coast festival tour. After struggling to reclaim her career, she finally found her stride, regardless of her looming regrets about selling the house to Martin and uprooting her boys from the only home they'd ever known. In her haste to end her relationship with Leland, she had candidly dismissed her own addiction issues and her self-centered views. Now she found herself alone on a custom coach with more accouterments than a five star hotel. She knew the demands of life on the road; how the lure of fame and fortune overshadowed any notion of an honest conversation about the unsettling monotony of the music business mired in poor judgment, bad taste, and chronic indulgence in illegal drugs. She had everything she wanted and more, with no one to blame but herself for feeling rejected at a time when she needed Leland the most.

Leland charged inside the Nashville recreation center to find Principal Hendrix engaged in conversation with a Davidson County Deputy. "Where's my daughter?" he vented loud enough to draw the principal's attention. "Abby's supposed to be here."

"Mr. Presley—"

"I want to see Abby now!"

Principal Hendrix maintained an aggressive stance with her large frame physically obstructing Leland's path. "Mr. Presley—"

"Where is she?"

"Abby's safe. Let's go somewhere private and talk."

A vein in Leland's temple throbbed. "I'm not going anywhere without my daughter. Bring her out here now, or this is going to get ugly."

Principal Hendrix waved off the deputy sheriff who took offense at Leland's fighting words. "Mr. Presley, I'm on your side. I realize you're frustrated. I promise you, Abby is safe."

Leland followed Principal Hendrix inside a small equipment room. "Whatever it is you think you're doing to protect my daughter, it's not helping."

"Mr. Presley, I've worked in education for more than thirty-five years, including most of my summers spent with youth programs like these. I've seen a lot in my tenure, and there are two things I know as certain truth: first, I don't believe you pose any threat to Abby; and second, I wouldn't be here if I thought otherwise."

"I'm taking Abby home with me."

"Right now that would do more harm than good."

"I disagree!"

"You're not hearing me, Mr. Presley. I'm on *Abby's* side. She has issues, of which I am well aware, but abuse at home is not one of them."

Leland drew a deep breath. "I'm not leaving here without her."

"Child services has a court order granting the state temporary custody until a hearing can be held to determine—"

"This is wrong! They have no right."

"They have the law."

"No law gives them permission to come in here and threaten to take my daughter!"

"It's not a perfect system."

Leland lunged for the door when he saw Abby emerge with a sheriff's deputy and a man in a tie with a government ID around his neck. "Abby!"

"Dad!" Abby screamed.

Leland approached the officer. "My daughter's coming home with me."

The officer reached for his taser gun. "Sir, I need you to step back."

"You said no one would take me away!" Abby cried.

"I'm sorry," Leland pleaded. "I'll figure this out. I promise!" He followed Abby and the officer until Principal Hendrix intervened.

"Mr. Presley! You're no good to your daughter in jail."

"This isn't right."

"You'll have your day in court."

Leland stood helplessly as the men ushered Abby from the building to a government sedan outside. He wanted Paula in a straight jacket, and the judge who sided with her case, in jail.

"Go home, Mr. Presley. Meet with your lawyer. If there's anything I can do to help, I will."

Sid entered Leland's house and followed the sound of acoustic guitar played at a heated tempo. "Leland?"

"*In here,*" he heard Leland call out.

Sid stepped around unpacked boxes and a curious orange tabby who jumped on a window sill for a glimpse at the squirrel festivities outside. "I'm sorry about what happened. I tried to get there before child services arrived."

Leland stopped playing when Sid entered the room. "They took her away from me."

"They had a court order."

"How soon will I get her back?"

"I'm working on it."

Leland picked at the guitar strings indifferently. "I feel empty inside."

"You can't blame yourself."

"I blame my wife!"

"The burden of proof falls on her attorney. Their case is flimsy. I've already filed a motion to dismiss."

"How long will that take?"

"Depends on the court's schedule. Maybe ten, twelve weeks at most. But there's no guarantee they'll grant it."

"I'm not waiting three months!" Leland set his guitar in the case. "There has to be something more you can do. This is my word against hers. There's no way the courts would side with Paula. You know she's lying."

"Only if we can prove it."

"You said the burden of proof was on her attorney."

"And her attorney will make a strong argument that you're not fit to be Abby's father."

"But I am her father."

"Not biologically, which makes the situation more complicated."

"Abby needs me."

"She'll be safe in the state's care."

"Bullshit! I've been in the state's care."

"We'll get her back," Sid assured him.

"How?"

"I'll worry about that. You stay close to your phone."

Leland reached for the bottle of bourbon stashed in the cabinet above the refrigerator. Behind him, the orange tabby sauntered from the hallway to Abby's room and howled. "She's not here," he told the cat and unscrewed the cap. He took a swig and left the open bottle on the counter. He retrieved his guitar and played through a new chord sequence, hoping to find the words to match the music. But every string played sharp or flat, out of tune and out of touch with every melody he composed in his head. Instead of solace in his music, he found emptiness, an emotional void where fear transformed into sadness, sadness devolved into anger, and anger appealed to apathy.

He clenched the guitar neck in both hands and raised the prized possession above his head. Rage swelled within him until he slammed the vintage instrument to the floor, again and again, pounding the handmade Gibson into a pile of splintered wood and broken strings.

CHAPTER 81

Melissa wiped her face with a towel backstage and guzzled a cold Evian. *Great show*, she heard someone call out as she advanced to her changing room and locked the door behind her. Her lower back throbbed more than it had the night before. Despite the prescription pills at her disposal, she refused to take them, opting for plain Ibuprofen instead. The pain was only temporary, she surmised. A result of her new routine, riding hours on end between outdoor shows along the East Coast festival tour.

She changed into a pair of loose-fitting jeans and an oversized shirt made from soft cotton weave. She let her hair down and approached a bouquet of pink roses inside an ornamental vase effervescing with the fragrance of fresh flowers. A white card poked out from the top with her name on it. "Who is it?" she asked when a loud knock startled her.

"Sorry to bother you," she heard her stage manager reply through the door. *"There's a guy out here who wants to talk with you. He says he knows you. He says it's important."*

"What does he look like?"

"He's clean. Should I tell him to beat it?"

"Just a second."

Melissa composed herself before she opened her room to find Martin holding a bottle of champagne. "What are you doing here?" she sighed incredulously. She stepped outside the room to see her manager flirting with a backup singer.

Martin raised the bottle of Cristal. "I thought you could use some company."

Melissa retreated inside. "You thought wrong."

Martin propped the door with his foot before Melissa could shut it all the way. "I didn't come here to argue."

"You're a lawyer. Isn't that what you do best?"

"I was in town. I miss the boys. I miss you."

"How'd you find me?"

"Brad Siegel said your crew would be in Raleigh for two nights."

Melissa grabbed the flower vase. "This was you?"

"I know pink are your favorite."

Melissa dropped the vase in the wastebasket. "Anything else?"

"I drove five hundred miles to see you. That should tell you something."

"It tells me you've got a long ride home."

"Where are the boys?"

"On my bus."

"By themselves?"

"No. I left them with Freddy Krueger."

Martin set the flat-bottom bottle of Cristal on the makeup counter and peeled the gold foil wrapping. "You look nice."

"I've been on stage for two hours with the heat and bugs. I smell like a sweat shop."

Martin opened the bottle. "How 'bout a toast?"

"Let's not."

"Come home with me, Mel. We both know you're not cut out for this life anymore. And our boys need a father."

"The boys had a father. He died in the flood."

"Your *chauffeur*?"

"Tomás was family, and he loved our boys like they were his own."

"Well they weren't. He was cheap labor from a third world country."

Melissa crossed her arms in disgust. "I think I'm going to throw up in my mouth. Get out!"

Martin raised his hand. "I didn't mean it that way. I liked Tomás. He was a good man, but I'm miserable without you."

"And I'm miserable *with* you. There's no place in my life for us anymore. Why can't you see that?"

"This is no life for you and the boys, playing hillbilly concerts with a bunch of B-list minstrels. If it weren't for me you'd be tied up in court with your record label or in jail on tax evasion. If I hadn't bought your house—"

"Save it, Martin. You're only digging the hole deeper."

"How do you think you got this gig?"

Melissa threw her hands in the air. "This was you? I should have known."

"Sid got his ten percent."

"If you didn't want us on the road, why did you set it up in the first place?"

"I wanted to make you happy. I didn't think you'd take the boys with you."

"And you thought what? I would just leave them in your custody to play house while I'm on tour? You couldn't even be a father for the one night I let you have them."

"I messed up. I own that. But I'm confident we can make this work. I wouldn't be here if I didn't care about you and our family. Like it or not, our sons need me in their lives. Not some honky-tonk cowboy living a lie."

"You're one to talk."

"I've made mistakes. And I know I've hurt our family, but I never lied to you about who I am or where I stand. When your career took off, I felt like I got left behind. I ran to California with another woman because I thought I needed her. I was wrong. She meant nothing to me. You're the only woman I ever really loved. I'm asking for a second chance here. A chance to do this over again. To do it right this time. Our boys deserve a normal life with a mother and a full time father."

Melissa rubbed her arms while the canned apology gnawed at her like a cancer in her bones. "Get out."

Martin held the champagne bottle in one hand. "Are you serious?"

"I don't trust you."

"Don't trust *me?* What about—"

"Please leave!"

Martin pondered Melissa's reaction. "Don't throw your life away with him."

"There is no more him, *or you*. There's only the boys and I."

Martin poured the champagne on the floor. "In case you get thirsty," he grunted bitterly. He emptied the bottle and dropped it on the makeup counter. Then he left abruptly and slammed the door behind him.

Melissa fumed inside her dressing room, recounting all the missteps she'd made in her life. More upset with herself than she was with Martin, she dismissed his comments as the words of a lying fool who occasionally spoke the truth when it served him. Her new recording contract had come too easy; a token gesture facilitated by her bitter ex and a power house label with no intention of supporting her career.

She gathered her things and walked to her bus to find her boys out cold in their bunks. She wanted them back in their own beds; in a house without wheels and land to roam. She had everything she wanted and only herself to blame. Her life had reached a paradox of epic proportion, where no amount of fame or fortune could restore her faith in the world as she knew it. She didn't need a man in her life, but she wanted one. If only the one she longed for had been honest with her to begin with.

CHAPTER 82

Leland woke up in bed alone and smacked the alarm clock to cancel the annoying beep. He pushed the covers aside and stepped carefully over Abby's cat flopped lengthwise on the floor with his tail thumping the carpet. Leland knew he'd come so close to having everything he ever wanted. Now the further he descended, the further the bottom fell away.

He checked his phone for messages and called Sid to leave a voice mail. A quick shower and shave preceded his efforts to feed the cat and brew a pot of coffee to fill his thermos for work. He drove the long commute to the new construction site near Franklin and met up with the surly foreman, a high-strung weather-beaten chief from Boston, who possessed all the warmth and charisma of a shovel.

"I hate to ask you this out of the chute," Leland started, "but is there any way you could float me an advance on my first paycheck?"

"I cut paychecks on Friday. You do your job. You get your check."

"What about a loan?"

"You got your own tools?"

"In the truck," Leland answered. He gestured toward his old Dodge Ram in the parking lot. "I take it that's a no?"

"Take it any way you want it. You need a loan, see a bank. There's a shitload of work to do, and you're thirty minutes late."

"I had a personal issue."

"Not my problem. You show up late again, and you can find another job."

Leland gathered his tools from the truck. He needed the work as much as he needed the distraction from his pending court date. The more he dwelled on the paternity results, the more he questioned his own existence. If he hadn't fathered Abby, why was she so prominent in his life? What did Paula have to gain by tearing his life apart? How much did Abby know? Would she see him in the same light if she knew the truth—or reject him the way Melissa had? Abby was a constant in his life, along with his love for music. Together, they'd kept him anchored through the tough times and brought him more comfort than one man deserved. Without Abby he had nothing. Without music, he was lost.

He made his way toward the construction zone managed by the same company he'd worked for previously and approached a cache of hollow metal framing posts. He acknowledged a coworker in a pair of Dickies and a short sleeve shirt. "I'm Leland."

"Miles," the man replied. He gave Leland a quick fist bump through his leather work glove. "You don't look thrilled to be here."

"Got a lot on my mind."

"Amen, brother. I've been working this site since they cleared the land. Not sure another mall makes sense in this part of town, but they don't pay me to think."

"You from Nashville?"

"Atlanta," said Miles.

"Were you here for the storm?" Leland asked.

"Every drop. Cost me five days pay when they shut us down. Lucky we didn't get hit as hard as some parts, or we'd be running pumps and hoses all day."

Leland rested his hand on his tool belt. "You have kids?"

"Two girls. Ten and twelve. I got an older boy from a baby momma, but I never see him much. His mom's got a new man. Doesn't like it when I come around. You?"

"A daughter."

"How old?"

"Thirteen going on thirty."

"I hear you. My oldest is the same. Too young to know better. Too old to take direction without giving lip to her mom or me." Miles lifted a section of hollow steel frame from the pile and propped it vertically in the track bolted to the concrete floor. "You been downtown since the flood?"

"Not much." Leland held the frame while Miles secured it to the track in the floor with a hammer drill. "How long have you worked for this builder?"

Miles stood up with the drill at his side. "Too long. But their checks always clear." He pointed at Leland with the drill. "You look familiar to me."

Leland repositioned his hold on the beam. "I did some work up in Nashville."

"I never seen you on site before."

"I must have one of those faces."

"Or you white guys all look the same," Miles jabbed with a big grin on his face.

Leland allowed himself to laugh. "You stole my line."

Miles grabbed another length of framing steel and held it upright. "Where're you from?"

"All over. I moved to Nashville a few months back."

"What happened? They run out of work in *all over*?"

"Something like that. I came here to sing."

"Then what are you doing here?"

Leland shrugged. "I got bills to pay like everyone else."

"We are what we believe. We all have a purpose in life. Some meaning. Some reason to get up in the morning and make it through another day. Do you believe in yourself?"

"I do," Leland replied. He held the metal stud for Miles to fasten at the track along the floor.

"Then what's keeping you here? And don't tell me about bills. We all gotta pay the man. For me, I got nothing but labor on my resume. This kind of work is in my blood. If you got the pipes to sing, use them. This work won't take you anywhere."

"You trying to talk me out of a job?"

"I'm trying to educate your mind. If you have a God-given talent, you should use it."

"Not that simple."

"It's only as hard as you make it," Miles countered. He helped Leland position the frame in place. "I believe in an honest day's pay for an honest day's work. I believe in God. I believe in family. I believe in myself to provide for them no matter how hard I struggle at times." Miles reached inside his tool pouch for another screw. "What do you believe in?"

Leland looked up at the concrete ceiling.

Miles tapped him on the side of the shoulder. "It ain't a trick question. If you got to think about it, you need to get right with your god. You follow me?"

"I follow you. But something you said got me thinking…"

CHAPTER 83

Sid waited inside his Escalade outside a gentlemen's club near Broadway and 12th Avenue, where a half-moon sky pierced the sunroof above his head and cast a shadow on the .44 caliber revolver on his lap. LEDs flickered from police chatter on the portable scanner inside the SUV.

He started the engine when Martin finally showed himself, and drove slowly with the headlights off. Tires crunched on fresh gravel as he followed his target to the BMW 850i sedan near the back of the parking lot.

He had the element of surprise in his favor. He also had what he needed to ensure the means justified the end result from the plan several days in the making.

He flicked on his high beams with his window down and gunned the motor to lurch beside his unsuspecting quarry. "Get in!" he demanded with one hand on the wheel and the other extending the large caliber revolver with a six-inch, ventilated barrel.

Martin faced the lighted cabin with his shirt untucked and his collar bent up. "Sid?" He froze at the sight of the bulbous hand cannon pointed at him.

Sid cocked the hammer. "I'm not going to ask you again."

Martin stumbled as he climbed inside the Escalade. "This is kidnapping and attempted murder."

Sid mashed the gas pedal and tore out of the parking lot to head west across the interstate toward Owen Bradley park. "I haven't attempted anything, yet."

"Jesus Christ!" Martin yelled, bouncing in his seat with a death grip on the door handle. "You drive like a maniac."

Sid reached for a manila folder beside his seat and dropped it in Martin's lap. "You should see how I shoot." He drove through the park entrance and cut the motor. The Escalade's xenon headlights illuminated the brick half-wall leading toward the bronze statue of Owen Bradley on piano.

Martin opened the file and skimmed the legal document. "What is this?"

"Leland Presley's divorce. You're going to make sure it happens quickly."

"It won't change anything." Martin plucked a cigarette from the crumpled pack in his pocket. "What are we doing here?"

"Exchanging information."

"By kidnapping me?" Martin put a cigarette to his lips. "You're out of your fucking mind!"

Sid raised the revolver to Martin's chin and watched the cigarette fall away.

Martin trembled. "What are you doing?"

Sid touched his finger to the trigger.

"Please don't kill me!"

Sid squeezed hard enough to produce a short, orange-yellow flame from the muzzle of the Smith & Wesson replica.

Martin swallowed dryly. A warm sensation spread through the front of his pants. "Are you insane?" he pleaded in a voice an octave higher.

"Depends on your definition."

"I just want Melissa back."

Sid lowered the chrome-plated lighter. "That's not going to happen."

"Oh it *will* happen," Martin decreed. He put his cigarette back in his mouth and lit up.

"You don't belong in her life."

Martin wiped the front of his pants. "*I* decide where I belong."

"Melissa mentioned your little impromptu visit on her tour. I told her to file a restraining order."

"Mel is my wife."

"Ex-wife."

Martin flashed a malevolent sneer and blew smoke through his nose. He glanced at the motion to dismiss Paula Presley's custody case. "What do you want from me?"

"Paula Presley's signature."

"The woman is cuckoo for Cocoa Puffs. She'll never sign this."

"She's your client. Get creative."

"What's in this for you?"

"Justice."

"Justice?"

"Paula falsified child abuse evidence against my client, Leland Presley."

Martin put his hand up as if he were about to give sworn testimony. "I had no part in that. As far as I knew, she had a legitimate claim. I never told her to falsify anything."

Sid produced another folder and handed Martin a signed page. "This is your signature, is it not?"

"Yes, but it doesn't prove anything."

"You wanted Leland out of Melissa's life. So you helped her attorney convince child services to get involved by promulgating false testimony about fictitious abuse. It wasn't enough to pull Leland away from Melissa. You wanted his daughter removed as well."

Martin took a long drag and blew smoke out his window. "You can't prove anything."

"Doesn't matter what I can prove. It's what I can convince the bar association to believe. You don't exactly have a spotless track record."

"And you're just a pretty fag in a cheap suit. I could end your career with one phone call. I have friends."

"Don't mistake me for someone who cares," Sid calmly replied. "This is not about my career. This is you doing the right thing for once in your miserable life."

"Since when did you grow a pair?"

"Since I uncovered your little scheme with Steven Harper."

"Who?"

"You both went to law school together. I know about your affiliation with his former employer. How much did you offer him to embezzle from Melissa's accounts? Or did you keep the money for yourself and use it to buy her house out from under her?"

"I have no idea what you're talking about."

Sid produced a copy of Harper's mug shot. "This one's a little outdated, but I can have the FBI forward a more recent version after Harper gives his formal statement about your involvement in the scheme to defraud your ex-wife."

"You're bluffing."

"The FBI has Harper in custody."

Martin took the mug shot photo and flicked his cigarette out the window. He dialed Harper's number and hung up when it went to voice mail. "How did you get this?"

Sid leaned back in the driver's seat, confident he had Martin on the ropes. "I have friends too."

"I didn't do it for the money. I just wanted to force Melissa's hand. Take her down a notch. Make her realize she needed me. I used most of the money Harper stole to buy the house."

"And the rest?"

"In a safe place. You're a business man. There's a deal to be had here."

"Only between you and the FBI."

"I'm not going to prison!"

Sid changed his tone of voice. "I hear it's not as bad as it sounds once you get acclimated to the new lifestyle. With the shared accommodations and all."

Martin clenched his fists. "You kidnapped me at gunpoint. I'm the victim here. No fault of mine, if I killed you in a struggle to get away."

Sid flashed his headlights. He pointed through the windshield at a pair of large men who emerged from the shadows with their faces disguised in nylon stockings. "Here's what's going to happen. You're going to return the remaining funds you stole from my client. Ownership of Melissa's estate will revert back to her. Paula Presley will accept the terms of her divorce and drop the child custody case against Leland. Paula will testify to falsifying the child abuse allegations, and Abby will be released to Leland's custody."

"Leland's not her father. The test results were conclusive."

"Paula Presley belongs in a mental health facility. You're going to help make sure that happens."

Martin shifted uncomfortably in his soiled pants. "Harper's a convicted felon. This case goes to court, it comes down to my word against his. There's nothing to tie me to him or his alleged embezzlement from Melissa's estate."

"If that were true, we wouldn't be having this conversation." Sid touched the digital recording device in his pocket. "*I used most of the money Harper stole to buy the house. And the rest? In a safe place.*"

"You son of a bitch!"

Sid started the engine. "I've already sent copies to my laptop and two private accounts online."

"None of which is admissible in court," Martin argued.

"But Steven Harper's testimony will be. On the up side, a goodwill gesture on your behalf might shave a few years off your sentence. As far as I'm concerned, you've got forty-eight hours to straighten this mess out, or your life is going to take a significant turn for the worse."

Martin's jaw muscles twitched. His nostrils flared. "This is blackmail!"

Sid unlocked the doors and motioned for Martin to get out. "Think of it as de-scoping your options. My colleagues will escort you back to your car. I'll be expecting your call."

CHAPTER 84

Melissa checked her phone for messages and powered on the flat screen television above her bed in the back of the private tour bus. She missed Tomás and all the chaos in her house with her boys running wild. She missed Belle Meade. She missed the smell of primrose and fresh-cut grass. She missed Tennessee and the strong-willed people coping with the flood's aftermath. She also missed the sound of Leland's voice and the way he made her feel about herself.

In the morning, the bus would leave for the next destination on the festival tour. Another city. Another crowd. Another scripted concert she could do in her sleep, followed by another night overwhelmed from the energy and excitement of a live audience, caught in an altered reality between the show world and the real world.

She flipped through several channels and paused when she heard her boys' muffled voices outside her small stateroom, their modulated banter punctuated by the sound of stifled laughter from a third voice she couldn't place. Her curiosity piqued, she left her private quarters to investigate the voice she attributed to excessive wine consumption—or the early onset of delusional paranoia. "Boys?" she called out.

The motor coach got quiet, emitting only the hum from the air conditioning.

She approached the boys' sleeping quarters, suspicious of the privacy curtains drawn across their bunks.

"*We're watching a DVD,*" she heard Adam reply before she opened the curtain to find her youngest son on his back, staring sheepishly at the video on the flip-down screen above his mattress. "What's going on?" she asked Adam.

"Nothing."

Melissa put her hand on the curtain above Jonathan's bunk and tugged it open. She stood silently for a moment, perplexed by the sight of her oldest son lying next to Abby in wrinkled jeans and a faded Hello Kitty shirt.

"Don't be mad," Jonathan started.

Melissa looked at Abby. "How did you get here?"

"She's a friend," said Jonathan.

"I know who she is. I'm asking how she got on this bus."

"I ran away," said Abby.

"From your dad?" Melissa asked in disbelief.

"From my foster parents."

Jonathan moved off the bed and stood up beside his mom. "Abby's mom wants her to live with her," he explained. "Her dad doesn't want her back."

"I doubt that very much," said Melissa.

"It's true," said Abby. "My dad doesn't call me anymore."

"I don't understand. Why aren't you with him?"

"My mom said he did some bad things, but they're all lies. The police made me live with another family. They said my dad couldn't see me anymore."

Melissa leaned against the bunk. "How did you get here?"

"I bought a bus ticket."

"Does anyone know you're here?"

Abby shrugged.

"I take it that's a no. We need to call the police."

"Don't!"

Melissa looked away, expecting her alarm clock to go off at any moment and signal the end of her bizarre dream state. "We need to call your dad and let him know you're safe."

"I'm not going back."

"You can't stay here."

"Then what am I supposed to do?"

"I'm not sure, but we'll figure it out together."

CHAPTER 85

Leland waited inside a construction trailer with his tool belt around his waist. The smell of burned coffee and cigarettes permeated the portable office wallpapered with building plans and a motorcycle calendar advertising topless women on custom bikes.

He acknowledged the foreman, who entered in his orange safety vest and yellow hard hat with a pair of leather work gloves and a dented Stanley thermos. "You wanted to see me?"

The foreman set the metal thermos on a file cabinet and unlocked the top drawer to retrieve a thin stack of envelopes. He parsed through the first few names before he found the one he wanted. "This is yours," he told Leland.

"My advance?"

"Severance."

"For what? I just started this job."

"We're over budget. Last to hire, first to fire. You know the deal. Other guys have seniority."

"Then put me on a different site."

"Not my call."

Leland tore open the envelope and scrutinized the dollar amount printed on the company draft. "This will barely fill my truck."

"There's FEMA work in the city."

"It pays half."

"More than you're getting now."

Leland followed the foreman outside the trailer and beat a path toward his truck. He unbuckled his tool belt and threw it across the seat. Then he climbed inside and contemplated his paltry earnings. With his rent in jeopardy and an empty refrigerator at home, he prayed for the daughter he sorely missed, for the woman he loved, and for the strength to press on. He prayed to endure what he knew was only temporary hardship; to look beyond the small setbacks and see the bigger plan.

He'd played more gigs on the honky-tonk circuit than he ever imagined he would. He'd also tasted his five minutes of fame and opened his heart to thousands of country music fans who'd listened to him perform, blissfully unaware of the pain that drove him to end his career.

He reached in his pocket when he heard his cell phone ring and noted Sid's name on the flip phone's display. "I left you three messages this morning."

"*I've been busy,*" Sid replied over the phone.

"I just got shit-canned from a job I can't afford to lose. If you're calling to kick me when I'm down, get in line."

"*I wouldn't worry so much anymore.*"

"What about Abby?"

"*That's why I'm calling...*"

"Did you talk to Paula's lawyer? I think Martin Hamilton's involved with her somehow."

"*I'm working on it.*"

Leland moved the phone to his other ear. "I'm getting tired of the waiting game."

"*Let's talk in person.*"

"Where are you?"

"*Look up.*"

Leland checked his rear view mirror to see a black Escalade in his field of view. He climbed out of his truck to meet Sid in a swirl of dust and diesel from a convoy of heavy equipment. "What's going on?"

Sid covered his mouth with his hand and pointed to the construction trailer. "Let's talk inside."

Leland followed him. "Is Abby okay?"

Sid entered the single-wide trailer on blocks and filled a paper cup from the water cooler. "She's fine."

"Where is she?"

"South Carolina. Myrtle Beach, to be exact."

"What is she doing there?"

"She ran away from the home in Nashville." Sid finished the water and crumpled the cup. "I just found out."

"How did she—"

"She lifted a credit card from someone's wallet and bought a bus ticket online. Melissa's boys emailed her their location."

Leland ran his hand through his hair. "Is she okay?"

"Melissa's escorting her back to Nashville. Their flight lands this afternoon."

"Then what happens?"

"You take her home."

Leland scratched his head. "To her foster home?"

"No, Dummy. *Your* home. You'll need to go downtown and sign some papers first. I'll come with you."

"What about Paula's case against me?"

"Her lawyer withdrew the case. Paula's returning to where she belongs. So is Abby."

"How?"

"I made some calls."

"Just like that?"

"Just like that."

"What if Paula tries to come after Abby again?"

"Paula needs long term care. By the time she's ready to even think about mounting another case, Abby will be of age and no longer a minor, free to choose with whom she lives."

"What about the test results? If I'm not her biological father—"

"You're her father, Leland. DNA doesn't change your commitment to your daughter. Paula's agreed for you to maintain full custody. Her falsified abuse allegations have been dropped. Child services will want to talk with you to make sure everything's above board at home and work."

Leland hugged him. "I can't thank you enough. But I need to find a new job."

"I would focus on your music instead."

"Music's not exactly in my future anymore."

"A few million people beg to differ. Your little stunt went viral. *A Man Like Me* has been blowing up the Internet. You've got three million hits on YouTube already. I have two major labels competing to sign you. Both are talking seven figures. *Country Weekly* wants an interview." Sid smiled wryly. "You're going to need a good agent."

Leland choked on his words. "Are you serious?" Tears welled up in his eyes.

"Your time has come, Leland. Lord knows you've earned it."

"I can't believe this."

"Believe it. You touched a lot of people that night. Before the concert, no one outside of Nashville, hell, no one *in Nashville*, knew the voice of Leland Presley. They do now."

CHAPTER 86

Leland waited inside the arrival area at Nashville International Airport with a large stuffed dolphin under his arm. Elated by the prospect of Abby's return, his adrenaline surged when arriving passengers began to trickle through the main terminal. His life-changing news about his pending record deal meant no more construction work, no more late nights in seedy bars, and no more stress to make rent every month. Everything he'd worked for, and everything he'd sacrificed had finally come to fruition. But as anxious as he was to see Abby again, he couldn't shake his looming anxiety toward the woman who'd showed him what it meant to give and receive unconditional love.

His expectations tapered by the last conversation he had with Melissa, he tried to imagine the situation from her point of view, escorting his stowaway daughter from a tour bus bound for the Sunshine State. Melissa owed him nothing, and yet in some ways, he owed her everything. Despite the circumstances, his confidence surged when Melissa emerged from the crowd with Abby. He waved when he made eye contact and rushed to greet his baby girl with open arms, clutching the giant dolphin by the tail. "I missed you so much!"

He hugged Abby tight enough to make her burp. Then he kissed her head and backed away to present the stuffed animal. "This guy belongs to you."

Abby poked the dolphin between the eyes. "I'm not five years old anymore."

Leland lowered the dolphin, deflated by Abby's response. "I missed you."

"We haven't eaten in a while," said Melissa in a subtle attempt to diffuse the awkward moment.

"Me neither," said Leland. "Why don't we grab a bite somewhere?"

"I have to go."

"You just landed."

"I'm on the next flight out. Show must go on, right?"

Leland forced a smile. "I'm really sorry. About everything."

"Me too. Abby told me what happened. Sid filled in the rest."

"You sure I can't buy you dinner?"

Melissa touched Abby's shoulder. "Take care of your dad for me. And make sure you keep him on a tighter leash this time."

Abby wrapped her arm around Melissa and said, "I will." When she saw her disappear among the masses headed toward the security lines, she looked at her dad and asked, "Can we go home now?"

"You sure you're not hungry?"

"I just want to go home."

"We will, but I need to make a quick stop first."

Melissa boarded her return flight and popped two Ambien before she checked her phone for messages. Nestled on a window seat in first class, she sent a text to her boys and skimmed the front section of the airline magazine she found in the seat pocket. She wanted what she couldn't have, and regretted what she didn't say. But she knew in her heart, old wounds never healed if she picked at them.

She laid her head on a travel pillow propped against the window and closed her eyes until a rotund elderly man in a sequined jumpsuit squeezed himself in the seat beside her. Assaulted by the copious application of Brut after-shave, she breathed through her mouth and did her best to ignore the late arrival.

"You headed home or leavin' town?" the stranger asked.

Melissa ignored the overt attempt to strike up conversation.

"You should answer your phone," the stranger continued, his voice deep and fervent. "I hear it buzzing."

"It's just a text message," Melissa said with her eyes still closed.

"How do you know it's not important?"

Melissa adjusted her position to maximize her personal space. "If you don't mind, I plan to sleep through this flight."

"I used to sleep when I traveled by plane. Not anymore. Too many damn distractions."

"Exactly," Melissa replied hotly. She moved her head away from the window and popped her eyes open to see an older Elvis impersonator in outlandish garb and fuzzy sideburns extending from a gray pompadour.

"I'm Jesse, Jesse Garon," the passenger introduced himself as the stewardess closed the main cabin door.

"Melissa."

"Pleased to make your acquaintance, Melissa…"

"Hamilton."

"You looked familiar," Jesse offered. He smiled to reveal perfect teeth and a ruggedly handsome face defined by thick eyebrows, a dark complexion with fine wrinkles, and prominent jowls.

Melissa stretched her legs. "Do you always fly first class?"

"Beats a shower on a moving bus." Jesse loosened his seatbelt strap around his bell-bottomed jumpsuit with Napoleonic collars and elaborate embroidery sewn with multicolor gems and rhinestone studding. "You never answered your phone."

Melissa read the text messages. "My boys are bored."

"How many sons do you have?"

"Two."

"I have an older daughter I haven't seen in years."

"You should see her."

"She's a fireball. Like her mother. Not sure either one of us is up for a family reunion. I'm not exactly father of the year material."

"It's never too late."

Jesse adjusted the air vent above his six foot frame. "What kind of work do you do Ms. Hamilton?"

"I'm a singer."

"Me too."

"I gathered…"

"Are you from Nashville?"

"Born and raised," Melissa said proudly.

Jesse contemplated her reply. "I was born in Mississippi. Grew up in Memphis until I joined the Army. What kind of music do you sing?"

"Country."

"I've done a little country western myself. With some gospel and good ol' rock and roll. There's nothing like a live audience. How long have you been divorced?"

"Pardon me?"

"I noticed you don't wear a ring on your finger, and you're much too pretty to be single. You had to be married at one time in your life. Divorce ain't nothing to be embarrassed about. I've been there myself."

Melissa leaned her head toward the window to see the plane taxi along the runway.

"Regrets?"

"I should have married the other guy," Melissa answered wryly.

Jesse cleared his throat. "I met my wife in the Army when I was stationed in Germany. Pretty young thing.

Unfortunately, my movie career lasted longer than my marriage."

"I thought you were a singer?"

"Among other things."

"How many movies were you in?"

"I lost count years ago. Most were made before your time."

"I wouldn't be so sure," Melissa teased, her inhibitions softened by the charismatic passenger whose voice had a soothing affect on her.

"If you don't mind me saying, you're as pretty as a Smoky Mountain sunrise."

"Are you hitting on me?"

Jesse laughed. "You don't strike me as a woman who falls for men too easy."

"You're very sweet."

"You should see me in the morning. I'm not the same man I used to be. The road can be a wicked mistress."

"You seem like you're in a good place, though."

Jesse nodded. "I've had my demons, but yeah, I'm happy with my life. Don't know what I'd do without music. Once you find it in your soul, there's no going back."

"You sound like someone I know."

"You got a man waiting for you at home?"

"Not anymore."

Jesse leaned across his armrest toward Melissa. "Not what I'm asking."

The plane accelerated, pressing Melissa against her seat as the wing-mounted turbo fan engine roared outside her window.

"Do you love him?"

"Who?"

"The man you can't bring yourself to forget. I can see him in your eyes. What is it you're afraid of?"

"I'm not afraid of anything."

Jesse scratched his sideburn and moved away from Melissa to adjust himself. "I used to think I was invincible. A heart attack taught me otherwise. At one point I thought

I'd lost everything. Funny how life can turn on you. One minute you think you got everything figured out. The next you're getting body slammed to the carpet. I'll tell you what, I'd rather live for the moment than wallow in the past."

"Good to know. Do you always wear your costume when you travel?"

"We all wear costumes, Ms. Hamilton. That's how we hide in plain sight."

Melissa looked through her window to see the plane fly through the clouds. She reflected on the friendly conversation until she finally put the pieces together. "What did you say your last name was again?"

"Ma'am?"

"Your name?"

"Ma'am?"

Melissa woke up when a hand brushed her arm. She blinked at the male flight attendant leaning over the empty seat beside her and yawned. "What's going on?"

"We're preparing to land. I need you to return your seat to the full upright position."

Melissa adjusted her seat. "Where's the gentleman who was sitting next to me?"

"Excuse me?"

"The guy dressed up like Elvis. I was just talking to him."

"Sorry ma'am. The seat beside you has been vacant since we left Nashville."

CHAPTER 87

Leland parsed through a box of old photos taken when Abby was born. Snapshots of Paula holding her in a white blanket, mother and daughter acquainted for the first time. He sorted the ones he could salvage from the flooded contents in his garage. He dismissed the ones too damaged to save, hoping his digital copies were still intact on his old PC. With Abby home, he wanted to leave the past behind and move forward with a new chapter in his life. With a future in music, he needed a permanent place to call home. And regardless of his affection for his truck, he could stand a new set of wheels. The money would never change what had happened with Melissa, but it would pave the way for a new start and a chance to prove himself in a city teeming with opportunity.

He put the photos down when Abby emerged from her room to approach him with the giant stuffed dolphin. "You okay?"

Abby hugged her arm around her dad with her head on his chest. "I'm sorry I was mad at you."

Leland felt Abby squeeze him. "You know I love you. That won't ever change."

"I love you too. I named him Orca."

"He's a dolphin."

"He's ginormous."

Leland felt Abby squeeze him tighter. "You going to let me go?"

"Never."

"I'm sorry about your mom."

Abby looked up at him. "What's going to happen to her now?"

"She's going back to the hospital."

"Forever?"

"Until she gets better."

"What if she never gets better?"

Leland ruffled Abby's hair. "One step at a time."

Abby let go and found an old photo from the pile on the dresser. "Is this Mom?"

"When you were little."

"I was tiny."

"We all start out that way."

"Are you going to divorce her?"

"I am. I hope you understand why."

Abby put the photo down. "When they took me away, I thought I'd never see you again."

Leland brushed his hand against the orange tabby rubbing at his ankles. "I'm sorry about what happened. I would have stopped it if I could. I hope you know that."

"It wasn't your fault."

"I should have protected you better. I wasn't supposed to call you, but I tried to anyway. Several times. Every day."

"They took my phone away," Abby said with her head down.

"I thought you were mad at me," Leland whispered.

"I thought you didn't love me anymore."

"We were both wrong."

Abby searched through a box of old school projects and found a science fair medal she'd won in third grade. "When are we moving?"

"As soon as I find a new house big enough for the two of us and this cat."

"I heard your song on the Internet again."

Leland reached for the box with the remnants of his vintage Gibson. "No big deal."

"What happened to your guitar?"

"It broke."

Abby poked through the scraps of splintered wood and tangled strings. "How?"

"I had a hard time when you were gone."

"We have to fix it."

"It's not fixable."

"We could Super Glue it."

"It doesn't work that way."

"Then why are you saving it?"

Leland thought to himself for a moment. "I have a hard time letting go of things."

"You miss her, don't you."

"I can always buy another one."

Abby looked her dad in the eyes and said, "I'm not talking about the guitar."

Leland closed the lid on the box and stacked it with the others against the wall. "Nicole's not part of our lives anymore."

"I get it. But she's not the one who made you happy. Melissa misses you."

"Did she say that?"

"She didn't have to. You should call her."

"She has a lot on her plate right now."

"You have to make time for the most important things."

"I'm not sure she wants me in her life right now."

Abby threw her arm up. "For someone your age, you haven't learned much about women."

"They are complicated creatures."

"You didn't write that song for Nicole."

"I didn't sing it for her either. Sometimes you have to play the cards you're dealt."

"Then you should ask for another deck."

"Did you clean the litter box?"

"Dad…"

Leland walked toward the kitchen. "I bought more cat food."

Abby followed. "But you do love her?"

"I do."

"Then your heart is open, but your eyes are closed. You're so caught up in the past, you can't see what's in front of you."

"I offered to buy her dinner at the airport, and she declined. If she wanted to stay, she would have stayed."

"It doesn't work that way."

"And how is it supposed to work, exactly?"

Abby fed her cat and filled the water bowl. "She cares about you."

"She has a funny way of showing it."

"Talk to her."

"Abby, I *sang* to her. You saw how well that panned out."

"I don't think she got the message." Abby sighed in frustration. "She's waiting for you to make a move."

"This isn't junior high school, Abby."

"And you're not twelve anymore, Dad. Would you rather live *with* her or spend the rest of your life without her?"

Leland rested against the counter and ignored the microwave beeper going off. "How did you get so smart?"

"I had a good teacher. Can I have a horse?"

Leland frowned. "Nice try." He left the kitchen to find his phone and called Sid to ask a favor. As much as he thought otherwise, Abby's advice resonated in a way he couldn't fully comprehend.

"Are you going to call her or not?"

"I'm working on it."

"You're stalling."

"Maybe I have something better in mind."

CHAPTER 88

M elissa glanced out her tinted bus window at the early morning traffic moving south along I-95 toward Melbourne, Florida. Alone with her boys and a driver who took kindly to kids, she noticed the familiar landmarks from the zoo to the Suntree Country Club along the Wickham Road exit heading east from the interstate, past the Maxwell King Center, toward Wickham Park. Years ago, she'd played the same location as a warm-up act for Vince Gill. She'd learned how to pace herself on stage, absorbing pearls of wisdom from accomplished singers and musicians willing to impart their knowledge for the sake of improving their craft. Eventually, her own musicians disbanded as competition escalated among major record labels vying for the strongest talent. Now, thanks to Sid, she found herself attached to an A-list team of professional musicians and seasoned crew members willing to endure the daily grind of back-to-back shows under less than ideal conditions.

She checked on her boys to find them snoozing in their racks when the bus entered the sprawling outdoor venue across from the community college.

"Where is everyone?" Melissa asked her driver.

"Don't know," the driver answered while several crew members offloaded equipment from a cargo van. "They must have got a late start."

Melissa felt the bus shimmy and jerk during slow speed maneuvers within the reserved parking area until it settled in its designated space. She stepped out to find Sid near a black limousine, in a pair of light blue golf shorts and a red Arnold Palmer shirt. "What are you doing here?" she asked, surprised by the unexpected visitor.

"I heard there's going to be a great show tonight."

"We deliver a great show every night. Why are you really here?"

"I wanted to tell you in person. Wharton Brothers decided to exercise an early termination clause. Translation…"

"I know what it means," Melissa acknowledged. "My tour ends here. And so does my career. Can't say I didn't see it coming. Good news travels fast. Bad news travels faster. What about my band?"

"They'll find work. Brad Siegel has other gigs lined up for them."

"I should have known he was involved in this."

"I tried to renegotiate," Sid explained.

"I get it. What about my new album?"

"You'll finish it. Just not with Wharton Brothers."

"What about my duet?"

"I'm still working on it."

Melissa followed Sid toward the main stage area, where crew members assembled racks of lighting gear. "How long have you known?"

"I got the call the other night. I booked a plane to Melbourne so I could tell you in person. Where are your boys?"

"Still snoozing on the bus." Melissa strolled toward a patch of shade. "This life's not for me anymore. The boys took to it at first. Then the novelty wore off. They miss their home and their friends and Tomás."

"Tomás misses you."

"Brad Siegel's a prick," Melissa vented. "And useless as a screen door on a submarine. I want a label who believes in me. A lot of women succeeded way beyond their prime. Bette Midler. Barbara Streisand. Cher. Celine Dion."

"Technically, Celine is younger than you."

Melissa gave Sid a heated glance. "Not funny." She followed him to a row of folding chairs near the stage. "Where's my band? I haven't seen them since we left Atlanta yesterday."

"They're around."

"Their bus wasn't in the parking lot. They better not be camped out in Cocoa Beach. We have a lot of work to do."

"Relax. Let life come to you for a change."

"This from the man who traveled eight hundred miles to tell me I'm fired."

Sid grinned. "If you could have one wish, what would it be?"

"Anything?"

"Anything…"

Melissa contemplated the question. "A better agent." She touched Sid's arm and chuckled. "I'm kidding." She looked at the stage prepped with drums, guitars, and a microphone stand. "What would you wish for?"

"A new client," Sid pushed back.

"Then I guess we'll both be disappointed." Melissa followed him to a pair of folding chairs near center stage with *RESERVED* signs hanging off the back. "What are you doing?" she asked when Sid claimed a seat.

"I'm tired of walking."

"You just got out of your limo."

Sid tapped the chair beside him. "Flatter me."

"What is this?"

"A surprise."

Melissa remained standing with her hands on her hips. "You know I hate surprises."

"Everyone always says they hate surprises, but people love them."

"I'm not most people," Melissa professed as she noticed her band members appear one-by-one on stage with Leland. She looked at Sid, then back at Leland. A moment later, she heard the bass drum pounding in rhythm with her elevated pulse. Her lead guitarist played edgy, up-tempo power chords while the bass guitar added a vibrant, southern-rock melody. The music pumped through her like the blood in her veins as Leland approached the microphone stand.

Leland admired the gathering crowd and signaled the band to take the volume down a notch. He slipped his arm through the strap on a white Stratocaster and spoke in a confident voice projected through a stack of Marshall amplifiers. "I have so much in my life. More than any man could ask for. More than I deserve. But I can't stand the thought of living one more day without you, Melissa Hamilton. You mean the world to me. I wrote this one for you. I hope you like it." He signaled the band to bring the music full force. Then he started to sing…

I believe in heav-en
And a life up above
I believe in des-tiny
And the value of love

I believe in freedom
And the power to choose
I believe in emp-athy
And a life without rules

We all go astray, but that doesn't change who we are
You are a-m-a-zing!
Like the sun that warms the earth, you warm my heart
You are everything a man could want and more…

I believe in karma

And the lessons I've learned
I believe in hon-esty
When the tables are turned

I believe in valor
And help from above
I believe in des-tiny
And the strength of our love

We all go astray, but that doesn't keep us apart
You are a-m-a-zing!
In everything you do
Like the faithful who believe in mir-a-cles...

I believe in you...
I believe in you...
I believe...in you...

Melissa ran to the stage amid a cacophony of cheers. Her eyes teared as Leland helped her up. She wrapped her arms around him and whispered in his ear, "I believe in you too."

Leland lifted her feet off the ground. He pointed at Abby in the flash mob audience and gave her a big thumbs up. "What do you think?" he asked Melissa.

Melissa raised a fist at her band. Then she relaxed her arm and waved at her boys in the crowd. "My boys are fakers!"

"They were all for it."

"What kind of name is Peter Blankenbaum, anyhow?" she razzed him.

"Irish-German."

Melissa laughed, her spirits high on love. "I had a dream about Elvis the other day. He was in his seventies, and I swear he sat right next to me on the plane. It all seemed so real."

Leland marveled at her candid jubilation. "Stranger things have happened..."

The End

SONG LYRICS BY JASON MELBY

"This Dance"

"Here Today and Gone Tomorrow"

"Favorite Honky-Tonk"

"All in Love"

"Nothing's Easy Anymore"

"Love is a State of Mind"

"Abby's Song"

"One More Day"

"American Pride"

"Between Lovers and Friends"

"A Man Like Me"

"I Believe"

NOVELS BY
JASON MELBY

Enemy Among Us
A Dangerous Affair
Without a Trace...
The Gauntlet

A graduate of Virginia Tech and Johns Hopkins University, contemporary fiction author, Jason Melby, draws heavily from personal experience and the raw emotions they evoke.

As a father who has lived and traveled throughout the United States and Europe, Jason enjoys creating characters who seem ordinary at their core but exhibit exceptional qualities when they find themselves confronted by their greatest fears and summon the courage to overcome them.

A former math major, inspired by a short story writing class in college, Jason discovered his passion for writing novels that appeal to a broad audience of men and women, young and old, who enjoy reading fast-paced books infused with humor, adventure, passion, and suspense.

For Jason, a life without art, without creativity or imagination, is a life without passion. And a life without passion is meaningless. To learn more about his work, visit www.jasonmelby.com.